SPIDER

'No threat, they said, the priest was no threat. And in any case, they said, they had him covered.'

At precisely twelve minutes to ten on the morning of Friday February 4th, 1983, in a bar in Lima, Peru, an officer of the CIA sanctioned, as a matter of priority, the immediate execution of a French priest, Father Jean Laporte.

Present were two other men: one, a CIA special envoy; the other, the representative of a fugitive Nazi war criminal whose network the execution was designed to protect.

That network was called 'Spider'. In their discussions, however, they overlooked one small detail . . .

'Spider' is the actual code-name of an underground intelligence system run by ex-Nazis in South America. Its web spans forty years. Its activities and political connections are a closely guarded secret. This book is based on some of its confidential documents and a series of clandestine meetings with a number of its operatives.

About the author

Gordon Stevens is a producer/director with ITV. A former journalist, he has worked in Fleet Street, as well as for two years as a freelance in South America, working for a number of agencies and papers including *The Observer*. As a producer, with the BBC and ITV, he has worked in Africa, Europe, Northern Ireland, the United States and Central America. He has won a number of awards for a variety of documentaries, on the death of IRA hunger striker, Bobby Sands, mercenary recruitment in the south of England and the moral and social implications of in vitro fertilisation. He filmed exclusively the birth of America's first so-called "test-tube baby". He also made the first television documentary to emerge from El Salvador. He is married with two children and lives in the New Forest.

SPIDER

Gordon Stevens

CORONET BOOKS
Hodder and Stoughton

Copyright © 1984 by Gordon Stevens

First published in Great Britain 1984 by Coronet Books

British Library Cataloguing in Publication Data

Stevens, Gordon
  Spider.
  I. Title
  823'.914[F]   PR6069.T4/

ISBN 0-340-36027-5

British Library Cataloguing in Publication Data

Printed and bound in Great Britain for
Hodder and Stoughton Paperbacks, a
division of Hodder and Stoughton Ltd.,
Mill Road, Dunton Green, Sevenoaks,
Kent (Editorial Office: 47 Bedford Square,
London WC1 3DP) by Cox and Wyman Ltd.,
Reading. Photoset by Rowland Phototypesetting Ltd.,
Bury St Edmunds, Suffolk.

For Marion, my wife, and Guillermo, whom we met in Lima, Peru, on his way from one struggle in Bolivia to another in Chile and who told us his part of this story.

I hope he is alive. I fear he is not.

With thanks to Ian and Deborah, for their faith and perseverance, and to Buck, Selwyn and Vera, and Brian and Bob, who told me what happened forty years ago.

And special thanks to Father John, Alastair, Dave and Chris.

Introduction

Lima, Peru

Close. Too close.

The cold of the night cut through his thin summer coat and shirt, slicing like a knife through the first layer of his body warmth, dissecting the muscle and tissue till it reached the bone, making him shiver like a child. In the city, ten kilometres down the long winding road behind him, he knew it would be warm. If he turned in the car seat, he thought, he would be able to see the reassuring halo of light hanging in the sky, almost hear the sound of the late-night traffic. He stared ahead, ignoring the instinct, blocking out the sense of isolation which threatened to engulf him.

Close. Too close.

He knew he should have stayed back, sent the contact in first, confirmed all was secure before he came near. But the trail had been too long, the prize too great. He wondered how long it would be. What they did to traitors.

He had been careful, carried none of the documents which would identify him, hired the car under a false name. So that if he had to run there would be nothing to lead them to Herbert Weissemann, born Stuttgart, Germany, 1943. Except they would know, as they always knew. And if they didn't they would find out. It was their way. It was why he was sitting in the car waiting for them.

The twin beams of light appeared from the wall, two hundred metres down the road, stretching like fingers across the corn fields on the left. He checked his watch. Just over an hour, about the time they had both calculated. Time for the contact to make his report and for the others to leave.

The lights swung round, up the road, and he heard the noise of the engine, the soft rumble of the Mercedes as it came towards him. He ducked, pushing his head low, cursing the fact that he had stayed in the car, counting the seconds it would take for them to pass him. He strained his ears for any sound, any change in the acceleration, which might mean they knew about him. Knew why he was there. Then the Mercedes was past, still accelerating, its headlamps momentarily lighting up the pale blue interior of his hire car, before the darkness closed in again.

He pulled himself up, feeling the sickness of the tension recede. From the point where he was parked he could see the junction where the side road joined the main highway to the mountains, four hundred metres away. He glanced at the rear view mirror then turned again to the front, eyes concentrating on the section of white wall from which the Mercedes had emerged. Ten minutes, they had agreed. Ten minutes after the others had left and the contact had been alone in the house. He fixed his eyes on the road ahead, afraid to look back, afraid even to look at his watch, afraid he would miss the signal.

The sickness was rising again in his throat, but now it was different. The nausea of triumph, not fear. The contact was good. He had always told himself that and now he knew. There had been no reason for them to suspect. And if anything had gone wrong, he reminded himself, there had been the insurance, arranged earlier, the last back door out. But nothing had gone wrong. The Mercedes had left and the contact was in sole charge of the house. He knew he was glad, not just for himself or the contact, but for Maria. He had tried to avoid involving her, had built in the safeguards, but in the end there had been no option. At least, he now knew, it was almost over.

In front of him the bright red of the brake lights blinked on and off, on and off. He started the engine, put the car in gear and eased it off the verge and down the road.

A hundred metres from the signal. He could taste the excitement, knew what the other man must be thinking.

The identity of the man in the house, the contact had said, was important enough. But that paled into insignificance with the rest. The organisation, the networks, the contracts. And Octavio, the contact had said, Project Octavio. The big one. The one that would expose it all. All on paper, all filed in the documents. Even the name. The link. The identity of the connection that would bring it all down. He wondered what Joe Corrigan was like, how he would react, whether he would ever meet him.

Thirty metres. His foot was on the brake, slowing down. The lights flickered in his rear view mirror. Someone coming home late from a party, he thought, too late for work. The contact was out of his car, standing at the rear, motioning him through the open gateway of the driveway to the house. To the evidence. Maria, he thought, he ought to phone Maria, tell her it was OK. He wondered again about the man called Corrigan.

Something different. Not wrong, just different. His mind detached itself, scanning, searching for the clue, wondering why he had noticed. Fifteen metres. He slowed almost to a halt, beginning to turn the wheel.

Something wrong. He looked at the contact again. Unsteady, weak on his feet, supporting himself against the side of the car. Too stiff to be drunk. Hand waving automatically, mechanically, as if any other movement hurt. Gesturing him into the garden. Urgently. Desperately.

The partygoer's car was slowing down.

He swore quietly to himself. Wrong time. Just when the road needed to be empty. Just when they wanted the night to themselves. The first bloody car of the night.

Christ. He saw it. Cursed himself. The black in the rear view mirror as he waited for the Mercedes which had left the house to reappear from the trees, turn off the side road onto the highway, slip into the line of lights moving towards the city. Nothing. There had been nothing. The car had not reached the main road. Never meant to.

The twin lights of the car behind were dazzling, almost blinding him. The big square front of the Mercedes. The

11

contact waving violently, almost pleading. The man's face came at him in the sudden blaze of lights: white, frightened, eyes wide and staring, mouth hanging disjointedly. The Mercedes was pulling out, cutting him off. He slammed the car back into gear and crashed his foot on the accelerator.

Chapter One

Monday, January 31st, 1983

The passenger in the black Citroen CX Prestige which
pulled off the Pan American Highway and headed up the
dusty track which served as the main street of the *barriada*
known as la Ciudad de Dios, the City of God, was young,
in his mid-twenties, well-dressed. The shanty town which
he was now entering, according to the population census
of 1981, housed some seventy thousand men, women and
children in conditions hovering around the poverty line, a
fact which, had he known it, would have neither interested
nor concerned him. His suit and shirt, as well as his
hand-made shoes, had been purchased in the best shops
in Paris. His watch, on the slim wrist of the hand which
held the map was 22 carat. The ring on the finger rivetted
to the red cross in the third section down, second in, from
the right margin of the map, was solid silver. Even the gun
which he carried in the soft leather holster beneath his
jacket was among the most expensive available, a hand-
made Korth .357 magnum purchased under licence in
Cologne, West Germany, for DM 2,000.

The time on the watch moved to 3.00 p.m., the figures
ticking away in luminous pink. To their right, in smaller
figures, was the date. He ignored both and concentrated
on the job ahead.

The priest, he had been told. In the schoolroom. Halfway down on the right. Third right after the water carrier.
Not the sort of assignment he normally did, but important.
He had already decided that. Very important. He wondered how they knew about the priest.

The heat of the desert penetrated even the air conditioning of the Citroen. The young man opened the window,

15

wiped the sweat from his hands, wondered what the weather was like in Paris. His companion, relaxed behind the wheel, seemed unaffected by the heat despite the heavier coat which concealed the standard issue MAB model D.

'I hope you know where we're going.' It was the first time the driver had spoken since they left the city.

'I know where we're going. I only hope he's there.'

'And if he isn't?'

'He has to be.'

'He's that important?' The question was almost a statement. The passenger checked his map again. 'Yes, that important.' He wound up the window, shutting out the smell of poverty from the luxury of their official vehicle. 'How do you think he'll react?' The driver hesitated. 'I don't know,' he replied at last, 'it will have been a long time.'

The passenger's finger was still on the red cross. He checked the map again. 'Right at the end of this block and it should be fifty metres down.'

'By the wreck?'

'Yes, by the wreck.'

The Citroen eased round the burnt skeleton of the car on the corner, crept quietly down the street, and slowed to a stop. The grey dust settled over it like a shroud, disguising the black in a thin coat, covering the number plate. Concealing the oval disc of the diplomatic corps.

The school was the only building on the street not made of cardboard. The concrete on the outside was rough and uneven, there were iron bars across the holes which served as windows, the wooden door which stood open to catch the faintest movement of air was unpainted. The red and yellow national flag hung limply from a makeshift pole nailed onto the wall. Already, on the opposite corner of the street, a small crowd was beginning to gather. Waiting expectantly. 'Two minutes,' said the passenger, getting out of the car, undoing his coat. 'No more.'

The children sensed his presence before their teachers

16

saw his frame fill the open door, blocking the light. Their chatter dropped then rose again, nervously. An elderly woman, black hair pulled back, stood to greet him. 'Good afternoon, can I help you?' The passenger stepped inside, eyes adjusting rapidly to the darkness. In the corner of the room farthest from the door the priest looked up. One day, he knew, had always known, someone like the stranger would come for him. He even knew the date. Monday, Monday the seventh. He looked at his watch. Confused. Monday the thirty-first. A week early.

The man in the doorway was equally confused. The sudden blast of heat as he stepped from the car, the blackness of the schoolroom, the smell and noise of the children. And the priests. The priest, he had been told, get the priest. But which priest? There was more than one. Five, he counted quickly, all the same, all sharing the same sense of peace and tranquillity, all bent over the groups of children clustered on the earth floor. His eyes adjusted and he knew immediately, even before the teacher pointed. The priest in the corner, the one who seemed to know, already rising, as if he had been waiting. Moving away from the children gathered protectively round him. Tall, late thirties, hair showing the first steeliness of grey, the white collar and purple shirt contrasting with the black of the suit he wore. The stranger stepped forward, through the children, his right hand reaching under his jacket.

He found his handkerchief, wiped his hands. 'Father Jean?' The priest nodded, the confusion overtaking him. The stranger was direct and formal. 'Father Jean, I am honoured to meet you. My name is Claude Bernard, First Secretary at the French Embassy.' A second priest had joined them, his face crossed with concern.

'Is there anything wrong?' The First Secretary sensed the depth of trust between the two. The priest he had identified as Father Jean shook his head.

'No, nothing wrong.' His manners overcame his nervousness. 'I'm sorry.' He introduced them. 'This is Father Michael, from Puerto Rico. This is M. Bernard, from the

17

French Embassy in Lima.' The newcomer acknowledged the second priest then turned back.

'Father Jean, may I have a word with you. In private. There is something important.'

Father Michael watched closely, hiding his concern from the children, as the stranger led Father Jean towards the door. The First Secretary was talking, the priest at his side white-faced, shaking his head, as if unable to comprehend what he was being told. Father Michael moved closer to the door, anxious, unable to hear, needing to know. Through the shrieks and screams of the children he heard the last snatches of conversation as the stranger led Father Jean to the car outside. 'The ambassador . . . confirming details now . . . anxious to speak to you in person . . . already informed Paris.'

2 *9.03 p.m. Paris, France*

Charles Chalbrand sank back in the seat, closed his eyes, and prepared to allow the strains of Mozart's 21st Piano Concerto in C major to weave their spell upon him. Schubert's 9th Symphony, which had opened the performance, had been even better performed than the critics had suggested. The champagne, the last extra surprise for his wife, had been served in the box during the interval. And now the 21st. His favourite piece. His wife's birthday. Their first evening together for three months, one of the few escapes from the pressures of office since the last election. And after, dinner at the restaurant where she had accepted his proposal of marriage so many years before. In the dark body of the auditorium the power of the music was creeping quietly but relentlessly forward. He pushed the last vestiges of work from his mind, forgot about the only other two people in the world who knew where he was, and waited for the slow movement.

The voice at his shoulder was discreet but insistent. He

half turned his head, still listening to the concert, only partially aware of his personal bodyguard standing behind him, bending close.

'I'm sorry, m'sieur, but the manager says there's a telephone message for you.'

'Can't it wait?' asked Chalbrand, knowing the answer, knowing it could only be one person.

'No, m'sieur, they said it was urgent.'

He whispered to his wife that he would be back shortly and followed the manager through a maze of corridors to the small office at the rear. His mind was still in the auditorium, drifting with the music he could no longer hear, thinking of the table at Claude's. The manager left the room, stealing one last glance at the tall, impressive-looking man in late middle age who now sat at his desk, and closed the door behind him. In the corridor, the bodyguard was hovering.

'Chalbrand.' His private secretary spoke immediately. 'M. Chalbrand, I'm sorry to disturb you, but the embassy in Lima has just come through with something you would wish to know about.' Chalbrand's mind left the music and picked up the subtlety of the words. Not a request for guidance or decision. Not information about a world event, a political scandal, an assassination, about which he, as Foreign Secretary of France, should be informed immediately. Something different. Something he would wish to know about. He leaned forward, elbows resting on the table top, the mouthpiece of the telephone cupped in his right hand, close to his lips, in the manner of those accustomed to both speaking and listening confidentially. Somehow, he did not know how, he knew what the man was about to say, the muscles of his jaw already hardening. 'Tell me.'

The private secretary spoke for fifty-five seconds, his precis sharp and succinct, omitting nothing of relevance, detailing the source and strength of the report from the Lima embassy. When he had finished he waited for Chalbrand to recover, fully aware of what he had just told him.

19

'Thank you.' Chalbrand's voice concealed the collapse of his mind and body. Already a thread was beginning to emerge from the blackness which had so abruptly and mercilessly engulfed him. 'Could you find out where the president is, please?' The secretary had anticipated the single request.

'I have a number.' Chalbrand wrote it in the notebook he always carried, thanked the secretary again, and put the phone down.

For the next five minutes he did not move, allowing the thoughts to sweep through his mind, allowing his mind to sweep through its memories. So long. It had been so long. And now it had happened. And so close. So close to the Monday. So close to the seventh. He took a clean white handkerchief from his breast pocket, wiped his eyes, ignored the number where he could contact the head of state, and lifted the telephone again.

3   *9.23 p.m. Melleran, France*

The air in the bedroom was cold. The old woman crossed to the dressing table, unsteady on her feet, her breath forming small clouds in the icyness. She pulled the woollen gown over her nightdress and sat down, listening to the harshness of the storm outside.

The face in the mirror was tired with more than age. She fingered the skin of her cheek, remembering how old she was, how young she had been, how young they had all been, thirty-nine years ago. Her hand reached for the face cream and she began to massage the lines round her eyes, her glance straying, as it always did, to the photograph holder at the base of the mirror, the two men looking at her from the elaborate silver frame. The photograph on the left was old, in black and white, the young man in it strong and handsome, the chain of prefectural office hanging proudly round his neck. The other photograph was new and in colour. The young man in it was also good-looking, the purple of his shirt making the white collar of the priesthood stand out, balancing the decoration of the other. The woman leaned forward and picked up the holder. The two were alike. Same eyes. Same shape of the face. Same smile.

It was getting colder. She put the photograph holder back in its place, took one last look at the mirror and slipped into bed, still wearing her dressing gown, welcoming the warmth of the blankets. The chocolate which Deidre had made for her was on the table, hot and sweet. Deidre had been with her, been good to her, ever since.

The ghosts began to drift back. They always did this week. Most of the year they tried. Most of the year she could push them away, hide them in the darkest corners of her mind. But not this week. It was too close. Too close to the Monday. Too close to the seventh.

The roar of the storm died away. In the sudden unfamiliar calm she heard the telephone ring, then Deidre's steps up the stone stairs. There was a gentle knock on the door and the woman entered. 'It's M. Chalbrand, madame.' She spoke hesitatingly, worried about the lateness of the call. The old woman stared at her, the fear suddenly growing in her mind. She got out of bed, found her slippers and tiptoed to the landing. The stairs were cold. She descended them slowly, leaning against the wall, her thin hands trembling.

The hall was large and tall, the stairs sweeping down, the floor below tiled and patterned. When she reached the bottom she took the telephone, listened for two minutes as Chalbrand spoke to her, thanked him, and replaced the handset. For two full minutes more she looked at Deidre without speaking, the tears filling her eyes then clearing, blurring then sharpening the figure in front of her. The knot in her throat loosened and she began to speak, the woman in front of her straightening, knowing what she was about to say. As the priest had known in the schoolroom of the shanty town on the other side of the world. As Chalbrand had known in the sudden quiet of the theatre office. As the mother had known when she had taken the telephone.

The words came of their own accord. In the stillness the old woman could hear her own voice, surprised at its strength. 'They've found him,' she said simply. 'They've found The Butcher.'

4 *Tingo Maria, Peru*

Corrigan watched as the Fokker Fellowship cleared the line of trees, wings unsteady, sun glinting on the body, dropped onto the dirt of the runway and slowed in a cloud of dust. Something happening, he knew, something building up, developing, which concerned him. Something which would involve him. And he was stuck in the middle of the jungle.

The fan on the ceiling of the waiting room was broken. The air was hot and sticky, the room smelt of people. He had planned to be back in Lima by the weekend, had been forced to break the plans he had made with his wife and children. Again, he thought.

The plane stopped fifty yards from the cluster of airport buildings at the side of the runway, locked in the clearing. The daily flight. Lima the capital, to Iquitos deep in the Amazon, and return to Lima via Pucallpa and Tingo Maria. A regular business service, he thought. Oilmen to Iquitos, cocaine dealers to Tingo Maria. It was like that, he thought again. Perhaps he was getting too old. He put down the bottle of lukewarm Coke, picked up his bag and walked to the plane, wondering what was waiting for him in Lima. Something happening, he was positive.

The French ambassador turned away from the window overlooking the Plaza Francia and looked back at the priest. Jean-Etien Lafayette was a career diplomat, a graduate of Saint Cyr, Mayor de Promotion de '59 before a riding accident ended a promising military career. Like any good politician he knew the importance of the man now slumped in the large easy chair in the corner of the suite, his fingers playing incessantly with the beads of a rosary, his lips moving in silent prayer, scarcely hearing the ambassador's explanation that he had sent the First Secretary because the news should be broken by a Frenchman.

The priest nodded, leaning forward, his voice soft and low. Not weak, decided the ambassador, remembering the priest's connections in high places, but not strong. 'Perhaps you could explain to me how you heard,' the priest said, the rosary stretched between his fingers.

The ambassador nodded. 'It happened this morning.' His instinct advised him to introduce the conditions he had intended holding back till later. 'There are complications, of course, but I am already dealing with them.' He opened a beige folder and took out a copy of a newspaper. 'We have been sent this as a matter of courtesy. The first editions go on sale in fifteen minutes. I think you should read it.' The paper was a proof of that day's *Expresso*. The priest remembered passing the offices on his way from the monastery to the cathedral. The words of the headline, in red across the top, filled the upper half of the page.

EXCLUSIVE . . . THE BUTCHER IS FOUND

The photograph beneath showed a house standing in its own garden, in what was clearly an exclusive residential suburb. The house lay behind a white wall which stretched along what seemed to be a side road, on the other side of which appeared to be a corn field. Two armed *guardia* stood at the front of the house, their machine guns pointing inside. The only words on the page, other than the headline, were in a small box beneath the photograph. 'See page three.'

He turned over, not noticing the secretary put the coffee on the table. The photograph on the right of the inside page was the one he had known since childhood, its definition obscured by age, taken in the early years of the war. The man in the photograph was smiling. The face was distinctive, the nose thin and the eyes piercing. On his uniform was a swastika.

Opposite was another picture of the house, showing more police ransacking what he thought was a library. Across both pictures ran another headline.

NAZI WAR CRIMINAL IN LIMA

The story itself was squeezed between the two photographs. His Spanish was sufficient to interpret the popular style of the paper.

The *Guardia Civil* today exposed the top Nazi war criminal known as The Butcher.

He has been wanted since he vanished ten days before Hitler committed suicide in 1945.

Since then he has been one of the world's most sought-after Nazi fugitives, second only to Martin Bormann and Joseph Mengele.

He heads the list of France's wanted men.

The Butcher received his title because of the atrocities he committed when he was head of the Gestapo in France during the 1939–45 war.

The crime for which the French particularly want him is the torture to death of the leader of the French Resistance, Charles de Gaulle's personal representative, Jean Laporte.

Laporte died on a train to Paris in February 1944.

The Butcher's real name is Josef Heiner.

The *Guardia Civil revealed that for the past eighteen years he has lived in Lima under the name Josef Klein.*

The ambassador rose from his chair, crossed to the cocktail cabinet and took out two glasses and a bottle of cognac. 'The wrong time of day, but necessary, I think.' He poured the brandy and two cups of black coffee. The priest read the newspaper again, ignoring the drinks: the details of the raid, the police assault at five in the morning, more information about Heiner himself, quotes from the neighbours.

The ambassador continued. 'Paris has already been informed. I have sent telexes to the president, the Foreign Secretary M. Chalbrand and the prime minister.' He waited to see if the priest would react. 'I have contacted the Peruvian government. They are in a cabinet meeting. I have left a request that they should be informed immediately. I have already requested the extradition of Heiner, Klein, whatever they wish to call him, and have an urgent meeting with the Peruvian president tomorrow morning. I am seeing the Interior Minister later this afternoon.' He selected two telexes from the folder and handed them to the priest. 'As you will see, I have also objected in the strongest possible terms to the fact that the French government was not informed of the proceedings, and that a representative of this embassy was not invited to accompany the *Guardia Civil*.'

The priest nodded, scanning the yellow of the telex paper. 'I must thank you, M. Ambassador, you have not wasted any time.'

Lafayette shrugged, the priest was taking it well. He sipped the cognac, choosing his words. 'There is something else of which you should be aware, Father Jean, though I clearly would not like it repeated outside this room.' Except, the First Secretary would have added had he been party to the intimacy, to the priest's friends in high places.

'Extradition is a dirty business. Times have changed, memories have faded. Governments and courts are no longer so willing to grant such orders as they were in the fifties and sixties. Not even the Israelis would be able to pluck the likes of Eichmann from Argentina as they once did.'

The ambassador sensed he had the full attention of the priest. 'Heiner, of course, will throw every legal obstacle in our path, will lobby his friends, which he undoubtedly must have here, to prevent his return to France. We must bear in mind that his contacts in this country must be well established for him to have survived undetected for so long. There is always the possibility, therefore, that the Peruvian government might reject our application for extradition.'

He paused, allowing the priest time to absorb the significance of what he was saying, what he was about to say. 'I have therefore begun some lobbying of my own.' He was pleased at the way the priest appeared to nod his understanding. 'Part of the job of any ambassador is to cultivate contacts. I appear to have been more than a little fortunate with mine. Individuals whom, quite frankly, the government of this country cannot afford to ignore. I am seeing them this evening.'

It was going well, he decided, allowing himself another cognac. 'Nothing can be permitted to stand in the way of getting The Butcher back to France.'

'Except, M. Ambassador, for one thing.' The priest's voice was low. Soft. Deceptive. The ambassador knew what he was about to say. 'Except, M. Ambassador, that they have not actually found Heiner.'

The words cut through Lafayette like a barb. 'I spoke to the Interior Ministry shortly before you arrived,' he twisted. 'They confirmed they have incontrovertible evidence that the house in Chaclicayo belongs to Josef Klein, and that Josef Klein is, in fact, Josef Heiner.'

The priest was patient, insistent. 'The newspaper says he is found. What it does not say is that he is in custody.

Where is he?' The ambassador fingered the rim of the glass, not replying. The priest continued. 'When the *Guardia Civil* raided the house, was he or was he not there?' The voice had an unexpected hard edge.

'No,' conceded the ambassador, 'he was not.'

'And is he or is he not in custody?' The cross examination was ruthless, without mercy.

'No.'

'And they don't know where Heiner is now?' The incisiveness had taken the ambassador unaware.

'No,' he finally admitted, 'nobody knows where Heinber is.'

The priest was still fingering the rosary. 'No matter, M. Ambassador, you have already done more than could be expected in such a short time.' The voice was soft again, as in the confessional. 'I can only express my most sincere thanks to you and your staff. I am sure my family will do likewise in due course.'

The ambassador relaxed. 'There is one other small thing. A local journalist has already been in touch with me. I don't know how he knows you are in Peru, but the fact of the matter is that he does. He asked whether it would be possible to interview you.'

The priest spread out his hands. 'Whatever you think best. If you feel it would be of help, then I'll do it.'

The ambassador nodded. 'Let's leave it for the moment. Will you still be going back for Monday?'

The priest was surprised that the man either knew or had remembered. 'Yes, I am always present for the seventh.'

He rose to leave. Lafayette wrote a telephone number on the back of a visiting card and gave it to him. 'My home number. Please phone me personally if there is anything I can do. Now, let me get my official car to take you back.

The priest smiled. 'No thank you,' he said, 'I would prefer, if you don't mind, to walk.'

Lafayette accompanied him to the front door and watched as the solitary figure walked down the steps and along the pavement. It hadn't gone too badly, he reflected, quite well in fact. And he was sure the priest had meant what he had said about the family showing its thanks. He pressed the intercom and asked for his car. Everything now depended on the pressure he could bring to bear for extradition. Should, as the priest had not failed to point out, they actually catch up with the bastard. He wondered where Josef Heiner was, then thought again of the figure shuffling along the pavement, remembered the sudden ruthlessness. Hard, totally unexpected. It had taken him off guard, but it had soon faded, the priest returning to the comfort of his rosary. At least, he told himself, the priest could lose himself in prayer. Strange, though, he thought, the memory of the ruthlessness refusing to leave him. Very strange.

6 *Lima*

Maria left the office early, pushed her way along Avenida Colmena, past the Hotel Bolivar and into the Plaza San Martin. A mime artist was performing in the centre of the square, face whitened as in death, arms and legs moving slowly, grotesquely. She remembered the last time she had stood in the square with Herbert Weissemann. Remembered the last time she had seen Herbert Weissemann.

No newspaper vendor, she saw, no newspapers. She watched the actor. Waiting. Worrying. As she had waited and worried through the previous night. The old man picked his way through the crowd, one-legged, right hand guiding the crutch which supported his body, the newspapers tucked under his other arm, and sat down. Maria pushed a five hundred soles note into his hand, took an

Expresso, ignored the change. Saw the front page, the headlines, the photographs.

The first tears of comprehension began to trickle down her cheeks.

7 *Lima*

Father Jean pushed open the wooden gates of the monastery, welcoming the peace he had known he would find inside, breathing in the cool air of the cloisters. The early evening sun was casting its long shadows between the arch of the pillars. He went into the church, seeking comfort, knowing he would find it in prayer. A single novice padded past him, leaving him alone. He entered a side chapel, took a candle, lit the slender wick and placed it before the statue of St Francis, the founder of the order in whose retreat he was now seeking his own refuge, watching the shadow of the flame dance against the black of the wall behind it. Remembering the words of the Franciscan prayer. 'Make me a channel of your peace.' At the rear of the church he heard the door open and close gently, then Father Michael sat beside him.

Father Jean reached in his pocket, pulled out the copy of the newspaper which the French ambassador had given him, and handed it to the other priest. Father Michael read it, slowly and carefully, looking across at Father Jean once, then folded the newspaper and placed it on the floor. 'Do you want to tell me?' he asked.

Father Jean hesitated. He had heard the others talk of it, heard his mother talk of it. Once, only once, heard his godfather, Charles Chalbrand, talk of it. But he himself had never spoken on the subject. Had maintained a silence. Almost, he thought, a vow. He nodded, welcoming the comfort, committing himself to Father Michael. 'It was thirty-nine years ago,' he said at last. 'Jean Laporte was head of the French Resistance, General de Gaulle's personal representative in occupied France. The cell to which he had originally belonged, and in which his wife and a number of his closest friends continued to fight during the war years, was in the small town of Melleran, in Central France.' The words were spoken as if in a report, with no personal connection or interest.

'In the last months of 1943 and the first weeks of 1944, Laporte went to North Africa and England, for briefings with de Gaulle and others on the Allied invasion plans, in which he was to coordinate the role of the Resistance, and for special training. He returned to France during the early hours of Saturday, February 5th and was taken by the Resistance to a safe house, where he planned to spend the rest of the day and the following night. His presence in France, for obvious reasons, was a closely guarded secret. He intended to move on the Sunday morning.'

Father Jean looked up, saw Father Michael watching him closely, diverted his look back at the flame of the candle burning in front of him, fingers feeling for the comfort of the rosary.

'At four o'clock on the Sunday morning the safe house was stormed by the Gestapo, led by the Gestapo chief in France, Josef Heiner himself, and Laporte was captured. Heiner, it was later suggested, was acting on the express orders of Adolf Hitler. For the rest of the Sunday Laporte was tortured for his secrets but later that day Heiner was ordered by Berlin to take him to Paris.' Father Jean hesitated, then continued. 'A special train was arranged, equipped with an electricity generator in one carriage, so that Heiner could continue his interrogation during the journey.

'Laporte was seen being carried onto the train. He had already been brutally treated. Their destination was known locally to be Paris, by the most direct route. Other trains were stopped to give them clearance. As they left, however, a signalman who was a member of the Resistance managed to divert it onto a longer route.' He did not know that the signalman was later executed. 'It gave the Resistance time to organise one attempt to free Laporte. By the purest coincidence the nearest group, the only group able to mount the operation, was Laporte's own cell in Melleran.' He paused, imagining the night. 'The attack failed, several of the group were killed in the attempt, at least one other was badly injured. Jean Laporte was never seen alive by a Frenchman again. When the train reached Paris, he was dead.'

'But,' Father Michael helped him on.

'But he never revealed any of the priceless secrets trusted to him by de Gaulle. He died without saying a word.' Again he paused. 'Except,' he said, 'for one thing.' Again Father Michael waited. 'Except that in the moment before he died, he said something. To this day, no Frenchman knows what.'

'How do you know?' asked Father Michael gently.

Father Jean looked at him. 'Present in the carriage were four Germans: Josef Heiner himself, his lieutenant, a man called Heinrich Schmeltz, Heiner's book-keeper and a corporal. After the war Heiner, Schmeltz and the book-keeper disappeared, but the corporal was traced. According to his account, in the last moments of his life Laporte summoned Heiner to him. He could hardly move, the corporal said. Heiner, Schmeltz and the book-keeper bent over him and he said something to them. The corporal was on the other side of the carriage and could not hear what it was. Then Laporte died.'

The Frenchman retreated into silence, the rosary tight between his fingers. 'There is something else?' Father Michael suggested. Father Jean nodded.

'You remember I said that Laporte's wife was a member of the Melleran cell?' Father Michael remained silent, afraid to interrupt. 'It was she who led the attack on the train. The snow round the track was four feet deep. She organised explosives and when the train stopped, albeit for a few seconds, she personally led the group forward, armed with a Sten gun.'

Father Michael waited.

'At the time,' said Father Jean, 'she was eight months and twelve days pregnant. During the attack she went into labour.'

His voice was low, barely audible. Father Michael strained to hear. 'When the attack failed one of the group, Charles Chalbrand, hid with her in a farmhouse while the Nazis scoured the countryside for them. According to the corporal on the train, her husband died without saying another word, at precisely eleven o'clock in the morning of Monday, February 7th.

'According to Chalbrand, and the couple who hid them, the wife completed her labour without making a single cry, to protect them from the patrols outside. She gave birth to their son at precisely eleven o'clock in the morning of Monday, February 7th.'

Father Michael sat still, as if transfixed, as the other priest finished his story, staring in front of him, the crucifix of his rosary tight in his hands, the skin of his slim fingers white. 'Jean Laporte,' he was able to say at last. 'You share a name. Were you related?'

'My father,' said Father Jean quietly. 'I was the son who was born the moment he died.'

The two sat in silence. It was Father Jean who spoke first. 'We remember him all the time.' He was holding the rosary, gazing at the flame of the candle. 'And if that is not enough, we remember him above all once a year.'

Father Michael looked at him. 'I'm sorry, I don't understand.'

'In the cathedral at Chartres. Once a year, on the seventh, a service to commemorate my father. To remember the others.' His mind was drifting again, to the cathedral itself, tall and imposing, spanning the years, the spires reaching into the sky.

'The service is still the same,' he continued, 'even after

32

so long. It starts at fifteen minutes to eleven, the organ and the choir. At eleven o'clock exactly the bell and the *Marseillaise*. At the moment my father no longer felt the pains of this life.' He lowered his voice. 'At the moment my mother no longer felt the pains of my birth.'

He pressed on, driving the thorns of the crown he had worn for thirty-nine years deeper into his head, into his soul. 'Always at eleven. Always on the seventh. This year it will even be the same day. Monday, February 7th.'

For one moment Father Michael remembered the date. Monday, January 31st. One week to go, he thought sub-consciously, more concerned with drawing Father Jean out of his anguish. 'And the others?' he asked.

'The others, those who survived, went into hiding. Chal-brand stayed with my mother, protecting her, moving her from hiding place to hiding place. The Gestapo were still looking for them, even though it was too late. Chalbrand risked a lot then, as much as when he was out fighting. They were almost caught twice, but escaped both times. When it was safe I was baptised and named after my father, Jean Laporte. My second name is Charles. Most people think it is after the General. It is not. It is after the man who delivered me and who saved my mother's life.'

'And after?' The prompting was gentle, persuasive.

'After? After, I think, many felt they had done enough. They went back to their jobs, their families.'

'And Chalbrand. What happened to him?'

'Charles Chalbrand was one of my father's most trusted friends in the Resistance. The other was named Henri Bellan. He was also a member of the Melleran cell and took part in the raid on the train.' He was twisting the rosary again, lost in the past.

'They were both younger than my father. They were also different from the others in the cell. Better off, their families had sent them to better schools, given them ambi-tion. So in a perverse way the war even helped them. Their service in the Resistance. Their closeness to my father. Their loyalty, especially Chalbrand's, to my mother. After the war they both worked hard. At their professions, especially at their politics.' His mind fluttered subconsciously along the path taken by the French ambassador that afternoon. 'I suppose,' he conceded, 'that Chalbrand and Bellan are now important people.'

'In what way?'

Father Jean thought of the tall, imposing figure of his godfather and the shorter but equally distinguished Bellan. 'Henri Bellan is editor of *Le Monde*, which many consider my country's finest paper.'

'And Chalbrand?'

'Charles Chalbrand is foreign secretary. Many people believe he will be our next president.'

'And your mother,' Father Michael asked, 'what happened to her?'

Father Jean was beginning to withdraw again, conscious of the unrelenting nature of the question, aware of the probing that would follow, escaping its impact by merging its answer into that about his mother. 'My mother was broken.' He could not look the other priest in the eyes. 'Not physically, you understand. She recovered from the pain and trauma of my birth. But mentally she continued to suffer.' He shook his head. 'It took time for her to recover, but when she did she was as strong as they said my father had been, managing the family's affairs, arranging my education.' He hurried on, as if he was admitting a great shame, as if he was seeking to avoid an answer. 'I myself felt it necessary to become a priest.' It was, they both realised, a strange way of expressing his vocation. He pressed on, not giving Father Michael time to question him, puzzled by the need he felt to explain himself. 'It was what my mother wanted, what I myself thought fit. A need in society, if you like, a balance to the violence which had gone before.'

'A witness to peace,' suggested Father Michael.

'A witness to peace,' the French priest agreed. Father Michael waited, sensing there was more.

'I even went to Germany.' Father Jean's voice was low. 'It was my mother's idea that I should demonstrate my forgiveness of those who killed my father by learning their language.' Father Michael was staring at him incredulously. 'I speak fluent German,' the Frenchman explained.

The confession was over. He finished the other answer. 'My mother is now getting old. She has a maid to look after her and someone to run the grounds of the house.' He paused, subconsciously aware of the importance of what he was about to say, unaware he was about to say it. 'I suppose,' he said at last, 'that she is like the others, though she would not admit it.'

'What do you mean?' asked Father Michael.

'Waiting.' There was no emotion in Father Jean's voice. 'I suppose that for all these years they've been waiting.' The candles flickered against the statue of St Francis.

'Waiting for what?'

'Waiting for The Butcher.' There was a sudden hardness in the voice, then it died away. 'He never returned from the train which took my father to Paris. After the war there was no trace. Bellan and Chalbrand tried to find him. When they came to power they searched the files, but there was nothing. He simply vanished. The government sentenced him to death in his absence, but they're all still waiting.'

'And now he is found.'

Father Jean looked back at the other priest. 'Not quite, my friend. They've found his house, found the name under which he has been living, but they haven't found him.' He stopped staring at the candle.

'How did he know?' The question was clear and brittle.

Father Jean tried to avoid it. 'How did who know what?'

'How did Heiner know how to find your father?' The silence pierced the still of the chapel. The smell of melted wax drifted from the altar and filled the air.

35

'They say there must have been a traitor. Not in the cell, of course, but close to it. That's what Bellan and Chalbrand thought. When he became Prefect after the war, as my father had been before, Chalbrand even held an enquiry.'

'But they found nothing?'

Father Jean shrank deeper within himself. 'No, they found nothing.'

A breath of wind blew softly through the church, snuffing out the candle. The Frenchman sighed and rose to relight it. 'And you,' Father Michael subtly changed his theme, 'Are you still waiting?'

Father Jean tilted the taper till it met the wick of the candle. In his mind he could see the priest, his hair white as snow, who had taught him his faith, as he had taught his father before.

'How can I?' he asked. 'How can a priest wait for that?'

He remembered again the priest's face, the passage of the Bible which the old man had told him was his father's favourite verse.

Roman's xii, verse 19. 'Not revenging yourselves, my dearly beloved, but give place unto wrath.'

8 *Lima*

The AeroPeru flight landed on time. Corrigan pulled his bag from beneath the seat and joined the line of passengers waiting to leave the plane. The wall of heat as he stepped outside almost took his breath away. Even the few days away, the trip to Tingo Maria, had dulled his memory of the heat. Dry. Almost overpowering. He walked down the steps, into the airport complex, cleared the police checkpoint while the other passengers were still waiting to collect their luggage, and made his way into the main body of the airport, welcoming the cool.

Something happening, he knew, something building up, developing. He turned left, walked down the concourse towards the parking lot at the far end where he had left his car. Something happening, he knew, something which would involve him. He passed the queues of passengers waiting for the afternoon flights, skirting the tail of the crowd, close to the newspaper stand. He stopped, glancing across the headlines. Nothing, he thought, nothing to interest him, nothing to concern him. A strike at Cerro de Pasco, an Andean Pact meeting in Ecuador, a photo of the president addressing foreign bankers. Funny, he thought, no *Expresso*. He wondered if they hadn't printed that day, if they'd already sold out. He walked back into the sun, unlocked his car, and drove towards the city. Something happening, he was positive.

9 *Lima*

Maria let the phone ring for five minutes before she put it down. Hoping for a voice, praying for Weissemann to answer. Knowing he would not. Not knowing what she would do, what she would say, if somebody else answered. She picked up the paper, put it into her handbag, and told her staff she was leaving early and would be home if necessary. Even in the late afternoon the sun was still hot. She collected her car and drove out of the city centre towards Miraflores. Already the sky was beginning to lose its blue, already the lines of people were waiting at the street corners for the *collectivos* to take them home. She drove past the American embassy, the traffic building up, past the Bar Hawaii at the head of the grassy park which served as the heart of the fashionable quarter of the city overlooking the sea, and turned into the street where Herbert Weissemann had his flat.

The street was busy, lined with cars and stalls, the pavements crowded with shoppers. She hardly noticed.

The blocks of flats and offices on either side seemed to hang over the road, blocking out the sun, drawing her in. Weissemann's flat was fifty metres on the left. She did not know what to do, whether to stop, park the car, go to the flat. No point, she told herself, no answer to her telephone calls, nobody at home. A message, she thought, he might have left a message. Pinned to his door. No message, she knew. He would have phoned her. At her flat, at work. No message since she had followed his instructions the previous evening.

She was in front of the flat, her car slowed by the traffic. She looked up at the windows. No reason to stop, she admitted. Every reason not to stop, she suddenly knew. She drove past, pulled round the corner, parked the car and found a public telephone box. There was still no reply.

10   *Lima*

At the side of the chapel, in the main body of the church, Father Jean heard the soft sound of the monks entering the choirstalls. He watched them, envying them their peace, mindful of the comfort and friendship he himself had received from Father Michael. He half turned, aware suddenly of the novice at his side, hands clasped reverently, partly because he genuinely believed it was a sign of piety, partly because he was in awe of the priest from another country who received messages from the other side of the world. He coughed, almost apologetically. 'Father Jean,' he stuttered, 'a telephone call for you. From France,' he added, emphasising its importance.

Father Jean excused himself and followed as the novice led him through the maze of passages to the abbot's room. Behind him he could hear the soft chant as the others began vespers. Through the window, the shutters open in the summer heat, he could feel the haze of the city and, far off above the roof opposite, see the first lights of the *barriadas* on the hills. 'Father Abbot has gone to choir,' the novice explained, 'he asked me to bring you here.' The novice had an almost old-fashioned way of speaking.

The study was in semi-darkness, only the desk lamp shining on to the hard wooden table, the telephone nearby. On the wall at the side was a painting of the Last Supper, the figure of Christ washing the feet of his disciples. The priest stood beside the abbot's chair, not wishing to sit in it, and picked up the telephone. In the faint light he could see the dark varnish of the oils glinting.

'Père Jean speaking.' He heard the hollow hum of the international call then, without knowing it, the calm tones of the multilingual telephonist at the Elysée. He wondered if it was his mother, heard the familiar voice of the Foreign Secretary.

'Father Jean, how are you, my son?' Chalbrand had always referred to him that way, it was a term of deep affection, though the politician had insisted on addressing him as Father, at least in public, after his ordination.

For the second time that day he pictured the man; white hair, tall, upright figure. 'You've heard?' he asked.

'Yes,' replied Chalbrand, 'I heard immediately the embassy in Lima reported the matter. I don't know what to say, except that we are trying all we can.' The voice began to fade. 'The line is bad,' said Chalbrand, 'we had better be brief while we can hear each other.' The priest agreed.

'Does my mother know?' he asked.

'Yes, I told her myself.'

'And is there any fresh news?' He knew, but could not afford to admit to himself, that he was in a better position to know than the foreign secretary.

'At the moment I am afraid not,' confirmed Chalbrand, 'but it is still early. I am with the president now. His response is no more or less than one would have expected.

Full diplomatic pressure for extradition once Heiner is found, full pressure to find him.'

The line began to break up again, till the priest could barely hear the words, isolated in his loneliness. In touch with, but barely able to communicate with, his one link with France. For one moment the line cleared and he heard Chalbrand distinctly. ' . . . very bad. I can hardly hear you. I will phone again tomorrow at this time.' He began to reply, the line broke up and went dead.

Father Jean replaced the receiver, staring at the small circle of light cast by the desk lamp on the hard wood table, the polish glinting in the yellow light. On the edge of the circle lay a book, cloth-bound, worn. His hands reached for it, needing to do something, his mind still lost. The pages fell open and he saw the words from St Paul to the Romans that he had quoted to Father Michael.

Chapter xii, verse 19. 'Not revenging yourselves, my dearly beloved, but give place unto wrath.'

There were those in France, he knew, who would be seeking revenge. As the ambassador had told him that afternoon. As Father Michael had tested him before the statue of St Francis. A slender beam of solace crept through the gloom, easing his burden. A message from Christ, he thought, from the Prince of Peace, that his priestly stance, his lack of desire for revenge, was correct. He closed the book, noting the page which carried the verse, running his finger over the faded lettering on the spine.

St Thomas Aquinas. 'Summa Theologica.' Volume Two. Part Two. The page he had opened was headed 'Question 40. War.'

The first silk thread of the spider's web floated unseen through the air, settling on his shoulders, wrapping round his body. Drawing him in. Ensnaring him. Committing him.

There were priests in the Third World, priests whom he would never know, who could quote the five-and-a-half pages of Question 40 verbatim. Catholics from the dictatorships of Brazil and Guatemala, Jesuits from the ruthlessness of El Salvador, to whom the Summa Theologica was as sacred and important as the Bible itself, but who called it by another name.

The Doctrine of the Just War.

The novice was waiting outside the door. Father Jean crossed the room and asked whether the abbot would allow him to borrow the book. The young man answered hesitantly but hospitably. 'If he knows you would be helped by it, Father, he would want you to take it.' Father Jean murmured his appreciation, said he would return it in the morning, and walked back down the corridor, into the main yard, and let himself into the street through the small door in the corner of the monastery's heavy wooden gate. The streets were quiet. He walked slowly, deep in thought, to the Plaza de Armas, the glow from the ornamental street-lights hanging like misty moons. A gaily painted bus clattered round the square, past the headquarters of the Municipal Police, the shopping precinct, the grim façade of the cathedral and the presidential palace itself.

The priest's mind was in turmoil. It had been good to speak to Chalbrand; he would have spoken to no-one else. Except his mother. He pictured her, alone in the château. He, at least, he thought, had the strength of his faith, the comforting words of St Thomas Aquinas to reassure him.

The red bus passed the statue of the Conquistador Pizarro, in the corner of the plaza, and disappeared beneath a cloud of oily smoke towards the Plaza Dos de Mayo. The square was almost empty, the last solitary shoe-shine boy sitting on his wooden box in the centre, hoping for a late-night customer. Father Jean crossed the road, strolled into the square and sat by the boy, unaware, playing with the rosary. The boy lifted the priest's right shoe onto the sloping front of his box, raised the bottom of his trousers and slid a sheet of newspaper against the black stocking to keep it clean. Then he dipped his fingers into the polish and rubbed them around the shoe, the palms of his hand black and shiny, spitting occasionally at the polish, coughing from its fumes.

Father Jean opened the book, still fingering the rosary, and turned to the page where he had found the quotation which had given him such comfort.

St Thomas Aquinas. 'Question 40. Of War,' he read. 'We must now consider war, under which head there are four points of enquiry: (1) whether some kind of war is lawful? (2) whether it is lawful for clerics to fight? (3) whether it is lawful for belligerents to lay ambushes? (4) whether it is lawful to fight on holy days?'

The words threw him off guard, stealing the comfort he had expected to find. He read on, anxiously scouring the page for the words he wanted, finding them.

Romans xii.19. 'Not revenging yourselves, my dearly beloved, but give place unto wrath.'

The shoe-shine boy patted the priest's right shoe, lifted it off the box and replaced it with the left. The priest looked up from the book, aware for the first time of the shoeshine boy kneeling at his feet, remembering the oil painting of The Last Supper in the room where he had borrowed the book, unsure what to do.

He turned back to Aquinas, ignoring the boy, shutting out the fact that he was probably no more than eight years old, searching for more words of comfort.

'In order for a war to be just,' he read, 'three things are necessary. First, the authority of the sovereign by whose command the war is to be waged.' Heiner had been tried by a court in France, albeit *in absentia*, found guilty of war crimes, sentenced. The authority was there.

He realised what he was thinking, tried to stop himself, passed to the next requirement. 'Secondly, a just cause is required, namely that those who are attacked should be attacked because they deserve it on account of some fault.' There were two voices in him, one arguing that the French court's indictment against Heiner itself constituted a just cause, the other pleading with him to stop the examination, to remember the words of St Paul to the Romans. The rosary was tight between his fingers. He passed to the last requirement.

'Thirdly, it is necessary that the belligerents should have a rightful intention, so that they intend the advancement of good, or the avoidance of evil. True religion looks upon as peaceful those wars that are waged not for motives of aggrandisement or cruelty, but with the object of securing peace, of punishing wrong-doers.'

The words leaped at him from the page. 'Of punishing wrong-doers.'

Three requirements, the voice in him argued. Each met. 'Not revenging yourselves, my dearly beloved, but give place unto wrath,' the other voice argued back. Three requirements, the first pressed him, each satisfied.

The thread of the rosary snapped between his fingers, spilling the wooden beads onto his lap, sending them cascading across the concrete. He lurched forward, grabbing, scattering the rest. 'Damn,' he swore, unaware he had done so, knelt to retrieve them, the shoe-shine boy at his side, scrambling together on the ground till they collected all they could see.

'Sorry, Father, so sorry,' the boy muttered, accepting the guilt as his own, desperately seeking a gesture of atonement. 'Look, Father.' He reached into the pocket of his trousers, and pulled out a length of cat-gut, strong and cutting, and pressed it into the priest's hands. 'Now, Father, you can mend your beads.'

The boy stuffed his polish and rags into the top of his box and began to hurry away, still afraid. The priest was still kneeling, staring at the beads. 'Hey,' he suddenly called, getting up, 'I owe you for the shoe-shine. How much?' The boy hesitated.

'A hundred soles, Father.' The priest held the beads carefully in one hand, felt in the pocket of his jacket and pushed five hundred soles into the boy's black hand. The boy began to protest but the priest silenced him.

'It's for the cat-gut as well,' he said.

43

For a moment he wondered why he had kept it, then pushed the thought to the back of his mind.

The first silky thread of the spider's web which had settled on him in the monastery tightened round him, drawing him in.

He sat down, threaded the beads onto the cat-gut, knotted it, pushed it back into his pocket and picked up the book again, finding immediately another quote from St Paul.

Romans xiii, verse 4. 'He beareth not the sword in vain: for he is God's minister, an avenger to execute wrath upon him that doth evil.'

Beneath the covered pavement at the side of the square he saw the blue tin surround of a public telephone. He closed the book, walked across, and found the card the French ambassador had given him that afternoon. The feeling was strange, as if he was about to restart something that had been halted many years before. He felt in his pocket for a coin, pushed it into the meter and dialled the ambassador's home number. He did not remember, as the ambassador would later remember, his exact words.

The telephone was answered by a maid. He gave his name and asked for Señor Lafayette. The ambassador came to the telephone immediately. 'M. Lafayette, I've been thinking about something you said this afternoon. You said there is a journalist who had asked for an interview.'

'Yes, Ricardo Pacheco. He runs a magazine called *Cartas*.'

'He must be well-informed if he knew I was in Lima.'

'He is. Probably the best informed journalist in the country.'

'In that case I'd like to see him as soon as possible.'

'For an interview?'

'Yes, tell him it's for an interview.'

The ambassador did not notice the difference in emphasis. 'Of course, Father, where can he contact you?'

'He can't. Tell him I'll see him at the house at nine in

44

the morning.' He gave the ambassador no time to think. 'I would also appreciate it if you could arrange for a car to pick me up, and get permission from the relevant authorities for the house to be opened for me.'

The ambassador was confused. 'I'm sorry, Father, which house?'

The reply was unexpected. 'The house in Chaclicayo where The Butcher lived.'

The ambassador returned to the lounge and helped himself to the cocktail which the butler had prepared. The request had taken him unaware though the priest, as he had confided to his First Secretary, was in such a state of shock that he might do anything.

He sat back, not enjoying the pisco sour, knowing something in the conversation had disturbed him. Not the requests, he decided, bizarre though they were. Something else. Something his trained diplomatic senses should have spotted. Something which chilled him without his being conscious of it at the time. He ran his mind through the conversation, detecting nothing, and retired to bed, the worry still eating at his mind. It was five hours later, in the still of the night, that it came to him.

Not the words of the priest. The words of the maid as she announced the call. His subconscious had spotted it immediately, thrown up a protective barrier, yet had been unable to conceal the chill of the warning. Now the chill spread again. He realised he was trembling, unable to control himself.

The name of the caller. Not Father Jean. He could hear the words again, could not stop himself hearing them, remembering the legend, that at the moment the father had died the son had been born. 'Señor Lafayette,' the maid had said, 'Jean Laporte for you.'

In the emptiness of the Plaza de Armas the priest stood alone and confused. 'Not revenging yourselves, but give place unto wrath,' the Bible told him. 'He beareth not the sword in vain, for he is God's minister,' the same Bible told him. He remembered the conditions of The Just War, wondered why he had overlooked that part of St Thomas Aquinas in his studies, wondered if he would ever abandon his old principles for the saint's philosophy. Wondered if he should.

11 *La Paz, Bolivia*

The man with the passport in the name of Anderson sat back as the black Peugeot 504, the yellow stripe denoting its status as an official cab, left the airport and began the drop into La Paz, its engine whining in the thin air. It moved slowly and in circles, following the road which descended towards the heart of the city nestling in the huge natural bowl which protects it from the harsh winds of the *altiplano,* dropping like the 727 had done above the rim of the capital thirty minutes before.

He checked his watch, felt in his pocket that his passport and money were still there. He had stopped for five minutes at the airport to change travel cheques into local currency. Though the rate was bad and he could have got a better deal on the local black market it was something he had not considered. His fee, payable into his Zurich account, made such trivia irrelevent. And there was always the threat of the book-keeper. He laughed, remembered the joking warning on the last job he had done for them, the job at Portachuela. 'Keep all your receipts,' they had told him, aware of the irony, 'the book-keeper is as tight as a Jew.' The cab stopped outside the El Dorado hotel. He paid the driver, picked up his case, and walked in.

He'd made good time, he thought, bloody good time. Less than twelve hours ago he'd been asleep, the quiet of the curfew outside, in the Camino Real Hotel, San Salvador, capital of El Salvador. The telex, re-routed via the company he used in Washington, had arrived at 4.00 a.m. It was lucky, he had thought then, that he had brought the other job forward, completed it the previous evening. At 4.30 he had phoned the Duvos brothers, apologised for waking them, booked their air taxi from the military strip in the city centre to the international airport forty minutes' drive outside. Nobody who could afford not to endured the drive any more, especially in the early morning. Too many guerillas. Too many right-wing death squads, the mutilated bodies of their victims littering the roadsides. The connection in Panama had been tight, just time to telex the confirmation he did not want to originate in San Salvador, and check his reservation at the El Dorado, then he had boarded his plane and fallen asleep.

The receptionist saw him coming, knew he had seen her. Attractive, he thought, very attractive. Mid-twenties, dark features, jet black hair. 'Good day,' he said, 'my name is Anderson, I believe you have a reservation for me.'

She smiled at him and checked on the computer. 'Yes, Mr Anderson,' her English was soft, with an Atlanta drawl, 'Room 513, on account,' she noted.

'Sounds nice,' he said, 'does it have a large bed?'

'I'm sure it has,' she replied, looking at him.

Carmen. He noted her name on the lapel badge. A good lay, he thought, a very good lay. A professional, she thought, the eyes empty, nothing behind them. The thousand-mile stare, she knew they had called it in Vietnam.

She wondered why he was in La Paz, who had brought him in. Sharp, he thought, sharper than she looks. He wondered if he detected a suggestion in her reply, signed the registration card she gave him. George Anderson, aged thirty-four. A resident of Houston, Texas. Occupation, travel tour retailer. Very sharp, he decided, and one helluva good lay.

'One thing,' he asked her, 'could you have some coca tea sent up?'

Only someone familiar with the country would ask for coca tea, she thought. '*Ceroche*?' she asked. 'Altitude sickness?'

He shook his head. 'Not yet, but there's always later.'

The man seated in the cluster of armchairs opposite the reception desk, his face hidden by a copy of the previous day's *Herald Tribune,* heard the conversation, smiled to himself as it ended on a lower note that he could not hear. He watched as the Texan caught the lift, gave him five minutes then followed, taking the lift to the floor above Room 513 and walking down the extra flight of stairs.

At the sound of the bell, Anderson walked softly to the door and peered through the spy-hole. The man outside was in his late sixties, tall and distinguished in a well-cut pale blue lightweight suit and open-necked matching shirt. The silvery hair, just long enough to touch the collar, was swept neatly back, contrasting with the deep suntan of the face. The nose was thin, almost aquiline. But it was the eyes which held Anderson's attention, even through the spy-hole.

He opened the door. The visitor stepped back one pace, an indication that he posed no threat to Anderson's security, then spoke in German.

'*Was ist in der Falle?*' It was the first line of the code which Anderson had expected from the wording of the telex.

'*Die Fliege.*' His German pronunciation was bad but the words were correct.

'*Was wartet immer?*'

'*Die Spinne.*'

He stood aside, let the man into the room. 'Thanks for getting here,' said his visitor, 'you made good time. When did you get the telex?'

'Four this morning.'

'How was the connection?'

Anderson remembered Panama, felt no surprise the man should have known. It was the sort of detail he expected from the organisation, as witnessed by the planning for the other job he had done for them, the job at Portachuela. 'The connection was tight,' he said.

'Thanks anyway,' said the man.

Anderson shrugged. 'Something else was pulled forward, otherwise I wouldn't have made it for a couple of days.' He knew it was more than he should have said. He could see the computer of his visitor's mind working. Outward flight from the United States, Central American connection in Panama, connecting flight from El Salvador. The archbishop shot dead as he said mass the previous afternoon.

'You're here as an insurance,' his visitor moved straight to business. 'At the moment I don't know what kind, or for how long.'

The Texan nodded. 'Do you want me to stay in the hotel?'

The other man shook his head. 'Not necessary, feel free to do as you please. Any messages will be left every hour on the half hour.' Anderson nodded again. He did not need to ask what kind of insurance he might have to provide, the organisation would tell him when he needed to know.

'Weapons?' he asked.

His visitor took a key from his pocket. 'Left luggage locker, central bus depot.' He gave the key to Anderson. 'All clean.'

'What?' asked Anderson.

'Handgun, plus a .22 Ruger.' The choice took Anderson by surprise. Built-in silencer, he began to think, working out the job, the selection interesting him. 'Night-sights, in case you need them,' added his visitor.

'Ammunition?'

'.22 hollow point.'

Anderson began to see the picture. Not like Portachuela, he knew. Not the Browning BAR, old but reliable, that he had been provided with for Portachuela, a Browning plus bi-pad, evoking memories of Vietnam. A different job entirely, he already knew. Probably a head job.

'Terrain?' he asked.

'Urban,' said his visitor.

'Range?'

'Probable maximum a hundred-and-fifty metres.'

49

It was almost, Anderson thought, that despite his denials his visitor already knew the exact location and circumstances of the job. Even the timing.

'Anything between me and the target?'

'Nothing.'

A head job, Anderson confirmed.

There was a knock on the bedroom door. 'Room service,' he said, 'it's on order.' His visitor nodded and went into the bathroom, leaving the door slightly open. Anderson checked, opened the bedroom door and let the waiter into the room. The man put the tray on the table next to the bed, accepted the small change which Anderson gave him, and left. The visitor came back from the bathroom. Anderson poured himself a cup of coca tea, his visitor declining, and waited.

'I suggest,' said the man politely, 'that you pick up the goods as soon as possible. There's no guarantee that your services will be required, but if they are there may be little warning.' Anderson nodded. He would have to zero the sights, load the magazines personally. He finished the tea quickly. 'If you wish to leave first,' his visitor offered, 'feel free to do so. I'll give you ten minutes, then leave.'

Anderson recognised the other man's logic. He would wait till Anderson was at the bus depot, verified by a look-out, then leave the hotel. That way there would be no danger of being followed. Or, thought Anderson, that was probably what he was supposed to think. 'OK,' he said, 'check calls every hour on the half hour.'

The visitor watched as he left the room. There was no-one at the bus depot. He, in fact, was the only person to know of the Texan's presence in La Paz. It was that kind of insurance policy.

He helped himself to a cup of tea and sat down to wait till Anderson had left the building. There was no danger, he knew, that the Texan would follow him, try to find out anything about him. But he was naturally careful. As an afterthought he lifted the telephone, waited for the telephonist to answer and asked for the delay in calls to

Lima, Peru. All afternoon he had been trying, all afternoon there had been no lines. To his surprise the international exchange said they would connect him immediately. He gave a number, knowing there were other calls to make but that they, even more than this call, should be made on the secure system on which he had spent so much money to set up, then swore softly as the call connected and the impersonal voice of an answerphone machine informed him the office was closed and invited him to leave a message.

'This is Heron Exports,' he spoke slowly and clearly in Spanish, 'the managing director speaking. I regret that due to unforeseen circumstances, service has been interrupted. Business will resume as soon as possible.'

He replaced the receiver, finished the tea and left the room. Ten minutes later he was five blocks away from the hotel, unlocking the door of the Mercedes. It had been worthwhile getting the Texan in, he decided. Expensive, of course, which the book-keeper would object to when it finally reached his files, but worthwhile. In any case, he thought, it was he, Josef Heiner, who had set up the organisation. So it was he, Josef Heiner, who would decide how it spent its money. And he was glad to have met the man; it confirmed what he needed to know, that the Texan was the right man to have around. The back door that nobody else knew about.

There was only one thing, he thought, that he had not asked. Whether Anderson had arranged to make it with the receptionist.

The hotel foyer was half empty. Carmen saw the Texan leave in a cab the porter called for him. George Anderson, she checked his registration again, a resident of Texas. She wondered who he really was, where he was from, why he was in La Paz. She took the card from the file, photocopied it, put the original back in its place, and slipped the copy into her handbag. Sometime, she knew, it would be important. Sometime in the next twenty-four hours, she also knew, Anderson would invite her to dinner. And after, he would invite her to his bed. The knowledge did not concern her, it was simply part of the job. She thought about him, wondered what he would be like. Good, she thought, he would probably be very good. She wondered if he would be as good as Guillermo.

12 *La Paz*

Guillermo Pertierro closed his eyes against the darkness. Outside, he knew, it was light. Two hours ago, he calculated, he had seen the light. Not the artificial glow of an electricity bulb, glaring, threatening. The light of a Bolivian afternoon, cold and clear, as he had been dragged up the stairs. He opened his eyes and looked at the darkness. Two many secrets, he thought, too many people to protect. One person above all. He wondered where Carmen was, what she was doing.

She was important, very important. To the cause, to himself. Few knew of her allegiance, her role in the struggle, her commitment to the revolution. To most of her friends she was just an hotel receptionist, yet even that had been invaluable. A good cover, a good contact point; she could talk to people, be approached by people, without rousing suspicion. More. She could check on the comings and goings of the strangers, the *gringos* who came from outside, draw the information out of them, report on them. Sometimes, he knew, he had not liked the methods she had been forced to use, had felt a jealousy, a resentment, at the exploitation to which the cause required her to turn her body. But the information was good, invaluable. For others as well as themselves. The movements and connections of the rich businessmen, the bankers, priceless to the brothers in Central America, who needed the ransom money from their multitude of kidnappings to finance the revolution in their own countries.

Sometimes the source had brought priceless benefits to the movement in Bolivia itself. The arms, the weapons with which they fought, had been secured from two European dealers whom Carmen had met, who believed her when she told them they were for the rich landowners to protect their properties against the peasants. Perhaps the men from Europe had not believed her, he knew, but they had taken her money, sold her their guns.

He looked again at the darkness, ran his fingers along its walls. Thought about death, wondered whether death was also black. Wondered if he was dead. Only the pain confirmed he was still alive.

13 *Lima, Peru*

The traffic lights changed to green. Joe Corrigan turned the Chevrolet right off Avenida Inca Garcilaso de la Vega, then sharp left, past the Marine guard, and into the underground car park at the rear of the red brick building which was the embassy of the United States of America. He found his usual space and took the lift to his office, the sign 'Commercial Attache' screwed neatly to the door, greeted his secretary, and turned up the air conditioning.

Something happening, he thought, something building up, developing. Something which concerned him, involved him. The instinct had not left him since he watched the plane clip the trees in the jungle strip in Tingo Maria. Something happening, he was positive.

The backlog of telexes, mail and newspapers was waiting in the outer office as well as the box, wrapped in plain white paper, which had arrived for him in the diplomatic pouch. He did not need to open it to know what was inside. Havana cigars, sent by a colleague, fresh, almost moist. Havanas, he sometimes joked, were his one folly. Havanas, his wife usually retorted, were his drug. In a way, he supposed, it was true. It was difficult to run the sort of

53

operations he ran, mix with the sort of people he mixed with, then switch off and go home to the white-washed villa he rented overlooking the city. The cigars, he had long found, soaked up his adrenalin when he did not need it, built it up when he did.

There were still half a dozen left from the last shipment, in the box in the bottom drawer on the right of his desk. He helped himself to one, savouring the flavour, phoned his wife to say he was back and would be home early, then pressed the intercom to Dick Mayer's office. The secretary answered immediately. 'Could you tell the boss I'm back, everything's fine, and I'll be up later.'

There was a surprise in her voice which puzzled him. Something happening, he thought again, something which concerned him, something which would concern him even more. He pushed it to the back of his mind, settled back in the leather chair and began the tedious process of catching up on the news before he briefed Mayer.

Joe Corrigan was thirty-seven. His name, like the job title on his office door, was misleading. There was not a hint of Irish in his accent or an iota of commerce in his profession. His grandparents had emigrated to Boston from Donegal just before the Great Depression. His father had worked during the day and studied at night, become a lawyer's clerk, and married the daughter of a Polish emigré who was similarly struggling to achieve the American dream. They had made sure that each of their three children went to university, two to the University of California in Los Angeles, the other to Berkeley. Their elder son, Edward, now lectured in law at the Harvard Business School. Their only daughter, Anna, had continued her law practice after marrying the local district attorney. For the past thirteen years, after service in an army Special Operations unit in South East Asia, their younger son, Joe, had worked for the American Central Intelligence Agency, the CIA.

The mail was uninteresting: updates on suspect groups,

movements of politicians. He turned to the batch of telexes, browsing through them in the order they had been received. It was only when he got to the second of the three messages received that afternoon in the embassy's communications room that he took notice. The coded message from regional head office in Caracas, Venezuela. It said simply that Washington required an immediate update on Heron Exports. He put the single sheet aside, noted that it would be something to raise when he briefed Dick Mayer later, and returned to the stack of local newspapers. Normally he would have left them for another day, but he wanted to familiarise himself with any local news in case Mayer raised it at their meeting.

La Prensa was official and uninteresting. He fingered his way through *El Comercio*, then moved on to the popular papers, remembering the news stand at the airport, satisfied there was nothing of interest. The afternoon edition of *Expresso* was at the bottom of the pile. The red headlines leapt out at him. He looked at the photograph, turned to the details on page three, scanned them as Maria had done in the Plaza San Martin that afternoon, as the priest had done in the ambassador's office, and sat back in his chair. 'Jesus,' he breathed slowly.

The Havana had gone out. He did not bother to relight it, chewing it instead, moving it round his mouth, between his teeth. He flicked on the answerphone machine attached to the private number into his office. Something happening, he had known, when the plane came in to land at Tingo Maria, when he himself had landed in Lima. Now he knew. Wondered already what had gone wrong. How he could start covering. The answerphone was repeating the messages it had stored during his days from the office. It spun on, the information interesting on any other day, unimportant today, till it was almost at the end of the tape. He reached forward to switch it off and heard the voice.

'This is Heron Exports. The managing director speaking. I regret that due to unforeseen circumstances service has been interrupted. Business will resume as soon as possible.'

The intercom buzzed. He answered, not waiting to hear who it was. 'I've just heard,' he told Dick Mayer, 'I'm on my way up.'

The Lima station chief was standing behind his desk, staring across the traffic to the park beyond. Even with the double glazing, the noise of the city crept into his office. He heard the knock on the door, shouted at whoever it was to come in, and sat down. Dick Mayer was in his early fifties, the front of his yellow shirt folding over his trousers where middle age had taken its toll on his physique.

The door opened and Corrigan came in. 'Nice to see you back, Joe, how was the trip?' Mayer lit himself a Winston. Corrigan settled himself in the chair in front of the desk, pulled a Havana from his shirt pocket and stuck it in his mouth without lighting it.

'Not bad, not bad at all. Until I got back. What the hell's going on?' It was the way the two men worked, worked well together, respecting each other, with no stalling. 'No bull-shit,' Mayer had told Corrigan when he had first arrived. 'Straight in, you cover me and I'll cover you.'

'Christ knows,' Mayer said. 'First I heard about it was when I read that goddamn newspaper report. Nothing we could do, of course, 'cept sit tight and keep our heads down. Couldn't even get the diplomatic boys to ask any questions. One sniff and everybody would have asked why we were interested.' The cigarette had gone out. He relit it. 'Then no sooner as dammit than Caracas is on the line wanting background, updates, the whole fucking lot. You've seen it?'

'Yes, I've seen it. And the paper.' Corrigan wondered how Mayer would take the news. 'Anyway, the man's OK.'

Mayer's face collapsed under the steel of his close-cropped hair. 'You've been in touch with him?' Oh Christ, the thought was simmering in his brain. Before was bad enough, but now. He could see the congressional enquiry, the television cameras.

'I haven't but he has. There was a message on my answerphone when I got back. He must have called less than an hour ago.'

'Jesus Christ, what did he say?'

Corrigan pulled a piece of notepaper from his pocket. 'He said, and I'm quoting verbatim, "This is Heron Exports. The managing director speaking. I regret that due to unforeseen circumstances service has been disrupted. Business will resume as soon as possible." ' He handed the paper to Mayer. 'That's it, nothing else, no clue as to where he is, what he's doing.'

'Jesus Christ,' Mayer repeated himself. Corrigan knew the expression denoted no panic. 'And you don't have any way of getting hold of him?'

Corrigan shook his head. 'Contact was always through the house at Chaclicayo.'

'So how do we stand?'

Corrigan was cautious but optimistic. 'At the moment we're standing pretty well. Only routine small stuff in the pipeline, all the big ends tied up.'

'What about Project Octavio?'

Corrigan indicated that he shared Mayer's concern. 'Politically the most delicate, but all the ends are sewn up.'

Mayer nodded, swung in his chair, faced out of the window for almost a full minute, then swung back again. 'And no other complications?'

'None that I know of.'

'OK, Joe. You're his case officer. You're the one who knows him. What do we do?'

Corrigan replied without hesitation. 'Like you said earlier, we sit tight. I'll draft a reply to Caracas to that effect, summing things up, and let you see it before I send it off. After that, there's nothing we can do.' Mayer nodded his agreement and lit another Winston. 'OK. We sit tight.'

The flat was cold and bleak. Even the wind off the ocean, normally warm, seemed chilled. Maria wrapped the sweater round her shoulders, hunched into the chair, and stared again at the newspaper. She knew what it would say, did not have to read the words again, looked at the pictures.

'Exclusive,' the garish red headline screamed at her, 'The Butcher is found.' It was the newspaper she had waited to buy in the square that afternoon, the newspaper the French ambassador had shown to the priest, the newspaper which had sent Joe Corrigan hurrying to his station chief. 'Nazi war criminal in Lima,' exclaimed the headline across the inner pages.

She wondered if they would find out, whether they would discover her involvement, what they would do to her when they did. In the street below she heard a police siren. The cup of coffee which she clutched tightly in her hands was cold. She got up, shut the window, and stared again at the newspaper.

The flames shot round the steaks on the barbecue. Corrigan prodded the sizzling meat with a fork and poured himself another glass of sangria. It was the type of spontaneous homecoming his wife often arranged for him, something that had started in the grim days in South-East Asia. They had both been young then, his first field assignment, and she had been thankful for every time he came back. Not knowing, in many ways glad she did not know, what he was doing. Growing accustomed to the way he came home, the Havana clamped in his mouth, the look in his eyes as he traced and retraced his tracks, covering himself. The trip into the jungle this time, he had explained, was routine, a business lunch he had called it. Pay up and invest for the future, a few jars of the local hooch, then home. But he had come home that evening with the Havana clenched between his teeth, chewing the end, the look in his eyes betraying him in a way nobody else would understand.

She looked across the back lawn of their house to where their two children were playing with those of the neighbours and friends she had invited for the evening. Modern American families like themselves, most of the husbands in the oil business, shipped in when the multinationals thought they'd struck it rich in the tree-covered Amazon, flying home when they could from the rigs in places like Iquitos, Pucallpa and Puerto Maldonaldo. The men knew about Joe, of course, or thought they knew. Out of town too much, they would say, to be the commercial attaché his visiting card said he was. Something else, something special. A troubleshooter, an oil man like themselves, they secretly believed, keeping an eye on developments, protecting interests. Corrigan had done his homework, slipped in the occasional line of technical jargon to confirm their suspicions, keep them quiet. A good guy, they all said, a good family. Stalwarts of the community, beer at the Saturday afternoon football replays at the embassy, regulars at the Church of the Good Shepherd in Miraflores. When, the men nodded knowingly, he wasn't away.

'Good trip, Joe?' one of the oilmen asked.

'*Huaraz*,' he said, the lie coming easily. 'Good for trout, bad for everything else.'

The man laughed. 'You missed a good match on Saturday.' He began to explain the details. Corrigan listened, nodding, teeth grinding the butt of the cigar, eyes fixed and interested in the conversation, mind on the police raid on the house at Chaclicayo in the misty hours of that morning.

Christ, he asked himself, where the hell is the bastard now? Should have left some clue, some indication where he could reach him. Pull him out of trouble if the going

59

got heavy. Jesus Christ, the voice in his head asked him. What do you mean, if the going got heavy? What the hell do you think it is now? Thank Christ he got out, though. Good contacts the old bastard had, bloody good. Tipped him off about the raid. So why the hell hadn't all those guys on the payroll at the *Guardia* HQ tipped him off as well on the private line with the answerphone? OK, he told himself, calm down. It was a good sign that nobody saw fit to tip him off. Cover. Fucking deep cover. What the hell would the good old US of A be doing with some Nazi war criminal who'd been on the run for nearly forty years? But somebody knew, the voice reminded him, knew enough to tip off the paper, knew enough to have a bloody photograph.

Something else, his instincts warned him. Nothing obvious, nothing immediate. But something else. It was like riding point in 'Nam, the sixth sense that something was not as it seemed to be. The sense that had brought him through, had made him a survivor. Made him good. Something else, the instinct confirmed. He wondered what the hell it was.

There was a tap on his arm. He turned round, his mind snapping back to the barbecue. His wife was standing beside him, the young wife of a neighbour with her, the freckles of the younger woman's suntan sparkling against the light blue of her loose dress, the contentment of recent motherhood beaming at him in her eyes. 'Mary Jane, you're looking slimmer every day. Too late in the summer for a bikini, of course. You'll have to organise it better next time.' He kissed her as she blushed.

'Joe,' his wife began, 'Mary Jane has something important to ask you.' He saw the seriousness in the younger woman's face.

'Sure, what is it?' There was a sudden concern in his voice. 'Nothing wrong, is there? The baby's all right?'

Check, the voice kept telling him. Go back and check. All the loose ends tied up, all the tracks covered. No way they can connect you. No way they can pick their way back to the Company. Something else, he knew, something else.

'No, Joe,' the young mother was smiling, 'nothing like that.' She hesitated. 'It's just that Daniel is three months old this week. He's being baptised on Thursday.' She hesitated again. 'We'd like you to be Daniel's godfather.'

He smiled back at her, giving her a hug, genuinely affected by the request. 'Can't you find anyone better than me?' he joked, kissing her. 'I'd be proud to be Daniel's godfather.'

Check, the voice told him again. Go back and check. It was OK in 'Nam. They all expected it there, the rough stuff, the dirty stuff. But it's different now, different times, too many liberals round Capitol Hill who didn't come up the hard way. OK to play games in some godforsaken corner of the world. But sometimes there's something big. Like Octavio. Then the dividends start rolling in. Then the liberals get ready to screw you.

'That's if you're not out of town, Joe,' the young mother was adding. 'We'd understand if something came up.'

He smiled again. 'I'll make sure nothing does come up,' he asserted playfully.

Over his shoulder his wife saw Dick Mayer loping towards them, his huge stride out of place behind the clipped footsteps of the maid who had let him into the house. 'Joe,' she alerted him, 'you didn't tell me Dick was dropping in.'

Corrigan half-turned and bellowed a greeting. 'I'm sorry, I thought I'd mentioned it. Better get him a drink, I suppose.' His wife knew he was covering. He kissed the young mother again, gave Mayer a steak and beer, and guided him to a quiet corner of the garden. Even in the semidarkness his wife could see the cigar moving between his teeth, sense the look in his eyes.

'The shit's hit the fan,' Mayer said without preamble. 'I was called back to the office tonight. Special message they couldn't give me over the phone, couldn't even send a messenger with.' He took a bite of the steak, almost choked, and tried to wash it down with a mouthful of beer. 'They're worried.' He took another mouthful. 'They're sending a special in.' He saw the look on Corrigan's face. 'Don't worry, they're not taking over the show. It's just insurance. It's just so big, they say, that they want somebody else in to oversee the whole shooting match, somebody closer to the big boys at the top.'

Christ, Corrigan felt the thought echoing through his head, they must think it's big if somebody in regional HQ in Venezuela had decided to send a special in. 'What else does Caracas say?' he asked.

Mayer took another mouthful of steak. 'Who said anything about Caracas?' he retorted. 'I'm talking about Washington.'

Chapter Two

Tuesday, February 1st, 1983

The residential suburb of Chaclicayo lies some ten kilometres from Lima, tucked into the western foothills of the
Andes, high enough to escape the mist which descends
upon the city for the three months of winter, from June to
August, low enough to enjoy the warmth of the coastal
strip. Most of its houses are owned or rented by wealthy
foreigners or even wealthier Peruvians, white walls surrounding the mock-colonial villas, guard dogs patrolling
the grounds.

The embassy driver knew the road well. On his free days
he took it up to the mountains themselves, sometimes
passing over the massive range to the tropical rain forests
on the eastern side. He wound down the window, enjoying
the fresh air. Behind him, unspeaking, sat the priest. The
driver left the main road, turning right, followed the sweep
of the side road for a little over a kilometre, slowed at a
junction while he checked the map which lay open on the
empty seat beside him, and took the left fork. The trees
on the right gave way to a line of houses, expensive
and exclusive, most as big as the ambassador's official
residence. There was no need to check for numbers. He
pulled in behind the police car and the green Audi and
switched off the engine. Two policemen, in the olive green
uniforms of the *Guardia Civil*, were lounging against the
patrol car. A man in slacks and open-necked shirt was
talking to them, another younger man with longer hair was
sitting in the other car.

The priest got out and approached the two policemen,
bidding them good morning. The man who was with them
held out his hand. 'Father Jean, my name is Ricardo

Pacheco. The ambassador phoned me last night and asked me to meet you here.' They shook hands.

'It's good of you to come at such short notice. Is it all right for us to go inside?'

Pacheco nodded. 'According to these people, you have complete access to the house.'

The priest smiled. 'Shall we go in, then?' A thought came to him. 'If that's your car, perhaps you could give me a lift back to Lima when we've finished and the man who brought me here could go?' Pacheco agreed. The priest walked to the embassy car and told the driver he could go. Different, thought the driver, already different from the man he and the First Secretary had collected from the schoolhouse in the *barriada* the previous afternoon. He started the car, Father Jean and Pacheco walked past the guards and into the gardens.

'Laporte,' the driver called, not knowing why he had chosen to address the priest by his surname. 'Good luck.' He did not know why he had said it. The priest looked at him.

'Thanks,' he said.

Pacheco was in his early forties, a little over six feet tall and well-built, the muscle of youth beginning to soften round his waist. His brown hair was thinning slightly and he wore hornrimmed spectacles which helped conceal the strength of his face. 'Have you been inside yet?' Laporte asked him.

'I was here for a while yesterday but there were too many people for a good look round. I didn't get past the front door.'

'In that case,' suggested Laporte, 'we could do that first, then talk.' The magazine editor agreed. The priest, he had already decided, was not as he had expected. The handshake when they had met was strong and firm and the suggestion that they should examine the house before talking was delivered with an air of confidence and authority.

The house stood at the top of a garden which was almost

a hundred metres long. Its sense of emptiness betrayed the fact that it had been occupied until the morning before. Even in the warmth of the summer it felt cold. Like a mausoleum, Pacheco thought, but more sinister. The front door had been opened by the police. They went into the large entrance hall, the lounge on the right, the study on the left. Each room had been torn apart, the furniture upturned, some of it damaged, the carpets pulled up and put on one side. A desk in the study was in pieces, its leather top sliced away. On the walls were light patches, some square, others rectangular, where pictures had hung. In one square the door of a wall-safe hung open. They went back into the hall and up the wide stairs to the bedrooms and bathroom on the first and second floors. Each in turn had been ransacked, the mattresses on the beds ripped open, the carpets torn aside and the floorboards prised up. Pacheco followed the priest down the stairs again and back into the study. The books on the mahogany shelves on either side of the fireplace had been piled in a heap in the centre of the room, covered with patches of soot, as if someone had examined the chimney. They went back through the hall and into the kitchen.

On the draining board was an electric kettle. 'Coffee?' suggested Pacheco. 'You look as if you could do with some.'

Laporte smiled an apology for his silence. 'Sorry if I'm not very talkative, I didn't sleep much last night.' Pacheco muttered that he understood, confirmed that the electricity was still switched on, and began to boil the kettle while Laporte searched in the cupboards on the side wall for cups and coffee.

'A bit bare, isn't it,' he suggested, looking around. The only items in the kitchen were a cooker which ran from a gas bottle, as is the custom in most Peruvian houses, a cupboard, a fridge, a small table, three chairs and, in one corner, an iron solid-fuel stove.

'You don't know much about Peru,' replied Pacheco, half serious, half joking. 'We're probably the first men ever to step into a kitchen in this country.' The kettle boiled, he began to make the coffee. 'In Peru, the only person who goes into the kitchen is the *muchacha*, the maid. Everybody has a *muchacha*, even the *muchacha* has her own *muchacha* at home.' He looked around. 'This is probably well-furnished compared with some.'

'What about that?' Laporte pointed to the stove.

'No idea,' said Pacheco, 'probably use it for hot water, it's always on.' He sat down, gave Laporte a cup.

'Nothing much left,' mused Laporte. Almost, Pacheco thought, as if he had either expected or hoped to find something. 'Who did all the damage?'

'The police, looking for evidence and the like. They certainly tore the place apart, but I think a lot of the stuff had already been removed.'

'How much did they miss him by?'

'Not much, as far as I can gather. Heiner was actually seen leaving the house late the night before, then someone was seen again in the house at about five, just before the police arrived. Whether or not that person was Heiner is unclear. The neighbours are very unsure. I've had my best reporters trying to piece the story together, but there's not much to go on.'

'What did you mean,' Laporte asked suddenly, 'when you said the stove was always on? How do you know?'

Pacheco looked across the kitchen at the stove in the corner. 'According to a couple of the *muchachas* who work for the neighbours and who occasionally visited the one here, the place was always cosy and warm, the stove was always on.' He sipped the coffee. 'And it was certainly burning when the police arrived.'

'What do you mean?'

'One of the squad told one of my people that it was blazing away. That was what made them think they only just missed them.'

'Any reason for that?'

'For the stove burning at night, you mean? I honestly

68

hadn't thought too much about it. Probably to burn something, documents and suchlike I'd imagine.'

Laporte looked at the stove. 'Did anybody check it?'

Pacheco shook his head. 'Not that night, as far as I know. Certainly nothing was found the next morning, or I'd have known.'

The coffee was strong. They sat drinking, lapsing into silence. Pacheco waited, watching the priest's eyes, confirming the impression he had already formed that the Frenchman was not as he had expected him to be. In some ways, he felt, the priest was there to ask questions rather than answer them. They finished their coffee and he made another two cups.

'The ambassador said you wanted to give me an interview.' It was not too far from the truth to be dishonest, Pacheco thought.

'The ambassador said you had asked for an interview and suggested that as you seemed to have good sources you might be able to tell me a little more about the affair,' countered the priest.

Pacheco recognised the offer of a deal. 'So which would you prefer first,' he asked directly, 'the interview or the information?'

Laporte smiled. 'The interview, then you won't feel under any pressure.' For the next hour they talked, Laporte's words taped on the cassette recorder Pacheco always carried, the Frenchman recounting the story he had told the night before to Father Michael. Without, he sensed, the involvement which had made the confession a form of torture. Without, though he could not admit it, the tentacles of self-doubt. When he had finished he explained the position of the French government as told to him by Chalbrand, and said what he imagined would be the reaction of those of his countrymen who had fought with the Resistance.

'And you,' asked Pacheco quietly. 'What is your reaction as a priest?'

'There are those,' began Laporte carefully, 'who argue

for what they call the Just War. That is to say, they set out the conditions under which it is permissable for men, even priests, to take up arms. In a way, that's what you're asking me about.' He continued the reference.

'Those who support this say there is a precedent, a justification, in both the Bible, mainly the Old Testament, and the action of the Church throughout history. They also quote the words of St Thomas Aquinas.'

Laporte smiled again. 'As I said, there are those who quote precedent, who quote Aquinas.' He got up and drew himself a glass of water.

Ricardo Pacheco switched off the cassette recorder. 'What do you want to know from me?'

'Whatever you think is necessary,' Laporte replied.

Pacheco made himself comfortable. 'As I said earlier, I don't know if the information will help you, but this is what I know.

'The article which appeared in the newspaper was written by a friend of mine, a German journalist called Herbert Weissemann.' He corrected himself. 'He did not actually write the piece, but he was responsible for it getting into the paper. And the fact that it did meant that something had gone very, very wrong.' Laporte began to ask who Weissemann was, why his nationality was significant, but Pacheco stopped him. 'Please, the story is complicated, let me tell it in my own way.' Laporte sat back.

'Herbert Weissemann is in his late forties, just old enough to have grown up in the chaos of post-war Germany, to have picked up the threads of nazism which went underground in 1945. He started working on a local paper in Stuttgart, then moved on to *Stern* magazine in Hamburg. He was good, very good. He became an international globetrotter for them. Any big wars, any big news stories, he would be there. But his great interest remained the Nazis. He made it his speciality. Finally the interest became an obsession, he was convinced he was going to find Martin Bormann. He gave up his job and moved to

70

Lima. On a retainer, of course. He still made a good living.

'Two weeks ago he came to see me. He said he had been on to something for a long time, but that he was only just learning how big it was. He was excited about it, especially for somebody who had been in the game so long. He said it involved an intelligence network and a top Nazi war criminal.' Pacheco laughed. 'I couldn't get out of him who the man was, which country wanted him. I suppose I assumed it was Germany since the Israelis seem to have forgotten.

'He was not his normal self, however. He was worried, said that it was so big that it carried more than the usual risks. Which, for him, was saying something. I remember he said something very strange, which he refused to explain. He laughed when he was talking about the risks, a nervous sort of laugh, and said something like, "They have a saying, remember what happens when the Spider sees you." Then he said he only needed one more piece to fit the whole web together. I remember that was the way he described it. He thought it was very funny, but I couldn't understand what he meant and he refused to tell me.

'I didn't see him for a week, then he came to see me, said he was going ahead with the project. He said he feared for his life, but that if they got him he had taken out an insurance, that they would still pay. He'd written an article, he said, exposing the part of the story for which he had the evidence. He said that if anything happened to him he was arranging for it to be sent to *El Expresso*.' Pacheco laughed again. 'I asked him why he wouldn't give it to me and he said he wanted to protect me.' He shrugged. 'A kind thought, but a pity.'

'So what happened then?'

Pacheco spoke slowly. 'I assume that the terrible thing which Weissemann feared happened. That somehow, somewhere, the people he was after found out about him. All I know is that his insurance plan was put into operation.

The article he had written was delivered to *El Expresso* and Heiner was exposed.'

'And where is Weissemann now?'

The editor looked at the priest. 'I imagine,' he said bluntly, 'that Herbert Weissemann is dead.'

Laporte waited for a moment then pressed on. 'But Heiner was the man he was talking about?'

'In retrospect, undoubtedly.'

'And you have no idea where he is at the moment?'

'Where Heiner is? No idea at all.'

'There's one thing I don't understand,' said Laporte. 'Heiner presumably left the house as soon as he was tipped off, which he clearly was. Yet somebody stayed, knowing the house was about to be raided by the police. Why?'

Pacheco gestured around him. 'To clean up, I suppose. The police did most of the damage, but I gather a lot of stuff had gone before they arrived: paintings, antiques, valuables.'

'The spoils of another war,' suggested Laporte.

'The spoils of another war,' agreed Pacheco.

They finished their coffee and rose to leave. 'There's one other thing,' said Pacheco, 'I have a photographer in the car. Do you mind if he takes some pictures?' Laporte agreed.

For the next ten minutes the photographer led Laporte from room to room, in the way he himself had led Pacheco earlier, photographing him both inside and outside the house. When he was satisfied they left, the photographer running in front of Pacheco and Laporte to snatch a last picture of the two together.

'How did Herbert Weissemann get the article to the newspaper?' Laporte suddenly asked. Pacheco stopped walking and looked at him, glancing round as if to confirm they would not be overheard.

'I'm not sure, but there's only one person he would trust. A woman he knows.' They began walking again. 'Not quite his girlfriend, more his confidante, somebody he had known for a long time and whom he knew he could trust, somebody he knew he could turn to when he needed help.'

'Can I meet her?'

'That's up to her,' said Pacheco. 'I'll phone her and ask. But the decision is hers.' He was aware of the web being spun round them, remembered Weissemann's joke about the spider. 'We can phone on the way back to town.' He saw the policeman looking at them from the bottom of the garden. 'It's safer than from the office.'

2   *Lima*

The special from Washington sat easily in a leather chair opposite Corrigan, on the right-hand side of Dick Mayer's desk in the station chief's third-floor office. The curtains behind Mayer were closed, the only light in the room came from a desk lamp. Each of the three settled comfortably in the half gloom. Jack Bailey had arrived in Lima earlier that morning, coming straight to the meeting, stopping only to shower and take a light breakfast in the basement restaurant. In his shirt pocket he carried a silver sheath from which he occasionally pulled a plastic toothpick. A packet of Winstons lay open on Mayer's desk. Three Havanas protruded from Corrigan's shirt pocket.

Mayer got up, drew a beaker of water from the cooler, and settled back behind his chair. 'Well, Jack,' his drawl was slower than usual, 'we've told you the little we know, the details of the raid, the man's phone message to Joe. Suppose you take it from there.'

The man from Washington began to speak, slowly and carefully, his delivery unable to conceal the clipped harshness of his East Coast accent. 'I'd like to make one thing perfectly clear.' It was a peace offering. 'Washington aren't looking for scalps, I'm not here as a head-hunter.' He looked at them both in turn, saw that they both appreciated the point. 'I'm here to provide any back-up that might become necessary if things go wrong. As far as I personally and Washington in particular are concerned, you remain in charge of the operation. You guys make the decisions.'

He moved in his chair, feeling the tiredness of the overnight flight. 'What happened yesterday,' he continued, 'was unfortunate. It happens. Not too often, thank Christ, but it happens. Our guy gets blown, we blow somebody else's. But yesterday was different.' He moved the toothpick between his teeth. 'As I began to say, Washington thinks the station has done a fine job. The output is sensational, the results make everyone else in the Southern Cone green with envy. In terms of hemispheric security you haven't just tightened up a small chink like most people, you've blocked a fucking big hole.' The familiarity was deliberate. 'But if it ever got out,' he began to shake his head, 'If some liberal jerk on Capitol Hill, some pinko journalist from the *Washington Post* or the *New York Times* got to know, then we'd all be in trouble. Heads would roll so fast you wouldn't be able to count them. And not just at our level.'

'So what are you saying?' the station chief asked.

'What I'm saying,' replied Bailey, the toothpick moving between his teeth, 'is the reason Washington sent me down to liaise with you.'

Corrigan began to ask what but stopped himself. Bailey continued. 'Washington sent me down to do, or to help you to do, two things. Firstly, to make sure that the shit doesn't get anywhere near Capitol Hill. Ever.' He paused for emphasis.

'And the second?' It was Mayer who intervened. Bailey turned to face him.

'And the second is to make sure we secure the system in a way that we can continue to use it.'

'We carry on as before?' There was a trace of amazement in Mayer's voice. Bailey continued to look at him. 'Why not?' he asked, 'What's suddenly changed?'

The introduction was over. The man from Washington moved on to the next phase. 'So let's start at the beginning.

It's on file, I know, but I'd like to hear your account of how it all started.' Mayer nodded and motioned for Corrigan to explain.

'Dick and I arrived here some eight years ago. Dick was here just before me.' He twisted in his chair so that he faced Bailey. 'You have to understand the times. We were both back from South-East Asia, fresh to South America. We thought we'd left behind a mess, but that was nothing to what we found here. Regionally, people were afraid to poke their noses above the bunker. The doves were screaming about what the Company had done to Allende in Chile, the hawks were screaming that we should have done it earlier. There were brooms in Washington sweeping people out, other brooms sweeping people in.' Bailey nodded, remembering the days.

'Peru was no different,' Corrigan continued. 'The country was supposed to be one of the cornerstones of the old Alliance for Progress, back in the sixties, but that fell apart. Allende got in in Chile. In 1968 the generals seized power in Peru, Washington breathed a sigh of relief when they thought they had another comfortable right-wing dictatorship, and the bastards went left. Gave the land to the peasants, nationalised the banks, kicked out the *gringos*.' Corrigan took one of the Havanas from his pocket and lit it. 'That's what we inherited. The generals, of course, began to change, moved to the centre, and we started building again, brick by brick, slowly and carefully.'

He had Bailey's full attention. 'Dick and I arrived when the process was under way, but still tottering. Allende was dead in Chile, but Peru was still unstable and Bolivia was as volatile as ever. There was even talk of a three-way war on the Chile-Peru border, mention that Bolivia wanted a land outlet to the coast. Anything in that area was vital, not only to South America, but to us if we wanted to retain some degree of influence here.

'One day we heard that somebody had some information on tank movements on the border. It was a particularly delicate time. The information held up, so we got ourselves

75

an introduction.' He remembered the long days and nights, the waiting in the cafés and boarding houses in Tacna and Arica, on the border. 'The more information we got, the better it became and the more Washington wanted. And the more we got, the clearer it became that we were not just dealing with a few locals trying to make a fast buck.'

Bailey pulled a toothpick and put it in his mouth. 'What do you mean?'

'It was obvious from the beginning that the information we originally received was only the bait. That there was in the background a highly organised system moving into what it considered an extremely profitable area. Which, of course, is what we confirmed when the contact was firmly established.' Bailey waited for Corrigan to expand. 'When we got to the top, got to know them, it all became clear. They had been operating in South America for a long time, using different names, moving around. Using their expertise in any number of fields. Starting in Argentina, laying low during the Eichmann scare, pulling out into Paraguay, then back into Argentina. When the trouble began to build up on the border with Chile, they saw the potential of moving their operations to the Pacific coast. They were already fairly active in Bolivia.' He did not say that he believed the people about whom he was talking may have had an involvement in fermenting the border dispute, in order to fulfill a contract with interests in Bolivia to gain that country access to the ocean. The suspicion had later been partly confirmed when he established that they had been involved in helping to set up a shipping line in Bolivia, a totally land-locked country.

Bailey picked at his teeth. 'But how long before you knew?' he asked.

Corrigan had anticipated the question. 'How long before we knew we were dealing with a bunch of ex-Nazis?' He shrugged. 'Not long, a couple of months. We had our suspicions, of course, but a couple of months to confirm it.' He did not wait for Bailey's next question. 'When we found out we filed a report on the identification of our source. Caracas passed it on to Washington and Washington filed back saying we were doing a good job and should continue. Like you're saying now.'

A reason, he began to think, a reason why Washington should send down a special. A reason why he was cross-examining them on something that was already in the files. Something, he began to think, that not even the special, not even Bailey, knew. Would ever know. A secret, the thought began to take shape in his mind, a secret that only Washington knew.

Bailey switched the subject. 'What do we know about the way they're organised?' Already in the files, thought Corrigan again, shrugging. 'Fairly obvious. Heiner, Klein, whatever you want to call him at the head. His number two is called Schmeltz, a good operator. Schmeltz was with Heiner in France during the war.'

'And there are no complications?' Corrigan shook his head, waiting for Bailey to tell them of the complication. 'No loose ends that we're aware of,' he said, changing the terms.

'And Project Octavio?' It was the question Dick Mayer had asked first in their meeting the previous afternoon, the day Corrigan had returned from Tingo Maria. 'Everything is tied up. The fact that the man has disappeared and that there have been no political repercussions proves the organisation works.'

'So there are no complications?' Bailey asked again.

Corrigan knew he was being set up. 'As I said, none that we are aware of.'

'What about the son?'

'What son?' asked Corrigan. His cigar had gone out.

Bailey leaned forward. 'As you know, Heiner is wanted in France for war crimes committed while he was head of the Gestapo there.' The voice was suddenly hard, abrasive East Coast. 'The specific crime for which the French would like to get him is the death of the then leader of the French Resistance, a man called Jean Laporte, whom Heiner personally tortured to death on a train to Paris.' Corrigan nodded. It was all in the file locked in the wall-safe in his office. Bailey continued. 'As you obviously don't know, Laporte had a son.' He paused for effect, as he had done earlier. 'Legend has it that the son was born the moment the father died.'

'How is that a complication?'

Bailey looked hard across the room. 'The son is in Lima at the moment.'

'Oh, Christ.' Dick Mayer gasped involuntarily, his words long, drawn out, curling into the dark like his cigarette smoke.

Corrigan took the cigar from his mouth, a line of teeth-marks clamped round the frayed edge, and crushed it in the ashtray. 'What do we know about him?'

Bailey selected a fresh toothpick. 'Fortunately, quite a lot. He's a priest. He left France three weeks ago on a study tour organised by a Catholic charity to give people an idea of what the Church is doing for the poor in the Third World. It's pure coincidence that he's in Lima at the moment. He arrived six days ago. He leaves on Sunday.'

'Pure coincidence?' queried Corrigan.

'An act of God.' Bailey chuckled, enjoying his own joke.

'Is he dangerous?' Corrigan asked.

'No,' replied Bailey firmly, then hesitated. 'At least, we don't have any reason to think so. He's led a peaceful, almost a pacifist, life. I don't think he'll be any trouble.'

'And if he is?'

Bailey smiled for the first time that morning. 'That, gentlemen, is what I'm in Lima to tell you about.'

3

The drive to the city centre took thirty minutes. Pacheco parked at the side of the Plaza de Armas and used the same set of telephones from which Laporte had contacted the French ambassador the night before. Two minutes later he came back, peering at the priest through his spectacles. 'It's arranged,' he said. 'A café called the Bar Hawaii in Miraflores. Five o'clock. You can't miss it, everybody knows the place.' Laporte got out of the car. 'What's her name?'

'Maria, Maria Cardones. She'll be sitting at a table outside.'

'Will she talk about it?'

Pacheco was honest. 'As I said, I'm not even sure it was she who was involved in getting Weissemann's article to the newspaper. She sounded frightened, but at least she's agreed to see you.'

They shook hands. 'Thanks for everything,' said Laporte, meaning it. 'I'll be in touch.'

4

Joe Corrigan locked his office door behind him, sat at his desk, turned off the telephone system so that no-one could disturb him, pushed a Havana into his mouth and lit it.

Bailey's arrangements were good, he thought, bloody good. He had felt an initial resentment when the special had outlined the scheme, an anger that he had not been consulted earlier. But he could see their point. His concern was Heiner, not the son. The son was someone else's responsibility. And as soon as it had mattered they had told him, sent Bailey from Washington to brief him on the plan, bring him into it.

More than that, he thought. They had given him the responsibility of the final decision. Whether or not to implement the plan. To allow Bailey and his men to do the fieldwork, the doorstepping, to keep him informed. And at the end of the day to turn to him for the final decision. He pushed the cigar from one side of his mouth to the other. It had been a surprise when Bailey had told him that Washington had instructed him to give the final sanction, the ultimate sanction, to him, but he was pleased. His concern was Heiner, Bailey had told him, the son was someone else's concern. But at the end of the day the two were so connected as to be inseparable.

He sat back in his chair, thinking of the plan. It was good, he reminded himself, bloody good. He remembered Bailey's words, the analysis of the details, the plan and the circumstances which would surround its final execution. Remembered, subconsciously and uncomfortably, Bailey's other words. No threat, the special from Washington had said, the priest was no threat. But if he did not pose a threat, Corrigan felt himself querying, why had Washington taken such precautions? A secret, he knew he had thought during the briefing. A secret denied to Bailey. A secret that only Washington knew.

He pushed the thought to the back of his mind, crossed the room, unlocked the wall safe, and pulled out his reference file on Josef Heiner. There was no reason Washington should not have a secret it wished to keep to itself; there had been few operations in which he had been involved where he had known the full details of the plan, the overall truth of its significance or connections. He sat down and opened the file. He would have it no other way, he thought, would not wish to know the secret Washington was keeping to itself. He pushed the cigar round his mouth and began to read. Washington would keep its secrets from him, just as he would sometimes keep his secrets from Washington. He concentrated on the document in front of him, remembering the details. The file was two inches thick, starting with brief details of Heiner's parents and primary education, going through his war record, with details of the converted liberty ship 'Corrientes' on which he had fled secretly to Argentina in the early fifties, his career in South America. Some of the information was public knowledge. Much of the background, Corrigan knew, was missing. Some of the information which he had gleaned over the years was deliberately omitted from the file. Either because Corrigan was unsure of its validity, or because he felt it was too sensitive to keep even in the American embassy in Lima. Details of Heiner's missing years in Europe after the war, a period which Heiner had occasionally referred to in the drinking sessions which ended some of their business negotiations. Details of Heiner's indiscreet reference, on one such occasion only, to the rat-line; an organisation, Corrigan had later checked, set up to spirit key individuals out of post-war Europe. An organisation, he had discovered, set up by Americans. Information on Corrigan's own operational relationship with Heiner were also kept from the file.

He returned to his desk, consulted the index on the rear pages of the file, and turned to the two pages which contained the nine long paragraphs of information on Jean Laporte. The closely spaced type detailed the background to the war crimes charges linking Heiner with Laporte, Laporte's political and military significance in occupied France, biographical details including date of birth and marriage, and a description of his capture and subsequent death.

The three long paragraphs dealing with his capture gave a more detailed account of Laporte's last two days than the son had recounted either to Father Michael the evening before or to Ricardo Pacheco in the house at Chaclicayo that morning. Corrigan read through the paragraphs quickly; condensing the information; playing, as he always did when he was concentrating, with a pen; assimilating the wealth of facts.

Jean Laporte, born 1905. Prefect. Head of French Resistance. Top secret briefings with de Gaulle and British representatives 1943, concentrating on Resistance participation in Allied invasion of Europe and political role after invasion. Special training December 1943/January 1944 with British Special Operations Executive. Returned to France by Lysander light aircraft, arriving 3.00 a.m. Saturday, February 5th. Picked up by local Resistance cell and driven to nearby town. Broke contact with first cell and established contact with second via hotel receptionist. Taken by receptionist to safe house. Intended to leave safe house next morning, Sunday. House raided by Josef Heiner 4.00 a.m. Sunday morning, February 6th and Laporte captured.

He had never realised, he thought, how important Laporte had been. Had assumed he was simply military head of the Resistance. He read the details again. Special meetings with de Gaulle in Algiers, mid-1943. Secret conferences in London, November 1943, with Dewavrin, code name Passy, overall director of the *Bureau Central de Renseignements et d'Action militaire,* and Buckmaster, head of F Section of the SOE. Top secret briefing, London, November 1943, with Winston Churchill. Jean Laporte, he was suddenly aware, was in charge of the political reorganisation of France after D Day. Was one of the few people, perhaps the only person, in occupied Europe with detailed knowledge of the Allied plans for the Normandy landings. It was little wonder, he thought, that Heiner should have taken so much trouble to capture him.

The Havana had gone out. He relit it, removed the two pages containing the information on Laporte from the Heiner file, photocopied them in his secretary's outer office, and returned them to the file. On the back of the thick wad of documentation was a cellulose envelope containing an assortment of indexed photographs. He fingered through them, found the one marked 'France. Laporte, Jean' and placed it in a separate envelope together with the two pages of photocopied information on Laporte. Then he returned everything to the wall-safe, locked it and went back to his desk, automatically straightening the pad of blotting paper on which he had rested the Heiner file.

In the top right-hand corner of the pad, he noticed, he had scribbled the time of the raid in which Josef Heiner

had seized Jean Laporte. He did not remember doing so.
The time was 4.00 a.m. He had circled it in red.

5

Maria left the office early, explaining to her staff that she
had a business appointment that evening. Colmena, the
avenue on which her office was situated, was already busy.
She walked to the Plaza San Martin, where the previous
day she had waited to buy the newspaper containing the
details of Josef Heiner's exposure. Remembering her reaction to the newspaper. Remembering her reaction to the
disappearance of Herbert Weissemann. Remembering her
reaction that morning when the magazine editor, Pacheco,
had telephoned her with a message that somebody wanted
to talk to her. A friend, he had said, a priest. But a priest
who shared something with her.

She had not wanted to go to the meeting. Had agreed
reluctantly, changed her mind and telephone Pacheco's
office. Had put the phone down before the magazine editor
had answered. Now she wished she had cancelled it. The
fact that Pacheco had telephoned her from a public box,
rather than from his office, worried her.

She collected her car from the parking lot off the side
street by the corner of the square and started the engine.
Nervously, almost frightened. The traffic was already building up. She knew she had one last chance, that she could
still phone Pacheco, call the meeting off. Could simply not
turn up, apologise later.

She decided she would go.

6   *La Paz, Bolivia*

Josef Heiner savoured the harsh taste of the Löwenbräu,
settled back in the large comfortable armchair and relaxed

83

to the strident passion of Wagner. *Der Ring des Ni-belungen.* The Führer's favourite.

The poor bastards back in Germany, he thought. The old-timers who lacked either the contacts or the courage to pull out, who had bowed to the American occupation, accepted the snivelling of the post-war apologies for national leaders, who could listen to Wagner and think only of the old days. And the exiles eking out an existence in some whorehouse in Buenos Aires or tucked away in some *hacienda* in a godforsaken corner of Paraguay, who could listen to Wagner and dream only of an impossible return to the old country. He was different. Not lucky. Different. He had the old days, the pride of the memories. But he also had the present. The organisation. The contacts. The power. He still had them all by the balls.

He looked round the room at the heart of the house he now occupied in a fashionable quarter of La Paz, the generals and industrialists his neighbours. Protected by high walls and political contacts; the thick carpets covering the floor; the oil paintings on the walls. Not ostentatious, relaxing and rewarding. Not priceless. Not the Van Goghs and Cézannes that the likes of Goering and Bormann had tucked away. But still highly expensive. Still sorely missed, even after four decades.

He watched the pattern of the beer on the side of the glass.

Schmeltz had just telephoned from the airport. His flight from Lima had been on time. He would be at the house within the half-hour. It was going well, he decided, beginning to think it was going better than they had a right to hope, correcting himself. They had earned it. The treachery which had exposed him in Lima was unforgivable, had not been forgiven. But the speed with which the organisation had countered it, the efficiency of the mop-up operation had been a success in itself.

The music in the background was low but powerful. Siegfried, he realised, the cloud passing across his mind, reminding him, taunting him. The hero, the colossus, with one fateful weakness. He looked again at the beer, not drinking. Concentrating. One weakness already. The worm in Lima. Already dealt with. He searched for any others, any flaws that would expose the organisation, threaten him.

None, he thought.

One, he decided. Not a weakness. Just a flaw. Not even a flaw. But not a strength. And if it was not a strength, it was a weakness. The bastard Guillermo Pertierro.

He considered the possibility for no more than five seconds. There was a danger and there was a solution. He put down the beer and made two telephone calls; one of information, the other of instruction.

7 *Lima, Peru*

Laporte saw the woman as soon as he stepped from the taxi. She was where Pacheco had said she would be, sitting at a table outside the café, the only table with one person. The others round her were crowded, even with the noise of the traffic he could hear the music from the bar. He crossed the road, dodging the cars which were packed into the evening rush hour, wondering if she knew why he wanted to see her.

'Father Jean,' he sat down, introducing himself. 'Thank you very much for coming.' A waiter appeared at the table. Laporte began to order a coffee then changed his mind. 'What are you drinking?' he asked her.

'A gin and tonic.'

He looked back at the waiter. 'Two gin and tonics, please.' The man wrote down the order and turned to go. 'Are there any tables inside?' Laporte asked him, not knowing why.

'I think so, señor.'

They followed the waiter into the café, choosing a table against the window, on the right of the door. Maria waited for the priest to pull the table out for her, let her sit on the inside. Instead he went first, taking the corner seat for himself, his back against the wall, his face in the shadows, his eyes just high enough to see over the curtains into the street outside. Unconscious of the fact.

The waiter brought their drinks, leaving the bill on the table. '*Salud*,' Laporte raised his glass, looking at her. She was as Pacheco had described her; mid-twenties, about five feet four tall, good-looking with long black hair tied back, her skin the bewitching brown of Brazil, her dark eyes staring back at him.

'*Salud*,' she replied, wondering why she had come. She remembered her doubts as she went to the parking lot that evening, how she had played with the excuses she could tell Pacheco, dominated by the fear that had hung over Herbert Weissemann the last time they had met. Pacheco had needed to persuade her, she remembered. The man is a priest, he had said, somebody you can trust. She had still refused. A priest with a good reason for needing to speak to her, the magazine editor had pressed her, apologising that he could not tell her why, even though he himself knew. Only that it was something important, something the priest himself should tell her. And she had agreed. 'Why did you want to see me?' she asked.

Laporte looked at her, undecided what to say. 'Pacheco said you might be able to help me,' he said finally, not committing either of them.

'Help you with what?' Maria raised the glass, hiding her face, trying to understand the man who sat with her. A priest, Pacheco had said. The clothes of a priest, yes, she told herself, an awkwardness at the greeting, as if he was unaccustomed to dealing with women. The trappings of a priest, she continued. As she had expected. But something more.

'Pacheco wasn't sure.' The words interrupted her thoughts, bringing her back to the conversation. 'He just said I should speak to you.' Laporte sipped the drink. 'About your friend. About Herbert Weissemann.'

Maria lifted the glass again, then put it down. She was trembling, the first sign of emotion betrayed by her hands; the fingers which had previously been held confidently round the drink now curled tight inside her palms. 'What do you want to know about him?'

'Whatever you think you should tell me.' His voice was calming and positive. Not, she thought, the voice of a priest.

'Why do you want to know?'

He looked straight at her. 'Yesterday the *Expresso* newspaper carried an article which said that a Nazi war criminal had been discovered here in Lima. Pacheco says that the editor doesn't know who wrote the piece, merely that it was delivered to the paper late at night, along with evidence to back up the allegations.'

Maria had stopped trembling. 'What else does Pacheco say?'

'Pacheco says the article was written by your friend, by Herbert Weissemann.'

Her voice was low. 'Why does Pacheco say that?'

Gently and patiently he told her Pacheco's account of his last two meetings with the missing journalist, how Weissemann had seemed elated but frightened. How the final conversation had seemed almost like a last will and testament.

Maria already knew what he was telling her, allowed him to continue, listening not so much to the words as to the way he spoke them. Deciding whether she could trust him, help him, whether in turn she could find solace in his friendship. 'So why did Pacheco send you to me?' she asked when he had finished.

'Pacheco said you were the one person Weissemann trusted.'

'Where does Pacheco think Herbert is now?' Laporte knew he was trapped, needing to be honest, aware of what that honesty might mean. His reply was direct, almost brutal. 'Pacheco thinks Josef Heiner killed him.'

He waited for the reaction. There was none. 'So why

did Pacheco send you to me?' Maria asked the question a second time.

'Because Josef Heiner also killed my father.' The shroud passed across his face, greying the pale triangle of skin beneath the eyes, frightening her, drawing them closer together. 'Tell me from the beginning,' she said.

He told her, remembering again those who were waiting in France; Chalbrand, Bellan, his mother. The cathedral at Chartres. The story he told was the story he had told Father Michael in the quiet of the chapel, the story he had told Pacheco in the mausoleum of the kitchen in the house at Chaclicayo. When he had finished she asked again. 'So why did Pacheco send you to me?'

He only half heard the question, aware it was the third time it had been asked. In the soft haze of his memory he recalled another question which had been asked three times. He was a schoolboy again, feeling the first warmth of the early spring, smelling its flowers. He was clutching his mother's hand, seated in the family pew in the church in Melleran. It was Palm Sunday, the priest was reading the Gospel. Matthew xxvi, verse 75.

'And straightway the cock crew. And Peter remembered the words which Jesus had said. "Before the cock crow, thou shalt deny me thrice." '

Three times he had told his story. Three times Maria had asked him why Pacheco had sent him to her.

'Pacheco said you could help me find the man who killed my father.'

'I met Herbert Weissemann three years ago.' Laporte looked up, surprised at the strength of Maria's voice.

'I had been working in Rio de Janiero for Varig, the Brazilian airline. They needed someone in their Lima office, as I spoke Spanish I was asked if I wanted the job. At first it was difficult. A new city, no friends. And Peruvian society is very traditional. With few exceptions they think that a woman who works and who lives by herself can only be one thing.' Laporte said he understood.

'After a while I began to make some friends. Mainly

through business. One of them was Ricardo Pacheco. Through him I met Herbert Weissemann.

'The more we got to know each other, the more he told me about his work, about what lay behind the stories he was writing.' She shuddered. 'Sometimes he wasn't meeting very nice people.

'After a while he didn't need to tell me. I could sense it. If we had a drink together, I could tell it in his eyes.' She looked at him. 'He would sit at this table,' she went on, 'his back against the wall, his eyes just high enough to see over the curtain.' There was no accusation in her voice, simply statement. 'Just like you.

'Six months or so ago, he began to change. He said he had a contact into something big. That much he told me, but no more. A contact into something so big, he said once, that even he was frightened.

'I think he meant by that that he was in awe, not necessarily physically frightened. In any case he took no notice. It was like a drug; the longer he spent on the story the more it seemed to suck him in, make him live for nothing else. I saw him once, in a café, talking with another man, younger than he was. Talking German. There was something about the way they were sitting that I knew immediately. The other man was his contact.

'I ignored him, pretended I did not know him. He saw me, ignored me also. That night he came to see me, said I had done well, done the right thing.' She thought back to the encounter. 'It was as if he was saying I had done the right thing for myself, protected myself.'

Her glass was empty. Laporte asked if she wanted another but she refused.

'Two weeks ago he came to see me. I think he needed to talk, as we had done before. He said it was almost complete. We went for dinner, but he said nothing. I wasn't sure what he wanted, asked him whether he wanted to tell me. Finally he said yes. We sat drinking coffee all night, then he told me.'

Laporte waited, allowing Maria time to tell him as Herbert Weissemann had needed time to tell her. The loneliness was deep in him. He knew how the other man had felt, running and alone, sensed why he had come back to Maria, sensed an envy that he himself was denied that help.

Maria's voice was distant, as if it no longer belonged to her. 'He said the contact had helped him uncover a Nazi war criminal, living here in Lima. He didn't give names, knew I understood him enough not to ask. He said the man was wanted, that he had been in the Gestapo. But he said there was more. The man still ran his own organisation. He was mixed up in spying, drugs, currency operations.' She was trembling again, her self-discipline beginning to disintegrate. Laporte stretched his hands across hers, feeling her coldness. 'No wonder Herbert Weissemann was in awe.'

She shook her head, holding his hands. 'There was even more, he said. He said the most important part was the people this Nazi worked for.'

'I thought you said he ran his own operation?' Laporte tried to keep the confusion out of his voice.

'I meant the people who employed his organisation, hired its services, paid for its information.' Her mind was drifting back to the night he had told her these things. 'We sat up all night, falling asleep in the chairs. Till morning. All he wanted was to be near someone.'

'And he said nothing about who employed the Nazi's organisation?'

'Nothing at all. In the morning we had breakfast as if nothing had happened and he left.'

'When did you see him again?' She was too close to the truth not to need guiding.

She shuddered. 'Three nights ago. Late at night. He phoned, saying he was coming round. He was tense, almost frightened. I think he must have been on his way to the house at Chaclicayo.' Her eyes were wide, reliving the meeting. 'I asked if he wanted to stay, but he said he was meeting his contact.'

'So why did he come to you?'

'He gave me an envelope. I asked what was in it but he said it was better I didn't know. He said that if I didn't hear from him by nine o'clock the next evening I should take it to the editor of *Expresso*. But he said it was important that no-one, not even the editor, knew that it was I who had taken it.'

'What happened then?' Laporte's voice was calm, reassuring.

'He left.'

'And you didn't see Herbert Weissemann again?'

Maria shook her head, the first glint of tears in her eyes. 'I waited all day, till nine o'clock. Then I took the cab into the city, left it two blocks from the *Expresso* office, and paid a small boy to deliver the envelope for me.' She was faltering, the words coming more slowly.

Laporte asked gently but quickly, before the resolve finally deserted her completely. 'What else did he leave, besides the envelope?'

The voice was beginning to choke in her throat. 'Nothing, nothing at all.' Her voice finally collapsed.

Laporte paid the bill and helped her to her feet. 'Come on,' he said, 'I'll take you home.' As he opened the door for her she saw a face looking at them from the street. When she looked again, it had gone.

8 *La Paz, Bolivia*

Anderson smiled as the wine waiter refilled his glass and looked back at Carmen. It had been no surprise when she had accepted his invitation to dinner, but she herself had been. Taller than he had thought, her legs longer. And intelligent. He made an excuse and went to the telephone.

Carmen watched him. Every hour on the half hour, the third time in the two-and-a-half hours they had been at the restaurant, the first within five minutes of their arrival.

As if he had planned it that way. She wondered what he was expecting from the check calls, assumed they were to the hotel. Wondered who had brought him in, what the job was.

Anderson returned to the table.

Still nothing. Twenty-four hours in La Paz and he still had no idea why he had been called in or what he was supposed to do. Not like the other job he had done for them, the job at Portachuela. The timetable for that had had a military precision. Even down to the number of hours he would need to acclimatise and recce the site. But this time nothing, as if the man himself still did not know why he had called the Texan in.

Carmen was talking to him, joking. Taller than he had thought, he was thinking again, longer legs. He had seen their outline as the waiter had taken her coat when they had arrived at the restaurant, the shape of the suspender belt through the silky texture of her dress. He thought about the Ruger he had collected the night before, the minor adjustment to the sights when he had tested the weapon that morning, could sense the soft area of flesh between the top of her nylons and her underwear. He had liked the feel of the .22, could already feel her damp warmth.

Carmen knew what he was thinking, knew she was also thinking about his body. Hard, she had already noted, no spare flesh. Tight with tension. His mind thinking about what he would do to her in bed, concentrating on the still unknown job for which he had been brought in, wondering what she would do to him.

She raised her glass. 'To your success,' she suggested.

He returned the toast. 'To you.'

A single shadow passed across her mind. 'To Guillermo Pertierro,' she thought.

The pain subsided as he knew it would, taking a long time, leaving his body sore and aching. Giving place to the wrath. The desire for revenge. Guillermo Pertierro allowed the anger to build, knowing it was inevitable, knowing he must control it. Knowing it was part of their weapon against him, part of the process he had to endure to maintain his silence.

The darkness around him was total. As it always was. He wondered what time it was outside. What was happening. Where Carmen was, what she was doing, whether she was safe. Whether the silence he had maintained had succeeded in protecting her.

For Carmen he had endured a great deal. She knew much about the movement, but not all. Not the details of his connections with the groups in other countries, the secret agreements and alliances which constituted the spine of the left-wing guerilla movements which stretched from South America, northwards, to the battlefields of Central America itself, to what the Americans called their own back yard. That, above all, was what they had tried to tear out of him. That, above all, was what he had not told Carmen. Yet by not sharing his secrets with her, he knew, he had exposed her even more should she also be taken. If she was caught, and succumbed, she could tell them a great deal, which would be bad for the revolution, but she could not tell them all, which would be worse for her. For that reason he had maintained his silence. To protect the revolution. To save his beloved Carmen.

The anger was mixing with the remains of the pain. Directed at them all. Particularly the one. The bastard in the corner. He thought again of the man, knew he would always remember him. Knew he would be back. Not often, but when it mattered. When his tormentors appeared to be giving up.

He tried to lie still, knowing it was impossible. Knowing it would not be long before they would be back and the process would start again. Already he could imagine the fresh pain, sense the anger that would come with it, the desire for revenge. Knew above all that he must control it, that if he allowed it to show they would know they were winning, that they would hurt him more.

He thought again of Carmen. Hoped it had all been worthwhile.

10 *Lima, Peru*

It was dark outside the café. The night breeze lifted off the sea, creeping up the cliffs, freshening the streets. Laporte smelt it as they walked through the park between the busy roads on either side, now bright with the lights of mid-evening, to the tower block where Maria lived. She stumbled as they walked so that at times he had to help her, ignoring the curiosity of the late shoppers.

The block was on the edge of the cliffs, overlooking the beaches three hundred feet below. The porter inside stared at the priest's clothing and wished Maria good evening. The lift took them swiftly and silently to the tenth floor and he followed her out, waiting patiently as she fumbled in her bag for the keys.

The lounge was spacious and comfortable, sparingly furnished: a large settee and two armchairs; a coffee table in the centre of the room and a sideboard along one wall. The wall opposite was of glass, sliding open to a balcony overlooking the Pacific. Laporte let himself out, welcoming the cool which the extra height afforded, while Maria went to the bathroom. The lights of the cars dipped and blinked along the road which ran round the top of the beach. To the right he could see the lights of Callao; to the left, before the coast curved out of sight, the solitary light at the end of a fishermen's jetty.

Maria came out of the bathroom and sat hunched in one of the chairs. The meeting had left her numb and speechless. She had not spoken since they had left the café. He wondered how much more she had to tell, how he could coax it from her. In a block of flats opposite someone was playing a *caena*, the thin sound of the Andean flute piercing the still. He turned back into the room. 'How about some coffee?' he asked lightly.

She smiled, getting up, grateful for something to do, and went into the kitchen on the other side of the entrance hall. Laporte followed her, watching as she filled the kettle, fiddled with the cups, occupied herself. 'What else did Herbert Weissemann leave with you?' The force of the question was wrapped in his velvet voice, comforting and relaxing. He knew he was taking a risk, but there was little time.

Maria reached for the coffee and unscrewed the jar, her fingers still trembling, aware that her reactions were split, thankful for it but confused. Part of her needing the physical strength of the man behind her. The rest needing the spiritual strength of his priesthood. She spooned the coffee into the percolator, the movement unlocking her, allowing her to answer. 'Nothing. He left nothing at all. Like I said before.' She screwed the lid back onto the jar. 'As I said, nothing except the envelope for the newspaper and the tape recorder.' She stretched for the cupboard, automatically putting the jar in its correct place. Already she was adding the details she had forgotten, the details he needed. 'That's right,' Laporte spoke softly, gently, 'you were telling me about the tape recorder.'

'Normally he left nothing here, he said it was too dangerous. He always said he wouldn't leave anything that would connect me with him.' Laporte waited as she poured the boiling water into the percolator, afraid to interrupt in case he broke the sequence, afraid to remain silent in case she stopped. 'The last night, though, he was in a hurry. He'd just left his contact and had to get back to him.' The story was again different, Laporte noticed. Only in small details, but different. He wondered how long she would keep talking, where she would lead him. Her fingers stopped trembling. 'I think,' she said, 'they were on their way to the house. I think he really called to say goodbye.'

His mind was screaming to interrupt, to ask for details. He stayed silent.

'He said things were moving so quickly he had to take some chances. But he was still careful. So he left his tape recorder here. He didn't have time to take it back to his flat, and he didn't want to carry it in the car in case they caught him.' Her mind was locked into the memory. 'If they found something like that on him, he said, they would suspect him immediately. If not, he might be able to talk his way out.'

The realisation of what she was saying was beginning to unlock the protective barrier she had created, exposing her mind to what it had tried to deny.

'What did he want at the house?' Laporte assumed they were talking about the same house, behind the white-walled garden at Chaclicayo.

'Documents. There was a secret place in the house where they kept the documents. The contact said it was like a library.'

'Documents proving Heiner's identity?' There was too much enthusiasm in his voice, too much expectation. He cursed, waiting for her backlash, fearing he had turned the key and locked her mind again.

The response slipped out before the doors slammed shut. 'Don't be stupid. Heiner was no longer important.' There was a resentment in her voice, harsh and bitter, as if he should have known what the documents were about. 'Documents tying the man with the people who employed his organisation, the people who hired his services.'

She turned, suddenly crying, hunching her shoulders, curling into him for protection, knowing she had hurt him but unable to apologise. He put an arm round her, unsure what to do. 'What else is there?' The question came automatically.

'Nothing else,' she answered.

'Are you sure?'

'Yes, I'm sure.'

He led her back into the lounge and brought the coffee. 'Is there a telephone?' He wanted her to be alone, give her time to recover. Allow himself time to think.

'In the hall,' she told him.

There was no answer at Pacheco's office number. Laporte dialled again, hoping the editor would be at home, relaxing with relief when he heard the familiar voice. 'Laporte,' he introduced himself, 'I'm sorry to disturb you, but I need some help.' He deliberately kept the conversation brief.

'Anything I can do.' Pacheco omitted any reference to Maria.

'Can you take me round Weissemann's flat?' Laporte asked. He did not want to torture Maria with the request.

'There's no point.' Pacheco's answer was sharp. Unexpected. 'What do you mean, no point?' Laporte was confused.

'There's no point,' repeated Pacheco, 'I've already been there. I went this afternoon. There's nothing there.'

Laporte refused to understand. 'What do you mean, nothing there.'

Pacheco was patient. 'The flat is totally empty. No documents, no books, no furniture. Absolutely nothing. I checked with both the porter and the landlord. The place has been vacated, the rent's been paid. Including a month's notice.'

Laporte thanked Pacheco, put the phone down, and went back into the lounge. Maria was sitting upright in the chair, her face dry, a small pocket-sized cassette recorder on the coffee table. 'I'm sorry,' she said simply, 'there's nothing on it.'

'Nothing at all?' It was, thought Laporte, an echo of the conversation he had just had.

'Virtually nothing,' said Maria. 'I listened yesterday and checked again while you were on the phone. No more than a few words in German. Somebody arranging a meeting, I think, my German isn't very good. But nothing more.'

'May I listen to it?'

'Of course.' She pressed the rewind button. 'It's a telephone conversation. Herbert always recorded the important ones.'

'Is it Herbert speaking?'

She shook her head. 'No, I think it's the contact. Probably at the contact's house, wherever that is, before Herbert left the machine here.'

Laporte sat back, sipping the coffee, watching the dark of the night invade the room through the windows to the balcony, the sense of isolation and loneliness building again in his body.

The tape clicked to a halt. Maria leant forward and pressed the start button. The first sound, as she had told him, was the telephone ringing, then a heavy voice answering in Spanish but switching instantly to German. The conversation lasted no more than ten seconds before it ended with an abrupt click as the telephone was replaced. He sat up, confused and disappointed. 'Is that all?'

Maria nodded reluctantly. 'Yes, that's all.'

They rewound the cassette and listened again, hearing the voices distorted by the size of the tape. Laporte concentrated, remembering the fact that his mother had sent him to Germany to study, hearing the ritual of the words, identifying the accents.

'Was ist in der Falle?'

'Die Fliege.'

'Was wartet immer?'

'Die Spinne.'

'What is in the trap?'

'The fly.'

'What is always waiting?'

'The Spider.'

He shrugged, stopped the cassette, rewound it and played the first words again, then listened to the rest.

The caller identified himself in German. 'I'm glad you phoned,' said the person who had answered the phone, 'we're leaving now. Can you take care of things while we're away?' The suggestion, Laporte suddenly thought, was too exact, as if it had been planned. Whoever the caller was, he knew, he was walking into a trap. 'I'll be with you in twenty minutes,' said the caller.

He stopped the cassette again and rewound it. 'Can I just clear my mind?' he asked Maria. 'Two simple questions. First, the tape is a recording of a conversation between Herbert Weissemann's contact and somebody at Heiner's house?' Maria nodded.

'Question two. That telephone conversation took place on the night Herbert Weissemann went to Heiner's house and disappeared?'

Maria agreed. 'That's right. He left the tape recorder here that evening. The next evening, when he had not returned, I did as he said and took the envelope to the newspaper. The following morning, at five o'clock, the *Guardia* raided the house in Chaclicayo.'

It was 8.30, he realised. Chalbrand would be calling the monastery in half an hour. He rose to leave, still disappointed at the taped message, explaining to Maria about the call from France, debating whether he should pass on Pacheco's information to her. He decided she should hear it from someone else and told her he would contact her the next day.

There was something she knew she should tell him, a memory eating into her mind, something he should know. Maria tried to remember, watching as he crossed the landing and waited for the lift. Something she had noticed. The lights at the side of the lift showed green and the doors opened. She remembered, stepped forward to tell him, suddenly questioning whether it was as important as she had thought, wondering if she had been mistaken. The face outside the café as they had left. The face that had disappeared. The doors of the lift shut and she went back into the room.

Josef Heiner poured two large glasses of schnapps, handed
one to the man seated opposite him, placed the bottle on
the leather-topped table between them and raised his glass
in toast. '*Salud,* my old friend,' he said, 'it's been a hectic
three days, but thanks to you we survived.'

Heinrich Schmeltz grunted and poured the drink down
his throat. 'Slightly hectic,' he conceded.

A white-aproned maid entered politely and placed a
silver tray of *empañadas* on the table. Schmeltz offered
his leader the plate then helped himself, biting through the
pastry, enjoying the strange mix of the sugar on the top
and the spicy meat inside.

Saturday already seemed as far away as the hills of
Bavaria where he had been born. They'd always suspected
the worm, of course, always thought he was dribbling their
secrets away, but not until they'd screwed the information
out of him three nights ago did they learn the full extent
of his treachery. He'd paid, Christ how he'd paid, till he
had no more to tell. And the journalist. The snivelling
fucker called Weissemann, ratting on his own countryman.
They almost got him as well, of course. He could see it now:
Weissemann's pathetic little Volkswagen pulling away as
Schmeltz's Mercedes closed in. But the bastard had twisted
out of their trap, then wrapped his motor round a tree.
Dead before they got him out.

They'd thought that was it. Till the next night. The
confidential call which the *Sturmbannführer* took in the
study of the house in Chaclicayo. The hate on his face
when he informed them that he, they, the organisation
had been betrayed and a police raid was planned for the
early hours of the next morning.

They'd got him away, of course. Priority. Protect the
leader. Fast car then private plane out of the country. Not,
the driver had reported back to Schmeltz, before Heiner
had spent ten minutes in the twenty-four-hour post office

in the centre of Lima. Then the rush to clear the house. Of everything. But especially the documents.

Heiner poured them each another drink. 'What happened after I left?' he asked. It was the first opportunity the two had had to talk since his flight in the early hours of Monday morning. Schmeltz half-drained the glass and began his report.

'We received the warning, as you recall, at about eleven on Sunday night, and you left immediately.' Schmeltz knew he could omit no detail whatsoever. 'After we had ensured your safety, I contacted as many of the boys as I could and ordered them to report to the house immediately, with as much transport as they could muster. I was assuming, of course, that your contact was as good as his word and would telephone us when he had more news.' He took another sip of the schnapps and continued. 'I assumed that the assault would be mounted by a squad from the *Guardia,* and that they would assemble at a garrison in the city, then come up the autoroute and stop for a final check and briefing, and probably a quick recce, at the junction where the road to Chaclicayo forks off from the main road. So I ordered one of the boys to find a telephone on the autoroute and to inform us when a large convoy of *Guardia* passed them. And I ordered another to a place just opposite the turn-off. There's a café there with a telephone at the side, with a good view of the road and house. He was to tell us when the convoy reached the turn-off and whether, as I imagined they would, they stopped for a final briefing.'

The *Sturmbannführer,* he could see, was relishing the account. 'Good,' said Heiner, leaning forward. 'Good.'

'When they moved off,' Schmeltz continued, 'he was to phone again. I told him there would be no time for us to reply. But in case we were still in the house he should keep phoning, letting it ring twice each time, till the first *Guardia* came through the gate. That way, if we were still there, we would know it was time to leave.'

Heiner refilled their glasses, his eyes shining.

'Your man was good,' Schmeltz told him. 'You left at about eleven, just after he phoned for the first time. He phoned again at two to say the assault squad was assembled and they were going in to the final briefing.' He laughed. 'It must have been a typical Latin affair, it went on for hours. Almost,' he added as an aside, 'as if the man giving it was determined to drag it out as long as possible.' He looked across at Heiner, waiting for a reaction. There was none. Even after so many years the *Sturmbannführer* kept some secrets to himself.

'The next time he phoned was just after four. He said they were on their way. Fifteen minutes later our man on the autoroute phoned the house to say they had just passed him. Twenty minutes after that the look-out at the café opposite reported that a group of cars had stopped at the junction and he assumed it was the *Guardia*.'

Josef Heiner could see it, smell it, feel it.

'It was tight.' Schmeltz's voice pulled him back. 'Your man warned us, but it was lucky we had the look-outs.' He paused, structuring the next part of his report with care. 'We loaded everything that could identify you in one of the trucks. We had to leave most of the furniture, I'm afraid, but that came from Argentina, so it was safe.

'The rest – the chandelier, the pictures, the cutlery and silverware – we managed to get away by about four. But the documents,' he shook his head. 'The documents were a bloody close call.'

Heiner leaned forward, anxious for an explanation.

'We couldn't get at them. Eventually Hernan managed it. Under orders, of course, but he did well. He's a good man. But Christ, you should have seen his hands after, no skin left at all.'

'But you got them out?'

'Yes, we got them out. I was just carrying the last bundle out of the house when we got the call that the *Guardia* had stopped at the turning.'

Heiner let out a whistle. 'Jesus, you're right, it was close.'

Schmeltz nodded. 'I got Hernan into a car. His hands were such a mess he couldn't do any more. Then I ordered one of the others to check there were no documents left. There wasn't much time, the *Guardia* hardly stopped at the junction. Almost before we'd got Hernan into the car the phone was ringing again, two rings then off, two rings then off. I closed up everything and got out.'

'But it was that close?' There was a trace of alarm in Heiner's question.

'Yes, it was that close. I didn't even stop to shut the gate. Just drove off up the road as they came down. No lights, of course, so they didn't see me. Thank God it was a cloudy night. Just as I got to the other end I saw their headlights.'

'What did you do then?'

'I got back to the main road at the top, which they had conveniently forgotten to seal off, headed east for a bit, then waited a couple of hours till there was some traffic about and came back into the city.'

'How's Hernan?'

'He's OK. His hands are an ugly sight. We might have to send him for plastic surgery, but the others had a doctor with him by the time I reached Lima.'

Heiner slumped back into his chair, his eyes ablaze. 'Fantastic, my friend, fantastic and brilliant.' He raised his glass in salute. 'I thank you, my old and dear friend, I thank you and toast you. I am only sorry I could not have been there alongside you.'

Schmeltz smiled. 'It would have been a pleasure to have had you there, but it was impossible. My duty was to stay, yours was to leave.'

Heiner shrugged. 'Perhaps, but I would have liked to have been there. Anyway, it's over.' He sat forward, alert again. 'And the documents. What's happening to them?'

'The boys in Lima are arranging a safe place for the other things. I thought it unnecessary to get them out of Lima. But the documents are on their way here. I ordered two of the boys to get some sleep, then leave with the documents. They should be here in the morning.

'Splendid, absolutely splendid.' Heiner was relaxed. Elated. Confident. The organisation, he was thinking. *Die Spinne.* Everywhere. All-seeing. All-embracing. Its web reaching out and drawing everything in. Resilient enough to survive. Strong enough to overcome. Schmeltz could see it in his eyes. The elation of success. Remembered the fire burning in France. The one morning in particular. The morning Heiner had reported personally to the Führer.

'And all because of the bastard worm.' Heiner's mood changed again. 'The bastard, fucking little worm.'

'At least he got what was coming to him.' Schmeltz's words released the pressure. 'And a little more besides.'

Heiner chuckled, sharing the memory. 'It was like a confessional, was it not? At the beginning he said there was nothing to say, and at the end we couldn't stop him.'

'You obviously keep your hand in,' suggested Schmeltz.

It was meant as a joke but taken seriously. Heiner feigned modesty.

'Not much, there's not enough time. And they're well trained here.' There was renewed enthusiasm in his voice. 'Plenty of instructors from Brazil and Uruguay, Argentina as well, but the Bolivians are training their own people now, even giving a bit of help to Pinochet in Chile.' It was as if he was talking about any professional in any profession. 'They've just devised a nice refinement here. Sensory deprivation, the theorists would call it. They just call it the coffin.'

He emptied the bottle, sharing its contents between the two glasses, the mood suddenly changing again. 'There could be a problem,' he said, his voice serious. Schmeltz left his glass on the table and waited.

'You remember Laporte?'

Schmeltz felt his stomach twist. They had been efficient. Under the *Sturmbannführer* they had been bloody efficient. You could count their failures on the fingers of one hand. Less than that. On just one finger. The bastard on the train. The bastard from Melleran. Even now he felt himself tighten at the memory, wondered why. Knew why. They had sweated over him. Christ how they had worked on him. Then the final twist of the generator handle and the bastard was gone. Without a word. Without a single bloody word.

Not quite, his memory reminded him. Not quite without a word. The bastard had said one thing. In the half-second before he died. Schmeltz still remembered the words, recalled them sometimes in the dark of the night when he woke up sweating.

'The one on the train?' He answered Heiner's question.

Heiner nodded. 'His son is in Lima.' He finished his schnapps. 'It's probably all right. He's a priest, apparently, on a study tour. Looking at poverty or some other noble cause. It's a coincidence he's in Lima at the moment.'

Schmeltz reacted the same way Joe Corrigan had earlier that day. 'Is he a threat to us?' he asked.

Heiner shook his head. 'I gather not. In any case, he's already taken care of.'

'How do you know?' It was a natural question. Even as he asked, Schmeltz knew he would not get an answer. There were some secrets, he knew, that would remain locked in his leader's head.

Heiner ignored the question. 'Because of this, I think you ought to return to Lima as soon as possible. When's the next flight?'

Schmeltz checked the details he carried in his wallet. 'Nothing tonight. The first one tomorrow is an AeroPeru flight at 12.45, arriving Lima 13.30.' He went to the telephone and reserved a seat. The maid reappeared at the door and informed them that dinner was ready. Heiner gave Schmeltz a polite arm. 'Come on,' he said, 'and I'll tell you about the coffin.'

Chapter Three

Wednesday, February 2nd 1983

The edge of light cut through the darkness like a knife. Guillermo Pertierro woke immediately, knew another day was about to begin. He tensed, glad to be reminded that he was still alive, already afraid of the pain it would bring, blinded by the sudden glare of the strip lighting above the coffin as the guard removed the lid.

He waited three seconds, giving himself time to adjust, giving the guard time to step back, the rule unwritten but sacrosanct. Allow the man time to recover, protect himself from any sudden movement. That way there was a chance the guards would be lulled into relaxing. That way there was a chance of survival.

He eased himself up, half turning so that he could pull on the sides of the wooden box, resting his weight against the edge, trying to protect himself from the soreness of his body.

It had been like this every day for two months, ever since they had moved him from the Interior Ministry in the centre of the city. He had been at the Ministry one day over six weeks, according to the calculations he had made. Forty-three days from the morning he had been taken on the street corner. He had known, as soon as he had seen the cars moving in, that he had been set up, betrayed. They had known everything about him, even as they handcuffed him, wrapped his head in a blanket, partly to frighten him, disorientate him, partly so he would not know where they were taking him. They had known his identity, the full details of his leadership of the MIR, the left-wing guerilla group, even before they began pouring the electricity through his body.

After two months he had been taken, again handcuffed and blindfolded, to the secret torture house in the suburbs. Each morning a special team from the Ministry came to work on him for between three and six hours. When he was not being tortured, Guillermo Pertierro was locked in a coffin.

The guard was standing three feet from the box, the Uzi pointing at him. Pertierro half rolled, half collapsed out of the coffin, knelt like a dog on the floor, summoned his strength and rose unsteadily to his feet. The sucker marks where they had attached the electrodes stung like open sores, his nipples burned and his testicles felt swollen and engorged. He supported himself against the wall and waited for the command.

'Breakfast.'

At first he and the other two guerillas he knew to be in the torture house had been passed bread and water in their cells or, in his case, the coffin. Gradually, however, the guards had allowed them to take breakfast with them in the kitchen, sharing their bread and coffee. He had wondered why they did it, whether it was from pity, or simply part of the process of weakening their resolve for the torture teams. Then he had shut out the search for an explanation and accepted it.

'*Gracias*.' He began to shuffle towards the door then stopped, knowing the guard had something else to say. Not turning. Sensing it was better not to face the man.

'Today is the last day. We heard last night.'

'*Gracias*.' The guard, he knew, was telling the truth. At least, he thought, it was better to know. At least there would be no more pain. No more tricks. No more mock executions, naked and trembling. '*Gracias*,' he said again. 'Thank you.' He edged forward and went down the stairs to the kitchen.

The room was twenty feet square, its two windows blocked off. A single naked electric light bulb hung over the table which filled the centre of the floor. To the right of the door through which Pertierro entered was a single bed, freshly made; to the left a dresser. Along the wall on the left was a sink, in the far corner on the left a cooker fuelled by a gas bottle at its side. The door out of the kitchen was in the far wall. The other guards and prisoners were already seated round the table.

The details, Pertierro forced himself to think, note the details. Even today they might be important. The sergeant, heavily built with a square face, sat at the end nearest him, back to the corner of the room on the left of the stairs, commanding a position from which he could dominate the whole kitchen. The captain, a younger man in his early twenties, sat at the far end. Two privates sat along the side on the sergeant's left. Another private sat facing them, on the captain's left. Between the sergeant and the captain, on the sergeant's right, was a space for Pertierro's guard. Squeezed between him and the other private on this side was space for the other two prisoners.

Pertierro knew them both, one better than the other. Lucho and he had trained together in the warmth of the Cuban sun, huddled together for warmth in the cold of the Bolivian night when they had returned to their own country, Lucho coughing up the blood of the tin mines where he had been recruited. The other, Paco, had been a student activist before he had gone underground. Both had been arrested in the same week as Pertierro.

'Coffee?' It was always the sergeant who gave the commands. The captain had seemed continuously embarrassed by his role of jailer.

'*Por favor, señor.*' The sergeant nodded at the coffee pot on the stove in the corner. '*Gracias, señor.*' It always paid to be polite. Especially to the sergeant.

Pertierro walked carefully round the table to his left, behind the sergeant and the privates to the sergeant's left, till he reached the stove. There was a tacit understanding that the other way, behind the captain, was forbidden. Not because of his rank. Because behind him, slightly to his left, beneath one of the blocked windows, the guards stacked their weapons. Though their captors still wore

111

their side-arms in their leather strap-over holsters, the guerillas studiously avoided that area of the kitchen.

Pertierro wrapped a towel round the hot metal handle of the coffee pot, poured a coffee into the thick enamel mug by the sink, and waited. Each morning he looked at the guns. Each morning he looked for a way of getting to them. Each morning he knew the sergeant would kill him if he tried.

'Bread?' Again it was the sergeant who spoke.

'*Por favor, señor.*'

The sergeant nodded to one of the privates to cut the guerilla leader a slice of bread. It was the last unwritten rule. The prisoners could eat with their guards. Help themselves, with the sergeant's permission, to coffee. But must not approach the stack of weapons or touch the jungle knife, normally tucked into the sergeant's right boot, that served to cut the bread.

Pertierro accepted the slice, thanked the guard, and took up his normal seat at the head of the bed, next to the table, on the sergeant's right. The coffee was steaming hot and strong. He dipped the hard bread in it and wondered how long he had to live. The other two guerillas were silent. He knew they had also been told, wondered what they were thinking.

The private to the left of the captain, on the side of the table nearest the nest of weapons, pushed back his chair, walked round the table, and turned on the transistor radio propped on the sink next to the stove, searching for a music station. The sergeant watched closely, his attention commanding the room. Pertierro scarcely noticed, was only faintly aware of Lucho asking for more coffee, the sergeant nodding. Lucho got up and walked the familiar route behind the sergeant to the stove. Pertierro sank the bread deeper into his mug and stared at the steam. At the stove, Lucho was wrapping the towel round the handle of the coffee pot. Beside him the guard who normally sat at the captain's left was still playing with the radio.

Christ. Pertierro saw it. Saw what Lucho had seen. Hoped to God he was right.

The route to the guns was exposed, for the first time since they had been allowed in the kitchen. The soldier whose position on the captain's left shielded the guerillas from the weapons was out of place, at the sink. Only the captain was closer than Pertierro. The route was not open, but there was a chance. He waited for Lucho, knowing what the other guerilla had to do, hoping to Christ he was right.

He looked round, calming himself down, keeping his movements slow. Looking for the weaknesses. The captain was a problem, but not the main one. That lay to his left. The sergeant. Close to Paco. Their strongest and your weakest, he thought, always the same. The tough veteran, rumoured to have taken part in the ambush at la Quebrada del Yuro, north of Valle Grande, where the legendary Che was taken, and the inexperienced student. It had been the same under torture. Pertierro and Lucho knew too much to talk, Paco too little.

He leaned forward, placed his mug on the floor freeing himself of any impediment to movement. Hoping Lucho would see the sign. Calculating the distance to the guns. Two paces, perhaps three. Uzis, he was thinking, no problem. Both he and Lucho had trained with them, slept with them, in the camps outside Havana.

He waited, knew all rested with Lucho. Whether he had read him correctly. At the radio the private had almost found the station, was about to return to his place. Seal off the chance. Do it, Lucho, he urged, for Christ's sake do it.

At the stove, Lucho began to put down the coffee pot. Pertierro relaxed, knew he had been wrong, knew Lucho had not seen the chance. He began to lean forward, pick up his coffee, resign himself to death. Heard the words. 'More coffee for you, sergeant?' He straightened, leaving the mug. Waiting.

Lucho stepped forward, behind the sergeant, so that he

could pour for him. The sergeant was picking up his mug, holding it forward. Lucho's hand was shaking with the weight of the pot. Pouring the coffee. Overfilling the mug. The hot liquid splashing onto the sergeant, scalding his flesh through the cotton of his shirt. Lucho was aghast, apologising. The sergeant was screaming at him, pulling back from the table, tearing at his shirt. The soldier at the radio was transfixed. The only person who was moving was the captain. Leaping up. Shouting for a cloth.

Moving.

Towards the sink.

Moving right.

Away from the guns.

Pertierro was himself moving. Off the bed. One pace. Towards the guns. The sergeant turning. Seeing. Two paces. The sergeant reacting. Almost there. Lucho was moving. The full contents of the coffee pot into the sergeant's face. Scalding. Blinding. The first Uzi, finger closing round trigger, thumb sliding safety catch off. Lucho hitting Paco, slamming him forward. Away from the sergeant. Clearing the firing line.

The attack had lasted barely six seconds. Lucho was already beside Pertierro, flicking an Uzi onto automatic fire. The sergeant was opening his eyes. Lucho stepped forward and slammed the butt across his head, knocking him out.

'Paco, get their pistols.' There was no guarantee the student's nerves would hold, Pertierro knew he had to take the chance. Paco removed the pistols from each of the soldiers, throwing them onto the floor between Pertierro and Lucho, careful not to stand between them and the guards. 'And the knife.' Paco threw the knife from the table, moved across and picked up a weapon.

'Turn around.' The guards did as they were ordered. 'You two,' Pertierro indicated the two nearest the sergeant, 'get him into the cells.' Lucho and Paco remained in the kitchen. Pertierro followed the two as they dragged the sergeant out of the room and into the small corridor

114

which led off it. Along the passage were a number of cells. They stopped at the first. 'Put him in.' The cell was two feet wide and four feet long, the walls lime green and stained with blood. The sergeant's body barely fitted. 'Get in yourselves.' The privates clambered over the body, trampling the wet clothes and scarred flesh. 'What time are they coming?'

One of the guards was unable to speak, the other managed to get the words out before he too froze with shock. 'Nine o'clock.'

Pertierro slammed the door shut, the whimpers of fear suddenly shut off by the soundproofing, pushed the bolt across and went back into the kitchen. The captain was white and trembling, the remaining guards also shivering. 'What time are they coming?' He needed to check.

'The normal time. Nine o'clock.'

'Car?' asked Pertierro.

'In the yard outside.'

The captain's voice was weak.

'Keys.' The captain took his hands off his head, moving slowly and nervously, and pulled them from his pocket. 'Watch and money.' The captain did as he was ordered. 'OK, put them in the cells.' Pertierro watched as Lucho and Paco escorted the captain and privates out of the kitchen, locked the privates in the second cell, next to the sergeant, and the captain in the last cell by himself.

The room where the guards slept was in the front of the house. The three hurried upstairs, ransacked the room till they found clean shirts and trousers that fitted, fresh socks, and laces for their own shoes. In a suitcase under a bed Pertierro found a sweater. In a locker he discovered a jacket that fitted him. For the first time since he had been captured and stripped he did not feel cold.

The captain's car was in the yard, a three-year-old Ford imported from America. Lucho loaded the guards' weapons and their own clothes into the car. Pertierro checked the front gate, made sure the street was clear, and told Lucho to drive through. When they were outside he pulled the gates shut till he heard the lock click into place and jumped into the front passenger seat.

It was six thirty-five. Fifteen minutes since the lid of his coffin was slid open and he had been told he was going to die. He wound down the window and breathed the crisp morning air.

'Which way?' Lucho's voice was anxious. Each of them had been driven to the torture house in the boot of a car or covered by a blanket.

The sun was to their left, he knew they were in the north of the city. 'Straight down, right at the bottom, and keep going till we see somewhere we know.'

Ten minutes later they were heading for the city centre. 'What are we going to do?' Lucho's question was a request for details. There was no panic in his voice.

'Two options,' said Pertierro, knowing time was against them. 'Either we hole up in a safe house, or we head for the border. Which do you prefer?'

Lucho drove steadily. 'I know you will have to leave for a while, tell those outside what's going on. I'll stay, keep Paco with me, make sure things are OK here.' He turned right, picked up one of the roads skirting the centre and headed west. 'You can drop us near the safe house. That will give you two hours to get to the border before they find we're missing and shut the place down.'

Fifteen minutes later Pertierro had left his two companions, keeping one Uzi and a pistol for himself, giving them the rest, and was heading north, out of the city, considering the option of routes open to him. Before leaving the bowl and beginning the climb to the *altiplano* he stopped at a market, bought a sack of potatoes, a second-hand poncho and an old hat, and put them in the boot. By the time he left the last straggle of houses he had decided his route. The road to the south-west of Lake Titicaca was shorter, faster, but it was the obvious route, the one they would block off immediately. The way to the north-east was longer, slower. And they could shut off the border before he got there. He turned west, trying to outrun them. Fifteen minutes after the execution squad were due at the house he reached the ferry-crossing at Tiquina, where Lake Titicaca narrows to less than two hundred yards, took one of the rafts, the boat with the outboard motor lashed to it, and turned north along the western shore of the lake towards Copacabana, close to the border with Peru.

Two miles from the town, calculating from the marker at the Tiquina ferries, he pulled the Ford into a small clump of thin trees and stopped the engine. Any closer, he feared, and he would be observed. Quickly he stripped off the clothes he had taken from his torturers and put back on his own stained shirt and trousers, aware again of the intense cold, and the poncho and hat he had bought at the market. He emptied the sack of potatoes, put the Uzi in the sack and threw back enough potatoes to conceal the shape, then tucked the pistol into the belt of his trousers.

The road was still clear. He started the car and drove four hundred yards to a point where the bank into the lake was steep and the water below dark and black. He unloaded the potato sack, put the car into neutral and rolled it gently forward, jumping clear when he was certain it would plunge into the lake.

The Ford gathered momentum and slid over the edge, striking the water thirty feet below with a crash that seemed to reverberate around the lake. For almost a minute it floated, then began to sink gently. Within another forty seconds it had sunk completely. To his annoyance he could still see the outline of the light blue car through the dark water. He comforted himself that it would not be spotted till he was safe, knew it was not the case, slung the potato sack across his back and began to shuffle up the road to Copacabana like the Andean peasant his father had been.

The town was farther than he had calculated. By the time he arrived in the main square it was five minutes to ten. The pangs of hunger, sharpened by the cold, were biting into his body. The walk had brought back the pains of his torture. At a stall in the corner of the square, by the steps of the church, he bought a potato, a *choclo* and a mug of coca tea. It was an hour after the execution squad were due to arrive at the torture house. Already, he assumed, they had discovered the escape, were checking, sealing off the border. He finished the meal, turned away from the lake, following a path that led inland from the town. When he had walked thirty minutes he turned right till he judged he was walking parallel with the shore. Two hours later, from an escarpment swept naked by the wind, he saw the border post half a mile behind him. Fifteen minutes later he picked up a path leading to the first Peruvian town on the lakeside, skirted round the edge of the cluster of houses, concealing himself from the Peruvian border post, and hitched a lift on a lorry heading for Puno.

At ten minutes past one, six hours and fifty minutes after he had been let out of the coffin, he knocked carefully on the door of a tin hut at the rear of a café in the port area of the town. Even later he could remember the words of the man who opened the door to him. '*Hermano,*' the man said. 'My brother, I thought you were dead.'

2   *Lima, Peru*

Laporte woke at six, put on the old red dressing gown his mother had given him when he first left home to train as a novice, and went to the showers on the floor below. They were empty. In the rest of the building he could hear the waking sounds of the brotherhood, the shuffling of feet and the echoing of whispers round the ancient stonework. After the shower he returned to his room, dressed and went downstairs to morning Mass.

Father Michael was already there. In the rear row, almost lost in the dark. When Mass was finished the two left the monastery and began walking towards the Plaza de Armas. The first bus of the morning passed them, its engine sending a cloud of exhaust into the air.

'You were late last night. I was concerned.' There was genuine compassion in Father Michael's statement. The Frenchman acknowledged the bond which had developed between them on the study tour.

'Don't worry, my friend. If there was cause for concern, if I needed help, you would be the first person to whom I would turn.'

They passed the double wooden doors of the cathedral, walked down the steps and along the wide pavement in front of the palace. In the centre of the square was the shoe-shine boy, as if he had never left. 'Have you found anything yet?' asked Father Michael.

Father Jean considered his reply. 'It goes much deeper than anyone thinks, much deeper than the mere fact that the man has been found and disappeared again.' He had always found the other priest easy to talk to, prepared to listen, to ask the questions to which he could provide the answers. Almost as if he was as involved as the Frenchman himself. 'They'll never find him,' he continued. 'Even if there was any real chance of finding him, I don't think anyone really cares.'

'And you, Father Jean, do you care?'

There was no hesitation in Laporte's reply. 'Of course. Very much.'

'Is anybody looking for him?'

'Not really. The authorities are going through the formalities, but nothing more.'

'And you, are you looking for him?' For the briefest of moments Lapore remembered the way he had anguished over St Thomas Aquinas and the doctrine of the Just War. 'He killed my father,' he said simply.

They had crossed the square, passed beneath the glass façade of the post office, and were almost back at the gates of the monastery. In the narrow street the noise of the buses was almost deafening, the thick pall of diesel smoke belching out of their exhausts was already draining the blue from the morning sky.

'Do you have anyone to help you?'

They arrived at the gates. 'I'm not sure. I've spoken to one or two people about the affair, but that's all at the moment.' Father Michael pushed the gate open. 'If you need anyone, remember me.'

Laporte was impressed by the sincerity of the offer. In their own ways both the magazine editor and the woman had already helped. But Pacheco had received a story in return, and Maria had been able to talk about her missing friend. Father Michael, on the contrary, would receive nothing. 'Thank you,' said Laporte, and followed him into the monastery.

The breakfast of bread and coffee was taken in the long refectory in the centre of the sanctuary. Laporte and Father Michael sat together but did not continue the conversation which had filled their attention during the walk round the square. After breakfast Father Michael joined the other members of the study group, waiting for the minibus which would take them to the concrete shell of the schoolhouse where the First Secretary of the embassy had brought the news.

Laporte watched the vehicle pull away into the swarm of traffic that was already congesting the city centre and went back to his room. The monastery had once again resumed its tranquillity. He lifted his briefcase from the top of the wardrobe, emptied it, stacking its papers and books at the foot of the bed, shut it, and carried it downstairs. When he left the monastery it was fifteen minutes past nine. Eight hundred miles away Guillermo Pertierro made the ferry crossing at Tiquina and headed for the border at Copacabana.

The main shopping street, between Plaza San Martin and Plaza de Armas was already packed with shoppers, the street vendors covering the pavements with their wares, the cars barely able to squeeze down the one-way system between the shops. Laporte pushed his way out of the crowd and found a clothes shop. Even in the morning the lights outside the shop were flashing and the music was filling the street. The dark suit was hot and heavy around him, the collar tight. He bought a jacket, two shirts and two pairs of lightweight trousers and put them in the briefcase, pushing the lid hard to shut it.

In the arched boulevard round the upper half of the Plaza San Martin, where the street of shops opened out onto the square, he found a cluster of telephone kiosks and a directory of the Lima area. There was no record of either a Klein or a Heiner with a house in Chaclicayo. He stepped back into the sun and began the half-mile walk to the block of offices, part of which housed Pacheco's magazine.

The magazine was on the fourth floor of a block over-looking a building site. The colonial façade of the exterior led into a large, marble-floored entrance hall from which a staircase swept to the floors above. In the right-hand corner was a lift. Laporte ignored it and walked up the stairs. On the first and third floors were women's toilets, on the second and fourth a gents'.

The editor was sitting at a large battered desk, a portable typewriter pushed to one side, three telephones on the top. The walls were covered with enlargements of the front pages which had made his magazine both famous and respected. Pacheco was reading as Laporte entered, scratching at a reporter's story with a red pencil. He looked up, saw the priest, and rose to greet him. 'Father Jean, sit down.' He cleared a space on a sofa to the right of the desk and shouted to his secretary to bring two coffees. 'So, Father, what news?'

'That's what I was hoping you could tell me.'

Pacheco shrugged. 'Nothing, I'm afraid. I've had a reporter working on the story, trying to get something on Heiner, but there's nothing. The neighbours say they heard singing sometimes, couldn't understand the language, but nothing else there. I've tried some police contacts, a few politicians I know, but nothing.' There was a break in the conversation. 'And Maria,' asked Pacheco, 'did you speak to her?'

'Yes, we spoke a great deal. A remarkable woman, very attractive.' It was a strange thing for the priest to say, Pacheco thought, knowing the statement had not been intended the way it seemed. He reached up to the desk and seized a bunch of photographs. 'What do you think of these? They're the ones we took at the house yesterday.' Laporte took them and leafed through them.

There was something about them that he knew he needed, not sure what it was.

'They're rather good. Can I have a couple?'

Pacheco was pleased at the priest's response. 'Take as many as you like. I was thinking of balancing one of you with one of your father, but we haven't been able to get one. I don't suppose you have one?'

'As a matter of fact, I do, though I'd almost forgotten about it.' He pulled out his wallet and took a photograph from the sheaf of papers and money. It was the same photograph which his mother kept on her dressing table.

Pacheco took it, fascinated, almost frightened by what he saw.

He recovered, and called for a photographer to copy the ageing print. 'Are you still leaving on Sunday?' he asked.

Laporte hesitated. 'I'm not sure, it rather depends.'

Pacheco nodded his understanding. 'As I said yesterday, if I can do anything to help, just ask.' It was the second such offer of the morning.

'There is one thing. You don't have the telephone number of the house in Chaclicayo, do you? It's not in the directory.'

Pacheco consulted a small leather notebook and wrote down a number. 'I made a note of it yesterday,' he explained. 'I had a man ringing every hour, in case anyone showed up, but there was no reply. I imagine it's the same today.'

Laporte took the number, put it in his wallet and rose to leave. 'Nice to see you again. I'll call back later for the photograph.'

Pacheco went with him to the office door. 'As I said, if I can help in any way, just ask.'

Laporte waited at the lift till Pacheco went back into the office, then walked briskly down the stairs. On the second floor he went into the gents' toilet, locked the door, unfastened his briefcase and stripped off his clerical collar. The cubicle was almost too small to turn round in. He pulled on a set of the clothes he had bought that morning, folded his priest's clothing into the briefcase, transferred his money and rosary to the jacket pocket and left, flushing the toilet after him.

At a shoe shop two blocks away he bought some more shoes. At a chemist he bought a pair of sunglasses, and at a newsagent's a pen knife, a street map of Lima and a copy of the Latin American Handbook. Then he walked to the Sheraton Hotel, situated between the former Palace of Justice, the front still showing the damage of the 1970 earthquake, and the American Embassy. He found a table in the Palscana Bar and ordered a breakfast of coffee and croissants, adding cognac as an afterthought.

While he waited for the order he unfolded the street map, found the road to Chaclicayo, and marked the location. Then he found Maria's address and noted it without marking the paper. When he was satisfied that he knew the general structure of the city, he turned his attention to the Latin American Handbook and began to study the road and air links out of Lima. There was little hope, he realised, of establishing how the fugitive had left the city, but he felt more confident knowing the options.

When he had finished breakfast he made his way to the Avis desk in the shopping precinct on the floor below the hotel foyer and asked for a car. The multilingual assistant smiled at him, gave him a price list, and asked which model he wanted. It was the first time in his life he had rented a car. His natural conservatism urged him to take the smallest and cheapest. He consulted the list and chose what he assumed was the fastest.

3 *La Paz, Bolivia*

The estate car passed through the security gate, up the driveway, and stopped in the parking area at the rear of the house. Heiner watched closely as the driver and passenger, assisted by two other men, unloaded the wooden boxes and carried them into the room which he had specially prepared, emptying it of all contents except a desk and chair. When all the boxes had been brought in he waited while the driver undid the metal fasteners with a wire-cutter, and ordered the guards round the house to be doubled. Then he closed and locked the shutters of the room, placed more guards outside the windows and door and went inside, locking himself in.

There were fifteen boxes, each containing a varying number of cardboard boxes which in turn contained either box files or loose-leaf folders crammed with documents. In the last minutes of the panic at Chaclicayo, however, some of the documents had simply been scooped up and stuffed into containers without order or logic, so that at least part of the minutely detailed filing system he had developed over the years had been destroyed. To organise the chaos, then to check the documents, he estimated, would probably take him two days. Thirty-six hours if he was lucky.

As an afterthought he placed a call to the international exchange, requesting a number in Lima.

The call came as he was halfway through the first box. He heard the ringing tone, then the noncommital grunt at the other end. Joe Corrigan, he knew, would almost certainly be chewing a cigar. If not, he would reach for one as soon as he heard Heiner's voice. 'Good morning,' he said, 'this is Heron Exports, the managing director speaking.'

Corrigan reached for a cigar. 'Good to hear from you. How's the holiday?'

'Everything's fine. I was simply phoning to say that all is in order and that my local service manager will shortly be returning to re-open our Lima office.'

'I'm glad to hear it.'

'Anything I should know?' asked Heiner.

'A couple of minor problems. I'll explain the details when I speak to your manager, but we're taking care of things.'

Heiner thanked him, put the phone down and answered the knock on the door. The chef was standing outside with a tray of lunch. Heiner allowed him in, watched while he placed the tray on the desk, and double-locked the doors again as the man left. He placed five more international calls then settled down to eat. Automatically he reached for the serviette, placed to one side of the tray the copy of that day's *Presencia* which the chef had also brought, and opened a bottle of chilled Löwenbräu.

The first of the international calls came through fifteen minutes later. He waited for the connection, found himself speaking to the switchboard of the Lima headquarters of the *Guardia Civil*, and asked to speak to one of the country's highest-ranking policemen. He waited while the general's secretary checked with her superior that the call could be connected, identified himself by a code name, invited the police chief for a drink, and terminated the call.

Twenty minutes later, precisely according to the timetable he had worked out, the international operator connected his second call, to the Sheraton Hotel in Lima. Heiner asked the switchboard to page a Señor Pascalles and waited while the police chief, dressed now in a smart civilian suit and wearing dark glasses, answered his fictitious name. Without querying the reason, the policeman confirmed that the *Guardia* watch on the house at Chacli-

125

cayo would be lifted between the hours of eight and ten that evening, and that before they took their extended break the guards involved would switch on the house lights.

The third international call was received by Heinrich Schmeltz fifteen minutes after the second. Only when the call was completed and Schmeltz had received his instructions did Heiner allow himself to relax and pick up the copy of the afternoon newspaper which had lain folded on his desk since the chef had brought his lunch. The face which stared at him from the front page had been lifted from a police file. The headline above the photograph was stark. '*Muere el Lobo.*' 'The Wolf Dies.' He turned his attention to the brief article beneath. The guerilla leader Guillermo Pertierro, known as 'The Wolf', had been killed that morning. He had stolen a car which was later found sunk in Lake Titicaca. It was assumed that the body had drifted out of the wreck on impact; police expected to find it later that day. There was no mention in the article that for the past three-and-a-half months he had been held in custody, that he had been tortured, or that he had escaped from that custody.

Heiner poured himself the remainder of the beer and walked to the curtained window, drawing aside the cloth, thinking about the man in the photograph. The paper, and presumably the authorities who had given Pertierro the bestial nickname, were wrong. *El Lobo*, or whatever they liked to call him, was not dead. By now he would be safe across the border in Peru. Heiner knew exactly what he had done. Driven as close as he could to the border, ditched the car, probably after changing his clothes to look like a *campesino*, then walked into Copacabana. From there he would have headed away from the lake, missing the border post three miles past the town, before dropping back onto the road on the Peruvian side. From there he would have hitched a lift on a lorry to Puno.

And from Puno he would head for Lima.

It was like a spider's web, he thought. The comings and goings. Each man, each movement, spinning the fine

126

threads of the trap. Himself from Lima to La Paz after the snivelling worm and the bastard journalist Herbert Weissemann. Heinrich Schmeltz from Lima to La Paz and now back to Lima. The documents from Lima to La Paz. The one they called *El Lobo* from La Paz to Lima. The Texan with the name of Anderson to La Paz.

The threads crossing, weaving, drawing them all slowly and inevitably together.

And the son, the one he had forgotten, from France to Lima. Not quite, he reminded himself. Not just from France to Lima. He remembered the words of the man on the train, the only words the man on the train ever spoke. Not just Laporte from France to Lima, he thought, not just strengthening the spider's web of the present. Extending it, taking it back, tying it to the past. To the man on the train.

And the bastard Guillermo Pertierro, he thought again, remembered his reasoning of the night before. One weakness, he had decided. Not yet a weakness, he had thought then, just a flaw. Not even a flaw. But not a strength. And if it was not a strength it was a weakness.

The international operator came through to say there was a delay in connecting the fourth and fifth calls. Heiner checked his watch and told the man to keep trying.

Pertierro, he thought again. Already in Puno. Already on his way to Lima. Thought he was fucking clever. Had managed to escape, had thrown the Bolivian authorities off his track, fooled them into thinking he was dead. But he, Josef Heiner, knew. He smashed his glass on the table. Fuck him, he thought, fuck Pertierro. He lifted the telephone and made a local call.

4 *Lima, Peru*

Corrigan left his desk and walked to the window. On the pavement to the right, three floors below, a man was selling chocolate and nuts from a case perched on a makeshift stand. Corrigan looked at him. No problems with Heiner, he thought, no panic on the telephone. Everything organised. As always, he reflected. Heiner was always organised. With good contacts, good enough to warn him of the *Guardia* raid on the house at Chaclicayo, good enough to help him get out. He wondered where he was, knew there were several alternatives. Probably La Paz, he thought. Heiner had excellent connections there. On both sides, he thought, remembering Octavio. Project Octavio, the one that Dick Mayer sweated about, the one that Bailey had raised first in the briefing the previous morning. La Paz, he decided, it had to be La Paz.

He turned from the window and went back to his desk. At least Washington was not pressing for an update on Heiner's whereabouts. On other occasions, he thought, he would have considered it strange; on this occasion he considered it to be a conscious decision, a matter of political expediency. If Washington did not know where Heiner was, Washington could deny knowledge of Heiner.

No problems with Josef Heiner, he thought again.

No problems with the son either, he thought. No word from Bailey's contacts that anything was wrong. No suggestion that the plan Bailey had brought with him from Washington should be implemented. He pulled a cigar from the drawer and thought about the son. The details Bailey had supplied in the several briefings they had held since the first on the Tuesday morning had never been far from his thoughts. He wondered again where the son was, what he was doing. Reminded himself that Bailey had the son under control. Wondered, he realised for the first time, what the son was like.

Something else, he suddenly remembered, something he had to do. Something he would overlook in what he knew would be the pressure of the next four days till the son left Lima on the Sunday. He switched on the answerphone machine of his direct confidential line, told his secretary he would be out of the embassy for no more than an hour, collected his car, and drove to an expensive jewellers in the San Isidro quarter of the city. There he spent fifteen minutes choosing a baptismal gift. The present he finally selected was a rosary. When the assistant offered to gift-wrap it for him he declined, explaining it was for his godson and that he would therefore like to wrap it himself. He paid for it and returned to the embassy. The day was hot and the traffic heavy. He turned off the main road, took a longer route back along the cliff tops, and stopped at a café overlooking the sea for a beer.

The rosary he had chosen was made of mother of pearl. He opened the box and looked at it again, the shell sparkling in the sunlight. The priest, he assumed, carried a rosary. He sat back, sipped the beer, and thought about the son. Bailey's brief had been good: age, education at primary and secondary level, family connections. What Bailey's brief had not told him, however, was anything about the nature of the person they were targeting, his beliefs and motivations. He watched the cold droplets run down the side of the glass and went through the points he knew would influence, if not ultimately determine, whether the plan against the priest would finally be implemented. What it had meant to grow up under the reputation of his father. Why the son had chosen to enter the priesthood. How his father's former colleagues-in-arms had reacted to the life of peace the son had chosen. What, at the core of the debate, the priest felt about Josef Heiner. Whether at any time in his life, whether at any time in the past two days in particular, he had entertained the notion of revenge. Or whether he meekly and unquestioningly welcomed the peace of forgiveness.

St Paul to the Romans, he remembered from his Catholic upbringing, chapter xii, verse 19. 'Not revenging yourselves, my dearly beloved, but give place unto wrath.'

Chapter xiii, verse 4, he also remembered. 'He beareth not the sword in vain: for he is God's minister, an avenger to execute wrath upon him that doth evil.'

In any case, he thought, if he, Joe Corrigan, Heiner's number one contact, did not know where Heiner was, how the hell could the priest find out? And if he did, what could he do, how would he know what to do?

The glass was empty. He paid the bill and went back to the car. No threat, Bailey had assured him, the priest was no threat. His life had been peaceful, almost pacifist. He started the engine and pulled away. Wondered, theoretically, what he would be thinking if he was the priest. What he would be doing.

5 *Lima*

The two *Guardia* outside the house in Chaclicayo paid no attention as he drove past. A mile further on he swung back onto the main road, turned back towards Lima for nearly three-quarters of a mile, then pulled to the right, up a rough track, to a garage almost immediately opposite the house. At the side of the garage was a small café; beside the café a telephone which an old man, a brown poncho over his shoulder even in the heat of the late morning, was using. Laporte went into the café, ordered an ice-cold Coca Cola, and examined the map again.

The side road on which the house was situated swung off the main road in a loop nearly two miles long. Three hundred metres from the point where it left the main road, however, the side road split, the lower fork passing in front of the house, the fork to the right forming another road to the rear. The two loops joined again before connecting with the main road. Halfway along the upper loop another road cut off at a right-angle to another suburb of the city, larger and more sprawling than Chaclicayo, three miles away. From this suburb an entire network of roads ran in different directions back into the city.

The old man finished his telephone call. Laporte paid for the drink and dialled the number which Pacheco had given him, letting it ring while he studied the house opposite. The telephone, he already knew, provided a perfect vantage point. The police car was some hundred metres away, the house beyond, at the top of the garden. Behind the house he could see an area of wasteground, then the backs of more houses which he assumed faced onto the upper of the two loop roads. He let the number ring for almost two minutes, then returned to the car and drove back to the main road, turning right towards Lima then almost immediately left into the side road. After two hundred metres he turned right, taking the upper fork, till he came to a house which he estimated was behind Heiner's. The houses in the road were newer and smaller than those on the lower fork. Many were still being built, the scaffolding clinging to them like skeletons.

The house which he had stopped at was a modern, two-storey building with a security gate in the front wall and an alsatian prowling its flat roof.

Two houses along, the building was only half-finished and empty. The road to the second suburb three miles away was forty metres past the house. Laporte pulled round the corner, locked the Caprice, checked there were no workmen on the site, and slipped through the rubble in the front of the house to the rear. The garden was ten metres long. On the other side of the wall at the bottom was the waste area he had seen from the telephone by the café, about fifty metres wide. On the far side, three houses to his left, was the house he had visited with Pacheco the previous morning. From the rear of the house to the garden where he now stood he could see a thin line across the waste area, as if someone else had crossed that way recently.

He climbed over the wall at the bottom of the garden and followed the line to the hedge at the rear of Heiner's house. In the foliage, at the foot of a small tree, was a hole. He crept through, concealing himself in the hedge till he was sure there was no-one in the garden, and hurried across the open space to the cover of the house. The door into the kitchen where he had sat with Pacheco was locked. The window over the sink was fastened by a simple latch.

He opened the pen knife he had bought that morning, slid the blade between the window and its frame, and eased the latch back, surprised at the ease of entry. Under normal circumstances, he assumed, there would have been a better guard system.

The house was quiet. He waited till he was sure he could hear no sound, no movement, then went through the kitchen and hall and into the lounge. Somewhere, he knew, there would be a hiding place. A safe, or a second safe at least, possibly something else. He remembered Maria's description in the Bar Hawaii, her account of Herbert Weissemann's mission to find the documents. The police, he mused, had had the same idea two mornings before. The entire area was as he remembered it from his earlier visit, the floor covered with debris, the furniture ripped, the pictures torn off the walls. The sunlight streamed through the bay windows in the front of the house. Laporte moved carefully out of the lounge and into the study, trying to envisage where he himself would conceal a hiding place, examining the walls and floors, moving the wrecked chairs and desks. When he was satisfied there was nothing, he moved to the next room. Ninety minutes later he was convinced there was nothing. Even the spare clothes in the airing cupboard in the bathroom on the first floor were pulled out, the framework of the cupboard torn apart. He went back to the kitchen, found a can of Löwenbräu beer in the fridge, took it back into the lounge and slumped disconsolately into a chair.

The police, he felt forced to admit, had been right and he and Maria, as well as Herbert Weissemann, had been wrong. There was nothing. There were no documents, and if they had existed, they had been removed.

The sharp tang of the Löwenbräu reminded him of the *Bierkeller* in Southern Germany, the long evenings he had spent in the mountain villages of Bavaria where his mother had sent him, first as a child, then as a student and teenager, to learn German. His German, he had been told at the time, had become flawless, so that he had spoken it

132

with the harsh rasp of the region. He sipped the beer again, remembering the nights at the *Rathauskeller* beneath the city hall, the folk songs echoing into the night and then, as the night grew older and the camaraderie closed in like a ghost, the songs turning to the marching hymns of the Reich, the *"Horst Wessel Lied"* and *"das Deutschlandlied"*, till he, the son of a French war hero butchered by the Nazis, knew the songs by heart. He remembered what Pacheco had told him. The neighbours had not been suspicious, not even of the occasional drinking sessions in the house. Of the singing. He looked around, knowing what the songs had been, hearing the words again, listening to the toast to the Führer.

He got up, the nervous tension suddenly consuming his body. He was wrong to think there was nothing in the house. There had been something. Was still something. He knew it, smelt it. He paced the floor, tasting the beer, hearing the songs. Think, he told himself, think like the bastard you're hunting. Think like your father.

The noise at the window jerked him round. His mind snapped back to the present. The sparrow scrabbled against the window, wings beating on the pane, and flew off. Beyond the bird, coming up the garden, Laporte saw the *Guardia*. He returned to the kitchen, climbed out the window, pulled it shut behind him, and crossed back over the wasteland. Five minutes later he was driving back to Lima. That there was something in the house he was adamant, except that he had missed it. He had the key. Somewhere in the past twenty-four hours, his instinct told him, he had been given the key. Except that he had not recognised it.

In front of him, the sun was dipping lower in the sky. The next time he visited the house, he knew, there was something else he would need.

By the time Laporte reached the city outskirts it was almost five o'clock. In the Plaza Dos de Mayo the traffic had come to a halt at a set of lights. He waited, jammed between a lorry of sugar cane and a bus, the fumes belching from both. On the corner opposite, an Indian woman, a small baby strapped to her back, was preparing *anticuchos*, the flames shooting into the air as she fanned the charcoal and splashed garlic and oil onto the marinated cow hearts. The lights changed and the traffic round him began to move forward. He eased his foot off the brake, his eyes still on the flames, his mind back in the kitchen at Chaclicayo.

He was sitting with Pacheco, hearing Pacheco's words as the photographer took his photographs, the flash lighting up the walls of the room. 'The police didn't miss them by much. The stove was still burning when they arrived. One of the squad told one of my people that it was blazing away.'

The strands were pulling together. He remembered the cooker in the kitchen, the gas bottle beside it, remembered assuming the stove was to heat the water. He remembered the bathroom on the first floor, the clothes pulled out of the airing cupboard, away from the tank and water heater. The realisation was descending upon him, slowly and inexorably. He knew he had the answer, allowed himself the pleasure of confirmation. A stove with no purpose burning fiercely in the early hours of the morning, of a morning in summer. Blazing was the word Pacheco had quoted. As if, thought Laporte, it had just been stoked. For no reason. Except one, Pacheco had suggested. To burn documents. Except another, he now thought. To stop anyone examining it too closely.

The cars behind him were blasting their horns at him. Laporte drove round the corner, bumped the car onto the pavement, pulled the briefcase from under the seat and took out the photographs which Pacheco had given him that morning. He flicked through them till he found the one he wanted. The two of them, the editor and himself, sitting at the table. Behind him, in one corner, the cooker with the gas bottle, and in the other the stove. He looked closely. No pipes led from the stove, no pipes which could

134

have been part of a heating system, no pipes which could have destroyed his thesis, only the flue leading into the wall. He knew he had the key.

The sky behind him, outside the city, was still deep blue. He checked his watch, wondering if he had time. Five-twenty. In seventy minutes, he knew, even less, it would be dark. No dusk, just the sudden transition from day to night. He could get to the house before then but did not know how long he would need inside. He had the key, but still did not know how to use it. But at night he would need a torch. And the protection he realised he had overlooked that afternoon.

Twenty yards along the pavement was a café. Laporte locked the car, walked to the café, ordered a beer and asked to use the telephone. The café was dark and cool, a row of seats and tables along one wall, the telephone on the marble top of the bar. For a moment he thought he was back in France.

He picked up the telephone and began to dial. Two people had offered him help that day, and a third had given help the night before. The airline office answered and he asked for Maria. Ten seconds later he heard her voice.

'Maria, it's Jean. Jean Laporte.'

There was a hesitation in her response. 'Father Jean?' she asked.

He remembered that she knew him as a priest. 'Yes, Father Jean. Can we talk?'

She knew what he meant. 'One moment.' He waited, hearing the sound as she shut the door, then the scuffle as she picked up the telephone again.

'I'm sorry,' she said. 'When you said Jean, I didn't know who you were for a moment.'

He knew he was trying to picture her in her office. 'Sorry, it was my fault.' He knew precisely what he wanted to ask her, why he was asking her. 'Is it possible to see you tonight?' The words, he realised, were terse and functional.

'Yes.' The response was instant. 'I had arranged something else but I'll cancel it.'

'Thank you.' He didn't ask whether she was sure, did not give her time to think about it. 'When do you finish work?'

'Seven.'

'Fine, where can we meet?'

'Do you want to eat?'

He realised he had eaten nothing since breakfast. 'That's a good idea.'

'There's a restaurant, the Café de Paris, on Nicolas de Pierola, the main avenue leading off Plaza San Martin. I'll meet you there at seven.'

He wondered at the irony of the name. 'There's one other thing.' He did not know how she would react. 'Can you get hold of a pair of night binoculars? They're not the sort of things a shop would normally sell.' She did not reply, unsure what he meant. 'There are different types,' he continued. 'Some use their own light source to view in the dark, others enhance the available light to improve vision. You can get binoculars, or special camera lenses.' He paused. 'I know it's difficult, but I hoped you might know someone who might have access to a pair of binoculars or a lens. Just for tonight,' he added. The conversation had changed.

If there was uncertainty in Maria's mind, her voice did not betray it. 'I'll see you at seven,' she replied, not committing herself.

Laporte left the café and returned to the car. For a moment he wondered how he knew about night vision equipment, how he knew there were different types. There was no answer.

Maria heard the click as he put the phone down. The outer office, which she could see through her door, was busy with a group of students asking about discount tickets to Rio. She sat back, ignoring the noise, and thought about the conversation. The way he had introduced himself. Not Father Jean, he had said. Jean Laporte. It had confused her, now it perplexed her. She wondered why he had used the name, what was happening, how she was becoming involved.

A pair of night binoculars, he had said, listing the types, detailing the differences. She wondered again what the priest would do with them, why he was asking for her help. Why he was asking for her involvement. More than involvement, she thought. With Herbert Weissemann there had been involvement. Weissemann had involved her, used her. As a confidante, as a hiding place for items like the tape recorder. As a delivery service for the article to the newspaper. But he had also protected her, always ensured that her involvement was superficial. The priest was asking for more. With Weissemann there had been points past which he would not ask her to go, past which she would not have gone. With the priest there were none. She wondered what right he had to ask her. What right she had to refuse. She looked at her watch. It was getting late. She closed the office door and telephoned a contact at the airport.

6

AeroPeru flight PL 616 from La Paz to Lima landed on time at 1.30 p.m. Heinrich Schmeltz cleared customs and immigration with the minimum of trouble, took a cab to the Hotel Bolivar, overlooking Plaza San Martin in the centre of the city, entered through the front door, walked quickly through the foyer, past the tea-room and lifts, and out the side entrance to the cab rank on Ocaña, where he took another taxi to the house in Miraflores which served as a temporary headquarters since the flight from Chaclicayo.

He checked with the three *Sturmmänner* that all was well and sat down to a late lunch of cold meat and beer which one of them had prepared. He had been in the house fifteen minutes when the telephone rang. Heiner's voice was distant but distinct, calm.

Schmeltz listened while the *Sturmbannführer* recounted the details of his conversation with Corrigan, mentioned that the minor problem to which he had referred the previous evening had been taken care of, and explained, almost as an afterthought, that the documents had arrived but were in such disorder that he would favour a check to confirm that nothing had been inadvertently left at the house. Schmeltz felt a professional admiration as Heiner went on to inform him that there would be no guard on the house between the hours of eight and ten that evening and that all the lights would be left on. When the *Sturmbannführer* had finished, Schmeltz informed him that all was well and that he would report back later that night.

The lunch was still on the table. He ignored it and summoned the three *Sturmmänner*. 'How many men can we have here in the next two-and-a-half hours?' he asked. Already his mind was working out the logistics of the night raid.

'Not many, three at most. The orders were for everyone to return to their zones and check there were no local breaches of security. So most are several hours away.'

'That's enough.' The plan was already established in his mind. 'Three of them, plus four of us. One man to stay here, that leaves six for the house.' He was thinking aloud. 'Contact them, tell them there's a briefing at seven.' He thought quickly, working out the timetable: how long it would take the three to assemble; how long he would need to have at the house; when he would need to leave. 'Make the briefing six-thirty.'

The afternoon sun was hot. He returned to his study, opened the door onto the garden to allow a gentle breeze to ventilate the room and rehearsed his tactics for the evening. When he was satisfied, he opened a wall safe concealed behind the cocktail cabinet, selected a false passport and an international driving licence from the several he kept, and took a cab to the Sheraton, taking with him one of the *Sturmmänner*.

The late afternoon traffic in front of the American embassy was already building up. He wondered about Joe Corrigan, imagined how the American must be worrying. In the shopping precinct beneath the hotel he picked his way between the tourists to the Avis desk. He would have liked to hire Mercedes, but there were none. He chose a Plymouth Volaire and a Dodge Coronet.

7

The traffic leaving the city was congested. Maria skirted round the Plaza Dos de Mayo, took a detour through the long line of commercial buildings strung in a circle round the outskirts of Lima, and headed for the airport. To the left she could see the lights of Callao, smell the warm sea air. In the old days, she thought, she would have smelt the fish meal, drifting over from the factories which filled the land between the port and the airport, processing the anchovy which the fleets brought in every day. Now the water temperature had changed, the cyclical phenomenon known as El Niño had altered, the anchovy had gone. And the factories were quiet.

A plane passed overhead, descending, engines screaming. She parked the car and phoned her contact from the Varig desk. Ten minutes later he met her in the bar on the floor above the departure lounge, handing her a box, explaining how its contents worked, not asking her why she needed it. She thanked him and returned to the city. It was all part of one long process, she thought, each move created a new commitment, tied the last one immovably into place.

The priest had started the process that day. Had committed himself to something, she did not yet know what, had

139

involved her by enlisting her help. Which in turn had cemented his own commitment.

It was like a web, she suddenly thought, like a spider's web.

She parked the car in a side street close to the restaurant where she was meeting the priest, put the box in her shoulder bag, and walked to the café. The evening was warm, the street busy. The Café de Paris was half full. A waiter met her at the door. She looked at the tables, searching for the priest. Apprehensive. Now confused. No priest, she could see no priest. She knew he would be there, would not be late, knew he would be waiting for her, but she could not see him. For a moment she admonished herself for choosing such a public place, feeling the weight of the bag on her shoulder.

In the far corner, in sight of the door, someone was standing, greeting her. A man, tall, dressed in open-necked shirt and jacket. She tried to remember who he was, where she had met him, afraid it would interfere with her appointment with the priest. She gripped the shoulder bag, politely acknowledging the man, still looking for the priest.

She recognised the man, her confusion growing. She sat down at the table, allowing him to help her with the chair, and put the shoulder bag underneath. 'What would you like to drink?' Laporte asked. She saw he was drinking white wine.

'The same,' she replied, still confused.

'I'm sorry,' he apologised, 'I should have explained about the clothes. It's just that sometimes it's a little impractical to go round looking like a priest.'

She nodded as if she understood. Like a web, she thought, drawing them all in.

The waiter brought a menu. They ordered. Maria pulled the shoulder bag from under the table, took out the box which the contact had given her, and handed it to Laporte. 'A little gift,' she explained. 'It's what you asked for this afternoon.'

'What sort?' he asked.

'The night glasses were impossible,' she said, 'there was only one pair and the security people at the airport have them. So I got a camera with a night lens, as you suggested.'

He thanked her. 'You didn't get into any trouble?' he asked.

'No trouble. I just owe somebody. But they have to be back tomorrow morning.' She waited for him to tell her why he needed them.

'Before I explain, there's something I have to tell you,' he said, 'something Pacheco told me.' He wished he had told her the night before, remembered why he could not. 'The day after you saw him, all trace of Herbert Weissemann vanished completely. Somebody paid the outstanding rent on his flat and removed all the furniture. It is as though he no longer exists.'

'I know,' said Maria, fingering the wine glass, 'Pacheco told me this morning.'

Laporte nodded, wondering whether he should continue the subject, deciding against it. 'I think I may be on to something,' he said. 'It may be nothing, or it may be too late, but at least it's a start.' He sipped the wine. 'I went back to the house this morning. There was a police guard there, but I went in through the back. It was empty, like yesterday, a complete mess where the *Guardia* had torn it to pieces.'

She knew she should have been surprised that the priest had broken into the house, knew she was not. 'But?' she asked.

'But I think the reason they didn't find anything is that they didn't look in the right place.' Maria waited. 'They were looking for a safe, a secret compartment, as Josef Heiner knew they would. Behind the pictures, inside the walls, probably the walls of the study or lounge. Even in the furniture. The police pulled the house to pieces but they didn't find a thing.'

Maria looked at him enquiringly, wondering why it

affected her, why it was important to her.

'I'm not sure if it will be of any use, but I now know where to look.'

She wondered again why it was important to her. 'How can you be so confident?' she asked. Laporte remembered the afternoon, thought again of the conversation he had had with Pacheco.

'Because this afternoon I sat in Josef Heiner's chair, drank Heiner's beer, thought like Heiner. I've sung the songs he sings and read the books he reads.'

'And?' asked Maria.

'And like Josef Heiner, I'm not a Peruvian.'

'What do you mean?'

'What's the only place in a house that a European would go that a Peruvian, particularly a Peruvian male, would not?'

'The kitchen,' she answered immediately.

Laporte nodded. 'Under the stove in the kitchen.'

The food arrived. He waited while it was served, then explained his theory, recounting Pacheco's description of the stove, blazing fiercely, when the *Guardia* had stormed the house two mornings before.

'Why didn't you look when you were at the house today?' asked Maria.

'Because I didn't see it until five minutes before I phoned you, and by then it was too late to go back. I had the vague feeling when I was in the house that I was overlooking something, but it took time to realise what.'

'So what do you intend to do?'

'I intend to go back tonight?'

'Why not tomorrow?'

'Tomorrow may be too late.'

'That's why you need the night vision?'

He wondered how she would react to what he was about to ask. 'That depends on you,' he said.

Like a spider's web, she had thought. Drawing her in, ensnaring her. Involving her, then committing her. She remembered asking herself whether the priest had a right

142

to ask her, whether she had a right to refuse. Knew it was already too late. 'Tell me what you want me to do.'

Laporte borrowed a pen from the waiter and drew a map on the serviette. 'It's now twenty minutes past seven,' he began to explain his plan. 'It takes about fifty minutes to get to Chaclicayo. 'We should be at the house at about eight-fifteen.'

8

The briefing which Heinrich Schmeltz had ordered began forty-five minutes late, at seven-fifteen, one of the three men he had recalled from outside Lima having been delayed by a road accident. At seven-thirty the two cars Schmeltz had hired for the operation, the Volaire and the Coronet, left the house in Miraflores. If anything went wrong, which he did not anticipate, there was nothing about the cars which would lead either to himself or to the organisation.

Schmeltz himself sat in the front passenger seat of the Volaire. The drive through the remnants of the Lima rush hour, he had estimated, would take them thirty-five minutes, the road to Chaclicayo another twenty-five. The guards would be away from the house between eight and ten. He consulted his watch. 'Plenty of time,' he said to the driver, 'we should be at the house by eight twenty-five.'

9

The road out of Lima was clogged with traffic. Laporte followed Maria's Datsun round the Plaza Dos de Mayo and onto the outer ring road. In the shallow hills around the city, the lights of the *barriadas* were twinkling like stars. Fifteen minutes later the traffic had thinned considerably. By the time they were halfway to Chaclicayo, the only other vehicles were the buses and the heavy lorries beginning their overnight haul into the Andes.

At twenty minutes past eight, five minutes later than he had planned, the two cars turned off the main road and bumped their way up the rough slope to the café and telephone opposite the house. The café was closed; Laporte felt a sense of relief. Maria was running enough of a risk without the staring eyes to threaten her even more.

The night air was chilled. Above them, to the east, the high rim of the mountains was scarcely discernible against the black sky. The moon was a thin, almost invisible crescent, its newness casting no light upon the landscape, so that in front of them the road and cornfield were a sea of darkness. Maria pulled a coat from the car, already shivering in the cold of the foothills. In the sky to the west, the bowl of light from the city reminded her of what she had left. Laporte left his car and walked to the telephone where that afternoon he had checked that he could see the house. The blaze of lights from the windows screamed at him across the narrow valley.

'What is it?' asked Maria.

'I don't know. The lights are all on. There must be somebody there.'

She looked across at the brightness of the house. 'There can't be. There are too many lights, every light in the place. It's something else.'

'Have you got the night vision?' She handed the camera with its night lens to him. 'No film in it,' she said, 'I've checked.' He raised it to his eyes, not knowing what the effect would be, hoping he would see something other than the total blackness which surrounded them. The effect of the lens was startling. Through the pale green of the vision he could pick out every detail of the house and garden, and the road in front. Something else, he realised, was different. He swept up and down the road, adjusting the focus slightly, then handed it to Maria for her to check. 'The guards,' he said unbelievingly, 'they've gone.' On the

144

grass verge at the front of the house, where he had passed the *Guardia* patrol car that day, there was nothing.

'Perhaps they're at the back,' she suggested.

He shook his head. 'I don't think so. They've been in the same place both times I've been here.'

'So what are we going to do?'

'Go ahead as planned. There's probably an obvious reason why the lights are on. The guards probably decided to take a break and switched them on to fool people into thinking the house is occupied.' The account satisfied neither of them.

'Why don't we ring and find out,' Maria suddenly suggested. 'At least if somebody answers we know we can't go in.' She consulted the number he had written for her and dialled, letting it ring for a full minute before she replaced the set in its metal cup.

'What time do you make it?'

She checked her watch. 'Twenty-five minutes past.' He synchronised his. In the cold their breath was forming small balloons.

'You're sure of the signals?' Maria nodded. 'OK,' he continued. 'If all goes well, I'll meet you back here. I'll drive down the main road first and flash my lights three times so you know it's me. If any car turns in here without that signal, if anything else happens, get out as fast as you can. If anything goes wrong, I'll meet you back at the flat.' He got into the Caprice, wondered whether he should kiss her good luck, and decided against it. 'See you later,' he said simply, and drove back into the blackness.

The lights of the houses in the upper loop road shone through the closed curtains. The street was quiet except for a drunk peddling down the road on a rickety push-bike. Laporte stopped near the junction close to where he had parked that morning, switched off the engine and lights, and allowed his eyes to adjust to the dark.

The half-built house was as he remembered. He made his way up the front garden, picked his way through to the rear and crossed the wasteland to the hole in the fence, using the blaze of lights as his guide. There were no unexpected figures in the lighted windows at the rear. He waited, checked, then crossed the exposed stretch of grass to the kitchen window. It was still unlocked from the afternoon. He pushed it open, horrified at the squeaking of the hinge, pulled himself in and eased the window shut behind him.

The light from the naked bulb in the centre of the ceiling was almost blinding after the black outside. He waited, listening for any sound, his eyes growing familiar to the light. On his left was the stove; on his right the door to the rest of the house. He listened again. Nothing. Somewhere, instinct told him, there should be a guard. He crossed to the door, opened it carefully, crept into the hall and waited again. Still nothing. Quietly, almost painfully slowly, he checked every room in the house till he was sure he was alone. The minute hand on his watch had reached eight-forty. He went back to the lounge and waited for Maria's check call.

11

The black weighed down upon her. Maria tugged her coat around her and waited, scanning the road with the night lens, wondering what she would do if someone suddenly appeared, asked herself what she was doing. She glanced at the luminous face of her watch. Ten minutes in. Eight-forty. Time for the check call. She knew the number, dialled it automatically, waiting while it rang, counting the number of rings. When it reached ten she broke off, waited twenty seconds and dialled again. The telephone rang three times before it was picked up. She heard the rattle of the pay tone and rang off. Laporte was safely in the house.

Even in the chill of the night the nervous sweat trickled down her back. She wondered what they would do to her

146

if they caught her, found herself wondering what they had done to Herbert Weissemann. Her left hand, in which she held the camera, was sticky; her right played with the car keys in her coat pocket. She remembered what Laporte had said. If a car pulled onto the ground by the telephone without the signal, if anything else happened, get out as fast as she could. The Datsun was three feet from her. She put the keys in the ignition, pushed the car into gear, and left the driver's door open.

Across the valley the windows of the house still stood out against the black of the night, throwing an eerie light down the garden. She raised the camera to her eyes again, methodically scanning the road in front, the garden, and as far into the darkness behind and on either side of the house as her vision would permit. She glanced again at her watch, surprised at the passage of time. Twenty minutes in. Eight-fifty.

12

Eight-fifty. Heinrich Schmeltz looked at his watch. If it wasn't for the bloody puncture, and the fact that the hire company had put the wrong jack in the Volaire, they would be at the house by now.

He had kept the briefing short, maintained his timetable despite the late arrival of one of the *Sturmmänner*. The traffic through the city had been as he had expected, but once clear and onto the ring road, then the autoroute, they had picked up time, the two cars sticking together, Schmeltz and one of his men in the leading Volaire, the others in the Coronet.

Halfway to Chaclicayo and they had been ahead of schedule, the only other traffic on the road had been the buses and the heavy lorries pulling into the mountains. And then the puncture. Which would have delayed them for five minutes, no more. Except that the jack was the wrong one for the car. He had checked that everything was present when he had picked it up at the Sheraton, made sure he had all the equipment and tools, plus a good spare tyre, but it had never occurred to him that the hire company would have got the bloody stuff mixed up, put it in the wrong bloody cars. So they had wasted another fifteen minutes while the boys had struggled and sweated to change the wheel.

They returned to their cars and moved off, Schmeltz erect in the front passenger seat of the lead vehicle. He checked his watch again; the delay had not been disastrous. They still had an hour.

The lights of the cars travelling in the opposite direction flicked past them. Schmeltz turned, checked that the boys were still behind, knowing they would be, the tension beginning to build in his body. Just like the old days. The feeling never changed. The taste in the mouth, the tightness in the gut. Some men tried to avoid it, some needed it to live. Thank God, he thought, that he was not still a farmer's boy in the fields of Bavaria, even in the windswept scrublands of Patagonia. Thank God he was where he belonged.

The Volaire pulled off the main road, barely slowing, passed the junction where the upper loop road forked right, and slid powerfully and menacingly down the long straight stretch in front of the house.

13

Maria's first check call echoed through the empty house like an alarm, taking him by surprise even though he was expecting it. Laporte waited while it rang ten times, admitting the sense of relief when it stopped. Thirty seconds later it began again. He let it ring three times and picked up the receiver. The line went dead. Maria knew he was safely in the house.

The telephone was in the lounge, on the opposite side of the hall to the kitchen. He stretched the lead as far as it would go, till he was able to place the telephone in the middle of the hall, as close as he could get it to the kitchen, and went back to the stove, putting a chair against the door between him and the telephone to make sure it would stay open.

The room was as he knew it from his previous two visits and Pacheco's photographs. The stove stood against the wall on the left of the window, the flue going straight into the ceiling, with no other pipes or attachments. Laporte pressed his weight against it, wondering whether it would move, disappointed but not surprised when it didn't. Slowly and methodically he began to examine the flue, pressing and pulling the screws and bolts which held it in place, hoping to find the key which he assumed would unlock the stove. Five minutes later he had eliminated the pipe and had started in the same careful manner on the stove itself. He had been at the stove seven more minutes when he began to wonder how Maria was, wished he had taken the number of the pay-phone so that he could check, glad that he could not.

Every part of the stove was solid and unmoving. After nine minutes Laporte stood back, knowing he was correct but thinking he might have to admit defeat. Wondering whether he had misheard or misinterpreted Pacheco's words. 'The police didn't miss them by much. The stove was still burning when they arrived. One of the squad told one of my people that it was blazing away.' The words provided no fresh clue. He felt the cold of doubt creeping over him, wondered again if Maria was safe.

The thoughts began to string together. If the stove needed to be secure, and heat was its primary security, then the key was as close as possible to the heat. He lifted the plate off the top of the stove and felt inside, running his fingers round the welded rim. At the back, where the flue connected, was a small, strong piece of metal which appeared to do nothing. He tensed his muscles, pulling the

149

metal up and down, left and right. There was a clicking sound and he felt the stove move with his body weight. Effortlessly he swung it round, using the flue as a fulcrum.

The stove moved three inches to the left and stopped. Carefully, afraid he might damage the mechanism, Laporte eased it to the right. The stove swung easily and loosely back till it was against the wall. In the concrete floor where it normally stood was a small iron ring. He lifted it, straining slightly, wondering what lay beneath. A section of the floor came up in his hands, revealing an opening two feet square, its edges camouflaged by the red tiles of the floor itself. Laporte picked up the torch and shone it down the opening. If there's a safe, he remembered telling Maria, they've probably taken everything; if there's more, they may have left something. The beam of the torch went down ten feet. Beneath the opening he saw a set of stairs, neatly made of wood and highly varnished; on the right was a light switch. He switched it on, suddenly surprised by the glare of the strip lighting, and let himself down the stairs.

The room he had entered was ten feet high, fifteen feet long and almost as wide. He guessed it matched the shape of the kitchen above. The walls were white, the floor covered by the same red tiles. There was no smell of mustiness. Along each wall, except that which supported the stairs, were rows of filing cabinets. For a moment his hopes soared. As he looked closer, however, he knew he was too late.

The room was a complete wreck. The drawers of the cabinets were open, on the floor between them was a pile of empty boxes, empty folders and files scattered on top. Whoever had left the house before the police arrived had been given sufficient time to clear the secret library. Not much time, judging by the chaos, but enough. He fought his disappointment and began to sift through the rubbish on the floor, still hoping to find a clue.

150

14

The house and gardens were quiet and peaceful in the soft green of the night lens. Maria moved the camera slowly, examining the garden, the walls around it, and finally the house itself, paying special attention to the dark recesses between the patches of brilliant light from the windows. There was nothing.

She looked again at her watch, noting the time, registering how long Laporte had been in the house, when the first spark of headlight flashed in the corner of her eyes. She jerked the camera up, searching frantically for the road in front of the house, establishing the wall, then sweeping right to where the pinpricks of light had suddenly emerged. She saw one set of headlamps, then a second. Automatically she began to dial the number, her attention diverted for vital seconds, gasping with relief when she heard the ringing tone and was able to focus again on the cars.

In the now familiar green of the night lens she saw the menacing shape of the Volaire, and the slimmer outline of the Coronet behind it. For a moment, unknowingly, she shared the fear Herbert Weissemann had experienced on the same road four nights before. As the convoy approached the house it seemed to slow. She pressed the telephone rest with her free hand, the other gripping the binoculars, trying to estimate how long the phone had rung, whether Laporte had heard the first warning that something might be wrong, beginning to dial again.

The cars slowed almost to a stop then accelerated away to the left, leaving the house as quiet and undisturbed as before. She breathed a sigh of relief and put the phone back on its rest.

15

The house was as unguarded as Heiner had promised. No police outside, lights blazing from the windows. Schmeltz checked his watch again. Five minutes past nine. Fifty-five minutes until the *Guardia* returned. Plenty of time, and no messing about with torches, trying to keep the beams away from the windows, trying to conceal the fact that someone was in the house. The *Sturmmann* slowed in front of the house, then Schmeltz waved him on. 'Right at the end, onto the upper loop road. We'll leave the Volaire there as a precaution in case we have to get out the back, and go in at the front with the Coronet.'

The driver nodded, accelerating away. 'What if we have to ditch the car?' he asked.

'No problems,' Schmeltz told him, 'it's hired under a false name.'

The loop road at the rear was empty except for a Chevrolet Caprice. They drove past the parked car, swung in a tight circle so they were facing the same way, prepared for the fast escape through the suburb three miles away to the right, from the junction just opposite, and parked thirty yards behind it. The Coronet had stopped on the other side of the road. Schmeltz and his driver got out and transferred to the other car.

'Listen carefully.' Schmeltz reminded them of the details of the early evening briefing. 'We go in through the front. Willy stays in the car, Rolf will position himself at the rear door of the kitchen, the rest of you will come in with me. If everything goes to plan we should be out in fifteen minutes, no more. That gives us plenty of time before the *Guardia* come back. If they're early, or if anything else goes wrong, Willy alerts us by blasting his horn, then he gets the hell out of it. The rest of us leave by the rear, and reassemble here. We should get here more or less together. We wait thirty seconds then pull out. Anybody not here gets left behind.' He laughed. 'As I'm the oldest, that should be me. The doors are unlocked, the keys are on the floor, just inside the driver's door. Understood?' There was a guttural agreement.

'OK,' Schmeltz said, 'let's go.'

16

The cold was numbing her fingers, seeping into her body. Maria rubbed her hands up and down her arms, then checked again with the night lens. Nothing. On the road to the right she saw again the pinprick of headlamps, tensed as she waited for the second set. The lights moved slowly down the road and she relaxed slightly, relieved at seeing no second car, dialling the number anyway.

The cold made it difficult. She blew on her fingers to warm them and continued dialling. By the time she could hear the ringing tone the car was halfway down the road. She focused the lens and swept the road till she was looking at the car, expecting subconsciously to see the uncompromising shape of the Volaire. The outline was lower and slimmer; she relaxed a little more, allowing the ringing to continue, waiting for the car to drive past the house and disappear.

In her imagination it began to slow. She told herself she was wrong, her mind suddenly sharpening as she remembered the second car of the convoy in the previous alert. Her attention had been focussed on the first car, the big square front of the Volaire, barely noticing the second.

Her fingers tightened around the camera. She wondered if she was right, how long she could leave it before ending the warning and starting the second vital call. She stared, fascinated, as the car slowed and stopped outside the house. In the green of the night vision she saw the doors open and the men beginning to get out. Her frozen fingers slammed on the rest and she began dialling again, her mind suddenly realising there was no dialling tone. She pressed the rest urgently, scared, banging the metal up and down, praying for the dialling tone. In the green of the night vision she could see one man opening the gate at the bottom of the garden and three more following him. Christ, she pleaded, please Christ, give me a dialling tone. Her fingers pressed the metal once more. She heard the low tone and began dialling, fingers shaking, trying to control herself, knowing she could not afford to make a single mistake. The six digits took a lifetime. She dialled the last, waited another lifetime, then heard the ringing tone. Ten seconds, Laporte had said, ten seconds between the warning and the alarm. She had taken twenty. More like thirty.

In the green of the lens Maria saw the first man, twenty metres inside the gate, still a merciful hundred metres from the house. Hear it, Jean, she was screaming to herself, for God's sake hear it! In the silence of the night, across the road and the corn field, she could hear the telephone in the house. She saw the man in the garden stop, hearing the telephone, turn towards her, as if he knew where she was, what she was doing. Then he turned again and began running up the garden towards the house.

The phone was still ringing. She dropped it and slid into the car. She wanted to stay, remembered Laporte's instructions. In one movement she had started the ignition, foot jammed on the clutch, and was accelerating away, wheels spinning in the dust, the door still open. She swung the wheel, wrenched the car down the track towards the main road and pulled the door shut. The blackness in front of her was total. She could see nothing. Automatically she leaned forward and flicked on the lights, still accelerating. The boulder at the side of the road was coming at her fast, the drop behind it rushing at her. She swung right, felt the sickening thud as the rear of the Datsun struck the stone, then she was on the main road, still accelerating, fleeing for the safety of the city.

17

The pile of cardboard boxes in the centre of the secret basement contained nothing. Laporte sorted quickly but carefully through each one, examining the folders, till he was satisfied they were empty, then switched his attention to the filing cabinets. Slowly and methodically he searched each drawer, feeling with his fingers at the top and back in case anything had wedged there. He had completed one row, and was halfway along the shorter wall at the end, when he heard the telephone. The blood began pounding in his ears, he wondered how long it had been ringing before he had heard it. The boxes in the centre of the floor were in his way. He stumbled over them, climbed the stairs and froze like a statue at the top, listening to the steady plastic ringing of the telephone he could now just see through the kitchen door.

If anything happens, he had told Maria, if a car appears on the road, start ringing. Merely as a precaution, as a warning of a potential danger. If the threat passed, she was to put the phone down and thank God. If the threat materialised, changed from potential to real, she should stop phoning, wait ten seconds, then phone again. And get the hell out of the place.

As suddenly as it had started the ringing stopped. He waited, not breathing, for the second call, the statement that the danger was real, that someone else was coming into the house. After a minute he relaxed and climbed back down the stairs.

Behind them, in the narrow space between the bottom rung and the wall, he saw a blue folder he had missed when he had rummaged through the mess on the floor, the darkness of its cover almost obscuring it from view. He reached behind the stairs and pulled it out.

The folder bore no title. He pulled it open and saw the papers inside, sensing the excitement rush through his body, then subsiding as he examined the contents. The twenty sheets of light pink paper inside were expenses

155

sheets, recording no more than destinations and mileages, meal allowances, entertainments and payments. At the top of each sheet was a name, beneath it a number and a project title. The signature on the bottom of each sheet was the same, as if someone had approved the expenses contained above. He flicked through the sheets, seeing some names, noting some words. The project title on five sheets in the middle of the sheath was the same, he noticed. Project Octavio. On another occasion, he thought, it might have made interesting reading, but it was not what he was seeking. He dropped the folder onto the top of the filing cabinet nearest the stairs and continued his search of the cabinets at the other end of the room.

He was working more slowly, he realised, spending only part of his time searching the drawers, the rest listening for the telephone. The realisation angered him, but he knew he could do nothing about it.

As he finished each cabinet, he pulled it off the wall to see if anything was lodged behind. The cabinets were solid and heavy, those on the remaining wall were older and taller, and he knew he would barely move them. He had finished examining the second of the final four cabinets and was struggling to lever it from the wall when he heard the first ring of the telephone. He stopped, taking the weight of the cabinet, straining to confirm the noise through the thudding in his ears, till he was forced to push the cabinet back against the wall and race up the stairs. He had been wrong. There was no telephone, no ringing. He climbed out of the hole back into the kitchen and checked that the phone was working, hearing the comforting sound of the dialling tone, then dropped back into the secret basement. The cabinet had jammed between the two on either side. Laporte heaved against it, trying to push it back into place, when he saw it. The small corner of white paper sticking out from behind the next cabinet. He pulled out the drawers to lighten the weight and began hauling at the next heavy metal frame. Slowly it tilted till he could see the paper. As he eased the cabinet from the wall, the paper slid further down. In the pounding of his ears he could hear the telephone ringing again. He cursed his stupidity and cowardice and ignored it. With a final effort he inched the cabinet forward, stretched an arm in, closed his fingers round the paper, and pulled it out.

On it were two lists. In one column on the left were a series of German names and military ranks; below was a second list of names and addresses in Spanish. He ran his gaze down the lists, hoping to find a familiar name, looking for the one name he wanted, recognising none.

Christ. The realisation hit him like an executioner's axe. The phone was still ringing. He hadn't been mistaken, had heard it in the strain of shifting the cabinet. He waited at the foot of the stairs, trembling with the physical effort of moving the cabinet, sweating with anxiety. The phone rang another four times then stopped. He waited, wondering whether it would ring again, counting the seconds. Ten, he had told Maria. Ten seconds then ring again. The time passed and he began to relax. Twenty seconds. He looked at the list again, wondered if he could gather the strength to shift the last cabinet. Thirty seconds. The sound cut through his mind like an ice pick. The sinister, impersonal ringing of the phone. The second ringing. Not the warning that something might be wrong. The confirmation that it was. He stuffed the list of names into his pocket, grabbed the file he had discarded earlier, and pulled himself into the kitchen. The phone was still ringing. No time to close the hatch, disguise the fact that he had uncovered their secret. He jumped onto the sink and out of the window, tearing his coat on the catch as he dropped onto the grass and scrambled for the hole in the hedge. The blackness was total, the hedge outside the circle of light from the window. He wanted to use the torch, knew he couldn't, remembered he had left it in the kitchen. The hedge was rougher than he had remembered. He tore at the thorns, found the hole, and squeezed through. The track across the wasteland was almost invisible. He followed it, trying to make as little noise as he could, aware of the commotion he was making as he crashed through the undergrowth.

The wall on the other side seemed higher than before. He wondered whether he had found the right place or whether he was simply more tired. He pulled himself up, feeling the strain on his muscles, then fell over. He was in the right garden. In front he could just distinguish the outline of the half-built house. He ran round the side, making himself move more slowly, more quietly, till he was in the front garden, then stopped. Behind him he could hear the telephone ringing. Then it stopped. Somebody else, he knew, was in the house.

The Caprice was fifty yards up the road to the left. He stumbled to it, almost bumping into the car parked behind it. He opened the door, fell into the seat, and pushed the key into the ignition. Thank God, he thought, thank God for Maria. The thought changed. Pray God she's safe, pray God she pulled out in time. The engine roared into life. Thank God, he panted, they came in the front way. He smashed the car into gear and accelerated away.

18

The driver cut the motor and allowed the car to drift to a halt outside the gate. Just like the old days, Schmeltz thought, silent and deadly. Hit them when they're not expecting it, before they know you're there. He got out of the car, pulled the key to the gate out of his pocket and let himself through, the others following. Pity, he realised he was thinking, pity it wasn't the real thing, pity there wasn't somebody in the house, pity they weren't after him. A hundred metres up the garden he could see the bright lights, the house quiet and ghostly in the silence.'Fifteen minutes,' he whispered back to the driver, 'fifteen minutes and we'll be back.'

The beams of light seemed to stretch down the garden,

drawing him towards the house. He had walked twenty metres when he heard it, froze as though he could not believe it. Concentrating. From the inside of the house came the sound of a telephone ringing.

He turned, looking across the valley at the telephone he knew was by the café, then spun round and began running up the garden. Fifty metres from the house he turned as he ran and looked back. The headlights were moving fast, away from the café, away from the telephone.

The back door of the kitchen was only thirty metres away. He ignored the key, crashed through the door, saving seconds, letting his body weight and brute power take him through the wood, sending it splintering.

The kitchen window was open. The stove lay against the wall, the clandestine hatchway to the secret basement open, the light from the strip lighting pouring up. In the doorway to the hall the telephone was still ringing. He picked it up, stopping the noise. On the loop road at the rear he heard the engine of the Caprice starting, then moving away.

'Jesus,' he moaned in German.

19

The night air grew warmer as Laporte dropped out of the foothills of the mountains and into the city, entering the way he had come that afternoon, crossing the Rimac behind the presidential palace. The drive from Chaclicayo had been fast, he had stopped only twice. Once, switching off the engine to check whether he was being followed, hearing nothing except the howling of the dogs. Once to phone Maria, to make sure she was safe. There had been no reply at the flat.

He parked at the side of the Sheraton, hurried to the public telephones at the side of the foyer and phoned the flat again. Maria answered immediately. 'It's Jean,' he said, 'is everything all right?'

'Yes, fine. And with you?'

'Yes.'

'Are you coming round?'

'I'll be in Miraflores in twenty minutes.'

Fifteen minutes later he had parked the car at the rear of the block where Maria lived and was pressing the door-bell of her flat. The spy-hole in the door darkened as someone on the inside looked at him, then he heard the sound of the lock and chain being undone and the door opened.

Maria had just stepped out of the shower. Her black hair hung round her shoulders, the water still glistening on her skin. A dressing gown was pulled across her body, tied at the waist. Laporte dug his hands into his pockets, unsure what to do, and stepped forward.

'We did it.' He was almost shouting, singing. 'We got something.' He was inside the door, hands in the air in celebration, smiling, laughing. Maria was sharing the elation with him, coming towards him, arms outstretched. They were in each other's arms, hugging, pulling themselves tight against each other, swirling in a circle. Triumphant. The movement stopped but the mood remained. He let her go, shut the door and came into the room, throwing the documents onto the coffee table. 'We did it, we bloody well did it.' They were too excited to say more. 'They came for us, but we beat them.'

'How about a drink to celebrate?'

'Cognac,' he answered, 'a big one.'

She knelt at the cocktail cabinet, reaching for the bottle and glasses, the dressing gown rustling. Laporte watched her, seeing the shape of her body through the silk, remembering the embrace. It had been one of triumph, he told himself, nothing more. Of colleagues greeting each other, congratulating each other, welcoming each other to safety as only those who shared a common danger could do.

Maria had poured the drinks, was coming across the

room, putting the glasses on the table. He remembered why he was with Maria. Tried to shut out the other thoughts. Knew she was thinking the same. 'I'll get dressed,' she said, suddenly serious, and went into the bedroom.

Laporte opened the file, spread the documents it contained, plus the separate white sheet, in a semi-circle on the floor, and relaxed again, sipping the cognac. Maria came back into the room wearing a light sweater and jeans and sat opposite him.

'I'm sorry,' she said.

'About what?' He was confused.

'About the delay in getting the second call through to you. I couldn't get a dialling tone. I thought it was going to be too late, that they would get you.' He remembered the long seconds at the bottom of the stairs, knew Maria also remembered them. 'They didn't, thanks to you.' He cupped the glass in his hands, enjoying the fumes of the drink, letting them seep into his head. 'Tell me what happened.'

For the next twenty minutes they recounted to each other the events of the evening: the details of the secret basement, the desperation at the telephone when Maria could not get the dialling tone, the realisation and animal fury of the man in the garden as he turned and looked at her. Twice Laporte filled their glasses. When they had finished he knew there was something he had to say.

'There was one thing I couldn't help being aware of this evening,' he began, hesitantly, almost formally. 'Driving to the house, in the basement, when we were both getting out. Not something I thought about at the time, because there was no time for such thoughts, but something that was always there.' He was unsure how Maria would react.

'Herbert Weissemann,' she spoke quietly but strongly. He nodded. 'I had the same feeling,' she admitted, 'a feeling rather than a thought. But when I was standing in the cold, I was aware of him waiting in the cold. When I

161

saw them going in for you, I was aware of them going in for him.'

'What does that mean to you?' asked Laporte. Wondered why it was important for him to know.

'You mean what does he mean to me, what do you mean to me,' she corrected him. 'Herbert Weissemann is dead and I mourn him greatly.' She drained her glass. 'His death was that of a very old and dear friend, but nothing more. A confidante, yes. A lover, yes. Once and long ago.' She wondered why she needed to be honest with him. He wondered why he felt a twinge of jealousy, knew he had no right. Remembered he was a priest.

'And me?' he asked.

'A very dear friend? You are already that. A confidante, a sharer of secrets? Of course.' A lover, she knew they were both thinking, knew it would not be enough, knew there would need to be something more. She stopped speaking. 'But?' he asked, knowing there was one other thing.

'But there is something more, something I never had with Herbert Weissemann. Something most people never have, probably that most people would never want, at least in the manner we have experienced it.'

He remembered the images he had carried with him since childhood, the fading photographs of those he knew had existed, but had never seen. 'With Herbert Weissemann,' he could hear Maria saying, half lost in the memories of the past, 'I was someone he could trust, someone to whom he could turn.' She remembered the afternoon the priest had asked her to get the night glasses, realised with a shock that it was only that afternoon, that it was only a little over twenty-four hours since they had first met. Remembered what she had thought about Herbert Weissemann and the priest. That Weissemann had asked only for her involvement, that the priest had required her commitment.

'I know you so well already,' she continued. 'Sometimes I know you better than you know yourself, know when

162

you're worried, almost when you're lying.' He began to reply and stopped, knew she had not finished. 'I know what you are, who you are. What you are thinking, what you are doing.' She paused, knowing what she was about to say, knowing she did not understand it. 'I know what you should be thinking, what you should be doing.' One day, she thought, she would know what she meant.

Laporte put down his glass, walked round the table, held her face in his hands, and kissed her. 'Let me show you the documents,' he said.

For forty-five minutes they studied the papers, checking and cross-checking, till they were both exhausted. It was one in the morning. 'Where will you sleep tonight?' asked Maria.

'I hadn't thought. The monastery will be closed by now.'

'Then you will have to sleep here.' She made a bed for him on the sofa and wished him good night.

20

Heinrich Schmeltz ground the stub of the cigar into the glass ashtray and waited for the international operator to connect his call to Josef Heiner. The *Sturmmänner* were in the lounge, helping themselves to the supper he had arranged for them after the operation. The operation. He almost spat the word out in disgust. There'd been a foul-up, an almighty big foul-up. The man in La Paz was not going to be happy, going to be even less happy than Schmeltz himself.

The ring of the telephone interrupted his thoughts. He waited while the operator told him she was connecting the call, then heard the iron voice of Josef Heiner. 'How did it go?' Heiner demanded immediately. Schmeltz sensed there was a reason for the directness.

'Badly. Someone else got there first.' He could hear the hiss at the other end of the connection.

'What the hell do you mean?'

Briefly and succinctly Schmeltz went through the events of the evening, emphasising the possibility of a double-cross, minimising the importance of the rear escape. 'I have an awful suspicion it could be your friends,' he concluded. 'It was a team job, at least two cars, probably more, and a good look-out, obviously using night-viewing equipment. They had us stone dead from the start.'

The voice from La Paz was hard. 'You'd better contact them in the morning. I told them you would, but I wanted to play them a little. Now I think you ought to sort it out immediately.'

'Of course.'

'One other thing,' Heiner said. 'Did you find anything, any documents, that the boys might have missed when they cleared up?'

'No, the place was empty. Plenty of boxes and rubbish, of course. But we checked everything.' He exceeded his status. 'Why?'

The reply was like black ice. 'There is a possibility that we have a problem. One set of documents is not in the correct place. I am checking, but we must accept there is a possibility it is missing.'

'Which one?' Schmeltz's sudden trepidation overcame his natural instinct not to question a superior.

'The book-keeper's file.'

For a moment Schmeltz felt a shudder in the very foundations of the organisation which he loved and served. Like a spider's web, he had thought that morning as he looked down from the plane from La Paz, observing the criss-cross of roads across the *altiplano*, like the threads of a web, drawing the world to its centre. Now, he suddenly thought, it was drawing in even itself.

'Including the details of Project Octavio?' He could barely recognise his own voice.

'Yes,' replied Josef Heiner, 'including the details of Project Octavio.'

Chapter Four

Thursday, February 3rd 1983

1

The dark was all around her. Carmen lay still, opening her eyes, limbs not moving, letting herself grow accustomed to the black. Gradually the objects began to form, taking shape, becoming firmer. She moved her head slightly so that she could look around, the rest of her body motionless, saw the shapes. Wondered, in her half sleep, whether they were real or imaginary. As Guillermo Pertierro must have wondered, she thought, lying still, in the blackness of his coffin. Not quite like Guillermo Pertierro, she corrected herself. At least she had the option, at least she knew the blackness was not complete, at least she knew she could get up and walk away. Her eyes grew more familiar with the black. She moved her head a little more, saw the shape of the bedroom. Five o'clock in the morning, she estimated, between five and six. She wondered where Pertierro was now.

The Texan called Anderson knew she was awake, felt the turn of the head, the slight tensing of the muscles in her body as she looked around. Between five and six, he estimated. The beginning of his third full day in La Paz, and still nothing. No phone calls. No word at all from the man. He wondered what was happening, if anything at all was happening. If the man would need his services. Or whether he would receive word to simply pull out.

He could smell the woman at his side. Still too dark to see her, dark enough to sense her. He half turned, brushing against her, rolled over, his tongue feeling along her shoulder, down her side. Her breathing did not change. The room was slightly lighter. She stretched, moving, raising her arms above her head. Exposing herself. His tongue

167

felt its way across her skin, picking up the channel between her pelvis and stomach. She moved again, her thighs opening, lifting. He wondered when the hell Heiner would contact him.

Carmen felt his movement, the intrusion of his tongue, his fingers. Felt his hardness. Pertierro, she thought again, where the hell was Pertierro. Anderson turned her, hearing her cry of surprise, entered her, the cry changing to one of satisfaction. Five-thirty, he thought, the check call, every hour on the half hour. Strange, he reflected, what a person thinks in the early moments of the day. He moved forward, slowly and teasingly.

Guillermo, she thought, crying out, part accepting the pleasure, part knowing it was what Anderson expected. She wondered again where Pertierro was, what he was doing. Knew he would contact her. As Josef Heiner said he would. She felt the penetration, moved again. Guillermo Pertierro, she thought again, the bastard Guillermo Pertierro.

She had only been partly surprised when Heiner had telephoned her two nights before, the evening of her first dinner with Anderson. Pertierro, Heiner had told her, had revealed nothing, was no longer any use. He had therefore taken the decision. Even then she had wondered whether Heiner was telling her the entire truth or whether there was another, more secret, reason. The decision had been too swift, the order given at the wrong time of day. If it had been concerned with the fact that Pertierro had revealed nothing, it would have been taken during the daytime, would have been discussed.

Anderson pushed into her, breathing hard. She gasped, half involuntarily, her mind divorced from her body. She had read the details of the car crash near Copacabana. Had known immediately, as Heiner had known immediately, that it was not accurate. Known as Heiner had known what Pertierro had done, what he was about to do, where he was heading.

Anderson's movements were strong and regular. She

168

rode with them, thinking about Pertierro, taking the rhythm, analysing the telephone calls, examining their significance. Two calls from Heiner after his initial call informing her that he had ordered Pertierro's execution. The first, on the day of Pertierro's escape, confirming what she was already thinking, confirming that he too assumed Pertierro was still alive and heading for the border. The second also reinforcing what she was already thinking: that Pertierro would contact her as soon as he was able. Would order her to contact the remnants of the movement in La Paz. Would betray himself again. The three calls, she thought, all connected. Wondered how. Wondered, suddenly, whether Anderson, sweating over her, moving rhythmically in her, was linked to them.

He pushed harder, taking her by surprise. She remembered the rape on the night she had been taken. The leering faces of the anti-guerilla troops as they gathered round her, holding her down, taking her one by one. The shock of the assault. The three days of torture that followed. Then Heiner. Intervening. Taking her out. Allowing her to bathe, to soak away the pain. Talking to her, turning her she now knew, as he had turned so many. Gently. Persuasively. Identifying her strengths and her weaknesses. Exploiting them.

The psychologists, she knew, would have a theory for it, would write papers about it if they could talk to her, if they could talk to people like Marta Bazan in Argentina, the former Montonero leader, now living clandestinely with her former torturer, the head of the Navy's School of Engineering, Rear Admiral Chamorro, betraying her former colleagues. She did not care a damn about them, about their explanations, knew only that at the end she was more committed to Heiner than she had been to anything else. Even now she did not know how it had happened. She remembered the soft days she had spent free from her tormentors in the sunshine of Northern Argentina, where Heiner had taken her, the evenings in the *haute cuisine* restaurants, the nights in the luxury apartment where he had become her lover. Only when he knew she admired his strength, despised Pertierro's weakness, had he sent her back into the movement, explaining away her absence. As Pertierro's confidante. As Heiner's source.

For nine months she had continued to fight alongside Pertierro, continued to sleep with him. Continued to be told his secrets. Passed them to Heiner.

Not all his secrets, she knew, not the secrets of his connections with the other groups, not his links with the tentacles of revolution that sought to embrace both South and Central America. Not the secrets they had tried to tear out of him in the torture rooms.

The strokes were longer, stronger. She took them, moving with them. The arms, she thought, the weapons she had arranged to buy from the two European dealers. The dealers to whom Heiner had introduced her. Even now she wondered why Heiner had arranged to supply the guerillas with the tools of revolution they so badly needed. Profit, she knew. He profited from everything, controlled everything. But something else, she knew, something he had not told her.

Then the *Sturmbannführer* had decided the time had come. And she had handed Pertierro to him.

Anderson came out of her, turned her onto her back, and entered her again. Something, she thought, that Heiner knew. Something, she suddenly thought, that Heiner was afraid of. Anderson was deep in her. She tightened her legs around him and wondered what it was.

2   *Lima, Peru*

Laporte woke with the light streaming through the open curtains of the balcony window and the sounds of the sea birds outside. He had not slept well. The names on the papers had spun through his mind all night, checks and cross-checks, till his head had been swimming in circles. And when he had forced them away, the smell of the woman in the next room had seeped into his nostrils, taunting his senses with its delicate perfume. He rolled off the makeshift bed, showered and dressed. It was six-thirty. There was no sound from the bedroom. He found a note-pad and pencil by the telephone, wrote a brief note to Maria saying he would phone her at the office, and left. Outside, the sun was already warm. He drove to the Sheraton, parked the Caprice, went to the gents' toilet at the side of the foyer and changed into his priest's cloth-ing, then took a cab to the monastery. By the time he pushed open the heavy wooden doors it was seven-fifteen. He went directly to his room, unlocked it, shaved, and went for breakfast, pushing the briefcase under the bed.

The other priests on the study tour were seated at two tables. As he entered they looked up at him. He wondered how he could explain his long absences to them, what he could tell them. Father Michael rose from the farthest table, spoke a few words, and met him at the door. They sat together, separate from the main group, and ate the bread and fruit. 'I felt you would not want to face them,' Father Michael said, 'so I told them that you were so moved by the poverty we have been witnessing that you wished to be alone, to consider what you could do to help.' He glanced upward. 'I trust the good Lord will forgive one such tiny untruth.' There was the gentlest hint of laughter in his voice. Laporte could understand why he was such a good priest.

'Thank you,' he replied, 'there was much to do.'

Father Michael fetched them both coffee. 'Have you made any progress?' he asked. Laporte hesitated, needing to speak to someone other than Maria about the events of the previous day, afraid to implicate her in anything he said, even to the other priest, knowing that anything he said would inevitably draw her into the web.

'Some progress,' he confided.

'What sort of progress?'

'I'm not sure,' Laporte admitted, more to himself than to Father Michael. There was something else he wanted to say. 'There's a problem.' Father Michael waited. 'The more I enquire into my father's death,' Laporte began, 'the more I feel I become his son. But the more I become his son, the more I am forced to compromise what I believe in as a priest.'

The rest of the group were preparing to leave. Father Michael rose to join them. 'It's a problem only you can solve. Only you can decide how many of the Commandments you can break and still go to Heaven.' There was the same slight trace of laughter in his voice. 'But if you don't ask me to break too many, remember my offer.'

The coffee was cold. Laporte went back to his room, retrieved the briefcase and left the monastery. It was eight-thirty. Maria, he thought, would be on her way to work. He returned to the Sheraton, changed his clothes again, bought a copy of the *Herald Tribune* and the morning's *Comercio*, and went for breakfast in the Palscana bar. The waiter showed him to a corner table. Laporte ordered coffee and croissants, with a large cognac, and began to flick through the newspapers.

On the right-hand side of the front page of *El Comercio*, squeezed between a story on anchovy fishing and an advertisement for Coca Cola was a small item from La Paz. It said simply that Bolivian police were still looking for the body of a guerilla leader called Guillermo Pertierro, nicknamed 'El Lobo', who had crashed in a stolen car into Lake Titicaca. He only read the item because it was from the office of the French news agency, *Agence France Presse*.

The breakfast arrived. Laporte folded the paper and began to eat. By the time he finished it was nine-thirty and the café was crowded. There were people waiting at the door for a table. He was draining the last of his coffee, preparing to leave, when a man walked into the café, looked around, saw that he was about to leave, came across to his table and sat down, ignoring the queue. The man looked tense and worried, thought Laporte.

'I'm sorry,' the newcomer apologised, 'I hope you don't mind, but today is already a bad day and it's going to get worse.' He spoke with an American accent.

Laporte shrugged, 'I don't mind if they don't,' he said, looking at the queue. The man looked up. He was more worried, Laporte sensed, than he looked. He rose to leave. 'Hope things get better,' he said.

The man smiled. 'They probably won't, but thanks anyway.' As Laporte left, the man pulled a cigar from his shirt pocket, put it in his mouth, and began to chew it.

The day was getting hotter. Laporte walked to Maria's office and asked if he could use the flat to study the papers they had retrieved the night before. She gave him a second key. As he was leaving she looked up from her desk. 'Take care,' she said.

He knew what she meant. 'You as well. See you this evening.'

The traffic in the city centre was cramming the streets. Laporte walked back to the Sheraton, picked up the hire car and took the longer route back to Miraflores, through San Isidro and along the clifftops, avoiding the congestion outside the American Embassy. The flat was calm and cool. He made a pot of coffee, spread the papers on the floor, and began picking his way through them, starting with the second document he had found, the list of names he had discovered, forgotten behind the filing cabinet.

The top of the sheet was torn. He assumed the paper had been mislaid in the panic to flee the house on the Sunday night. The first fifteen names were German; opposite the names were ranks and job descriptions. The names below were South American; surname first, with addresses opposite. There was no way, he had decided the night before, of knowing what the names represented. None of the addresses, he noted, were in Lima. He pored over the sheet for fifteen minutes, hoping to find a clue, toying with the idea of checking on the list of South American names

173

and addresses, wondering how he could ask them if they were connected with a war criminal called Josef Heiner, then abandoned the idea and switched his attention to the pink expense sheets he had found in the dark blue folder.

After another fifty minutes he was still disappointed. The sheets were nothing more than expense returns, details of job titles and reference numbers, locations and mileages, restaurant and hotel bills, names of clients entertained. Most of the sheets were copies of personal submissions for approval and refunding. Each in turn had been authorised by one man, Laporte assumed, whose initials were scribbled on the bottom. None of them referred to Josef Heiner.

He turned his attention to the locations, then to the names of what he assumed were clients or contacts entertained. Twenty-eight of the thirty-four names were Spanish, seven were German and one was either Irish or American. There was no way, he realised, of knowing whether the names were correct or merely codenames. Several appeared twice, four appeared three times. Only the Irish/American name appeared more than three times. He checked through the sheets again. The Irish/American name was the only one which appeared under what he assumed were project titles at the head of the page. He wondered who Joe Corrigan was.

After a further three hours he had made no advance. He put the documents back in the folder, hid it in the kitchen and left the flat. At a café off the main street, at the foot of the tower block, he bought a sandwich and a can of Coca Cola, climbed down to the beach at the bottom of the cliffs, stretched in the sun, and fell asleep.

3 *Lima*

Joe Corrigan had been in his office for nearly an hour when the red telephone on his desk rang. It had been a long sleepless night; at six he had rolled out of bed knowing it was pointless to stay. He pressed the recorder switch and picked up the phone. 'Yes,' he said, noncommitally.

'Good morning. This is Heron Exports, the local service manager.'

'Nice to hear from you.' Corrigan hid the relief in his voice. 'We were expecting a call from you. How's business?'

'Business is fine but there are a couple of problems. We ought to meet.'

Corrigan wanted to know more. 'I think we mentioned one small problem to your managing director, and told him we were taking care of it.' He waited to see how Heinrich Schmeltz would react.

'I realise that, but there's something else. What time?' The urgency was clear in the German's voice.

'Breakfast at nine-thirty,' said Corrigan. Schmeltz agreed. 'One other thing,' said Corrigan, 'I have to bring an associate.' Schmeltz asked if it was necessary. 'Yes,' Corrigan told him, 'he's from head office.' Schmeltz grunted his agreement and terminated the call. Corrigan gave himself a line, dialled the Sheraton and asked for the man from Washington. Bailey answered immediately. 'They've called,' Corrigan said, 'I'm seeing them for breakfast, told them I'd be bringing a colleague.'

'What time?'

'Nine-thirty. The Palscana.'

Corrigan replaced the telephone, reached into the top drawer, opened the wooden box, pushed one Havana into his shirt pocket and another into his mouth. Something had happened. He knew by the urgency which Schmeltz had not even bothered to conceal in his voice. He wondered what it was, how it would affect things. Wondered somewhere, deep in the recesses of his mind, whether the son was involved.

At twenty-five minutes past nine he entered the Sheraton, went through the foyer and into the Palscana bar. The restaurant was crowded, there was a queue of people waiting at the door. In one corner, alone at a table, a man was draining a cup of coffee, preparing to leave. The man, he thought, looked tense and worried. Corrigan ignored the queue, walked to the table and sat down. 'I'm sorry,' he apologised, 'I hope you don't mind, but today is already a bad day and it's going to get worse.'

The man at the table shrugged. 'I don't mind if they don't,' he said, looking at the queue, rising to leave. 'Hope things get better.'

Corrigan returned his smile. 'They probably won't, but thanks anyway.' He pulled the Havana from his shirt pocket, put it in his mouth, and began to chew it. A waitress came up to the table, pocketed the tip which the man had left, swept away the crumbs and cleared the coffee cup and large brandy glass which the man had left. Christ, Corrigan thought to himself, how some poor bastards have to start the day. The only difference, he acknowledged, was that he would have preferred Jack Daniels.

Forty seconds later Heinrich Schmeltz arrived; two minutes later they were joined by Bailey. The waitress finished clearing the table. Corrigan and Schmeltz ordered full breakfasts with coffee, Bailey ordered continental. In addition, Heinrich Schmeltz ordered a large schnapps.

'So where do we start?' Corrigan allowed Schmeltz to dictate the subject of the discussion.

'Let's start with last night,' replied Schmeltz. The response took the two Americans by surprise.

'Why last night?' queried Bailey, 'why not the fuck-up on Sunday night?' It was not the diplomatic start to the conversation Corrigan sensed was necessary. He saw Schmeltz's temper was already rising.

'Because on Sunday night there was no fuck-up; we had a warning and we got out. Nobody was caught with their pants down. Last night was the fuck-up.'

'What happened last night?' asked Corrigan, ignoring Bailey.

Schmeltz tried to calm himself. 'When we left on Sunday night we took everything that might incriminate us.

Or anybody else.' He paused, looking at Bailey, allowing the significance to sink in. 'Last night, just as a check, we went back to make sure we hadn't missed anything.'

Corrigan waited.

'But somebody got there first.'

'Oh, shit.'

'And you thought it was us?' It was Bailey who interrupted.

'Well, who else could it have been?' retorted Schmeltz.

'Plenty of people.' Bailey's face was almost white. 'The house is all over the papers.'

Schmeltz's voice had become low, almost menacing. 'There's one thing nobody could have got from the papers.'

'What the hell's that? There's photos, the address, the lot.'

The calm had returned to Schmeltz's delivery. 'Whoever went in last night knew what they were looking for. They found the place where we kept the documents.'

'Sheeet.' Bailey's nasal East Coast accent accentuated the word. Corrigan felt the conversation in the rest of the café numb into silence. 'Was there anything for them to get?' he asked quietly.

Schmeltz leaned forward, elbows on the table. 'We're still checking, we're not sure.'

'But?' asked Corrigan.

'We think, or at least we thought, that we had removed everything.'

'But?' Corrigan asked again.

'But there's one file that might be missing. It's not in the correct place but it could have got mixed up with something else, other documents. The man himself is checking.'

'But unless you find it, we must assume that whoever was in the house last night has it?' Corrigan summed up their fears. Schmeltz nodded. 'Unless we find it, we must assume that.'

'Any idea at all who it was?' Bailey interrupted the logic of the discussion. Schmeltz shook his head. 'No idea at all.

It was a team job, stake-out at the front, bolt-hole at the back.'

An awareness was seeping through Corrigan's mind. 'What's in the missing file?' he asked.

'Details of expenses, the book-keeper's accounts.'

'Project Octavio?'

Schmeltz's answer was bleak, delivered without emotion. 'Yes,' he said, 'Project Octavio.'

The waitress arrived with the breakfast. 'Sorry,' Corrigan smiled at her, slipping a five dollar bill onto the tray, 'we've changed our minds. Another large schnapps and a large Jack Daniels.' He turned to Bailey. 'What do you want?'

'The same as our friend here.'

'Two large schnapps.' The day already felt old. Corrigan remembered the look in the eyes of the man from whom he had taken the table. 'Is there any good news?' he asked.

'Possibly. We're not sure what good the documents would be to anyone except those directly involved. The details in them are meaningless.'

'Are we mentioned?' Bailey asked.

Schmeltz lied. 'Not directly,' he said.

The waitress delivered their drinks and the conversation relaxed. 'When did you get back?' Corrigan had held the question till Schmeltz was off guard and Bailey would not notice.

'Yesterday, early afternoon.'

'Good flight?' It was asked as a matter of fact.

'On time, bad service.'

'And the man was OK when you left him?'

Schmeltz smiled. 'The man is always OK.'

Corrigan changed the subject, too experienced to press his questioning further. 'You know about the son?' Schmeltz nodded. 'I understand you've made arrangements to take care of him if necessary?' It was Bailey's turn to nod.

'What arrangements?' asked Schmeltz.

'Let's just leave it at arrangements,' replied Bailey.

Corrigan remembered his thoughts as he had sat drinking beer after buying the baptismal present for his godson. Remembered wondering what he would be thinking if he was the priest, what he would be doing. 'Any chance it was the son last night?' he asked.

Schmeltz considered the point. 'No chance at all,' he said at last. 'As I said, it was a team job. One, almost certainly more, in the house. Stake-out at the front, bolt-hole at the back. Communication worked out in advance. Probably back-up somewhere.' He thought again, shook his head. 'No way it could have been the son.'

Corrigan was relieved, did not know why. 'How do we get hold of you?' he asked, gesturing for the bill.

Schmeltz wrote a number on a piece of paper. 'The house in Chaclicayo is dead,' he said. 'Until further notice, this is the contact.' They shook hands and left separately, Schmeltz followed by Bailey. Corrigan paid the bill, explaining to Bailey that he had some local business to deal with and would join him later.

Like the strands of a web, he mused as he waited for the change. Heiner and Schmeltz, himself and Bailey, whoever raided the house, the son. The waitress returned. He tipped her and left the bar, crossed the foyer to the public telephone booths near the reception desk and dialled a local number. There was one connection he needed to make, needed to know, even though Schmeltz was back in Lima. The whereabouts of Josef Heiner.

The man who answered was a paid contact in the under-cover narcotics division of the PIP, the *Policia de Investigaciones del Peru*, the country's plainclothes police force. Corrigan arranged a meeting in a café in the Parque Universitario, at the side of the Plaza San Martin, ten minutes' walk from the Sheraton, then dialled the embassy number and asked for the secretary who ran the building's travel arrangements.

'Mary,' he identified himself, 'it's Joe Corrigan from the commercial section. I need a small favour. Can you check

179

what international flights came into Lima early yesterday afternoon?'

Four countries, he thought. Schmeltz would be coming in from one of only four countries: Chile, Argentina, Bolivia or Paraguay. 'I'm really interested in flights from Santiago, Buenos Aires, La Paz and Asuncion,' he told the secretary. La Paz, he knew instinctively, remembered Heiner's most recent connections, remembered Project Octavio. It had to be La Paz.

He began the walk to the meeting place. The streets were crowded, the sun already hot. He wondered why it was necessary for him to look for Josef Heiner, discover where he was hiding, if he was already in contact with Heinrich Schmeltz. Wondered why he was doing it this way, the back door way, rather than officially. Why he was shutting out even his own people.

In the Plaza San Martin, at the telephone kiosks on the edge of the square opposite the Hotel Bolivar, he rang the secretary again.

'Four flights in early yesterday afternoon,' she told him, reading from a list she had prepared. 'Nothing from Asuncion.' Paraguay was out, he thought. 'Two flights from Buenos Aires, an Avianca flight which arrived on time at 13.10 and an AeroPeru flight which arrived half an hour late at 13.55.' Argentina was still a possibility, he thought. 'One flight from Santiago, an AeroPeru flight landing at 13.25, an Avianca flight due in at 13.10 was cancelled.' Also a possibility, he thought.

'And La Paz?' he asked.

'An AeroPeru flight PL616, left La Paz 12.45, arrived Lima 13.30,' she told him.

'On time?' he asked.

'On time,' she confirmed.

La Paz, he knew. Heiner had to be in La Paz. Obvious, he told himself, bloody obvious. For a whole number of reasons. And Schmeltz had virtually confirmed it. Except, he thought, that Schmeltz might have come in on a private plane. 'Good flight?' he had asked Schmeltz. Matter of fact. 'On time,' Schmeltz had answered, 'bad service.' La Paz, he was positive.

'Mary,' he told the secretary, 'you're an angel.'

The narcotics agent was already at the café. Corrigan ordered coffee and papaya juice. 'Do you have a reliable contact in La Paz with access to records of international telephone calls?' he asked immediately, knowing that neither he nor the contact had time to spare. 'Not the contents,' he added, 'just the numbers involved.' The undercover agent did not bother to ask why Corrigan could not use his embassy equivalent in La Paz.

'When do you need to know?'

Corrigan shrugged. 'Yesterday.'

The contact laughed. 'This afternoon.'

They left separately. Corrigan returned to his office, closed the door, and arranged for an engineer to change the number of his confidential direct line.

At 3.30 in the afternoon the narcotics agent telephoned him with a name and number in La Paz. Corrigan took the details, told him that from the following day the number of his private line would be changed and that he would notify him of the new number, then telephoned the number in La Paz which the contact had given him. The international exchange took ten minutes to connect the call. It was answered by a male voice. The conversation was brief and to the point. 'Juan, this is Sam in Lima, Miguel said you might be able to help me.'

'I can. What do you want?'

'Two calls were made to a number in Lima in the past three days. I want the details of where those calls came from.'

'The numbers they came from?'

'Numbers, plus names and addresses.'

'OK, I'll see what I can do. What was the Lima number?' Corrigan gave him the number of his confidential line which he had just arranged to change. 'Any information which might help?' asked the La Paz contact.

Corrigan thought. 'The first call was made sometime on

181

Monday afternoon.' He remembered the words on the answerphone, recalled his reactions, 'probably mid to late afternoon. The second call was made yesterday at one-thirty in the afternoon.'

The contact did not ask Corrigan how he could be so accurate about the timing of the call. 'That will help,' he said.

For the next two minutes they discussed payment: how much, how, where and when it would be made. At the end they were both satisfied. 'When do you want to know?' the contact asked.

A secret, Corrigan suddenly thought, remembering his reaction at the Bailey briefing two mornings before, a secret that Washington was keeping to itself. A secret, he thought, that Washington had guarded for a long time. 'As soon as possible,' he replied, 'tonight if you can make it, tomorrow at the latest.' He wondered why he was in such a rush.

'I'll try,' said the contact, 'how can I reach you?'

'You can't,' Corrigan told him, 'I'll reach you.'

4

Fool. Bloody fool.

The thought woke him immediately. Laporte blinked, wide awake. Stupid, unseeing, bloody fool. He picked up his jacket from the sand where he had been using it as a pillow and hurried up the beach towards the steep track up the cliff.

The chance was a slim one, but a chance none the less. He pushed his way up the slope, cursing himself for not seeing it before, wondering how long it would take Josef Heiner to discover he had found the documents, how long it would take Heiner to discover he had the material to make the connection. His mind began repeating the details he had studied that morning, the names on the single white sheet, the one common factor on the twenty-three pink ones. God, he hoped, please God, may I be right. He looked at his watch. Three-thirty already. He had slept for two hours, two precious hours when Heiner might have spotted it and closed the gap. The sweat ran down his back, the sun beat down on him and the nervousness filled his stomach. Please, God, he thought again, please may I be right.

He took five minutes to climb the hill from the beach and another five to reach the flat. The folder was behind the cooker where he had left it. He opened it, spreading the papers on the table in the small kitchen, not having time to go back into the lounge, checking the initials of the man who had signed each of the expenses sheets. J. S. V. His fingers were trembling, the first part fitting, the prayer that he would be right thudding through his head. He turned to the sheet of white paper, the two lists, one above the other, running his finger down the first column of names, those in German, not alphabetical, not in any order. The first time he missed it, panicked, started again, the nausea welling in his throat. Finger searching. Finding it. Halfway down, tucked away as if he was never meant to find it. Johann Sebastian Vogel. J. S. V. The last list, on the bottom half of the page, was in alphabetical order, the Spanish surnames first, followed by the christian names. Please, God, please, let me be right. Valdez. Jaime Stefan. He felt the thrill surge through his body, did not know how to deal with the sudden excess of nervous energy, wished Maria was there so he could hug her in congratulation as he had done the night before.

The oldest trick in the world, he told himself, the oldest bloody trick in the world. Change the name but keep the same initials. Simple. And absolutely bloody stupid. He calmed himself, checked the documents again, knowing he was correct, the doubt suddenly filling his mind, wanting a final confirmation.

It was there. In German. On the top list, next to the name itself. Rank and occupation. He ran his finger down the list again, stopping at the name Johann Sebastian Vogel. Rank, *Scharführer*. Occupation, book-keeper. Alias, Jaime Stefan Valdez. Address, Hotel Escobar, Mollendo. On Maria's bookshelf he found a road map of the country, scouring it for five minutes before he found Mollendo, a tiny fishing town south of Lima, almost two hundred miles south, he estimated, along the long dusty road known as the Pan American Highway.

The excitement was still pulsing through his body. He checked the time again. Ten past four. Two hundred miles, he thought. An hour to get out of Lima, four hours drive on top, perhaps three and a half. Getting there by mid-evening. As long as Heiner didn't get there first, wait for him as he had waited for his father. He paced the room, calming himself, giving himself time to work out his plan, then phoned Maria. The number was engaged. He waited thirty seconds and phoned again. The señorita, he was told, was out of the office with a client. The office did not know what time she would be back that evening, if she would be back at all. He felt a sting of resentment, thanked the secretary, and put the telephone down.

It was already late, getting later. He wrote Maria a note on the pad by the telephone, saying he would probably not be back that night, wondering at the significance of the word night instead of evening, but that he would contact her as soon as he returned. It was too dangerous, he thought, to give any details of what he had found or where he was going.

The Pan American Highway left Lima to the south. Laporte drove back into the city, unable to avoid the congestion, joining the Pan Americana just before it swept past the ancient ruins of Pachacamac before straightening on its three-and-a-half thousand miles to Punta Arenas. The road clung to the coast, deviating from it only to cross the neck of a peninsula, rarely more than a mile from the swell of the ocean. The country on either side was desert, coloured by the occasional oasis, bordered by the sporadic groups of houses. Twenty miles south of Lima he slowed for a police check point, realised they were examining only the passenger lists of public vehicles, and drove through. Two hours after leaving the city he pulled into a service station, filled the Caprice and quenched his thirst with a bottle of ice-cold, lime-green Inca Cola.

An hour later the sun fell below the horizon on his right in a blaze of red and orange and the darkness closed swiftly and abruptly around him, even faster than in the city. He turned on the car radio, enjoying the feeling of limitless space around him, listening to the American and European records that dominated the programmes, calculating he was another hour from Mollendo. When he estimated he was thirty minutes from the town he pulled off the road, switched off the engine and got out of the car. In the exhilaration of the discovery and the sudden freedom he had enjoyed during the drive, he had not questioned what he was planning to do, how he was planning to do it. He thought carefully for ten minutes, breathing in the warm night air, thinking of the cold just twenty-four hours before in Chaclicayo, then got back into the car and drove on.

He knew what he had to do, how he had to prepare himself for the book-keeper. He wound down the window, felt the air rushing through his hair, across his face, switched off the radio, filled his lungs, and began to sing. Not the plastic music of the radio, the inconsequential rhymes that would be forgotten in the morning, but the power of the hymn that immortalised the martyr, sending a message through the ages. Already he sensed, he was beginning to think as he would have to think that night. Singing louder, with more conviction, losing himself in the fervour of the *"Horst Wessel Lied"*, the bass of his voice striking out across the dark of the desert.

The words he had known for so long. Now the language came back to him, as it had done in the destruction of the lounge in the house at Chaclicayo. He sang till he was thinking, breathing, sweating in German, till he was back in the *Rathauskeller*, smelling the beer, joining the old men in their memories of the great days that had gone for ever. Then he closed the window and shut himself off from the world.

5

Heinrich Schmeltz's instinctive sense of preservation had stood both himself and the organisation in good stead through the years. As he left the meeting with Corrigan and Bailey the instinct flooded through his body, occupying his entire span of concentration. He returned to the house in Miraflores, relayed the news and his interpretation of it to Josef Heiner in La Paz, and began to prepare for the storm which every ounce of his vast experience told him was about to break.

The three *Sturmmänner* who had reported to the capital the previous evening were ordered to stay. *Scharführer* and *Sturmmänner* within three hours' drive of Lima were contacted and ordered to report immediately to what was fast becoming a fortress. He arranged for the hire cars which they had needed the night before to be returned, and for their own vehicles to be serviced by the organisation's mechanics. As each of the others arrived, so their vehicles in turn were checked. Schmeltz did not want a delay like the one they had experienced the night before.

At three in the afternoon, behind closed and guarded curtains, he held a briefing, speaking tersely, summarising the danger they all faced. Then he drove to an isolated area five miles from the city and spent half an hour on target practice, feeling the thud of his favourite sub-machine gun, a short barrel Heckler and Koch MP 5K in his hands as he practised with live ammunition, snapping the 9mm clips into the 30 round magazine. Preparing himself. Then he returned to the house, checked that his arrangements were in order, took a light meal with the boys, and retired to his study with a copy of Schiller's *Wallenstein* to wait for what he knew would be the inevitable phone call.

6

The town of Mollendo lay two miles off the main road, a cluster of two thousand people living round the port which formed the focal point of the community. The houses which sloped down to the sea were single-storey, washed with off-white or lime paint, their tin roofs red with rust. A hundred yards from the sea one street forked left to where the curve of the coast formed a beach, the other bent to the right, to the small jetty which served as a port. The smell of fish hung in the night air. As long as the town suffered the odour, Laporte knew, there would be life. In the bay off the beach, and outside the black outline of the jetty, the lights of the fishing boats bobbed in the gentle roll of the ocean.

The dust rose in swirls round the car. He slowed, looking for the address. On the street corner in front of him, visible in a single pool of light which broke the darkness, was an old man, a small boy crouched beside him, boiling a pan of water over a pitifully small fire. Laporte stopped the car and wound down the window. 'Hey, *compadre*,' he said. '*El Hotel Escobar, donde está?*' the old man muttered something he could not understand, waving his hand carelessly in the direction the car had come from. '*Que dice?*' Laporte asked the boy, 'what's he saying?'

'He doesn't know,' replied the boy, rising from his haunches.

'Do you?'

'*Claro*,' said the boy, 'of course.' Laporte pulled a five hundred soles note from his pocket and showed it to the boy. 'Follow me,' he was told.

He rolled forward and followed the young guide down the slope of the hill, towards the sea. Fifty metres down they turned right for one block, then left again into a street that led to the harbour front. The boy stopped outside a wooden building, two storeys high, painted white, leaning slightly to one side. Three steps led to the verandah from which a set of double doors led into the building. Above

187

the doors, in garish green neon lights, shone the words 'Hotel Escobar'.

'*Gracias, compadre.*' Laporte handed the boy the note. The boy thanked him and wished him good luck. It was, thought Laporte, a strange thing to say.

'*Una cosa más,*' he asked the boy, '*hay otra salida del pueblo?*'

'No, señor,' said the boy, 'there's no other road. The way you came in is the only way out.'

Laporte reversed up the hill two blocks and backed the car into a side street. The small boy was still watching him. 'Hey, *compadre*,' he called him over. 'You want to earn some more money?' The boy nodded. 'Look after my car then. If anybody comes, thieves or anybody, let me know.' He handed the boy another five hundred soles. 'You'll know where to find me.'

The boy nodded. 'Si, señor, at the hotel or somewhere.'

Laporte smiled. 'That's right, at the hotel or somewhere.' He pointed to the note. 'That's just a deposit. If everything is OK when I come back, there'll be another five hundred.'

The boy smiled. 'OK, everything will be OK when you come back.'

Laporte locked the car and walked down the street to the hotel. The double doors were locked, a splinter of light showing between them. He knocked and waited till a large woman, her hair pulled back behind her head, her pendulous breasts seeming almost to overbalance her, came to the door.

'Hotel Escobar?' he asked. She nodded. 'Do you have any vacancies?' She nodded again and let him into the small room that served as an entrance hall. The wooden floor was bare; the only furniture was an armchair, patched and worn, and a reception desk behind which the woman now stood. She was not German, he had already decided.

'Is Señor Jaime in?' he asked.

'Señor who?' she queried.

'*El dueño*, the boss,' he replied.

'Who wants him?'

'An old friend.' He did not know what else to say, suspected the woman had been told the same thing in the past.

'He's not here.'

A panic swept over him, replaced by an instinctive suspicion.

'Where is he?'

The large woman looked at him. From a room in the rear he could smell cooking. 'Where he always is when he's not away. Down the road.'

Laporte picked up the reference to the man being away, sensed his identification had been confirmed, and pressed on with the game of question and answer. 'Where down the road?'

'The Bar Atlantico.'

'The Bar Atlantico,' he repeated, wondering who would name a bar on the edge of one great ocean after another two-and-a-half thousand miles away.

'Si, señor, the Bar Atlantico. Down the road and along the front. About two hundred metres.'

'*Gracias.*' He turned to go.

'Señor,' she stopped him. 'I thought you wanted a room.'

He turned back and signed the register which she pushed across the wooden counter, using the name Maldonaldo, for no other reason than he had once seen it on a map of Peru. He was, he noted, the only guest in the hotel that night.

'How many nights?' the woman asked him.

'Three, at least. Probably more.'

'Pay each morning,' she told him, giving him a key from a row of hooks on the wall behind the desk. 'Any bags?'

'In the car,' he told her. 'I'll bring them when I come back with Señor Jaime.'

7

The telephone call which Heinrich Schmeltz knew was inevitable came at precisely three minutes past eleven.

'It is confirmed,' Heiner told him without introduction, 'the expenses documents are missing.'

'Shit,' breathed Schmeltz, knowing there was worse to follow.

'Something else is also missing, a list of the addresses.'

'But there is no way of linking the name on the two lists.'

'There is one link.' Heiner's voice was bleak and ominous. 'The book-keeper. His is the only name that appears regularly on the expenses, or at least his initials. And the name and cover are on the other list.'

'But there is no way of linking the two on the other list,' Schmeltz repeated. 'The names are not in the same order. We insisted on that for security reasons. There is no way anyone could decide which German name goes with which Spanish name.'

'Think of the names.' There was irritation in Heiner's voice. 'Think of the initials on the expenses sheets.' Schmeltz saw it immediately, knew why the tension had been coiling tighter inside him all day. 'Christ, the stupid bastard.' Changed his name, he thought, kept the same bloody initials. 'I'll check right away.'

'I think you had better,' said the fugitive in La Paz.

The telephone at the Hotel Escobar rang for two full minutes before it was answered. Schmeltz recognised the voice of the large woman whom the book-keeper employed as a housekeeper. He had never understood why the man had chosen someone so unattractive. At least, he had thought on previous occasions, none of the others would be chasing her. 'Is Señor Jaime there?' he asked.

'No, señor,' said the woman, her voice sleepy. 'It's half past eleven at night. Phone back tomorrow.' She began to put the phone down. The sudden ice in the caller's response jerked her awake.

'Listen to me, woman, I want him now. Where is he?'

There was fear in her reply. 'Sorry, señor, sorry.' The strange unspeaking men who visited Señor Jaime had the same effect on her. 'He's not here.' She was panicking, trying to find an answer that would satisfy the voice that did not need to threaten her. 'He's gone out, to the bar.'

'Which bar?'

'The Bar Atlantico, señor, down by the harbour. Where he always goes.' Her voice was strained, pinched. 'That's what I told the other man, didn't he tell you?'

Schmeltz's senses froze. He cupped his hand over the mouthpiece. 'Start the cars,' he shouted to a *Sturmmann*, then turned his attention to the woman. 'What other man?' he asked.

'The man who came looking for him this evening. I thought . . .' her voice trailed away. She knew what she thought, but was afraid to say it, afraid to say that she had noticed the men in their Mercedes, who visited the hotel in the dark of the night.

'You thought what, woman?' Schmeltz's voice was low, menacing.

'I thought . . . I thought he was one of you.' She knew she had said the unpardonable.

Her caller appeared not to notice or to mind. 'What time did he come?'

'Two, three hours ago, this evening, señor.'

'Where is he now?' Outside Schmeltz could hear the rumble of engines.

'At the café, I suppose, with Señor Jaime. He asked me where it was.'

'Is there a phone at the café?'

'No, señor, no phone at the café.'

Schmeltz's mind was racing. 'One man, you say, no more?'

'Si, señor, one man.'

'Are you sure?'

The woman hesitated. 'Well, señor, one man came into the hotel and then left.'

Schmeltz's questions were staccato, interrogative. 'You didn't look outside to see if he had any friends?'

'No, señor. He said he wanted a room then asked for Señor Jaime.'

'He took a room?' asked Schmeltz, a sliver of hope piercing the bleakness.

'Yes, señor.'

'What name did he use?' He waited while she checked the register.

'Maldonaldo, señor.'

Schmeltz knew that further questions were futile. He was already wasting time. He considered sending the woman to the bar to warn the book-keeper, knew it would only warn off the other man, or men.

'Listen, woman, and listen carefully. When Señor Jaime comes back, tell him his brother from Lima phoned. Tell him I said to phone me back immediately, no matter what the time. Do you understand?'

'You're his brother?' the woman asked hopefully.

Schmeltz ignored the question. 'I asked if you understood.'

She was whimpering. 'Si, señor, I understand.'

Christ. Schmeltz swore in exasperation, put the phone down, trying to control his anger, the plans already clear and cool in his head. 'Rolf,' he ordered one of the *Sturmmänner*, 'stay by the phone. If the book-keeper rings, tell him that the man who visited him this evening is a spy. If the man is alone, tell the book-keeper to hold him there till we arrive. He has enough boys, doesn't he?' The *Sturmmann* nodded. 'If the visitor is not alone, which is more likely, tell the book-keeper to stall till we get there. Tell him it's imperative we get the man.' The *Sturmmann* understood. 'If the book-keeper doesn't phone, phone him in half an hour's time, then every fifteen minutes until you get him.'

He ordered a second man to stay in the house, leaving him eleven for Mollendo. Then he checked that those he was taking with him were prepared, selected his personal

192

Luger and the Heckler and Koch with which he had practised that afternoon, and began to leave the house. The journey, he estimated, would take three hours, plus half an hour to get out of Lima.

There was just time, he decided as an afterthought, to spend fifteen seconds on another telephone call.

8

Corrigan woke at the first ring of the telephone, recognising Schmeltz's voice immediately. 'There's an emergency, no time to explain.' The voice was controlled and precise. 'I'll pick you up at the café at the top of the Pan Americana in ten minutes.'

Corrigan was already getting out of bed. 'I know the place. Shall I get Bailey?'

'No time,' Schmeltz told him and put the phone down.

The night air on the desert strip south of the city was warm. Corrigan had time to park the Chevrolet at the side of the café and light a Havana when the three Mercedes screeched off the road. Schmeltz leapt from the front passenger seat of the lead car, opening the rear door for Corrigan. Without stopping to ask what was happening, Corrigan got in. The driver slid his foot off the clutch and the car moved away before he had time to shut the door. There were two other men in the rear seat, both armed. Schmeltz turned back to face Corrigan as the three cars accelerated across the road and headed south.

In front of the café a group of men watched, nodding their heads as if they understood.

Schmeltz saw Corrigan's quick glance at the Uzis the others had laid across their knees. 'Don't worry,' he said, 'we're carrying for you as well.'

Corrigan ignored the reassurance. 'What's happened?' he asked.

For the next two minutes Schmeltz briefed him on the

events of the evening and the plan he had already formulated in his mind.

'And Project Octavio is mentioned in the missing documents?'

Schmeltz nodded, 'Apparently so.'

'What time do you estimate we'll arrive?'

'About three. '

Corrigan looked at the speedometer. The needle was hovering at one hundred and eighty kilometres an hour. Two-thirty, he decided they would arrive, probably earlier.

9 *Mollendo*

The Bar Atlantico was ten metres from the Pacific, in the centre of a row of shops and houses which ran along the waterfront at the end of the street in which the Hotel Escobar was situated, to the top of the jetty. It was dark, there were no lights between the street and the solitary lamp swinging at the end of the jetty. The windows of the bar were covered by thin curtains, the door was half open. From within came the sound of men laughing and drinking.

Laporte hesitated, trying to look unobtrusively through the door, wondering how he would identify the bookkeeper. There was a tug on his trouser leg. He looked down and saw the small boy. 'I thought you were looking after my car,' he said, half jokingly.

'I am, but I thought you might need some help.'

'Why might I need some help?'

The boy shrugged his thin shoulders. 'No reason, I just thought you might.' Laporte remembered the shoe-shine boy in the Plaza de Armas.

'OK, which one is Señor Jaime?' The boy peered through the door. For the second time that evening Laporte smelt fish cooking.

'The old man, thin with a bald head. He's sitting by himself on the farthest wall from the door. He looks like an eagle.'

Laporte wondered how the boy knew what an eagle looked like. 'OK, *compadre*,' he said, 'now go and look after the car.'

The book-keeper was as the boy described, sitting alone by the far wall. Small and sharp-eyed, a glass of beer on the table and beside it a bottle of Crystal, the beads of water rolling down the side. The table next to him was empty. Laporte walked in and looked around. The bar was bigger than he had expected from the outside, some fifteen tables on the wooden floor, most of them occupied by two or three men, most of them obviously fishermen. A piano, its lid closed, stood against the wall to the right, the bar to the left of the door. He nodded at the barman, the faces turning to identify the stranger who had suddenly appeared, and ordered a Crystal, the beer which bore the same name as one of Lima's football teams, the same beer as the book-keeper was drinking. The barman was polite and friendly. Laporte supposed he was also the owner. He poured the drink into a tall glass, the white froth running down the sides, and put the half-empty bottle on the top of the bar.

'Passing through?' asked the barman.

'*Si*,' replied Laporte, 'just passing through.' He ordered a plate of fish and took the drink to the table next to the book-keeper, bidding the man good evening as he sat down. The book-keeper returned the greeting and continued drinking. Laporte waited for the barman to bring his supper, wondering how long the book-keeper would stay, how long he had to make the contact.

'Nice place,' he tried to start a conversation, 'plenty of fish, anyway.'

The old man looked at him shrewdly. 'That's about all.'

'I don't know, plenty of sun, nice beach. What more could you want.'

195

'What are you doing here, on holiday or something?' the book-keeper asked. Laporte wondered if there was the hint of suspicion in the question that he feared.

'Yes, on holiday, and yourself?' Laporte was unsure if the man wanted to continue the conversation, wondered how he could prolong it.

'I live here,' said the book-keeper, draining the glass in front of him. Laporte gulped his own down thirstily and beckoned to the barman. 'Another Crystal, *compadre*, make it a large one.' He turned to the book-keeper. 'Same for you?'

The old man turned his empty bottle upside down and looked at the last of the white froth running down the neck. 'Yes,' he said, 'why not.' He pushed out a chair. 'Why don't you join me?' Laporte accepted the offer and waved to the barman to make it two bottles. The contact had been made.

'Where are you staying?' the book-keeper asked.

'Place up the road, the Hotel Escobar.'

The old man laughed, a thin crackling laugh. 'In that case the next round's on you as well.'

'How come?' asked Laporte, sharing the joke.

'I own the place, so anything I pay tonight will be going on your bill tomorrow.' They laughed as the barman brought the beer.

'In that case,' said Laporte, 'I may as well know who's giving me the pleasure of entertaining him.' The book-keeper held out his hand. It was larger than his body would have suggested, his grip bony but firm.

'Jaime,' he said. 'Jaime Stefan Valdez.' Johann Sebastian Vogel, thought Laporte, *Scharführer*, one-time member of the most feared squadron in France.

'Good to meet you,' he said, introducing himself. 'Ricardo, Ricardo Maldonaldo.' He used the name he had entered in the hotel register.

'You're not from Peru,' the book-keeper observed, a shrewd glint in his eye.

'Gibraltar,' lied Laporte, 'so my parents couldn't decide

what nationality I was, English or Spanish, or a bit of something else. And yourself?'

The book-keeper shrugged, helping himself to the beer. 'A bit of something else,' he said.

Laporte's fish arrived. He ate it ravenously, forgetting the tension in his stomach, agreeing when the book-keeper called for more beer. For the next twenty minutes they talked about the town, the fishing, women and football. The atmosphere in the bar was contagious. They laughed with the crowd as the bottles filled the table, till Laporte felt he could delay no more. He ordered more beer, waited till the barman had left it on the table, then raised his glass, feeling the nerves coil in his body.

'Your health, Jaime Stefan Valdez,' he announced, bending closer to his companion. The book-keeper raised his own glass in response. 'Not bad beer really, Jaime,' he continued in Spanish, switching suddenly to German. 'Not as good as the old stuff, of course, Johann.'

'*Nein . . .* ' the book-keeper began to reply in German then froze.

'Your health, *Scharführer* Johann Sebastian Vogel,' Laporte continued his toast, looking into the startled expression of the book-keeper's yellow eyes. To his right he sensed someone was rising, coming towards them, closing in on him. He wondered how many other Nazis were in the bar.

'*Was ist in der Falle?*' he asked, repeating the words from Weissemann's tape, knowing he was already committed, knowing it was too late to pull back, hoping he was right, filled with sudden and awful dread that he was wrong. The book-keeper stared at him blankly. Behind him, Laporte felt a massive presence by his right shoulder.

'*Die Fliege.*' The book-keeper's reply was barely audible.

'*Was wartet immer?*' The Bavarian accent rolled off his tongue.

'*Die Spinne.*' The response was stronger. The expression in the old man's eyes had changed, the yellow of age had vanished in them, the blue of youth suddenly burning brightly. From the corner of his eye Laporte saw the old man wave his hand, as if calling off a guard dog.

'You are one of us?' the book-keeper asked in German.

'*Ja*, I am one of you.'

'But you said you came from Gibraltar?'

'My Spanish isn't as good as yours. I need a cover story.'

The book-keeper nodded. 'But why are you here? Who sent you? Someone from Lima?' There was only one man in the Lima organisation whose name Laporte knew. Josef Heiner. He lied.

'*Nein*,' he said, 'not from Lima.' He bent even closer. 'From Germany.'

The old man's eyes shone. 'From Germany,' he said, 'from the Fatherland.' There was an urgency, a conspiracy in his voice. 'So why have you come? What are you doing here?'

Laporte spun another thread to his lie. 'I flew in yesterday, special orders, to help out after the fiasco in Chaclicayo.'

The old man was enthralled. 'You came in specially? From Germany? Who sent you? Somebody big?' There was a plea in his voice, a cry for someone to tell him that the exile was worthwhile; that in Germany there were still people, important people, who cared. Cared about the old days. Cared about exiles like himself. Somebody to tell him there was a future.

'*Ja*,' Laporte lied again, 'somebody big.' There was something in the way he said it that made the old man understand he could say no more.

'But you're young, so young.'

Laporte nodded. 'I was born in the milky days after the war, when the shits who bombed Dresden and Hamburg made us all stand in the docks at Nuremberg.' He slipped easily into the role he had rehearsed in the car, allowing the rasp of the Bavarian accent to slide round his tongue and through his teeth. 'I went to school and was told to wave when the Americans drove their tanks over our fields;

198

to cheer for Adenauer when he opened his arms to the West, and for Brandt and Schmidt when they opened their legs to the East.'

The book-keeper's eyes were glowing. He picked up the unmistakable accent of the Bavarian hills. 'And so you were recruited?' he asked, almost breathless.

'And so I was recruited,' confirmed Laporte, feeling the hot breath upon his face.

'And you are from Bavaria itself?'

'*Ja*,' nodded Laporte, 'I am from the old country itself. How did you know?'

The book-keeper winked slyly. 'I know,' he said, 'I know.' He was talking excitedly. 'Tell me about the *Keller*,' he demanded. 'Tell me about the one you used to go to.' Laporte told him, remembering the days in the old university town, remembered them as he had remembered them in the house at Chaclicayo. Remembered the way the others in the cell had remained tight-lipped when his mother had insisted he should study German at the birthplace of the movement which had slaughtered so many of his countrymen and butchered his own father.

'You mean the *Rathauskeller*, by the clock, next to the statue.' He did not name any of the famous beer cellars, knowing that was what the old man expected. The book-keeper was impressed. '*Ja*,' he remembered, '*der Rathauskeller*. Do you remember the barmaid with the big boobs?' He gestured with his hands. 'Heidi was her name, the one who could carry more glasses in one hand than a man could drink in a night?'

Laporte laughed, '*Nein*,' he said, 'but if she was anything like the girl who is there now.' He puckered his lips.

'*Der Rathauskeller*,' the old man was caught in the vortex of his memories. His expression had changed. 'You really are one of us, aren't you,' there was awe in his voice, 'you really have come from the Fatherland.'

'*Ja*,' the Frenchman replied, 'I really am one of you.'

'*Mein Herr*.' The book-keeper called to the barman, still in German, sweeping the empty bottles and glasses off the table. The entire café was suddenly still. 'Two beers for me and my friend here.' He turned to the man at the centre table, the man Laporte had sensed was the watchdog. 'What are you waiting for?' he shouted. 'There's a piano.' The barman understood, laughed a reply. The man in the centre got up, also laughing, and went to the piano. The noise returned to the bar.

'"*Das Horst Wessel Lied*,"' Laporte said quietly, 'let him play "*das Horst Wessel Lied*."'

'"*Das Horst Wessel Lied*,"' the book-keeper called to the man at the piano, 'he wants to hear "*das Horst Wessel Lied*."'

Slowly, eerily, the strains of the anthem rose from the keyboard, filled the room, floated across the road outside, and drifted into the dark above the water. The pianist played two lines, then waited for the book-keeper. The old man stood erect, staring ahead, no longer in the winter of his years, back in the spring, in the Germany of the thirties. There was a silence in the room. Slowly his thin, quavering voice reached out of his lungs, gaining strength at every note. Laporte let him sing the first verse by himself, then the second. When he came to the third, Laporte rose and sang with him, aware that every man in the room was watching him.

The song ended, the book-keeper returned to the present, the tears streaming down his face. The pianist leaned across. 'Careful, old man,' he said in German, 'careful.'

The book-keeper tapped his chest. 'The doctors say I have a bad heart, give me little pills, dynamite pills, to take if anything happens. But how do they know what it means to sing "*das Horst Wessel Lied*."' Laporte knew what he was going to say, hoped he would say it. 'How do they know what it means to meet another member of the organisation.'

The pianist was playing Wagner. From the far side of the café a voice began to sing in German, then another, and another.

Laporte wondered how many fugitives were in the bar.

'The organisation,' he picked up the book-keeper's words. 'In Germany they talk of it, how they talk of it.'

The moment had come. 'How they talk of its exploits, its operations. Minos, for example, simple but effective.' He slipped in the first of the project titles on the sheets of expenses.

'Ah,' the book-keeper shrugged, drawn in, 'not a bad little job. Efficient but not very big. Just two businessmen in the hotel with a couple of whores. Simple blackmail job, nothing else. Except, of course, that the whores worked for us and the businessmen worked for an arms company.'

'Exactly,' agreed Laporte, pouring them each another drink. 'Or Minos.'

The book-keeper was laughing. 'You're right. Not bad, not bad at all that one.'

Laporte tried to remember the figures. 'Five thousand to Marabella,' he said casually, as if it was unimportant.

The book-keeper looked hard at him. 'Who are you, that you know so much?'

Laporte smiled, raising his glass. 'Just a messenger. Just somebody who sits at the right hand and is told how good the organisation is.'

The book-keeper nodded, accepting the praise, his mind drifting back. 'Aries, of course, that was good. And profitable too. Two birds with one stone. Bought out the politicians and set up a good deal on the white stuff.' He laughed feebly, remembering an incident. 'Too much of the white stuff. All right for some people, helps you go all night.' He made an obscene upward movement with his lily-white forearm, simulating a male erection. 'Youngsters like you don't need it, of course.'

Laporte laughed, poured him another drink, passed the bottle to the pianist.

The old man was mumbling, caught in the flow, pouring out details of operations and deals, filling in the muscle and blood of the thin frameworks Laporte had pieced together from the sheets of expenses. Sometimes his mind slipped, drifting back to the old days, reciting the poems and myths of a bygone era, the life-blood of his youth, the saga of Siegfried, songs from the 'Ring'. Each time Laporte drifted with him, let him sway, then brought him gently back, till there was only one operation left to deal with.

'But Project Octavio,' he said glowingly, 'in Germany the one they really talk about, when the curtains are drawn and the doors are locked, is Project Octavio.'

For an instant there was a look of fear in the book-keeper's eyes. 'You even know about Project Octavio, about *all* of Project Octavio?' he asked incredulously.

'Amazing,' continued Laporte, not letting the man stop to think, 'amazing how you built it up, brick by brick, slowly and carefully, like craftsmen.'

The book-keeper picked up his theme, changing the analogy. 'Like fishermen,' he said, 'like fishermen.' His voice was slower, more tired. Laporte wondered how much longer he would last. 'Easy really, though, just give them the bait, let them nibble, then draw them in.'

Laporte tried to remember the names on the sheet. 'But Corrigan,' he continued the book-keeper's analogy, 'how did you hook Corrigan?'

The book-keeper's confidence had already been won. 'We'd been working for the CIA for some time, of course, anywhere they'd pay us. Except it took Corrigan to work out who we were. It didn't seem to matter, they were still eager. Like virgins in a whorehouse.' He chuckled at the thought, his voice fading away.

Corrigan, thought Laporte, remembering how many times the name had appeared on the book-keeper's lists. The CIA. His mind fought to put the two together. Corrigan and the CIA. Corrigan was the CIA. Corrigan knew that Heiner had killed his father, but still used his services. The CIA knew that Heiner was a wanted war criminal but still employed his organisation.

The book-keeper was still talking. Laporte listened, aware of the growing ache in his bladder. Slowly and carefully he edged the old man on, drawing the details from him. 'But Portachuela,' he said at last, haphazardly

202

picking another name from the files, 'was it worth it?' The tightness of his bladder was turning into a pain across his stomach. He needed to step outside, was afraid that if he did he would allow the old man to slip from his recollections. The book-keeper was mumbling, shaking his head.

'Portachuela was necessary,' he said, his voice almost lost, 'but Portachuela. Christ, oh Christ.'

Laporte was surprised at the response, wanted to press the questioning, knew he could not. 'I have to go outside,' he made a joke of it, 'the beer here is too good, even for a Bavarian bladder like mine.'

The book-keeper's eyes were closing; he was slumping into the seat, sliding into a drunken stupor. 'Will you be back?' he slurred his words.

Laporte bent down, till he was looking the old man in the face, could feel the hot breath on his cheeks. Answering. Surprised at the words he chose.

There was a recognition in the book-keeper's face which Laporte could not understand, a spasm of fear in his eyes, as if Laporte had uttered a forbidden word. Then he passed into unconsciousness.

The piano player and the barman came across the room and lifted the thin frame off the seat and onto the floor. Laporte helped them carry the old man along the waterfront and up the street to the hotel, banging on the door till the fat woman answered, then laying him gently and carefully on the bed in a rear room on the first floor.

The book-keeper's breathing was shallow and irregular, rattling from the bottom of his throat. Laporte loosened the shirt and took off his shoes, the waves of tiredness sweeping over him, the drink numbing his mind. He stood up, suddenly barely able to keep his eyes open. The fat woman was looking at him.

'I'll get my bags from the car and be back in a minute,' he told her. She nodded, still looking at him. He was so tired he fell against the frame of the door as he went out.

'I'll leave the front door open for you,' said the woman and turned back to the book-keeper.

10

Eight minutes earlier than Corrigan's earliest estimate, the three cars pulled off the main road and began to bump down the rough track to the town at the foot of the low cliffs. A hundred metres from the first lights of the township, at a point where the track passed between two shoulders of rock, they stopped. The driver of the third Mercedes pulled across the gap, blocking it entirely, sealing off the only entrance to and exit from Mollendo and disappeared into the darkness with one of his passengers, taking positions on either side of the road so that anyone forced to stop by the obstruction would be caught in their cross-fire.

The other passengers squeezed into the remaining cars. The drivers switched off their engines and rolled gently into the first cluster of houses, turning right where one limb of the community forked the other way to the beach, past a small fire with an old man and small boy huddled over it, turned right and left, and stopped one block from the Hotel Escobar.

The square windows at the front of the hotel were black except for the solitary light at the side of the door. Corrigan eased himself silently from the car and moved up the steps of the hotel and across the porch, the Uzi which Schmeltz had given him on automatic. Behind him, the *Sturmmänner* were taking position, two to cover the rear, two covering the front, the others falling in behind.

The night air was warm. Corrigan could smell the fish-meal in it, hear the sounds of the ocean two hundred metres away.

The front door was unlocked. Schmeltz joined him, pushed it open and went inside. Upstairs Corrigan heard the sound of moaning, of a man breathing against his own body. He knew the sound of old, the last sound before the rattle of death.

The small reception area was filled with men. In the light of the lamp, Corrigan saw the book which served as the hotel register on the wooden desk. He turned it round and opened it to the latest entry. There was only one name against the date. The name Schmeltz had told him in the car. He looked up, saw the row of hooks on the wall behind the desk, the keys hanging from them.

One missing.

He checked the room number above the empty hook with the register. 307. Schmeltz was already moving up the stairs, no noise disturbing the silence of the night except the rattle of the breathing from the room on the first floor. As they passed the room, Schmeltz indicated the door and two *Sturmmänner* took their positions outside.

Room 307 was at the rear of the hotel on the next floor. Corrigan eased his weight over the creaking boards of the last stair and crossed the threadbare carpet which covered the landing. The only light came from a wall lamp down the corridor. The door to the room was loose on its hinges, warped by age and heat. Corrigan turned the door handle, feeling Schmeltz at his side, and gently pushed against the wood. The door gave slightly but did not open. Behind him he felt the breath of the assault squad. Schmeltz moved Corrigan aside, drew a knife from his pocket, eased the wood strip of the door-stop away from the frame and slid the blade into the opening between the lock and the door frame. In the warmth of the night the smell of fish-meal pervaded even the walls of the hotel.

Slow, Corrigan thought, too slow. He felt isolated, exposed. Christ how he wished he had a stun grenade, even a frag, to send in first. Schmeltz grunted and the lock gave. Silently, he thought, how silently they were suddenly in the room, himself and Schmeltz first, the others behind. Instinctively he and Schmeltz dropped low, moving away from the door. Giving themselves a minimal protection. His eyes were adjusting fast to the darkness of the room. Lighter than he had anticipated: the soft, almost primrose yellow of the moon through the open window. He could almost see the dust. Half a second and no response. He felt safer, searched for the bed.

In the corner, next to the window. He knew Schmeltz shared his bewilderment. The bed. Empty. Not even slept in. No sign of disturbance, the sheets and blankets as unmarked as when the bed was made. He felt behind him, found the cord hanging at the side of the door and switched on the light, tensing himself for the concealed trap away from the bed.

Nothing. The room was empty. Corrigan switched off the light and moved out of the room and down the stairs. Behind him, Schmeltz ordered two of the team to cover the top corridor then followed him. The two *Sturmmänner* who had remained below were still by the door behind which came the slow rattle of death. As Corrigan reached the last stair onto the landing Schmeltz hurtled past him, ignoring the men at the door, dipping his shoulder as his body-weight crashed through the wood and into the room. By the time the frame had splintered against the wall, Schmeltz and Corrigan were already in the bedroom, followed by the remainder of the assault squad.

The woman with the large breasts was sitting in the hard-backed chair at the side of the double bed, moaning.

'Where is he?' asked Schmeltz without ceremony.

The woman looked up, eyes and face red with tears. 'Gone,' she said, 'gone. He brought the señor home with the others, put him to bed, then went to get his bags. But he never came back.' She turned away and looked again at the thin figure on the bed.

'The pills,' she explained, as if they had asked her, 'he lost the pills.' She looked up at them again. 'They brought him back, said he was drunk. But I knew, looked for the pills.' She wiped the old man's face. 'They weren't there.'

The book-keeper looked up, unseeing, knowing who was in the room, beckoning Schmeltz closer. 'He knew,' he said, his voice barely audible. 'Knew everything. About Heidi with the big boobs. *Der Rathauskeller*, the "*Horst Wessel Lied*", Siegfried and *die Spinne*.' The breathing was shallow, painful. 'Where is the fly?' he asked, 'where is the fly?' The dying man repeated the code of the organis-

206

ation for the last time. 'In the trap, I told him, in the trap.' His breath smelt of death. The voice was trailing away, leaving Schmeltz behind.

'Why, old friend, why?' he asked.

The book-keeper could barely move his mouth, tried to tell the *Hauptsturmführer* why he was dying. 'He knew, knew everything. Minos, Aries, knew Corrigan.'

Behind Schmeltz, Corrigan heard his name, remained silent.

'Knew Octavio?' Schmeltz was almost too afraid to ask.

The book-keeper's voice was even lower. 'Everything.' He knew he had little time left. 'The Swiss bank account, Portachuela, everything.'

'Why?' Schmeltz still needed to know. 'Why?'

The book-keeper's eyes were pleading forgiveness. 'I should have known, should have recognised him.' The last clot of blood was moving upwards, relentlessly and unmercifully. 'He was the same: same eyes, same mouth, same face.'

'Who?' Schmeltz wanted to know, needed to know.

'He said he was from the Fatherland, from Bavaria. He knew the *Rathauskeller*, the one with the big tits. but I should have known.'

'Known what?' there was desperation in Schmeltz's questioning. The clot moved closer, passed the ventricle, into the pulmonary arteries, closing in on the junction to the lungs.

'I asked him and he told me, then I knew.' There was renewed terror in the dying man's eyes.

'Asked him what? Told you what?'

'*Ich fragte ihn, ob er wieder kommen würde.*'

Corrigan wished he could speak German, wished he could share the secret.

'*Ich fragte ihn, ob er wieder kommen würde.*' The words were repeated. The clot was almost there, reaching for the cord that would bring down the eternal darkness. The book-keeper was sliding away, down the long dark tunnel from which he would never return. Schmeltz went with him, reached down, found him, tried to pull him back. The book-keeper fulfilled his one last duty.

'*Ich fragte ihn und er sagte "Ich habe gesagt, dass ich wieder kommen würde."*'

The tunnel closed. Schmeltz stood back, allowing the fat woman her last moment with the book-keeper. Corrigan watched him, seeing the realisation descend upon him. He should have known, thought Schmeltz, like the book-keeper should have known. Should have known when the dying man told him of the eyes and mouth. Should have seen it in the torture of the book-keeper's soul as he passed into the tunnel. '*Ich fragte ihn,*' the old man had said, '*Ich fragte ihn und er sagte mir. Dann wusste ich.*'

'*Was haben Sie ihn gefragt?*' Schmeltz had asked, stretching out for the *Scharführer,* pulling him back, till the old soldier had been able to hear him, tell him. '*Was hat er gesagt?*'

He heard the words again, not the thin words from the sweating, smelling body on the wet bed in the hotel, but on the train to Paris, the man in the corner beckoning them to come closer, weakly, as weakly as the book-keeper had done. The *Sturmbannführer,* the book-keeper and himself. Bending over the tortured remnants of the man, the *Sturmmann* ready again at the handle of the generator, the book-keeper ready with his note-pad. All ready. For their moment of triumph. Then the words. The last words of the Frenchman on the floor as they waited over him. The only words they had pulled out of him.

The coldness swept over Schmeltz. He turned from the book-keeper and gestured to Corrigan to join him outside.

Chapter Five

Friday, February 4th 1983

The grey of dawn was turning to blue; the first of the lorries were already trundling into the city. Somewhere between the *barriada* of la Ciudad de Dios and the city centre Laporte lost his way, so that it was past six when he reached Maria's flat. He parked the car behind the tower and took the lift to the tenth floor.

He had wanted to sleep. God, how he had wanted to sleep after he had carried the book-keeper back to the hotel. He had gone to the car to fetch his bags before he realised he had no bags to fetch, had sat slumped behind the steering wheel for a full five minutes before he had seen the small boy staring at him from beneath the wooden pavement. The small boy who had looked after the car. The small boy who had pointed out the book-keeper to him. The small boy, the alarm bells had begun to sound, who had confirmed that in Mollendo there was only one road in and the same road out. He had pulled a bunch of notes from his pocket, paid the boy, then slipped out of the town. Expected at any moment for the road to be cut off, to see a Mercedes lurch in front of him. Twice during the drive back he had fallen asleep, once only waking when the car bumped off the road. He wondered how the book-keeper was, thought about the look of terror in the old man's eyes when he had risen to go to the toilet and the old man had asked him if he would be back. The dust of the desert filled his eyes, making them sting when he rubbed them.

He waited for almost two minutes, ringing the doorbell only once, till he saw the light of the spy-hole black out and Maria opened the door. She had not slept, he could tell. The dressing gown she had worn two evenings before was loose over her shoulder.

He went past her, into the lounge.

'Are you all right?' The concern was deep in her voice. He nodded.

'I know everything,' he said wearily, without enthusiasm, collapsing into a chair. 'I found the key to the papers, drove to Mollendo to find someone I hoped could help.' She saw his weariness was more than physical.

'Could he?' she asked.

Laporte looked at her. 'He was the book-keeper for the organisation, the man who approved all its finances, the man who knew everything.'

'And he told you?'

'Yes, he told me.'

Maria knew he would tell her in his own way. She helped him up and led him into the bathroom. 'Have a shower, you'll feel better. I'll make some coffee.'

He undressed, turned on the water and stepped under the hot spray, feeling its needles bite into his body. The massage was sharp and invigorating. He sat down, allowing the water to run over him, ignoring the stream that seeped around the curtain and onto the floor, till he could smell the fresh coffee. Only then did he pull himself up, lather his body with soap, and allow the spray to wash it off. Then he switched off the water and stepped out. Maria had left him a large towel and a cloth dressing gown. He dried himself, pulled the gown round him, and went back into the lounge.

Maria was still wearing her silk dressing gown. For a moment, Laporte knew he was looking at her the way he had done two nights before. Then he sat down opposite her and began to drink the hot, strong coffee. She went back into the kitchen and returned with a plate of warm croissants, allowing him to eat and drink as much as he needed before she asked him what had happened during the night, listening without speaking as he led her through it, step by step, beginning with his realisation of the codenames, how he had traced the book-keeper, how he had persuaded the old man to talk, what the exile had told him.

'Josef Heiner,' he said, 'runs a network of former Nazis called *die Spinne*, the Spider. The message which was on Herbert Weissemann's tape is the code to the group. They operate in a number of countries, mainly doing clandestine, illegal work, but putting the profits, or at least a percentage of the profits, into legitimate front activities.' He sipped the coffee again. 'The Spider's activities include the operations we saw on the expenses sheets, and a great many more. Operation Minos was, and still is, a currency racket. Aires was an illegal trade in ancient pottery. Apparently there is a great deal of money in that. Spider has contacts with some very prominent museums and auction houses both in Europe and North America. Others included a cocaine smuggling operation and a blackmail system, using sex parties to trap businessmen, then blackmailing them for commercial secrets.'

Maria poured him another coffee.

'That way,' he continued, 'they could sell the information to any number of bidders. They're also involved with the arms trade and military intelligence, which I suppose is logical considering their background. That's how they first came into contact with the CIA.'

Maria interrupted him for the first time. 'They work for the CIA?'

'According to the book-keeper they work for anyone who will pay them, even though people seem to know who they are.' He remembered the Irish/American name on the book-keeper's lists. 'Their CIA contact is a man called Corrigan. Corrigan knows who they are but still uses them. The CIA know who they are, but still use them.' For the first time he wondered about Corrigan.

'What about Project Octavio?' Maria asked.

'Even dirtier,' Corrigan began to explain. 'Even the book-keeper did not know all the details.' For ten minutes he explained the tangle of intrigues and counter-intrigues that made up Project Octavio, listing the web of plots, dissecting facts from interpretation, till Maria knew it as well as he did.

'But does it help you?' she asked when he had finished.

'Help me to do what?' He knew what she was asking, knew he had chosen to ignore the question on the drive back from Mollendo.

'Help you find the man who killed your father. Help you find Josef Heiner?'

He felt the tiredness return to his body. 'No,' he admitted, 'it doesn't. I now know everything about the man I am hunting except the most important thing. Where to find him.' The exhaustion was turning to despair.

'Come on,' said Maria gently, 'you're tired, come to bed.' He looked at her, hearing her words, misinterpreting them, thrown into sudden confusion, feeling the tightening of his stomach. 'It's almost seven,' she explained, 'I should be getting up anyway.'

He followed her into the bedroom. The light of the day was coming through the cotton of the curtains. Maria went out, shutting the door behind him, leaving him alone.

He lay on the bed, resting his head on her pillow, his tiredness suddenly gone. Moments ago, he knew, his whole body had been craving rest. Now he could not sleep. The perfume of the woman rose from the pillow, from the sheets, from everything around him, seeping into him, filling his pores, as it had done the night he slept on the sofa in the lounge.

Two nights before, he remembered, the night of their assault on the house at Chaclicayo.

He remembered how he had returned to the flat then, torturing himself with the image. Maria had just stepped out of the shower, her black hair wet around her shoulders, the water still gleaming on her skin, the silk of the dressing gown pulled across her body. He had not known what to say, what do do. They had held each other, pulling tight against each oher. He had told himself it was the elation of the danger they had shared at Chaclicayo, the way he had trusted Maria with his safety, the way she had protected him. Afterwards they had talked, discussed their feelings towards each other, Maria having the courage he lacked, stating those feelings. 'A very dear friend?' she had queried. 'You are already that. A confidante, a sharer of secrets. Of course.'

'A lover?' she had said of Herbert Weissemann. 'Once, long ago.' She had not asked the question of their relationship.

He remembered now, as he had remembered then, the embrace of triumph at the door.

A priest, thought Maria, stepping onto the balcony, looking at the blue of the morning sea, thinking of the man in her bed, hardly smelling the last freshness before the heat of the day. Remembering the first time he had come to the flat, the evening she had first met him, the evening he had asked her for help and she had told him of Herbert Weissemann, of the tape recorder. Part of her needing the physical strength of the man beside her, she remembered, the rest needing the spiritual strength of his priesthood. She had been confused then, was confused now. 'Damn him,' she thought, 'damn his strength, damn his priesthood.'

Laporte rolled on the bed, the sheets tight around him, his body alert, his mind confused. He was a priest, a man of the cloth. Yet each decision he had taken since he had first seen the shadow of the First Secretary in the schoolroom in the *barriada* of the City of God had taken him further from the priesthood. Each action he had taken had prepared him, committed him, to move even further away. Maria included. And each step had been natural to him, welcomed by him. Maria especially.

'He is God's messenger,' a voice quoted Romans from The Just War, 'an avenger to execute wrath upon him that doth evil.'

'Not revenging yourselves, my dearly beloved,' a second voice reminded him of his father's favourite passage from the same Book of Romans, 'but give place unto wrath.'

215

More sins to commit, the first voice pursued him. More priestly vows to break before the evil was punished.

Laporte got off the bed and left the room. Maria was standing on the balcony, looking across the sea, watching the clear blue line of the horizon smudge with the heat of the new day. Her hands clasped the rail, her shoulders were hunched. Her knuckles, he saw as he approached her, were white with the force with which she held the metal bar. He took her shoulders, turned her gently till she faced him. 'You as well?' he asked.

She nodded. 'Yes, me as well.'

2   *Lima*

'It's the son.' Schmeltz was adamant. Bailey waited impatiently while the waitress served them breakfast, starting with coffee, schnapps and Jack Daniels. He had joined Schmeltz and Corrigan immediately they arrived in the Sheraton.

'Why?' he asked, as soon as she left.

Slowly and carefully, without omitting a single detail or point of background information, Schmeltz took Bailey through the last words of the book-keeper as the dying man fought to pass on his warning.

When Schmeltz had finished, Bailey ordered another round of coffee and drinks and stuck a toothpick between his lips. 'It's not much to go on,' he commented.

Schmeltz disagreed. 'For me it's enough.' Bailey turned to Corrigan.

'What about you, Joe,' he asked, 'remember what Washington said. You're the one who makes the big decision.'

Corrigan swilled the Jack Daniels in the glass. Not his decision, he knew, it never had been. He would simply rubber-stamp whatever recommendation Bailey made. He wondered why they did it, why they were trying to draw him in. Almost, he thought, like tying him deeper into the web. He was not sure whether or not it worried him, concentrated on the problem facing them.

'Heinrich is positive that the man who visited the book-keeper was the son. Like you, however, I'm not convinced.' He remembered the night before, the assault on the hotel. Less than six hours ago. His reaction when Schmeltz had finally explained his reason for believing that the book-keeper's visitor was the son. Bailey was nodding.

'I'm not sure either,' he repeated. 'And I don't think Washington would be too pleased if we went ahead on such evidence without consulting them first. There'll be a hell of an outcry anyway if the son dies, even if it is an accident. The press boys will be swarming round like flies. Washington will need to be convinced.'

'There's an obvious check,' suggested Corrigan. 'Presumably you have a photograph of the son?' Bailey nodded. 'In that case,' continued Corrigan, 'it's easy. Some of the book-keeper's boys were in the bar. They saw the man who visited him. So did the old woman at the hotel. It'll take a few hours, but we can get a photograph there by lunchtime, then we'll know for sure.' Bailey agreed. Schmeltz nodded his head.

The food arrived. Bailey ordered more coffee. 'It's funny,' Corrigan suddenly remembered, 'but the book-keeper's boys in the bar thought the visitor was a German.' Bailey looked up from his breakfast.

'What the hell do you mean?'

'Apparently he spoke German with the book-keeper, they even said he had a Bavarian accent.' He remembered something else. 'One of the boys also told Heinrich that the visitor seemed to know Munich. He mentioned a beer hall called the *Rathauskeller*, which apparently isn't on the normal tourist track.'

Bailey downed his schnapps and put the glass on the table. 'In that case,' he spoke slowly and deliberately, 'there's no need to check with Washington, or with the boys in the bar.'

Corrigan wondered what he meant, what had changed

his position. Schmeltz began to mutter that he still thought the visitor was the son.

'It was,' said Bailey, 'it was the son.' Corrigan reached for his Jack Daniels.

'The son, the priest, call him what you want, speaks fluent German,' Bailey said at last. 'It was not something that was greeted with any degree of enthusiasm by those in France who knew his father, but before he became a priest his mother sent him to Germany to learn the language.'

'And the Bavarian accent, the *Rathauskeller?*' asked Corrigan.

'The *Rathauskeller* is a beer hall in a village on the outskirts of Munich,' said Schmeltz. 'It has, shall we say, certain historic connections.'

Bailey nodded. 'And the son went to university in Munich.' He moved the toothpick between his teeth. 'It's all on the son's file: the university, the *Rathauskeller*. It's the son.' He sat back, looking at Corrigan. 'As Washington said, it's your decision.'

Not his decision, Corrigan knew again, it never had been. Not that it mattered who made it. They were all equally involved. Heiner and Schmeltz, Bailey and himself, on one side. The son on the other.

Something else, he thought. The secret. The secret Washington was keeping to itself. Not Project Octavio, he knew. Something else. Bigger. Dirtier.

No reason, he thought, for Washington to tell him. No reason for him to know. Except that he had been getting close. Sensed it when he talked to the telephone contact in La Paz, when he listened to the words of the book-keeper in the stinking room in Mollendo. Now, he knew, it was finished.

His decision, they had told him. As if, he suddenly thought, they always knew he would suspect their secret. As if, in some twisted way, they wanted him to be the one to shut the doors on the only way he would find out what they were guarding. 'How long will it take?' he asked.

218

Bailey's voice was without emotion. 'The boys are ready.'

'OK,' Corrigan made the decision. 'Tell them it's on. As fast as they can.'

'When will we know?' asked Schmeltz.

'This evening,' Bailey told him. 'This evening and it will all be over.'

The three finished breakfast. Bailey and Corrigan allowed Schmeltz to leave first then walked outside together. 'You'll be in all day?' Bailey asked. Corrigan said that he would. 'Good. I'll be in my room. I'll contact you as soon as I know anything.'

The traffic on Avenida Inca Garcilaso de la Vega was at a standstill. Corrigan left his car, which he had picked up on the return from Mollendo, and walked to the embassy. His secretary, in the outer office, was wearing a new white dress. On the filing cabinet at the side of her desk was a new hat. 'New boyfriend?' he asked jokingly. The woman looked at him acidly.

'I hope you haven't forgotten,' she rebuked him.

He stalled. 'Your godson is being baptised this lunchtime.'

He groaned silently. 'Of course not,' he laughed, 'I've even remembered the present.'

He went into his room, telephoned the Sheraton Hotel and asked for Bailey. The man from Washington answered immediately. 'Jack, it's Joe Corrigan. I've just been reminded that there's something I have to do this afternoon that will be very difficult to put off. If it's all right with you I'll be at home between eleven and twelve, and on the car radio after that. Somebody will be manning the radio. I'll never be more than fifty yards from the car. They'll know exactly where I am.'

Bailey was in a hurry to clear the line. 'What the hell are you doing?'

Corrigan wondered how the special would react. 'A baptism,' he said weakly, 'I'm going to be a godfather.'

He heard Bailey laugh, 'Sounds just like you, Joe. I'll see you later.'

He waited for another line and telephoned his wife, telling her that he was back in Lima and that he would be home at eleven to shower and change before the christening. It was twenty minutes to the hour. He felt tired, wished he had not drunk the Jack Daniels at breakfast. The son, he thought. All the time it had been the son. In the house at Chaclicayo. In the hotel in Mollendo. A team of professionals, Schmeltz had said. The son was no threat, Bailey had maintained. And all the time it had been the priest. After Heiner. Just as Corrigan was now after him. The same thing, he thought, but different sides.

He walked to the cafeteria, helped himself to coffee, and brought it back to his office. In the outer room the secretary was talking to someone on the telephone about the baptism. He moved the blotting paper into the centre of his desk and rested the coffee cup on it. In the top right-hand corner were the figures he had scribbled three days before. 4.00 a.m. He had circled them in red. The time of the raid in which Josef Heiner and Heinrich Schmeltz had seized Jean Laporte thirty-nine years before. He sipped the coffee and stared at the figures. 4.00 a.m. The time of the raid in which he and Heinrich Schmeltz had tried to seize the son.

He got up, left his office, locked the door, told his secretary he would be at home for the next ninety minutes, and saw her smile approvingly when he assured her he would not be late for the baptism.

3

The warmth of the sun penetrated the blue and white pattern of the curtains and settled on the bed. Laporte woke slowly, checked his watch. Though he had been asleep for little more than two hours he felt alert and awake. In the kitchen Maria was making coffee. He rose, wrapped the dressing gown around him, and phoned the monastery. It was over two days since he had spoken to France. He wondered if there were any messages for him. Yes, he was told, somebody in France had been trying to get hold of him, had been phoning every six hours. And somebody else had telephoned for him that morning. A man called Pacheco. Less than an hour ago. Could the Holy Father call him immediately. And a message from Father Michael, concerned about him, asking him to meet him for lunch, suggesting a time and place. He left a reply for Father Michael, confirming he would be there, glad at the thought, and dialled Pacheco. The magazine editor was engaged, said his secretary. He waited while she interrupted him, then heard Pacheco's voice. It was a little difficult, the editor explained. He was busy, could he phone Laporte later? Laporte knew what he meant, but was reluctant to involve Maria.

There was, he decided, no alternative. 'I've been away,' he said. 'I only got back an hour ago and dropped in to see a friend.' Pacheco said he understood.

Ten minutes later he phoned from a public telephone. Maria took the call and gave the telephone to Laporte. 'Thanks,' said Pacheco, 'the office isn't always a good idea.'

'What do you want?' asked Laporte, looking through the lounge door at Maria.

'I have something which might interest you. When can we meet?' Laporte estimated the time. 'I could be in town in an hour.'

'OK, I'll see you in the Café Amarillo, in the Calle Cuscena, at twelve. How will you be arriving?'

Laporte was puzzled. 'What do you mean, how will I be arriving?'

Pacheco's response was short and sharp. 'I can't explain, but I need to know your precise movements for the next six hours.'

Laporte tried to work them out. 'I'll be leaving my friend's in three quarters of an hour. My friend will drive me to the café. I have no way of knowing how long I will be there. That's up to you. But I have to meet another friend for lunch at one. After that I don't know.'

'Fine,' said Pacheco, 'it won't take long.'

Laporte went back to the lounge. Maria was finishing her coffee. 'What did Pacheco want?' she asked.

He sat down. 'I'm not sure. He says he has something that will interest me, wants to see me at twelve.'

Maria put down the cup, remembering something. Something she had noticed, had meant to tell him, three days before, the evening they met. 'I think somebody's following you,' she said. The words took him by surprise.

'What do you mean.'

She told him of the man on the pavement opposite the Bar Hawaii, the face that had disappeared when she looked a second time.

'Are you sure?' he asked. She felt lost, unsure. On the night she had known, three days later she was not so confident, told herself she might have made a mistake, might have still been upset at the disappearance of Herbert Weissemann.

'I don't know,' she admitted.

4

Corrigan stepped out of the shower, dried himself, pulled on a fresh set of clothes and joined his wife in the garden. She had prepared a lunch of salad and meat, two bottles of cold beer on the side. He sat down with her and relaxed in the sun. A secret, he could not wipe the thought from his mind, a secret that Washington had tried to keep to itself, that he had almost prised open. A secret he now would not know. He knew it was connected with the son, the priest. The man whose execution he had sanctioned less than ninety minutes ago.

'Is everything all right, Joe?' His wife's voice interrupted him.

'Sure,' he smiled, pouring them both a drink, 'why do you ask?'

'Sometimes,' she said, 'I know you better than you know yourself, know when you're worried, know when you're lying.'

He began to reply and the phone rang. Bailey's voice was flat and factual. 'It's on,' he said. 'The boys have been in contact. It's all set up. You'll be at home?'

'Or on the car radio.'

'Good,' said Bailey, 'I'll be in touch.'

His wife looked at him as he put the phone down. 'Well?' she asked.

He did not want to lie to her again. 'Come on,' he said, 'or we'll be late.'

5

The street on which the Café Amarillo was placed was one-way. Maria arrived at ten minutes to twelve, pulled the car onto the pavement to avoid blocking the traffic, and waited while Laporte got out and walked round to the driver's door. 'Shall I see you tonight?' he asked. She nodded. He bent down and kissed her goodbye.

The man slumped low in the rear seat of the car parked unobtrusively thirty yards away on the other side of the road turned to his companion in the driving seat. 'That's him?' he asked.

Ricardo Pacheco nodded.

'I thought he was a priest,' said the man in the back.

'He is, it's the first time I've seen him dressed like that.'

The passenger stared up the road. 'I wasn't talking about his clothes,' he said. He waited, watching as Maria drove away and Laporte went into the café.

'It's on,' he told the magazine editor, 'set it up for two-thirty.'

Laporte chose a table on the right of the door, near the

223

counter, and ordered a black coffee. He had waited for ten minutes when Pacheco joined him and asked for a beer. 'How's it going?' the editor asked casually.

'Well,' replied Laporte, trying to remember how much Pacheco knew, whether he had told him about the documents. 'I know why Herbert Weissemann was killed, what he was after.' He wondered why Pacheco had not commented on his clothes, not asked why he was not dressed as a priest. Someone on the pavement, Maria had said, somebody looking at them.

Pacheco nodded. 'And how's Maria?' A face that had disappeared, Maria had said, that had faded into the night.

'She's fine.' He knew he had to lie, unsure why, the suspicion growing. 'I was away all last night, she gave me breakfast this morning.' He knew he had said too much. 'Anyway, you said you wanted to see me.'

Pacheco nodded. 'There's someone in town who would like to see you,' he said carefully, 'I suggest you meet him.'

'Why?' asked Laporte. Only three people knew of the meeting on the Tuesday evening he thought: Maria, himself and Pacheco. A face, Maria had said, a face that had disappeared.

'Because it is possible he could help you.'

'Who is he?' asked Laporte. 'What can you tell me about him?'

'Nothing,' replied Pacheco, 'I can tell you nothing.'

'Where and when?' Laporte remembered the need for the back door in the house at Chaclicayo.

'Cinco y Media at two-thirty. Room twenty-six.'

No time, thought Laporte, no time to recce, no time to check it out. No-one to guard his back. 'What's Cinco y Media?' he asked. Not Pacheco, he thought, please not Pacheco.

Pacheco laughed. 'Cinco y Media is a whore house. It gets its name because it is exactly five and a half kilometres out of town.

Laporte could hear the thumping in his ears as he waited in the secret basement, Maria's warning call, the flight from the back of the house. The one road in and out at Mollendo. 'OK.' He knew there was no option, 'Cinco y Media at two-thirty.'

6

At forty minutes past twelve, Jean Laporte finished his coffee, left the Calle Cusceña, walked to the Plaza San Martin and picked up a cab to the café where he was to meet Father Michael. At forty-three minutes past twelve, Joe Corrigan and his wife left their house, the marine guard in civilian clothes in the rear seat, and drove to the Church of the Good Shepherd on Avenida Santa Cruz in Miraflores.

The mother and father were already waiting, the child who was about to become Corrigan's godson sleeping peacefully in his mother's arms. The smell of lilies filled the church.

Corrigan felt in his pocket and took out the gift. The mother of pearl glistened in the light of the candles. He laid it on the child's breast and watched as his tiny fingers began to play with the beads of the rosary.

The mother slipped her hand through Corrigan's arm. 'I hope you don't mind, Joe,' she said softly, 'we meant to tell you but you were never at home. We asked the priest to change the service a little, to include the Lord's Prayer in the baptism. It's an old family custom.'

Corrigan looked at her with affection. 'I think it's a lovely custom,' he said.

The sky outside was brilliant blue and burning hot. Laporte arrived at the café, in a narrow street behind the National Stadium, at five minutes to one and selected a corner table away from the door and counter. From the kitchen came the familiar smell of fish. He was early, there were no other customers as yet.

He ordered a beer and looked round. It was the sort of place he could have guessed Father Michael would have chosen, removed from the severity and conservatism of most of the other priests on the study tour. He wondered how his friend would react to his appearance, to the fact he was not dressed as a priest, trying to decide how he could explain.

The beer was chilled, like the beer in the café at Mollendo. The evening with the book-keeper already seemed a lifetime away; he remembered it was less than twelve hours. His fingers felt inside his right pocket, touching the rosary, playing with the beads. Finding a strange assurance.

The door opened and Father Michael came in. Laporte rose to greet him, poured him a beer and ordered *cebiche*. Father Michael looked at him across the table. 'I've been worried about you,' he said. 'You come at night, you go at night. I was relieved to see you yesterday morning; when I went to your room the bed had not been slept in. The same this morning. Is anything wrong?'

Laporte shook his head. 'No, nothing's wrong. In fact everything is going quite well.'

'So tell me what's happening.' Father Michael started his *cebiche*. Laporte waited for the waiter to leave them, then began.

'As you know, last Sunday night the local police raided the house of Josef Heiner. They had the right man. But they missed him.' He was glad to talk to a friend. 'They don't know where he is. I don't either, but I now know practically everything else about him. Who he works for, what he does.'

Father Michael looked puzzled, asking him to explain. The waiter brought two more bottles of beer. Quietly and efficiently Laporte told the story, beginning with his visit to the house, ending with his trip to Mollendo and the mystery meeting that Pacheco had arranged for him that afternoon. The only thing he did not tell Father Michael about was the depth of his relationship with Maria.

In the church two miles away, the priest began the Lord's Prayer.

> Our Father, Who art in Heaven,
> Hallowed be Thy name . . .

'Glad to see you . . . concerned about you.' The words were coming back. Laporte lifted his beer, hardly drinking. 'When I went to your room the bed had not been slept in.' He poured them each another drink, saw himself the previous morning, unlocking the door to the humble accommodation at the rear of the monastery. Locking it again after. More words. 'Lucky to have Maria; who is she? Where does she live?' And more. 'What documents, what detail?' The ice began to spread through his brain. Remembering. Dissecting.

> Thy kingdom come, Thy will be done
> On Earth as it is in Heaven . . .

A face, Maria had said, a face that had disappeared into the darkness. Not Pacheco, he had pleaded at the Café Amarilla, please not Pacheco. The plea had been answered. Not Pacheco. Father Michael. He knew why he had gone to Maria that morning, why he had needed her. She had taken the tiredness from him, enabled him to see. As his father had not been able to see nearly thirty-nine years before. He remembered his other thought as he wanted Maria, smelt her perfume on the bed, seen her anguish on the balcony. Remembered what he had thought as he wrestled with his own conscience. As if the breaking of each vow, of each commandment, took him closer to the truth.

> Give us this day our daily bread
> And forgive us our trespasses . . .

He had been bled, calmly and professionally, sucked dry of information as he had sucked dry the book-keeper. Not an act of friendship, not the hand of peace. An interrogation. And he had succumbed, told all. Names and addresses, meeting places. Betrayed those who had helped him. He remembered the legend of his father, that he had not spoken a single word. Too late, he thought. Not too late, he told himself, still time. All the information had been bled from him that day, all the names betrayed that lunchtime. Not too late, he knew. He came to the sixth Commandment.

> As we forgive them
> that trespass against us . . .

He stood up, making an excuse about the beer. Seeing it, seeing the set-up, knowing why the café was empty. He moved round the table, behind Father Michael, hands in pocket. Remembering the shoe-shine boy. Feeling the cat-gut of the rosary.

> Lead us not into temptation
> But deliver us from evil . . .

The movement was sharp and swift, the beads bruising the flesh, the cat-gut biting deep into the hard muscle of the windpipe. The knee between the shoulder blades, straightening the condemned, serving as a lever.

> For Thine is the Kingdom
> The power and the glory . . .

Father Michael's fingers were on the beads, fighting them, feeling their death-grip round his throat. He had thought about death. Known it too often not to recognise it. Wondered sometimes how he would meet his own. Softer than he had thought. And warmer. He felt his strength ebbing. He was going back. Through the years. Through the places he had served his God. Guatemala. East Berlin. El Salvador. Vietnam. Chile. Sometimes the United States itself. The feeling was warmer, blacker. He was a young man again, enjoying the sunsets and the girls. Into childhood, the poverty of his youth. The way his mother had fought for survival. Cried herself silently to sleep each night.

For ever
And ever . . .

He was almost there. The long black tunnel waiting for him, beckoning him. He was hurrying, going home. As if it was the one thing, the only thing, he had always wanted. He was being baptised, his mother crossing herself, her breasts large and comforting, taking the hunger from his stomach, dispelling his fears. Almost there, almost home. There were tears in his eyes. Not of pain of execution, almost of happiness, as if he had discovered the true meaning of the cloth he was wearing. His fingers stopped playing with the beads, stayed still. He was there. Back in the eternal darkness, warm and comforting around him.

Amen.

Laporte straightened, removed the rosary from Father Michael's neck, and allowed the body to slump gently back into the seat. The panic was spreading through him like a cancer. He backed away, hardly able to look. Oh God, forgive me, please forgive me. He looked down at his friend. Of course there was an explanation. Of course Father Michael had asked a novice to unlock his door. He looked desperately round the café. Still empty. But open. The sign on the door said so.

Damn them all. Damn Pacheco. Damn the ambassador. Damn the shoe-shine boy. Damn Chalbrand. Damn Maria. Damn even his own father. Theirs was the guilt, not his. Damn them all for the sins he had committed.

The door was locked. He looked again at the sign,

hanging from a nail. OPEN. He saw it, the ice closing in again. OPEN to anyone on the inside, CLOSED to anyone on the outside.

In the street he saw two men sitting in a parked car. As he looked, one of them nodded. They got out and began to walk to the café. He slipped the lock and let them in, passing them in the doorway.

'Where's the priest?' the man in front asked. Laporte nodded to the figure sitting peacefully at the table.

'Where's Corrigan?' he heard himself ask.

'He'll be along later to see the body before we dump it.'

Laporte stepped into the sunlight and walked away.

In the choir loft of the church the organ began the recessional. The priest handed the child back to his mother. Corrigan looked at his godson, saw the marine sergeant enter and hurry towards him. He bent down and kissed the child. At his side the young mother was red-eyed with happiness.

'A message on the car radio, sir,' the marine told him. 'They said it's done, they said you should be there in half an hour.' He handed Corrigan a piece of paper on which he had written an address. 'They said you would understand.'

Corrigan saw his wife looking at him, avoided the stare, looked down again at his godson. 'Yes,' he said, 'I understand.'

7

The address which the marine gave Corrigan was in the Jesus Maria quarter of the city. Corrigan kissed his godson goodbye, avoided his wife, and drove to the street. The house was a detached two-storey building, the yellow paint peeling from its front, a side-entrance protected by a gate. He parked the car outside, checked that the doors were locked, and rang the front door bell. It was answered by the first of the men Laporte had passed in the doorway to the café.

'Corrigan,' he announced himself. 'Is Bailey here yet?'

The man who had opened the door shook his head. 'He's on his way.'

Corrigan followed the man through the hallway into the kitchen at the rear. Through the windows, in the courtyard at the rear, he could see a large black car which he assumed had been used for the pick-up. Leaning against the bonnet, drinking a Coca Cola, was a second man.

The body was stretched on the red-tiled floor where the table had previously stood, covered by a white sheet. The priest's legs protruded from one corner, the black shoes flopped against the tiles were threadworn and dusty, the socks grey and woollen, hanging in folds round the ankles. Blessed are the meek, thought Corrigan, bending down and lifting the sheet from the face, staring at the man whose death he had approved. His decision, they had said. Not his decision, he knew but he had made it anyway. He was glad he had taken it. Not because it was the right decision, but because he would not have to take it again.

The eyes were twisted, protruding, in the agony of the garrotte. Corrigan stretched forward and eased down the white collar which had risen up round the neck. Underneath, partially concealed by the shirt, were the marks of death. He bent closer to look at them, smelling the man, smelling the body.

'Sometimes,' his wife had told him less than two hours before, 'I know you better than you know yourself, know when you're worried, know when you're lying.' He remembered her look in the church, the way he had avoided her stare as he left. Looked back at the marks on the neck. Not clean, not the thin red line he had so often seen. Pitted and bruised, as if the assassin had used a necklace. Or, he realised he was thinking, a rosary. Even in the cool of the kitchen he could hear the buzzing of the flies. He pulled the sheet back over the priest's face and joined the men in the rear garden. A car horn sounded in the street. One of the men opened the side-gate and Bailey drove in, parking his car behind the makeshift hearse.

'How'd it go?' he asked enthusiastically, nodding a greeting at Corrigan, accepting a Coca Cola.

'Smooth,' the bigger of the two men replied with equal enthusiasm. 'Like clockwork. That guy in the café was good. No fuss, no mess. Told us to be there at one-thirty, and at one-thirty he comes out the`door and nods like he's passing the time of day. Then walks off down the street as if he hasn't a care in the world.'

'The best,' said Bailey, following them into the kitchen. 'A natural. Been everywhere. Guatemala, East Berlin, Vietnam, El Salvador.' He laughed. 'Sometimes a bit closer to home.' He stood over the body. 'Wire man mainly. Good with anything, of course, but best with the wire.' The words echoed through Corrigan's brain. He remembered the marks on the neck, the pitted holes of the rosary, the first fingers of the frost beginning to touch his body.

Bailey knelt, savouring the moment, the triumph, and lifted a corner of the sheet. There was silence in the room.

'Christ. Oh Jesus Christ.' The words slipped out of Bailey's mouth, low and unbelieving. He stared at the face, unable to move. 'Christ. Oh Jesus Christ.' The words came out again. Bailey looked up, staring. 'What did you say happened?' The two men who had made the pick-up shuffled uneasily, knew something was wrong, did not know what.

'The meet was at one. We got there early, parked up and waited. Our man arrived first, then the priest. Like we said, it was a smooth operation.' An element of uncertainty had crept into his voice. 'Half-one, bang on schedule, our man comes out and we go in and collect the priest.'

Bailey stared at them, repeated their words. 'Our man arrives, you say, then the priest.' It was as if he was hypnotised. 'Our man comes out, you go in and collect the priest.' The undertakers nodded.

'Did you ever meet our man?' Bailey asked them.

232

'No, he arranged everything on the phone.' Corrigan looked at Bailey, the frost hardening. Cold. Deep.

'But,' he heard Bailey say, 'this is our man.'

8

The secretary was already in the outer office when Corrigan returned to the embassy. He and Bailey had left the house together, leaving the undertakers to deal with the body of their dead colleague. Bailey had gone straight to the communications room to report to Washington.

'Wasn't it wonderful?' the secretary said with a hint of tears in her eyes. Corrigan smiled and locked himself in the inner office.

No threat, Bailey had said at the first briefing, the son was no threat. A priest, he had emphasised, a man of peace. Then the night raid on the house at Chaclicayo. Definitely not the son, Schmeltz had said. A pro job; stake-out at the front, bolt-hole at the back. A team job; back-up somewhere else.

And the missing documents. No use to anybody, Schmeltz had said. But the son had done the job, made use of the documents, traced the book-keeper through them, learned all their secrets from him. 'He knew everything,' Schmeltz had said the book-keeper had whispered, 'even Project Octavio.'

And the Agency assassin, the man on the inside, the best in the business, Bailey had said. Stretched out beneath the sheet on the kitchen floor with his socks round his ankles and the kiss of the garrotte round his neck. No threat, Bailey had said, no threat at all.

A secret, he thought again, a secret known only to Washington, a secret denied even to Bailey.

The new box of Havanas was in the top drawer of his desk. Corrigan took one, opened the wall-safe, took out the envelope containing the information on Jean Laporte which he had previously removed from the Heiner file, laid the sheets of paper on his desk, and began to read the nine lengthy paragraphs. He had almost finished the first page, concentrating on every detail, when his secretary called on the intercom to say that a Mr Bailey was outside. Corrigan slid the sheets back into the envelope, returned it to the wall-safe, and let Bailey in.

The man from Washington was looking grim, as if his entire future depended on the next few hours. 'No feedback yet,' he said tersely, sitting down. 'They're assessing the situation. Will come back with instructions in an hour.'

'How do things look?' asked Corrigan. 'Awful,' said Bailey, 'fucking awful.'

'You have a photo of the son,' Corrigan changed the subject. 'I'd like a copy.' Bailey nodded, still thinking about the reaction in Washington.

'Anything else?' Corrigan asked.

'Some details on the son, nothing much. I'm taking a shower at the hotel. I'll bring them back in an hour.'

Corrigan chewed on the Havana, walked to the front of the embassy building, and watched as Bailey left. He wondered where the hell the son was. What the hell was going on.

He returned to his office, opened his note-book, found the number of the La Paz contact, and dialled international. The operator took twelve minutes to connect him.

'Sam here,' he introduced himself, wondering what was happening in Washington, 'any luck?'

The contact was brief and succinct. 'The calls were made from different numbers. The first was made from the El Dorado hotel. That was easy to trace. The second was from a private number in the city. The private number is interesting. It is actually credited to a name which does not exist, even though the bills are paid promptly.' Like Heiner, thought Corrigan, just like Heiner. 'I've had no luck with an address so far,' continued the contact, 'but I'll keep trying.' Corrigan thanked him. 'There's one other thing that might interest you,' the contact added, 'a number of other international calls were made from the same number at more or less the same time, suggesting that the caller gave the operator a list of numbers to get.'

'Wait while I get a pen,' Corrigan told the contact. He put the La Paz connection on hold, pressed the intercom to his secretary and gave her two numbers, one in Washington, the second in New York. 'Urgentmost,' he told her.

The La Paz contact was waiting. 'I'm ready,' said Corrigan, 'give them to me slowly.' The contact read through his list. Corrigan recognised the old number of his private line, plus the new number in Lima which Heinrich Schmeltz had given him, relieved to have the reliability of the La Paz contact confirmed, sensing there was an immediate explanation for some of the others, already apprehensive about the rest.

The secretary was calling him. Corrigan thanked the man, said he would phone back the next day for any more information the contact could uncover, and took the call he had requested to Washington.

'Dave, this is Joe Corrigan. I need some help and fast.' He wondered why he was in a hurry, why he was behaving as if he was caught up in a timetable. 'I have some international numbers and I need to know who they belong to.' The man in Washington asked the obvious question. 'No,' Corrigan told him, 'I'm not in a position to check them myself and no, I can't just call the numbers. Do you know anybody who could make some enquiries and keep his mouth shut about it?' He waited while the other man found pen and paper, then read to him three of the numbers from the list supplied by the La Paz contact, omitting Heinrich Schmeltz's new number and that of his previous confidential direct line, plus one other. 'Thanks, Dave, I owe you.'

The call to New York was connected eight minutes later. The conversation followed a similar pattern; Corrigan giving the man the one outstanding number about which he knew nothing and which he had not given the Washington contact to check. When the call was finished he sat back in his chair and stared at his desk, wondering what he should do next, knowing there was no more he could do. The Havana was in the ashtray on the top right of the blotting paper. He picked it up again, saw the idle scribbling.

4.00 a.m. The lines around the time like a web. He pushed the thought to the back of his mind and wondered again where the hell the son was.

9

Three blocks from the café, Laporte picked up a cab, took it to the Bar Hawaii, where he had first met Maria, walked the remaining half-mile to her flat so that it could not be connected, collected the hire car, and began the drive to the meeting at two-thirty. Exactly five-and-a-half kilometres from Lima he recognised the two-storey complex of grey concrete, the walls without windows, of the brothel known as Cinco y Media. He turned right, off the road, behind a factory, and followed a maze of side streets into the complex itself.

'Where's Corrigan?' he had asked the man in the doorway to the café.

'He'll be along later to see the body,' the man had said.

Laporte drew the strands together. The name on the book-keeper's lists, the confirmation by the old man himself, the words of the men as they came to collect the body of the priest. As they came to collect his body. Corrigan, he thought again. Corrigan had protected the man who had butchered his father. Now Corrigan had tried to kill him.

An armed guard, a pistol stuffed into the top of his trousers, manned the metal barrier across the entrance to Cinco y Media. As Laporte approached, he raised the

236

metal bar, let him through, then closed it behind him. The brothel was a series of single rooms, each above its own garage, so that vehicles could not be seen once they had entered. The numbers of the rooms were painted on the whitewashed walls of the garages. Laporte drove slowly till he found number twenty-six, the doors of the garage open, and drove in. As he switched off the engine, the doors closed. He got out of the car and faced the man standing in the shadows. 'Laporte?' the man asked.

He nodded. 'Yes, I'm Laporte.' The man turned to his left and walked through a small doorway and up a narrow staircase to the room above. Laporte followed him, sensing that his host was not as unprotected as he seemed.

The walls of the room were lined with red velvet. The thick carpet was also red, the large pear-shaped bed which occupied most of the floor-space was draped in red covers. Discreet wall-lights cast a warm glow into the room. In the ceiling, over the bed, was a large mirror. There were more mirrors at the foot and head of the bed. On a table at the foot of the bed was a television with a video attachment. Laporte imagined its use. The only furniture in the room were two armchairs. In a small room to the side was a shower, bidet and toilet.

'Drink?' the other man asked.

'What is there?'

'In this place,' said his host in a resigned voice, 'I imagine there's anything.' He picked up a telephone which was concealed in a small alcove behind the head of the bed and ordered two beers. Almost immediately the telephone rang again. The man pulled aside the curtains at the back of the alcove to reveal a small door in the wall. He unlocked the door and opened it. In a small space beyond stood the beers. He took them, shut and locked the door, and closed the curtains. 'As I said,' he sighed, 'in this place I'd imagine you could get anything.'

Laporte was growing accustomed to the setting. The other man read his mind.

'Cinco y Media is a brothel,' he explained, 'a very special

sort of brothel. You can't buy a woman here, you bring your own, hire a room on whatever basis you want.' Laporte opened a beer. He had no idea of the identity of the man, though he supposed there was a reason for the clandestine nature of their meeting.

'Isn't this a dangerous place to meet then?' he asked.

The other man shook his head. 'The safest place in the world,' he said. 'Most of its clients are high up in society. Most of the generals and politicians use it, as well as the police chiefs and the mayors of Lima. If the place was raided this afternoon, they'd probably catch half the cabinet here.'

Laporte's eyes were adjusting to the bizarre lighting. His companion was only slightly younger than himself, about the same build. Even in the red of the semidarkness, however, there was a strange pallor about the man's face, as if he had been deprived of natural light for many months. 'So you,' said the man, 'are the son.'

Laporte nodded. 'Pacheco told you?'

'Yes, Pacheco told me. He also said you were a priest, but after seeing you with the woman this morning, that is something I find difficult to believe.'

It was no surprise to Laporte that his movements had been monitored. He now knew the consequence of Pacheco's enquiries, though not as yet the reason. He also knew that the man was about to ask something else, as if he could see inside Laporte's soul. 'I am a priest, yes,' he replied.

'Not just an ordinary priest, however.' The man's look was rivetting. 'Something else has happened since I saw you with the woman this morning.'

'They tried to kill me. Sent an assassin after me.' There was no need to explain who they were.

The other man's stare remained immobile. 'What happened?'

'I killed him.'

The other man nodded as if it was the answer he had expected. 'What did Pacheco tell you about me?'

238

'Very little. Nothing in fact. He didn't even say who you are.'

The stranger poured himself a beer, took one sip, then put down the glass. 'My name,' he said, 'is Guillermo Pertierro. I am a commander of the *Movimiento Izquierdo Revolutionario*, the MIR, in Bolivia. Until Wednesday morning I had been held captive for three and a half months. Then I escaped. I arrived in Lima late yesterday afternoon.'

Laporte remembered the article in *El Comercio*. '*El Lobo,* The Wolf,' he said.

'Yes,' said Pertierro, 'the one they called The Wolf.'

'Pacheco said you had some information that could help me.'

'I do. I know where the man who killed your father is.'

The words cut deep into Laporte's brain. He allowed himself time to hear the words again, repeating them to himself, dissecting them, understanding what they meant. 'Where?' he asked.

'La Paz. He spends quite a lot of time there.'

'How do you know?'

Pertierro breathed deeply, remembering the man who had stood in the shadows of the torture room as the electric pain arched through his testicles into his body. 'Because the man who tortured your father to death also tortured me.'

It was like a spider's web, Josef Heiner had thought. The comings and goings, each man, each movement, spinning the fine threads of the trap. Himself from Lima to La Paz. Heinrich Schmeltz from Lima to La Paz then back to Lima. The documents from Lima to La Paz. The son into Lima. The Texan with the name of Anderson into La Paz.

And now, he could have added, the one they called El Lobo from La Paz to Lima. The son to the bookkeeper. The Americans to the son. The son to Guillermo Pertierro. The threads crossing, weaving, drawing them together.

239

Laporte digested the information, allowing it to settle into the framework of knowledge he had gleaned from the documents and the book-keeper. 'Tell me,' he said at last.

'I have been a militant since I was ten,' Pertierro began. 'My parents were peasants. After the death of El Che in 1967 I began working with the unions, organising the miners, but still remained a guerilla. As others were killed or captured so my role changed till I became leader.' He took another drink. 'That area is best left untouched, in case you yourself are taken.

'Three months ago I was captured as I waited to meet a contact. For a while I was held in the Ministry of the Interior in La Paz, where they have a special torture room. Later I was moved to a torture house in the suburbs of the city. Two *compañeros* were also held there. We were tortured daily by a special squad that came to the house. When I was not being interrogated I was locked in a coffin. Two mornings ago, I and my companions managed to escape.

'And Josef Heiner?' asked Laporte.

'Present during many of the early sessions, or those when my torturers were desperate for information, was a man who rarely spoke, who tried to keep in the shadows. He spoke with a foreign accent, advising them what to do, how long to do it. Sometimes, however, he seemed to love his job so much that instead of just instructing my torturers he came forward and did it himself. I swore that I would never forget his face and I did not. When I arrived in Lima yesterday I saw the face on the front of the newspaper. He was younger in the photograph: thirty, nearly forty years younger perhaps. But the same man, without doubt.'

'And I could find him in La Paz?'

The guerilla leader hesitated. 'I said Heiner was in La Paz. I didn't necessarily say you could find him.'

'What do you mean?'

'In Bolivia, Heiner enjoys massive political protection.

As I said, he works for the government, tortures for them. God knows how else he is involved. So when you get to Bolivia, you have three problems. One: how to find him. Two: how to deal with him. Three: how to get away after. It won't be easy.'

'What do you mean, "When I get to Bolivia"?' asked Laporte, pouring them each a drink. The *guerillero* took the glass.

'I have already made arrangements for you to go to La Paz.'

'How?'

'I myself left La Paz in a stolen car, walked across the border and was flown into Lima by plane. That plane is still here. The pilot, in any case, could not have left last night. When I saw the newspaper this morning and spoke to Pacheco, I asked the pilot to wait in case he had a passenger for the return trip. I have also arranged a guide to take you across the border and transport you into La Paz. After that, you break contact with that cell of the movement.'

'And when I get to La Paz?'

'Already arranged, by telephone. A *compañera* is already expecting you, someone who is very trusted, a very dear colleague in the struggle.'

'What's his name?' asked Laporte.

'Her name,' said Guillermo, 'is Carmen.'

10 *La Paz, Bolivia*

Carmen finished checking in the honeymoon couple from Norfolk, Virginia, went to the side of the reception desk, and picked up the phone. It was the third time she had tried the number since she had received the call fifty minutes before. Each time it had been engaged. She dialled the number and waited for the ringing tone, leaning against

241

the desk. She felt tired, the inside of her thighs stiff. She smiled at a guest and heard the ringing tone.

Not that she could complain about the way her muscles ached. Anderson was good, very good. And though he had said nothing, everything about him confirmed the suspicion that had been growing in her mind. The Texan was waiting. As she was waiting. Knowing something was building up, not knowing what. Anderson knowing he would soon be involved. She knowing she was already involved. The bastard Guillermo Pertierro, she thought.

Heiner answered the phone without identifying either himself or the number.

'He's been in contact,' she said non-commitally.

'When?' he asked.

'Nearly an hour ago. International. He didn't say where he was.'

'What did he say?'

'He said he was sending someone to La Paz, had instructed them to make contact with me at the hotel.' It was, she suddenly thought, as if Heiner already knew what she was telling him.

'Who?'

Heiner already knew who, she was certain. 'He didn't say.'

'When?'

'He said the man will arrive sometime tonight. He'll contact me here at the hotel sometime tomorrow morning.'

Pertierro's route in reverse, Heiner thought. Light plane to the Peru-Bolivia border, cross into the country at night, and car into La Paz.

'That's good,' he said. 'He'll probably show at around nine o'clock, want a safe house, somewhere to hole up till the following morning.'

It was as if, Carmen thought again, Heiner knew what was happening, what was about to happen. Without, she suddenly thought, being aware that he knew.

'Let me know the moment he contacts you.' He thanked her, put the phone down, closed the door of the study and

242

returned to his desk, sitting hunched in thought in the chair. Schmeltz had telephoned that morning, confirmed it was the son, informed him that the Americans were taking care of him. That evening, Schmeltz had said, and they guaranteed it would all be over. He got up, walked to the window. But now Carmen had telephoned to say that Guillermo Pertierro had been in touch, that Pertierro was sending somebody to her. He knew it was the son, had known all along that it would happen, from the first moment he had read the details of Pertierro's supposed death in the car crash. So how could Pertierro be sending Laporte if the Americans were taking care of him? Either, he considered, Pertierro had begun his arrangements before the Americans had completed theirs. Or, the cloud passed over his mind, something had gone wrong with the American plan.

He turned back to the desk. Three calls to make, he knew. One to the Texan called Anderson, putting him on stand-by. The second to Schmeltz, to check what was happening in Lima, to recall him to La Paz if necessary. To recall him to La Paz as a matter of urgency, he decided. The third call, if Schmeltz confirmed that the Americans had screwed their operation, to have Corrigan and Bailey pulled off. To let the son come to him. For him to take care of him. Personally. As he had taken care of the father.

11   *Lima, Peru*

The secretary's voice on the intercom woke him up. In the fraction of a second before he was fully conscious, Corrigan was back in the Mercedes, leaving Mollendo, trying to sleep, the significance of what the book-keeper had told Schmeltz, of what Schmeltz had repeated to him, keeping him awake.

He crossed the room and opened the door. Bailey was

standing outside. Corrigan brought him in and shut the door.

'What's happening?' he asked.

Bailey helped himself to a chair. 'Everything and nothing,' he replied, the relief beginning to show in his face. 'I've just heard from Washington. Apparently they're not happy with the fact that the boys fucked up on the operation this afternoon, though they've cleared both of us of responsibility for that.'

'So what's happening now?' Corrigan asked again.

'I'm being pulled out, you're back in charge.' Bailey's delivery was flat and without sentiment.

'What do you mean?'

'What I've just said. I've been ordered to return to Washington and you're back in sole charge of the case. Apparently Washington feels that the local station is perfectly capable of handling the entire affair. I'm flying out tonight.'

'And your boys?'

'Pulling out as well. Separate flight, of course.'

'What the hell's going on?' Corrigan was already reaching for a fresh Havana.

'Christ knows,' conceded Bailey, 'I certainly don't.' He reached into his jacket pocket and handed Corrigan an envelope. 'The son,' he said. 'Good luck.'

The phone on the new confidential number rang. Bailey shook hands and left. Corrigan closed and locked the door behind him, put the unopened envelope on the desk and picked up the receiver.

'I have the information you want.'

The contact in Washington did not identify himself. Almost, Corrigan thought, as if he did not wish to be associated with the information he was about to pass on. Corrigan reached for a note-pad, knowing he had been correct in splitting the enquiries on the La Paz phone list. 'OK, I'm ready.'

The caller read out the numbers Corrigan had given him earlier that afternoon, following each with an identification

244

and an address, spelling each word to avoid mistakes. When the list was complete Corrigan thanked the man and began to put the phone down.

'Joe,' there was concern in the caller's voice, 'I hope you know what you're playing at.'

'Routine,' Corrigan told him, 'just routine.'

He put the phone down and stared at the list. Five calls, five different numbers. A sixth to come. He could imagine Heiner, safe in his fortress in La Paz, making the calls. Lunchtime, he remembered, Heiner probably taking a glass of Löwenbräu.

He remembered what else had happened that day, what other information Heiner would have been in possession of. The documents would have arrived, Heiner would have had them stacked neatly in an inner sanctum, the guard doubled. And the mid-day paper would have carried the first article about the supposed death of the guerilla leader, Guillermo Pertierro. He wondered why he had thought of the Bolivian, whether it was relevant, how it would fit in to the tangle of moves and counter-moves, then concentrated on the telephone calls.

Five calls at the moment, he thought again, five different numbers. Two he already knew, three new, one to come.

From a drawer he took a sheet of paper and wrote the numbers again, grouping them into sections. Beside each number he wrote a description of the identification of the number. In the first section he wrote two numbers. Call number one: the previous number of his direct line, the number that had made the check possible. Call number two: Heinrich Schmeltz's new contact number in Lima. End of Section One, he thought. Entirely logical.

He switched his attention to the next section, the next series of calls. Call number three: the headquarters of the *Guardia Civil* in Lima. Heiner contacting his source in the local police. Corrigan remembered what had taken place later that night, knew what the call was about. Heiner arranging to remove the guard from the house at Chaclicayo for Schmeltz to check for missing documents. A

245

dangerous call to make at the source's office. Call number four: the Sheraton Hotel in Lima. The suspicion crossed his mind that the call had been to Bailey. He dismissed it, seeing the connection with the previous call. Heiner's contact in the *Guardia Civil*, obviously high-ranking, probably a general. A coded call to the general's office. The general leaving his headquarters in a prearranged procedure and taking the real call at the Sheraton twenty minutes later, using an assumed name and wearing civilian clothes. End of Section Two, he thought. Entirely logical.

He turned his attention to the next section. The next call. Call number five. Entirely illogical.

The confidential phone rang. He picked it up, heard the voice of the contact in New York, wrote down the details the man gave him, thanked him, and transferred the information to the sheet of paper under the next heading, Section Four. Call number six. Entirely illogical.

He stood up, staring at the numbers, concentrating on the last two, trying to make sense of them. They had taken him by surprise when he had received them from the La Paz contact. Now his new knowledge confused him even more. He chewed on the Havana, thinking of the calls separately, then as part of a pattern, listing them mentally under the same section. He pushed back his chair and walked to the window, looking back at the sheet of paper, beginning to see a connection. Knowing it was not possible. The Havana was in shreds. He returned to his desk, took another, went to the wall-safe, and took out the envelope containing the biography of Jean Laporte, the father. He read it, re-read it, then checked the relevant pages of the full Heiner file. When he had finished reading he locked the safe and returned to his desk.

Slowly and deliberately he drew a box round the fifth and sixth calls, placing them in the same section, grouping them as he had grouped the others. Then he went to the window and looked back at the last connection.

Logical, he thought, entirely logical.

A secret, he thought, a secret too precious for even

Bailey to know. A secret known only to Washington. To a handful of people in Washington. Now he knew. He looked at the list again. 'Jesus Christ,' he breathed, reaching for another cigar. 'Jesus fucking Christ.'

The strands were pulling together, becoming stronger, forging into a pattern. A definite pattern. Corrigan allowed his mind to play with the connections, then transferred the outline to paper, confirming the strengths, eliminating the weaknesses, till he was satisfied he was correct. Only then did he reach for a match, light the paper, crumple the burnt remains into the waste basket and telephone Heinrich Schmeltz.

The voice that answered spoke Spanish with a harsh guttural accent and confirmed what Corrigan expected. Schmeltz was no longer available. It was not known when he would return.

His secretary was not in the outer office. Corrigan telephoned airport enquiries and asked about flights to La Paz that evening. There were two flights, he was told, a scheduled AeroPeru flight at 18.30 arriving 21.15 and a Lloyd Boliviano flight, not scheduled because of delays, estimated departure 20.00, arriving La Paz 22.45. He picked up the confidential line and dialled a contact at the airport. By the time a colleague of the man fetched him from the international departure lounge it was ten minutes past five. Corrigan asked him to check two flight lists: passengers on AeroPeru flight PL 616 from La Paz to Lima on the Wednesday, and that evening's AeroPeru flight PL 615 Lima-La Paz. The computerised check took less than a minute. The name Heinrich Schmeltz did not appear on either list. The only name which appeared on both belonged to an Argentinian, a native of Buenos Aires.

When the passenger had made the booking for the flight that evening, the contact confirmed, he had been asked as a matter of routine for a telephone number in case of flight changes. The number the passenger from Buenos Aires had given was the Lima contact number for Heinrich Schmeltz.

Corrigan put the phone down, waited for another line, dialled Lloyd Boliviano and reserved a seat on the eight o'clock La Paz flight.

'Your reservation is confirmed, sir,' the official at the airline desk informed him. 'What name?'

'Donaldson,' said Corrigan, 'Michael James Donaldson.'

His secretary knocked on the door, pushed it open and said she was leaving. He wished her goodnight then telephoned his wife, uncertain what he was going to tell her. They talked briefly about the christening, then he said he had been unexpectedly called away for a few days. For the first time in their married life, he knew, she wanted to ask him where he was going, what he was going to do. Knew she would not. For the first time in his life, he knew, he wanted to tell her. Knew he could not.

Sometimes, she had told him earlier that day, she knew him better than he knew himself, knew when he was worried, knew when he was lying.

'Is it anything to do with the telephone call when we were having lunch?' she asked.

'Yes,' he replied.

'And the message you got at the baptism?'

'Yes,' he replied again.

'Joe,' there was fear in her voice, 'do you know what you're doing?'

His decision, Bailey had told him. Not his decision, he knew. He remembered standing over the body in the kitchen, glad he had made the decision, glad he would not have to make it again.

'I'll take care.' He knew he had not answered her question.

'When will you be back?'

'Monday afternoon,' he told her, not knowing how he knew. He said goodbye and put the phone down.

The building was quiet. He opened the wall-safe and took out a large brown envelope containing three passports. He selected two, one in the name of Michael James

Donaldson, and replaced the third. From a box in the safe he chose three rubber stamps bearing the insignia and letterings of the immigration services of certain countries. He adjusted the dates on the stamps, and on the passport of Michael James Donaldson stamped the information that the bearer had left Canada on January 11th, transitted the United States the same day, and arrived in Lima, Peru on January 12th. In the second passport he stamped the information that the holder had left Bogota, Colombia on January 2nd and arrived in La Paz, Bolivia the same day. If he was using one name on the outward trip, experience had taught him, it was always useful to have the insurance of a different identity for the run home.

From another envelope in the safe he took ten thousand United States dollars in used notes. He placed the passport in the name of Donaldson in his jacket, folded one thousand dollars into his wallet, and concealed the second passport and the remainder of the money in the false bottom of his briefcase.

As an afterthought, he tucked the envelope containing the sheets of information and photograph of Jean Laporte, senior, which he had removed from the Heiner file, plus the envelope containing the information on the son which Bailey had given him but which he had not opened, into the inside pocket of his jacket, and left for the airport.

It was logical, he thought as he drove out of the city towards the lights of Jorge Chavez, that Heiner should be in La Paz. It was logical that Schmeltz should be hurrying to join him. It was also logical, according to his interpretation of the events of that afternoon, that Laporte would also be heading for La Paz.

The only thing that was not logical was that he, Joe Corrigan, was also going there.

Chapter Six

Saturday, February 5th 1983

Laporte paid the cab driver, tried to fight off the headache of the altitude sickness and the waves of fatigue and entered the foyer of the El Dorado hotel. He wondered how the contact would react, what use the contact would be.

He had travelled non-stop since he had left the brothel at Cinco y Media with the guerilla leader, Guillermo Pertierro, in the middle of the previous afternoon, retracing in reverse the route the Bolivian had taken earlier in the week. The last contact had dropped him in the main presidential square fifteen minutes before, breaking the chain, satisfying Pertierro's request that no-one who helped him enter the country clandestinely should know a single detail about his next point of contact.

There were two receptionists on duty: a middle-aged man smartly dressed in the yellow and gold livery of the house, and a young, attractive woman wearing a yellow dress and matching chiffon scarf. Laporte settled in the circle of chairs round the foyer, waited till the woman was alone at the desk, then walked quickly forward. The receptionist looked up at him. On her lapel was a badge. On the badge was the name he was seeking.

'Carmen?' he asked cautiously.

'*Si, señor*, I'm Carmen.'

Laporte's manner was relaxed and confident, disguising the tension he felt. 'A friend of mine said you might be able to help me.' He kept his voice low, under control. The receptionist looked puzzled.

'I'm sorry, I don't understand. What friend?'

'His name is Guillermo.'

The woman's expression did not change. 'I'm sorry, Guillermo who?' The other receptionist returned to the desk, passing behind Carmen. Laporte changed the subject, suddenly afraid he was wrong, had the wrong Carmen.

'And how much is a double room?' She told him. The other receptionist went to the far end of the counter. 'Guillermo Pertierro,' said Laporte.

She wondered who he was, why Heiner wanted him. Knew what Heiner would do to him. Wondered how Heiner knew. Nine o'clock, he had said, the man sent by Guillermo Pertierro would arrive at nine o'clock in the morning. She passed the stranger a registration card to fill in.

'I've been expecting you,' she said quietly, saw him relax a little. 'What do you want?'

For the first time he knew he had the right contact, knew he was safe. 'Somewhere to hide up, probably until tomorrow. After that, a little help. I'm not sure.' He would ask for a safe house, Heiner had said, would say he wanted to hide up till the following morning.

'Go outside, turn right,' she told him. 'There's a small bar, the Café Apurimac, two blocks up. I'll see you there in fifteen minutes.'

Carmen watched him leave, removed the card he had completed, and went to the telephone at the end of the reception desk. Heiner answered immediately. As if, she thought, he was waiting.

'He's here,' she said. 'He signed the hotel registration card in the name of Velasco.'

Heiner ignored the name. 'Where is he now?'

'At a café two blocks away. He wants a safe house till tomorrow.' Again, Heiner did not seem surprised. 'What do you want me to do?' she asked.

Heiner swivelled in his chair, considering the options. Get him while you can, his caution urged, take him on the way to the safe house. Too dangerous, his instinct told him, too many unknowns in the street, wait till he's in a corner. He saw the middle way, the reason for taking it.

254

Let Carmen take him to the safe house, let him talk to the four men Carmen had told him were there. He needed to know what the son knew, what the son might not tell even his tormentors. What he might tell the men in the safe house. Run him into his hole, he decided, take him at the proper time. Cover him in case he moved.

'Take him to the safe house,' he told Carmen. 'I'll have it staked out in fifteen minutes.'

Carmen confirmed the address and went into the rear office. The chief receptionist was inside. 'Alfredo,' she said to him, 'I have to slip out, can you cover for me?' The man nodded.

'No problem, it's very quiet.' She thanked him and left. It was two minutes to ten.

2

Joe Corrigan let the phone ring for two minutes before he was satisfied the La Paz contact was not in his office, then finished the black coffee and fruit juice which he had had delivered to his room on the fourth floor of the El Dorado. He had arrived later than he had planned, the flight to La Paz had been delayed and he had not got to bed till nearly three.

The remainder of the breakfast was cold. He showered, dressed and went downstairs to collect the hire car he had ordered. At the reception desk, where he had registered under the name Donaldson, he placed the envelope containing the US dollars in the hotel safe and bought two maps from the middle-aged man at the desk. The attractive dark-haired receptionist at the other end of the counter was busy with two Guatemalan tourists. Then he left the hotel and drove out of the city, following the road Guillermo Pertierro had taken three mornings before.

It was a route he knew well. Less than fifteen minutes after leaving the hotel he saw the familiar outline of the escarpment. He drove two hundred metres past, parked the car off the road and skirted back, checking there was no one around. The cache was as he had left it. He satisfied himself that the hiding place had not been discovered then reconstructed, returned to the car and drove back to the city. At the hotel he parked the car, deciding to take a walk, acclimatise himself again to the feel of La Paz, before he called the contact. He left the parking lot, turned right out of the hotel and walked up the street. It was two minutes to ten.

3

Jean Laporte had finished his second coffee when he saw Carmen at the door of the café. He paid the bill and joined her outside. 'We have to hurry,' she said, 'I can't be away from the hotel too long.' On the corner she waved down a taxi. The streets and pavements around them were jammed with cars and people. Carmen gave the driver an address and the cab pulled away, then stopped at a set of traffic lights on the junction. They waited ten seconds, then the lights turned to green.

Joe Corrigan was halfway across the road when he saw the lights begin to change. He hurried to reach the pavement, sandwiched between an Indian woman with a baby strapped to her back and a tourist with a large Nikon camera. A cab which had stopped at the lights began to edge forward. For half a second Corrigan was staring straight into the back of the vehicle. Two passengers, his mind registered automatically: one in semi-profile in the shadows on the far side; the other, a male, looking in his direction. Looking at him. He knew he had seen the face somewhere before. Then the cab pulled away.

Jean Laporte saw the man in the street looking at him, knew he had seen the face somewhere before, then the cab pulled off, down the street, past the hotel, and he relaxed back into his seat.

4

Joe Corrigan walked to the end of the block then turned back to the hotel. As he reached the reception desk a tall man with a tanned, healthy complexion left the lift and handed in his room key. There was, Corrigan noted, only one receptionist on duty.

'No Carmen today?' joked the man. Though his Spanish was fluent, Corrigan sensed it was a second language, that the other man was a North American like himself.

The male receptionist shrugged his shoulders. '*Las señoritas*,' he returned the joke, 'you know what they're like. She had to slip out for a moment.'

Corrigan asked for his key, glancing down as the other American handed in his key, and went to his room.

The telephone rang twice before the contact answered. 'Any news?' Corrigan asked.

'Some,' replied the contact, noting that Corrigan had come through on a direct-dial local call rather than a long distance call connected by an operator. 'No luck so far with the private number. I should have some more on that this afternoon. But the call from the hotel is a different matter.' Corrigan waited, pen ready.

'The call was made from a room registered to a Mr George Anderson, aged thirty-four, from Houston, Texas.' He spelled out the details of the name and address in full. At Corrigan's request the contact repeated the information, together with the passport details which had been entered on the hotel registration form.

The fact that an American, or an alleged American, was involved did not concern Corrigan. 'When did he check in?' he asked.

'The day the calls were made. Last Monday.'

'And when did he leave?' The assumption was automatic.

'He didn't. He's still there.'

Corrigan's reply did not betray him. 'Which room?' he asked.

'513.'

The pieces tumbled into place. The number on the key at the reception desk. The American who spoke fluent Spanish, joked with the clerk, asked about someone called Carmen. The number of the key on the desk. 513.

'One other thing,' the contact added. 'It's probably not important but you may as well know. My source says that Anderson is screwing somebody at the hotel.'

'Who?' Corrigan already knew, had to ask.

'The receptionist, someone called Carmen.'

'Any significance in that?'

'Probably not,' said the contact. 'Anderson is an American, plenty of dollars. Carmen is probably just a good lay.'

Corrigan thanked the contact, said he would be in touch, and went downstairs to the foyer. The key to Room 513 was in place, there was still only one receptionist at the desk. He chose a large, comfortable armchair, ordered coffee and the day's newspapers, and settled down for his one lead to return.

5

The safe house was a flat above a shop, entered by a flight of stairs on the left-hand side of the shop, at the foot of a gently sloping street. Carmen introduced Laporte to the four men inside and left, wishing him luck.

The men locked the door behind her and settled back round the table in the middle of the room overlooking the street. Round the room were beds which also served as seats. To the left was another room which he assumed

258

was the kitchen, a table in the centre and a camp bed on the opposite wall.

The guerilla whom Carmen had introduced as Lucho pulled Laporte a chair and the Frenchman sat down. He remembered the name. Lucho had been with Guillermo Pertierro in the torture house, had escaped with him. He remembered what the guerilla leader had said about Lucho, how he coughed up the blood of the tin mines as he slept. He looked at the other three. Another man, the one Carmen had introduced as Paco, had also been in the torture house. The other two, whom Carmen had called Jaime and Roberto, had not been mentioned by Pertierro.

Lucho pushed him a coffee and some bread. 'Guillermo said we could help you. How?'

The coffee was sweet and reviving. Laporte drained it and asked for another. For the next fifteen minutes he told them his story, omitting any information which might incriminate anyone.

When he had finished, Lucho asked one question. 'Why does Guillermo think we can help you?'

'Because the man who killed my father also tortured Guillermo, and probably you.'

They waited for him to explain. When he had told them, Lucho made more coffee and returned to the table. 'We will do what we can. But there are other things. You entered Bolivia illegally, so your passport won't have the correct stamps.' Laporte nodded. 'It's important for you to have them,' continued Lucho. 'If you're stopped, even for the most innocent reason, and you don't have them, then you're in trouble. You have the passport?' Laporte gave it to him. 'Jaime has a good connection in the business. He and Roberto will arrange it this afternoon. Until it's done, you should stay here. Besides, you need a rest. When did you last sleep?'

The altitude sickness throbbed in his head, slowing down his mental process. Laporte tried to remember, calculating backwards. 'Three nights ago,' he said.

'Tomorrow, perhaps even tonight, you can start work again. But today you sleep.'

The bed in the adjoining room was hard but welcome. Laporte lay between the rough blankets, allowing the sleep to overtake him, relaxing from the altitude sickness. The last time he had slept, he realised, was in Maria's flat. Now he saw her face again. The sleep closed in on him. He panicked, his body jerking. Her face faded, replaced by the thin face of the book-keeper, then of Josef Heiner. The faces were drifting before him. Guillermo Pertierro and the meeting at Cinco y Media.

The last face he saw was the face of the man on the pavement that morning. He suddenly remembered where he had seen it before. The face of the man in the Lima Sheraton, the man who had taken his table at breakfast. The man who looked as tired and worried as himself. He wondered who the man was, what he was doing in La Paz.

Beneath the table in the centre of the room was a wooden box. In it he saw six sub-machine guns and a cluster of hand grenades. Then he fell asleep.

He woke only once. Some time, he guessed, in the middle of the afternoon. The sun was slanting through the crack in the curtains. He lay still, hearing the voices in the other room, counting them. Four voices. Jaime and Roberto had returned from dealing with his passport. He rolled over, pulled himself up and struggled to his feet. The thudding in his head had eased slightly and his body was beginning to shake off the nausea of the altitude sickness. He stumbled into the front room and flopped on to the sofa beneath the window.

'How do you feel?' asked Lucho.

'Could be worse, but could be a lot better. How did it go with the passport?'

It was Jaime who answered. 'Fine. They'll be ready tonight.' Laporte muttered his thanks and went back to bed.

6

Corrigan got up, stretched his legs, and returned to the seat in the foyer. Four hours since he had known the identity of the contact. Four hours since he had begun his wait at the hotel. Changing his position occasionally, partly to throw off suspicion, partly to relieve himself of the anxiety which he knew was inevitable. But four hours nevertheless.

He ordered more sandwiches and coffee and resumed his wait.

7 *Lima, Peru*

No news. No news at all.

On the beach below the cliffs she could see the sand and sea crowded with people enjoying the weekend. Maria turned away from the balcony and went back into the lounge.

No news since yesterday afternoon.

And then nothing except the message, left in a hurry at her office, saying that he would contact her as soon as he could. No indication where he was, what he was doing. She had only been out of the office for forty minutes, less than forty minutes, and in that time she had missed him. She sat down, did not know what to do. In a void, she thought, as if she was in a void. Waiting. As if they were both in a void, the thought suddenly changed. As if they were both waiting.

The telephone rang. She picked it up, heard Pacheco. He was in his office, he said, wondered if she was doing anything, if she wanted to join him. She knew he was also waiting, knew she did not want to leave the flat in case Jean phoned, in case Jean came back. Knew, she did not know how or why, that he would not. Knew something would be served by seeing Pacheco. She told him she would be at the office in half an hour.

The streets in the commercial section of the city were quiet, almost deserted. Even the Plaza San Martin was almost empty. Partly because of the *siesta*, it would come back to life when the shops re-opened in the late afternoon. Partly because of the heat of the summer day.

Pacheco let her in and offered her coffee. She knew immediately there was a reason for inviting her, knew he was worried like her. Knew there was a reason for his worry. He made them both a coffee from the electric kettle in the corner of the next office and stood by the window, looking out. Something had happened, he began, something which might involve Jean. She waited.

A priest had disappeared, he said. Not Jean, he added immediately, but not just any priest. One of the priests on the study party of which Jean was a member. She remembered Laporte's original reason for coming to Peru. Not just any member of the study party, Pacheco went on. The one that the teachers in the school in the *barriada* had told his reporters had been Jean's best friend. The one they called Father Michael.

More, she knew, there was more.

He had been worried. Of course he had been worried. The last anyone knew of Father Michael, he said, had been a message he had left at the monastery on Friday morning, suggesting Jean met him for lunch. Maria recalled Jean telling her of the arrangement, knew it was one hour after he had been due to meet Pacheco himself in the café in Calle Cuscena, the meeting about which he had said Pacheco would tell him nothing.

'And?' she asked.

He assumed, Pacheco continued, that if there was a link between the disappearance of Father Michael and Jean it had to be connected to Jean's hunt for Josef Heiner. He had therefore assumed that someone was after Jean, had meant to deal with Jean, but had got Father Michael instead. Maria could not understand the logic, asked him to explain. Simple, said Pacheco, think of what Jean was wearing. Ordinary clothes, not dressed like a priest. If somebody had been told to get the priest, they would have got the one dressed as a priest. Would have got Father Michael.

She knew it was logical, knew there was more.

Except, he went on, he had checked with the monastery, got the name and address of the church in Puerto Rico where Father Michael was a community priest.

She knew what he was going to say.

He had phoned them. Had been told they had not heard of a study tour of the Third World. That they had not heard of a trip to Peru. That they did not know a Father Michael.

'So where does that leave Jean?' she asked. Pacheco knew something, she sensed, something he was not supposed to tell her.

'Jean's lunch with Father Michael was at one o'clock yesterday afternoon. Father Michael must have disappeared somewhere round that time because he left the study tour at twelve and said he would be back at two-thirty.'

She knew he was about to tell her why he had asked for the meeting in the café in Calle Cuscena.

'Jean had another meeting afterwards,' he spoke quietly. 'At two-thirty. I cannot tell you where, or with whom, but he made that meeting.'

The same time, Maria thought, that Father Michael was due back with the study party. 'How do you know?' she asked.

'I cannot tell you,' he said, 'partly because it is better for you that you do not know, partly because I myself do not know much more.' The coffee was cold. 'All I know,' he went on, 'is that Jean made the meeting, and that at that meeting certain arrangements were made. I do not know the details of those arrangements. But I do know that later yesterday afternoon Jean kept them.'

After, she thought, he had left the message for her in

her office. 'So what does that mean about Jean and the priest who disappeared?' she asked.

'What it means,' said Pacheco carefully, 'is that somebody, I don't know who, knows Jean is after Heiner, knows he is getting close to him, that Father Michael was ordered to deal with him.' She knew who. Remembered Laporte's description of the network, remembered the organisations, the one organisation in particular, that Laporte had said Heiner worked for.

'I think,' said Pacheco, 'that Jean now knows they are after him.' He hesitated, unsure how to phrase his next statement, 'I think Jean dealt with Father Michael.'

Something else, she thought, something she ought to know, did know.

'And where is Jean now?'

'I think,' said Pacheco, 'that Jean is in La Paz.'

She knew she could not ask him any more. 'Sometimes,' she remembered she had told Laporte, the evening after their assault on the house at Chaclicayo, the evening they had found the documents, 'I know you better than you know yourself. I know what you are, who you are. What you are thinking, what you are doing.' She had paused, she remembered, knowing what she had been about to say, knowing she did not understand it. 'I know what you should be thinking, what you should be doing.' One day, she had known then, knew again now, she would know what she had meant. Until then she could only wait.

She wondered who else was waiting.

8 *La Paz, Bolivia*

The Texan lunched late, following the Spanish tradition, in a small but expensive restaurant in the centre of the city, drinking mineral water instead of alcohol. Halfway through the main course he rose, asked the head waiter if he could use the telephone and, precisely on the half-hour as instructed, made his hourly check call to the hotel. He waited patiently while the clerk checked.

'*Si, señor*, there is a message.'

'Tell me,' said the Texan.

'A friend of yours called a few minutes ago. He said you would be phoning. He asked that you leave a number where he can contact you.'

Anderson had been expecting the call since Heiner had put him on stand-by the previous afternoon. He gave the hotel clerk the number of the restaurant, slid ten dollars into the hand of the head waiter, told him there would be a telephone call in the next few minutes, and resumed his lunch.

Three minutes after the check call the head waiter informed him he was wanted on the telephone. The Texan left the table, recognised the voice immediately, and listened carefully to the instructions. At one point he was asked if he wished to write down any of the details. He replied that he did not. The information was good, he thought, the organisation as strict and as regimented as it had been at Portachuela. Different, of course, entirely different, but the same systematic approach. He remembered how the details had worked at Portachuela. The position to which he had been directed was perfect. The helicopter had arrived precisely on time, hovered for thirty seconds while an obstruction on the ground was cleared, precisely as Heiner said it would. Giving him the time he needed. The four five-round bursts from the Browning BAR, the tail rotor disintegrating. The assassination looking like an accident, just as Heiner had planned. One problem, he had learned later, one last minute change of plan which had rendered Portachuela an expensive failure. But it had not been a fault of planning. He hoped the details of the operation on which Heiner was now briefing him would go as smoothly.

At the end of the conversation he returned to his table, finished the main course, paid the bill, making sure he asked for a receipt, and left.

9

Precisely five minutes after the hour, as he had done every sixty minutes since he had taken his position in the foyer, Corrigan crossed to the line of the telephones, dialled the hotel number, and asked to speak to reception.

'Good afternoon,' he repeated the familiar procedure. 'I'm expecting a message from Mr Anderson, Room 513.' He made the request vague, waited while the clerk checked, expecting the answer he had received four times already.

'Are you the gentleman who left the message earlier?' The question took Corrigan by surprise. 'That's right,' he replied instinctively.

'No, *señor*,' said the clerk, 'no more messages since he left the telephone number for you to phone him back as you requested.'

Corrigan did not hesitate. 'That's why I'm phoning again,' he said, 'it didn't seem to be the right number. I don't suppose you could check it for me?'

The first lead, he was thinking, probably the only one. He wondered what he would do with it. 'I'm sorry, *señor*,' said the clerk, 'I threw it away.'

Something moving, Corrigan cursed, something picking up. And he was out of it. Did not know what, or where, or when. He returned to his chair and ordered a beer. The first lead, the only lead, and it had gone from him. Anderson, he thought, the man from Texas, the man from whose room Heiner had made the telephone call. A private job, he assumed, brought in by Heiner in case of trouble. Probably without anyone else in the organisation knowing. A back door if anything went wrong. Or, he thought, an insurance if everything else failed. It was unlikely, he conceded, that Anderson would return to the hotel before the job, whatever it was, was done.

He cursed again, told himself to calm down, think it out. Made himself sit back, work it out. Ask himself why he hadn't done the obvious. He wanted the son, wanted to get to Heiner because that was where he knew the son would eventually show, was using the Texan called Anderson to get to Heiner. But he already had Heiner's telephone number in La Paz. He wondered why he had not simply called the man, arranged a meeting. There was a reason, of course. The manner in which he had found the number. He could explain that away, of course, even explain away his presence in La Paz. But there was something else, he knew, without knowing exactly what. Connected to the secret he had untangled from the web of telephone calls Heiner had made earlier that week. Connected to the secret Washington had kept to itself.

He thought again about the telephone calls, about the two calls that mattered. Calls five and six. Remembered the box he had drawn around them, linking them, exposing the secret. Illogical, he had thought when he had considered them separately. Entirely logical, he had decided when he had considered them together.

The foyer was quiet. He remembered the envelope Bailey had given him, the brief on the son, the priest whose execution he had ordered, which he still had not read. He opened it, put to one side the smaller cellophane envelope stapled to the report which he assumed was the photograph Bailey had also promised, and read the three pages in full, read them again, then concentrated on the biographical details contained in the fourth paragraph of the first page.

The first fingers of frost touched him, alerted him. He knew the feeling, read the words again, looking for the link. From his jacket pocket he took the second envelope, containing the report on the father which he had copied from the Heiner file, removed the smaller envelope in which he had placed the photograph of the father, and began to read. Concentrating on the paragraphs covering the father's biographical details. Then checked again the biographical details of the son.

The ice was spreading through his body. He opened the two cellophane envelopes, one containing the photograph of the father, the other the photograph of the son, laid

267

them side-by-side on the table and studied them for a full minute.

'*Ich fragte ihn, ob er wieder kommen würde*,' the book-keeper had struggled to tell Schmeltz in the hotel room in Mollendo, '*Ich fragte ihn und er sagte, "Ich habe Ihnen gesagt, dass ich wieder komme."*'

'Jesus Christ,' he breathed, seeing, comprehending. Knowing at last why he had come to La Paz. 'Jesus fucking Christ.'

He returned the photographs to their cellophane envelopes and read again the full briefs on the father and son, concentrating this time on the section covering the father's return to occupied France and his subsequent capture and death. Then reconstructed in his own mind the events of the Friday afternoon and Saturday morning, beginning with Schmeltz's sudden departure for La Paz and ending with the telephone message to the man called Anderson which he had failed to intercept.

He knew it. Knew it all. As Carmen had sensed Heiner knew it all when she had relayed to him the movements of the stranger whom she had taken to the safe house. What would happen. When it would happen. The only thing he did not know was where.

He thought for two minutes, re-read two sentences in the father's report dealing with one specific stage of his return to France, and turned his attention to the reception desk in the foyer.

Anderson was screwing someone at the hotel, the La Paz contact had told him, a receptionist called Carmen. He remembered asking whether the information was significant. 'No,' the contact had said, 'Anderson is an American, plenty of dollars. Carmen is probably just a good lay.' Now Corrigan looked differently at the receptionist.

When he had left the hotel that morning there had been three receptionists on duty: the middle-aged man and two women, one more attractive than the other. Dark-haired, he remembered, matching scarf and dress. He had returned at ten, the Texan jokingly asking about Carmen.

He remembered the words of the male clerk. 'She had to go out for a moment.' Between the two times he had been in the street. At two minutes to ten. The man in the back of the cab at the traffic lights. The man in the photographs.

Jean Laporte.

Two faces in the cab. The second a woman, sitting back in the shadows as if she did not want to be seen. Dark hair. Attractive. Matching scarf and dress. A hotel uniform.

Carmen.

The foyer of the hotel was becoming busy. He looked across to the reception desk, where Carmen was booking in a French couple. Wondered whether she had indeed been the person in the car with Laporte that morning. And if so, how long it would take Josef Heiner to find out through her contact with the Texan. There was, he decided reluctantly, one short swift way of finding out. At least, he told himself, it would last no more than five minutes.

He crossed the foyer to the porter's desk, tipped the man for a sheaf of hotel notepaper and envelopes, and returned to his seat. On the paper he wrote a simple message, printing it in capital letters in case the receptionist had seen Anderson's handwriting.

> Carmen. Must see you urgently. Please
> come up immediately.

He signed the note with the initials G.A., put the time on the bottom of the page, placed the note in an envelope, sealed it, and addressed it simply to 'Carmen,' marking it urgent.

The foyer was still moderately busy. He waited till Carmen had left the reception desk to check something in the rear office and the middle-aged clerk was busy with a couple, then went to the desk.

'Excuse me,' he interrupted the clerk, friendly but firm, 'Room 513.'

The clerk reacted instinctively and gave him the key, turning back and smiling his apologies at the other guests.

Corrigan thanked him, waited till the man's attention was back on the couple, slipped the envelope onto the desk and went to the lift. The room was large and smelt of pine. He placed a 'Do Not Disturb' sign on the door knob, assuming Carmen would ignore it, switched on the bedside lamp and radio, pulled the curtains, then went into the bathroom and turned on the taps.

From the bedroom he took two chairs into the bathroom and placed them two feet apart and facing each other, jamming one between the toilet and wash basin so that it could not fall over. On the basin beside the chair he put a glass of water. In the fitted wardrobe in the bedroom, beneath a neat row of clothes, were two pairs of shoes. Corrigan took the lace from one shoe and laid it on the bedside table, on the side of the bed nearest the door. In a drawer he found a large handkerchief which he rolled from the corners and placed beside the shoelace. When he was satisfied with his preparations he took his position behind the door and waited.

The knock he was expecting came three minutes later. Corrigan checked through the spy-hole and saw Carmen outside. He opened the door, standing behind it, and she walked in, smiling and laughing. He stepped forward, one hand shutting the door behind her, the other smashing, open-palmed, onto the side of her head, almost knocking her out.

In the same movement he double-locked the door, caught her as she fell and carried her quickly to the bed, dumping her face down. She was groaning, not yet conscious enough to struggle. He knelt on top of her, right knee thrust into the small of her back, pinning her down, reaching for the handkerchief at the bedside, knotting it round her mouth, gagging the scream that would soon come. She was stirring. He reached for the shoelace, pulled her hands behind her back, tying the thumbs together, then picked her up as if she was weightless, carried her into the bathroom and dropped her on the chair which he had jammed between the toilet and wash basin. She was moaning, her eyes staring, fighting for consciousness. Corrigan shut the bathroom door, put Carmen's feet on the second chair so that her legs bridged the two and sat on the ankles, locking her in position.

She began to recover. He waited till she was looking him straight in the face, unable to avoid his stare, then spoke for the first time.

'I'm sorry, it was the only thing I could do.' He wondered why he felt the need to explain. 'Listen to me carefully. You're completely helpless. No-one is going to help you. The door is locked, so no-one can come in. We're in the bathroom, the music is turned up and the taps are on, so no-one will hear you if you make any trouble.'

He paused, allowing her time to consider what he had told her. 'I'm going to undo the gag, but I don't want you to scream. Is that understood?' She nodded. He bent forward and undid the handkerchief. Her head dropped, her mouth gulping in the air, the deep sobs engulfing her. He leaned forward again, took the glass of water from the basin and held it to her lips, gently helping her to drink.

'What do you want?' she asked at last, her body jerking with fear.

'Where is he?' Corrigan asked softly but firmly.

Carmen stared back at him, the spasms still convulsing her frame.

'I asked you. Where is he?'

She shook her head, wide-eyed, sobbing again. 'I don't know what you mean. Believe me, I don't.'

Corrigan repeated the question, using the same words, giving no clue to the answer he wanted. 'Where is he?' Her mind was going back to the last time.

'Where's who? Who are you talking about? Who are you?'

More words, Corrigan thought, each answer more words. She was already thinking, working out a strategy. He wondered what her mind was planning, which way it would turn.

'Where is he?' he asked again. 'That's all I want to know. Where is he?'

'I don't know.' She changed her answer, her confidence growing. He hadn't hurt her, except at the door, but not since he had started questioning her. Perhaps he was soft, perhaps he didn't want to hurt her.

He knew what she was thinking, edged forward a little, so that he was sitting on her knees, taking his feet off the ground. He raised his hand, as if to strike her. She recoiled, unable to move, locked into place.

'Don't worry,' he said in the same voice. 'I promise you I'm not going to touch you.' He took the glass of water and held it to her lips again. Soft, she thought, too soft. Time, Corrigan thought, running away.

'All I want to know is where he is, then you can go.'

'I don't know what you're talking about.'

Corrigan placed the glass back on the basin and sat still, watching her, not speaking. Don't worry, he had told her, I'm not going to touch you.

She returned his stare, knowing he had told her the truth, wondering why. Soft, she thought again, too soft. His face was eighteen inches from hers, his weight on her stretched legs, over her knees. She felt the load on the tendons at the back of her legs, waited for the question again, wondered how long it would take for him to lose his patience and ask her again.

He looked at his watch, then back at her. One minute.

The tendons were tighter, she could feel the pain. Soft, too soft. Two minutes. The pain was passing up her legs, into the base of her spine. Christ, she thought, why doesn't he speak, why doesn't he say something. Three minutes. Her body was screaming with his weight. The back of her legs, her spine, her back. Oh Christ, why doesn't he get off, do what the others did. Four minutes. The pain was excruciating. She wanted to turn away, move her body. His weight locked her immobile. She looked for a way out, the pain increasing. The plan came to her.

'Jiron Ica, number four. A flat above a shop.'

'Who?' he asked, not moving.

'You know who.' The pain was breaking her body. 'The man from Lima. The man Guillermo sent.'

He sat back, taking his weight from her knees, still pinning her feet to the seat, but allowing her to bend her legs. The pain subsided as it had come. 'How many are there?' he asked.

'I don't know,' she lied. 'When I was there only two. I think one of them was about to leave.' The strategy was forming in her mind. Get him there, get the bastard there. The boys will be on guard. One warning would be all they would need. She had seen them in action before.

He stared at her again. 'Listen to me for the last time. I want you to take me there. If I'm satisfied you're telling me the truth, you'll come to no harm. Otherwise I'll kill you. Do you understand.'

She nodded, the plan developing, seeing him walking into it.

'We leave by the trade entrance,' he said, 'then walk to the car park. You walk slightly in front of me. Now get up and turn around.'

Carmen did as she was instructed. Corrigan untied the shoelace from her thumbs, allowed her to massage the circulation back into her hands, then re-tied them in front of her. The corridor outside the suite was empty. He let her walk first, holding her by the arm, to the trade lift at the end. The hotel was quiet. They took the lift to the ground floor and left the building by a side entrance, meeting only one chambermaid on the way. When they reached the car he opened the passenger door and she slid in.

'Behind the steering wheel,' he told her.

She moved across and he got in beside her.

'You drive. But remember what I said. Any trouble and I'll kill you.' She nodded, not speaking. He untied her thumbs and gave her the car keys. Carmen started the engine and pulled away.

273

The sun was dropping in the sky, casting the shadows of the houses across the streets.

Five seconds, she thought. Less than five. Two seconds and the boys will know. Let us go past, let me get away. Then they'll take him.

They stopped at a set of traffic lights. Less than two seconds. One second, she thought. The lights changed and they moved off.

Corrigan sat sideways, watching her. Too quickly, he thought, she had begun to think too quickly in the bathroom. Given in too quickly, even under the pain of his body-weight. As if she was planning something. As if she was leading him into a trap. Half a second, less than half a second, was all she would need. Not that he would expect anything else. The people in the safe house would have arranged a warning system anyway. He just had to watch for it, not give her even a quarter of a second.

They climbed a hill, turned left at the top, swung to avoid a child playing in the road, and began to move downhill. On the front of the house on his right he saw the street sign. Jiron Ica.

'Is this it?' he asked. She nodded. 'Stop.' Carmen did as she was ordered. 'Tell me where it is.' She looked straight ahead.

'On the left, about a hundred metres down, on the corner of the junction. You can't see it very well from here. The house above the shop is painted lime green.'

He looked down the street, dropping gradually in front of them. In the late afternoon it was almost deserted. 'OK,' he said, 'but slowly.'

She nodded, started the engine and edged the car forward, steering the automatic with one hand, her left elbow resting casually on the open window of the driver's door. One second, she thought, just one second was all she needed. She saw the stake-out cars, measured the distance. Fifty metres.

Half a second, thought Corrigan, just half a second. He

274

saw the flat on the corner, measured the distance. A hundred metres.

Half a second, she brought the time down. Forty-five metres to go.

Something wrong. Something he should have seen. Something he had missed by concentrating on the woman. He glanced away from her, down the street. Still ninety metres to go.

Forty metres. She tensed herself.

She was on the wrong side of the road to signal the house. Coming from the wrong direction. Should have come along the road by the plaza opposite the safe house, exposed him to the watchers there, given them a chance to see him. Eighty-five metres to go. Still time to work it out.

Thirty-five metres to go. Thirty-five metres and she would have the bastard.

Christ. He saw it, saw them. The two vans. One only thirty metres in front of them, parked, apparently empty. The other at the bottom of the street by the plaza. Not just one traitor, he thought. Two. His hand whipped up, crushing her windpipe, doubling her up, chopping the slender curve at the back of her neck as she jerked forward, left hand jamming on the handbrake, stalling the engine.

Avoiding the stake-out. Avoiding Heiner's men.

Bastard. He cursed himself, cursed Heiner, cursed Carmen. She was gurgling, her lips tinged with a frothy red. She would be unconscious for three minutes, he estimated, perhaps four. He pulled her away from the wheel, the sudden exertion making him breath hard in the thin air, twisted her onto the floor, then slid across into the driver's seat.

The street in front was quiet, there had been no reaction from the look-out vehicle closest to them. The watchers, he knew, would be concealed in the back, concentrating on the safe house. He re-started the car and drove down the hill, past the first van, slowing at the crossroads, glancing at the safe house. Looking left and right, seeing the stake-out vehicles, saw they were placed exactly where he would have placed them, then accelerated away slowly, not drawing attention to himself, past the last stake-out car down the hill from the flat. The plan already forming in his head, his brain noting the geographic details he would need later. He had already decided his position. The tall building site, the tower block still under construction, overlooking the entire area, the heavy wire mesh surrounding the site.

Carmen was beginning to stir. He drove two blocks, bound and gagged her, then drove out of the city, following the road he had taken that morning. Near the point where he had stopped earlier he checked that the road was deserted, pulled off, and switched off the engine. The flat, almost horizonless, country around them was bleak and hard, swept by the winds of the *altiplano*.

Corrigan knelt on the seat, held Carmen under the arms and pulled her up till she was facing him. Her make-up had smudged across her face, the blood colouring the soft tissue of the skin round her lips. Her dress, the matching chiffon scarf still round her neck, had ridden up over her thighs. He reached forward and pulled it down, covering her legs. No reaction, he noted, no jerking away from the physical contact, no fear at what might have been the threat of sexual abuse. Almost, he thought, as if she was immune.

'One question,' he said, his voice as flat and unemotional as it had been in the bathroom. 'One question.'

The first tinge of doubt began to seep into her mind, touching her soul. For the first time she wondered how he knew so much, how he had found her in the first place, discovered her secret. Who he was.

'Fuck off,' she said.

He knew she had to die, knew there was no alternative. She had set him up, tried to kill him. And if that was not enough she could recognise him, identify him. He wondered if there was another reason, asked the question.

'You betrayed him,' he said, 'just like the other one.' It was not a question, more an indictment.

She looked back at him, her eyes laughing in defiance, the matching scarf round her neck. Corrigan lifted his hands, wrapped the ends of the scarf round his fingers, and began to pull. Slowly and gently.

Too weak, she knew, too weak to do what he had promised. Too weak, she made an assumption, to avenge a friend.

The scarf was tightening. Too weak, she knew, too weak. She knew he would stop soon. Tighter, much tighter. Too weak, she repeated. Not like Heiner, not like the *Sturmbannführer*, the one they called The Butcher. Not like herself.

The scarf was tight. No air. A splinter of fear shot through her, the light of day misted into red. Then the red diffused into black.

Corrigan opened the passenger door and pushed her out, watching as the body rolled into the ditch at the side of the road. Then he started the engine and drove to the escarpment he had checked that morning. The landscape was still deserted. He parked the car five hundred metres further on, off the road, took a pair of gloves and road map from the glove compartment and the handle of the wheel-jack from the boot, and walked back. For fifteen minutes he crouched motionless among the rocks of the escarpment. Only when he was confident that he was alone did he move in on the cache.

He picked up the first marker, lined up on the second, the remains of a tree deformed by the winds of the *altiplano*, and paced out thirty metres. He checked his position, making sure he was in the direct line between the third and fourth markers, and paced fifteen metres towards the fourth. Then he turned half left, till he was facing the second marker again, this time on a different line, measured another ten metres, and began to dig with the handle of the wheel-jack.

It was six months since he had buried the cache. The ground was firmly packed, almost hard. He had dug almost a metre before he struck the top of the Schermuly box.

He stopped, put on the gloves, and began clearing the earth away. He had left no fingerprints on either the box or its contents when he had buried them, no link between its secrets and the CIA man in Lima. Tonight above all nights, he knew, he had to continue that care.

The box was grey plastic, the top signal-red. Not standard issue, he had purchased it himself. Originally manufactured to package flares, frequently used by yachtsmen to store dry clothes at sea. Perfect for caching arms. Watertight. The plastic concealing the smell of weapon-oil from intruding animals.

He unscrewed the lid. The contents were packed neatly and tightly. He took out a Belgian-made 9mm Browning, loaded two magazines, clipped one into the handgun and placed it on the earth at his side. If he was disturbed, it was too late to pull out.

The cache was not the only one he had concealed in the area. Its contents, however, satisfied both the logistical requirements and the stringent security conditions of the night's operation. From the earth at the side of the box he prised a rifle box, wrapped in two layers of polythene. The rifle inside, like the handgun he had selected, had no link with United States manufacture or supply. There was a more than reasonable chance, he had already calculated, that he would have to abandon his weapons on site in the next few hours. Which was why he had chosen nothing with an American connection. Why he was already wearing one pair of gloves. Why he would wear another, special, pair later.

The rifle was a Yugoslav M76 semi-automatic sniper rifle, its most effective killing range up to eight hundred metres. The killing that night, he already knew, would be done at no more than a hundred and fifty. From the Schermuly box he took a West German Orion 80 image intensifier for night use, the mounting adapted for use with the M76, and clipped it into position.

It was cold, getting colder. He loaded two ten-round magazines with 7.9mm Soviet-made hollow-point ammunition, and a third magazine with only four rounds, clipping the last magazine into the rifle. The sights had been zeroed before being cached. As a precaution, he marked a cross on the back of the road map, propped it up with a piece of wood on the top of a small rock, paced out a hundred metres, and pressed off the four-round magazine from the prone position. When he checked, the beating zone was tight, the holes grouped in a one-inch circle round the centre of the cross.

He reloaded the magazine with ten rounds and snapped it back into the rifle. From the Schermuly box he took a set of wire-cutters, a pair of Cape leather gloves and a hand-warmer, purchased in a hunting shop in Hamburg, plus two solid-fuel sticks. His vigil, he knew, would be long and cold. His hands and fingers, at least, needed to be warm.

It was even colder. He screwed the lid back on, filled in the hole, stamped the earth hard and tight and took his selection back to the car. The sky above showed the first tinge of purple. He started the car, turned in the road, and headed back to the city. By the time he drove past the ditch where Carmen lay a condor was already circling in the sky. It would be morning, he knew, before the body was found, cold and stiff, rigor mortis firmly established.

And by morning, he knew, it would be over.

10

The streets were still busy. Corrigan parked at the hotel, locking the weapons in the boot, and walked to the city centre. At a car rental in one of the tourist squares he hired another car using the second passport he had taken from the wall-safe in Lima. At a market stall he purchased a poncho, returned to the hotel, and made his final call to the La Paz contact.

The man was excited. 'The bastard,' he spoke quickly,

excitedly. 'He hid it, tried to lose it in the records, but I got it. Got the address.' Corrigan knew how he felt. 'It will cost,' said the contact, 'I had to pay more than expected. But I got it. Not the real name, the bastard has that well covered. But I got the address.'

Corrigan wrote it down, thanked the man, arranged an additional payment. Wondered how it would have affected events if he had known it earlier. Knew it was now too late for him to use it. Wondered if it would have saved Carmen.

It was mid-evening. He took a light dinner of steak and salad, declining the wine list, then transferred the weapons to the rear seat of the second hire-car, covering them with the poncho.

Before he left the hotel he emptied his pockets of all personal possessions including cigars and the keys of the first hire-car which, if they dropped from his clothing, might give a clue to his identity. Then he drove to the street on which the safe house was situated.

The temperature was falling.

At the bottom of the road the building site stood empty against the night sky. At its base, outside the perimeter fence, the family who had been hired as statutory guardians were clustered round a small fire in front of a one-room tin shack, preparing the mash of potatoes that was their only meal of the day.

Corrigan avoided the stake-out cars, still in position, drove to the rear of the block, parked the hire-car among the site machinery and cut his way through the perimeter fence, bending the wire back in position after he had passed through.

The building was ten storeys high. He examined each in turn before choosing his position on the eighth, selecting a balcony directly opposite the corner on which the safe house was placed and from where he could see both the front and back of the house as well as the web of streets which led from the corner.

The streets below were already lost in the night. He put

on the Cape leather gloves, picked up the M76, able to feel the trigger as if the thin leather of the gloves did not exist, took off the lens cap of the night sights, and surveyed the ground around the house. Scouring the streets. Picking out the door, crystal-clear in the green of the image intensifier. The door through which the assault team would enter. The door out of which they would bring Laporte.

It was even colder than he had expected. He adjusted his position, calculating how the cars of the assault team would obstruct his line of fire, put the lens cap back on the sights, lit the hand-warmer and wrapped the poncho around him.

Then he settled down to wait.

11

Laporte woke slowly, allowing himself time to enjoy the warmth of the blankets, aware that the tiredness had been drawn from his body and the aching from his head. He turned over. Ten minutes to midnight. From somewhere, he could not be sure where, he could smell the spice of the *anticuchos* being grilled. From the front room he could hear the sound of voices.

He rolled out of bed, pulled on his shoes and went into the other room. The four guerillas were seated round the table in the centre of the floor, drinking beer from bottles. Lucho offered him a chair and he sat down. Jaime went into the section of the rear room which doubled as a kitchen and came back with a plate of corn and meat, and a thick slice of bread. Laporte accepted it gratefully, remembering that the last time he had eaten properly had been lunch the previous day. Lunch the previous day, he paused, knowing what had happened. Roberto opened a bottle of beer and passed it to him across the table. He took it and drank from the bottle, letting the cold of the alcohol erase the memory.

281

'You're feeling better?' It was Lucho who asked him.

Laporte mumbled that he was, nodding his head, dipping the bread into the thick gravy of the meat and pushing it hungrily into his mouth. 'Much better. And the passport?'

It was the guerilla's turn to confirm that all was well. 'Jaime and Roberto collected it this evening. The stamps are all in order.' He opened Laporte another beer. 'Now let us see how we can help you.'

For the next hour they talked through his hunt for Josef Heiner, the four guerillas poring over the details Laporte gave them, discussing then discarding the possibilities. Gradually the disappointment settled, till there were only two names left.

'What about Project Octavio?' he asked, 'what do you know of it?' The four shook their heads. 'Or Portachuela?' he suggested hopefully, remembering the fear in the eyes of the book-keeper when he had talked of it, anticipating a positive reply.

Lucho shrugged his shoulders. 'An accident,' he said, 'the wrong person dead, of course. It was a pity it was only the wife. But it was no more than an accident. We had nothing to do with it. No-one did.'

Laporte felt the wave of depression sweep over him. He listened as Lucho chronicled the events of Portachuela, barely hearing the details, then excused himself and crawled back to bed.

Once and only once during the following hours did he wake, calculating the time at around 3.30. All was quiet. In the bed next to the door he could hear Lucho coughing up the blood of the tin mines.

Chapter Seven

Sunday, February 6th 1983

Five minutes to go. Corrigan tightened his fingers round
the hand-warmer, feeling its heat through the thin skin of
the Cape leather gloves. The rest of his body was stiff with
cold, the skin of his face white. He checked his watch
again, peeled off the poncho in which he had huddled for
the past six hours and surveyed the street below. Quiet.
He stood up, stretched, placed the spare magazine in front
of him, slightly to his left, picked up the M 76, took the
lens cap off the night sights, and settled into position. The
night, he sensed, was about to surrender its black to the
first light of dawn. Below him the city was still. Even the
dogs were asleep.

'*Ich fragte ihn, ob er wieder kommen würde,*' the book-
keeper had said. '*Ich fragte ihn und er sagte "Ich habe Ihnen
gesagt, dass ich wieder komme."*'

Four minutes to go. The street still empty. He thought
of the telephone calls. Calls five and six. The connection
which had endured through nearly four decades. The secret
which Washington had tried to keep to itself. The secret
he had prised from them. Remembered again the moment
in the hotel foyer, the moment he had read the two files;
one on the father, the second on the son. The moment he
knew what was going to happen. The moment he knew
the exact time it would happen.

'*Ich fragte ihn, ob er wieder kommen würde,*' the book-
keeper had said. '*Ich fragte ihn und er sagte "Ich habe Ihnen
gesagt, dass ich wieder komme."*'

Three minutes to go. The street still empty. Corrigan
thought of the photographs accompanying the two reports.
The two photographs the mother had looked at in the cold

of her bedroom. The two photographs the magazine editor Pacheco had seen in his office. The one face he had seen in the breakfast room of the Sheraton Hotel in Lima and in the back of the cab in La Paz. He thought again of the dates on the two reports. Jean Laporte, father. Born 1905. Died 11.00 a.m. Monday February 7th 1944, aged 39. Jean Laporte, son. Born 11.00 a.m. Monday February 7th, 1944. Tomorrow would be Monday, February 7th. Tomorrow the son would be 39.

'*Ich fragte ihn, ob er wieder kommen würde,*' the book-keeper had said. '*Ich fragte ihn und er sagte "Ich habe Ihnen gesagt, dass ich wieder komme."*'

In Lima the night air was hot, almost suffocating. No breeze from the sea. Maria turned on her bed, dogged by the images which refused to go away. Laporte. The photograph of Heiner. The man in the garden, turning to her, hating her. She tried to sleep. Could not. Tried to wake. Could not. Remembered the night they had got the documents from the house at Chaclicayo. Her fingers trying to phone the warning to Jean. No dialling tone. 'Sometimes,' she had told him, 'I know you better than you know yourself. Know what you are, who you are. What you are doing, what you are thinking.' The night pressed down on her. 'What you should be doing, what you should be thinking.' The images crossed and re-crossed her mind. She remembered that she had not understood the words then, remembered she had known that one day she would. She tried to tear herself away from the images. Tried to wake up.

Knew the time had almost come.

Two minutes to go. The street still empty. Corrigan thought of the timetables he had analysed as he had sat, suddenly aware, in the hotel the previous afternoon. Jean Laporte. Resistance hero. Martyr. Returned clandestinely to France during the early hours of Saturday, February 5th. Contact with local Resistance cell via hotel receptionist approx. 9.00 a.m. and escorted to safe house. Already betrayed. Seized by Gestapo squad headed by Josef Heiner and Heinrich Schmeltz 4.00 a.m. Sunday February 6th. Jean Laporte, priest. Entered Bolivia clandestinely during early hours of Saturday February 5th. Contact with MIR guerilla group via hotel receptionist approx. 9.00 a.m. and escorted to safe house. Already betrayed. He checked his watch. It was almost time.

'Ich fragte ihn, ob er wieder kommen würde,' the book-keeper had said. *'Ich fragte ihn und er sagte "Ich habe Ihnen gesagt, dass ich wieder komme."'*

One minute to go. The street still empty. Corrigan thought of another raid. On the hotel in Mollendo. He and Schmeltz at the head of the assault team. The scribbling he had seen on his blotting paper when he had returned from the raid. 4.00 a.m. The numbers circled in red. He thought again of the secret of the telephone calls. The short but sincere conversation with his wife before the baptism. Thought for the last time of the words of the man on the bed in Mollendo.

'Ich fragte ihn, ob er wieder kommen würde,' the book-keeper had said. *'Ich fragte ihn und er sagte "Ich habe Ihnen gesagt, dass ich wieder komme."'*

The secret which had haunted the book-keeper, Heinrich Schmeltz, even Josef Heiner himself, when they thought of the man on the train. Calling to them. Beckoning them to come closer to him.

'Ich fragte ihn, ob er wieder kommen würde,' the book-keeper had said. *'Ich fragte ihn und er sagte "Ich habe Ihnen gesagt, dass ich wieder komme."'*

'I asked him if he would be back and he said, "I told you I would return."'

The last words, the only words, the man on the train ever spoke.

'I will return.'

Maria woke with a start. Cold. Frightened. She got up and went to the balcony. Remembered the priest's story. The dates. Knew what was happening. What was about to happen. The moment he had waited for. The moment they had all waited for. For thirty-nine years.

4.00 a.m. Sunday February 6th. At the top of the street, Corrigan saw the two blunt-nosed Mercedes, massive grilles and distinctive emblems, bumping their silent way down the slope. In the green of the night sights he picked up the lead car, knew it contained Heiner and his personal chauffeur, the rear seat kept empty, Schmeltz and the assault team in the second car. He swung round, scanning the side streets which spread like a cross from the corner on which the safe house was situated. At the end of each road, emerging from the dark, he picked out the rest of the assault squad. Closing in, sealing the web. Just as they had done thirty-nine years before. For the briefest moment he remembered Anderson, the Texan, Heiner's back door out, Heiner's own personal insurance if all else went wrong. Knew Anderson was also there, in the dark, waiting like himself. Then he swung the rifle back, targeting the window of the safe house, then the door. Waiting for the moment they would bring out the son.

The two Mercedes braked to a silent halt beneath the flat. Corrigan watched as the doors of the rear car opened and four men slid out, the driver remaining in position, and moved like ghosts across the pavement. Classic assault formula, he thought. Schmeltz, the man Heiner could always trust, trying the door of the stairs to the flat, easing it open, waving the three assault men inside. The front of the lead car opened. He watched as Heiner got out, an Uzi hanging from his right hand, walked carefully round the front of the car to the rear passenger door nearest the entrance to the flat, and opened it.

In the east, behind the building site, the dawn broke. Corrigan looked down on the street, thought of the son, remembered the father's file. Jean Laporte. A French citizen. Briefed in Algiers by the exiled de Gaulle and in London by Churchill. A man of peace. Trained by the British Special Operations Executive at Beaulieu in

Hampshire and, for five awesome, unending weeks in the depths of winter, at the SOE Group A school at Arisaig in Scotland, in the dirtiest of the arts of war.

2

The sound was almost imperceptible. Laporte woke, not moving, not breathing. Hearing it again. The almost silent noise of heavy wheels freewheeling on an unbroken surface. Then the squeak of a car suspension and the soft click of a door opening. He waited, hearing nothing more, telling himself he had imagined the sound, allowed himself to be sucked into an illogical paranoia, as he had been sucked into the nightmare of faces earlier that morning. He waited. Still nothing. Moved deeper into the warmth of the bed, tried to think of Maria. His mind still on the noise. Slipping back into sleep.

Maria knew why she had said it, what it meant. 'Sometimes,' she had told him, 'I know you better than you know yourself.' Remembered Laporte's story of his father's death, his own birth. Remembered the dates. Remembered what he had said about his father, the secret visit to Britain late in 1943, into January 1944. 'Know what you should be doing,' she had told him, 'what you should be thinking.' She gripped the balcony, stared at the sea. Knew what was happening, could see it, feel it. Knew he could not. Wake up, Jean, she urged. She was gripping the balcony even harder, the urgency giving her strength. Wake up, Jean, she was shouting at him, screaming at him, for Christ's sake wake up. Now. Remember who you are. What you are. What they taught you to be.

Quiet, he thought, too quiet. Not even the sound of dogs.

He rolled out of the bed, moved across the room and peered behind the corner of the curtain covering the front window onto the street. In the half-light below he saw the square tops of the two cars, three doors of the rear car open, a man with a sub-machine gun walking round the front.

He remembered where he had last seen the man.

On the train to Paris thirty-nine years ago.

In the bed by the door Lucho was still coughing, the handkerchief he held clutched to his mouth spotted with red. Laporte crossed to him, shook his shoulder. The guerilla woke instantly, making no noise. Laporte indicated with his hand to the front window and the street below. Behind him Jaime was already crossing the room, checking, nodding to Lucho. From the other beds Paco and Roberto were rising, picking up their weapons.

'I want one of them.'

Lucho nodded his agreement, not asking why. Laporte pulled on his shoes and took his position against the wall on the immediate right of the door into the flat. Jaime and Roberto covered the front and rear windows, Paco slotted himself behind the partition wall, at the head of the bed where Laporte had slept. Lucho placed two grenades on the table in the centre of the front room and crouched beside it, an AK 47 in his hands.

In the night outside the dogs were still silent. Laporte bent across the door and drew back the bolt. From the top of the stairs came the scratching of a key sliding into a lock. The catch turned and the door swung open.

In the street below Josef Heiner knew the time. Four in the morning. Sunday February 6th, 1944. Get the bastard, the Führer had urged him. Get Laporte. Now, he urged, in now. The muzzle of a Heckler and Koch penetrated the room, followed by the shape of a man. Now, Lucho urged the Frenchman at the side of the door, for Christ's sake now.

Laporte drove up with his foot, into the genitals, rupturing the hernia. The leader jackknifed with shock and pain, clearing the firing line. Lucho smashed the trigger of the Kaleshnikov, maintaining the pressure, taking the figures behind by surprise, cutting them in two. The screams echoed down the concrete stairs and into the street. Laporte slammed his clenched fists onto the neck of the man doubled in front of him and pulled him into the room. The bodies of his two companions were still moving, cartwheeling backwards with the force of the bullets. Lucho pulled the pin from the first of the two grenades on the table, lobbed it into the stairwell, and slammed the door.

Heiner's driver was already pushing the Mercedes into gear, easing away, removing his leader from the line of fire, Heiner himself hanging from the rear door. Lucho pulled the pin from the second grenade and lobbed it through the front window. Schmeltz saw it, screamed a warning, dived for cover behind the bodies of the *Sturmmänner* in the stairwell. The driver heard, smashed his foot on the accelerator, pulling Heiner in, the car swinging wildly. Schmeltz heard the grenade bounce off the roof of Heiner's car and onto the bonnet of the rear Mercedes. The second driver had time to register its presence before it exploded, scything off his head. From the corner opposite came a burst of fire, smashing the window, sending a shower of glass fragments into the room. In the seconds that followed a longer burst kept the occupants from the window while a figure sprinted across the road, ignoring the wreck of the Mercedes, and took up position, out of sight of the window, on the corner beneath the front of the flat.

In the silence that followed the dogs began to howl.

Inside the flat Jaime was pulling the table from the centre of the front room, half covering the window, speaking quickly in a Spanish Laporte could not understand. 'What's he say?' asked the Frenchman.

'He says we've had it, Father,' replied Lucho. 'The only way out is down the stairs and the bastard on the opposite corner will finish us off as soon as we step outside.'

'What about the back window?'

'No way. A twenty-feet drop and they'll have that covered anyway.'

The man on the floor was still writhing in pain. Laporte

pulled him up, shouting at him in German. *'Wo ist* Heiner?' 'Where's Heiner?'

'Fuck off,' the man screamed back. In German.

In the middle of the kitchen floor Lucho was pulling clips of ammunition from the box beneath the table.

'How long before the police get here?' Laporte asked. In the front room Jaime was firing intermittently from the window, dodging back as the gunman on the opposite corner pinned them down.

'Who the hell do you think he is,' retorted the guerilla, pulling the box from beneath the table.

'From Heiner, the one I told you about.'

Lucho ignored him, pulled an empty magazine and a handful of clips from the box. 'You load for me, Father, this is what you do.' Behind them Jaime was exchanging fire through the front window. 'This is a sten gun,' Lucho began to explain, quickly but patiently. 'This is a magazine, it goes into the gun. You load the magazine with these clips.' He began snapping the clips into the magazine, explaining it was easy, encouraging, protecting, then stopped. Looking at the man he knew as a priest. The Frenchman had whipped the rounds from the clips, was loading them individually into the magazine, snapping them into place faster than the guerilla had loaded with the clips.

'What the hell are you doing?' the guerilla asked.

Laporte heard his own voice, replying, explaining. Unaware what he was saying. What he was doing. His fingers moving fast. Automatically. 'Safety. Clips probably loaded too long, springs might be faulty. Impede the loading.' The metal felt familiar in his hands. He finished one magazine, loaded the sten, filled a second.

'Six minutes, probably seven,' Lucho answered the original question. 'No more. Then the police will be here.'

Laporte pulled on his jacket and shoved the spare magazine into his pocket. 'I'll take the one on the corner. As soon as he's down, get out.' He pulled the wounded stormtrooper towards the rear window. 'He'll draw their fire. As soon as he goes out you'll get their position. Just keep them pinned down. But for Christ's sake make sure you're firing through the top half.'

The German was wide-eyed with fear, trying to pull away. Lucho was staring at the Frenchman in disbelief. 'Good luck, Father,' he whispered.

Laporte lifted the captive off the floor, surprised by his own strength, and pushed him through the window into the darkness outside. The volley of shots hit the body the moment it filled the frame, following him as the man fell screaming to the ground. At his side, Laporte heard the roar as Roberto and Lucho opened fire on the tell-tale flashes of white, pulled himself to the window, and dived through.

Corrigan watched as the figure filled the window space, moving forward into the emptiness, doubling and jerking as the first burst caught it. Instinctively he traced the source of the shooting to a balcony sixty metres away. Almost immediately the source was silenced by a prolonged volley from the window. As he watched, a second figure catapulted out, ducking under what Corrigan calculated was the line of fire, and dropped to the ground. 'Jesus,' he breathed.

Laporte hit the hard ground, rolled instinctively, letting the whip of his body absorb the shock. At the same moment, Corrigan saw the figure on the corner. The gunman who had sprinted across the road had crept forward, concealed by the shadows on the pavement, clinging to the wall so he could not be seen from the flat. As Laporte hit the ground the man rounded the corner, concentrating on the window above, seeing at the last moment the figure on the ground ten metres away. Laporte saw him, remembered that he had never held a gun in his entire life, saw the surprise on the face opposite, the gun coming down, finger closing on the trigger. He rolled again, presenting a moving target, jerking suddenly to the kneeling position, the sten already on target, and squeezed the trigger.

One two three four, he was counting, not knowing what

or why. One two three four. The gunman was still moving forward, his chest shattered, falling slowly, his Uzi discharging harmlessly into the night air. Four and four, Laporte knew he was thinking. Two fours. Twenty-four.

Along the streets below Corrigan could see the assault teams moving closer to the house. He focused again on the son. Laporte had turned right, back towards the crossroads, not away from the safe house as he had somehow expected, using the same cover of pavement that his victim had taken. A burst of firing splintered the plaster on the wall above the Frenchman's head. He dropped low, spun round. Two *Sturmmänner* from an assault car fifty metres to his rear had spotted him, identified him, were closing in, sandwiching him between themselves and the single gunman still in position on the opposite corner of the crossroads. Corrigan watched as the two crossed the road, momentarily exposing themselves, remembering the way he had automatically counted the number of rounds the son had fired seconds before. Standard Special Forces training. Two bursts, four rounds each burst. Counting each round. Eight rounds from the sten's thirty-two-round magazine. The son still had twenty-four rounds left in his gun.

Laporte pressed the trigger of the sten, bracing himself for the shock.

There was a sudden lull in the firing. In the unnatural silence, Corrigan heard the grating sound, knew instantly that the gun had jammed, knew also that the gunmen had heard it, recognised it. They closed in, straightening up, protected from the flat by the angle of the corner. In the distance, Corrigan heard the wail of the first police siren. The gunmen also heard, broke into a run, guns ready, intent on taking their quarry alive. Corrigan sensed their elation, knew the feeling. For a moment he remembered the timetable. Two times, two dates. 4.00 a.m. Sunday February 6th. 11.00 a.m. Monday February 7th. The son had not made his thirty-nine years. Then remembered again the father's file. Jean Laporte. Trained by the British SOE, December 1943–January 1944.

A month before the man on the street was born.

The priest heard the sound, knew what it was, saw the triumph in the faces of the gunmen. Instinctively he reached for his pocket, searching for the comfort of the rosary, the hard wood beads of the prayer chain. Finding instead the spare magazine. Remember what you are, Maria urged him, what they taught you to be.

'Gun jams, Frenchie,' the instructor was shouting at him, 'what the fuck do you do.' He was back in the room, pitch black, no light, his body beaten, his mouth tasting his own blood. His mind befuddled, fingers frozen from the five hours they had made him stand motionless in the ice-cold river. 'Fuck you, Frenchie, scum, bastard,' the instructor's screams were confusing him, disorientating him, the sound of gunfire crashing through his head. His left hand moving. Automatically. Right thumb depressing the mag catch. 'Five seconds, Frenchie,' the instructor was screaming at the best pupil he had ever had, 'five seconds and you're dead.' Left hand still moving. Not thinking. Jerk out mag, cock weapon, fresh mag in. 'Three seconds, Frenchie, and they won't know what hit them.' He was straightening. Two and a half seconds, more like two. They were still coming forward, laughing at him. The bastards who had made sure he would never see his only begotten son. Fire.

The arc of his bullets was tracing a line across them, cutting them down. One two three four, he was counting. One two three four. Two bursts. Eight rounds. Twenty-four rounds left. Christ, why hadn't he loaded a second spare mag?

To his right he heard three sharp bursts from the gunman at the crossroads. Six minutes, perhaps seven, Lucho had said, then the police would arrive.

He could hear the sirens getting closer. He moved forward, hiding himself in the darkness, knew he would not be able to see the gunman concealed in the black opposite, remembered the sounds of the bursts. Three fours, the man was firing, always three fours. He brought the sten up, waiting, hearing the sirens closing in. No sweat, he told himself, no rush. Sounds carry at night. Still two minutes, perhaps three, before they get here. Come on, you bastard, fire. The sirens were closer still. From the corner opposite he caught the first sound of the first four-round burst, saw the white flash, adjusted his aim fractionally to the right and pressed off two four-round bursts. There was a cry from the darkness, a staccato of fire as the gunman's finger jerked haphazardly on the trigger, then silence.

He paused. Sixteen rounds left. Waited for the back-up, straining to hear any tell-tale noise behind him, from the street to his left. Nothing. Then the sound of a door opening, feet thudding on wood, to the right, at the entrance to the stairs to the safe house, a sustained burst, a long scream, and the sound of someone running.

He moved to the corner, checked, and ran to the right, to the entrance to the stairway. Lucho was lying over the bodies of the two stormtroopers, the top of his head shot away, the other three guerillas trying to drag him clear. Twenty metres up the road a man was running.

'One we didn't see,' Jaime was telling him. 'Lucho was the first down the stairs, the bastard was at the bottom.' The guerilla stepped across the bodies, raised Lucho's AK47, finger closing on the trigger.

Laporte looked up the street, saw the man running, fleeing. Shoulders heaving. Old shoulders. Forty metres from him, almost fifty.

Knew who it was.

He pulled up the Kaleshnikov, stopping Jaime from firing. 'He's mine, I need him.' Jaime was confused. Laporte remembered the two men who had tried to take him when his sten had jammed.

'There's a car round the corner, fifty metres, perhaps a hundred. Get Lucho there. Get him out.' He was already running, Schmeltz now forty-five metres in front, slowing down, the gap closing.

Laporte was moving as fast as he could, uphill, feeling suddenly the strain of the altitude, the breath already bursting his chest, head pounding. He was gaining, forty metres, thirty-five. The sten heavy in his arms, slowing him down, legs dragging. Thirty metres, twenty-five.

Schmeltz had almost reached a corner, Laporte knew he would turn right, did not know what lay behind. Knew he must catch him before that. Twenty metres. In the half-light he saw that Schmeltz had dropped his Uzi, reduced his load. Schmeltz was gaining on him, slightly but crucially, drawing away. His lungs were exploding, his throat on fire. He dropped the sten, moving faster, lighter, gaining. Ten metres, five.

Schmeltz had turned, was looking at him, coming forward. A knife in his hand. They circled, eyeing each other, two metres apart. Schmeltz lunged, slow with fatigue, Laporte swinging aside, also tired, just avoiding the blade. Schmeltz struck again, breath rasping, hatred in his face. The oxygen was returning to Laporte's blood, clearing his brain, making logic fight through the headache.

Dirty, the SOE instructor was shouting at him. No rules. Just take him. He reached in his pocket, felt the rosary, fingers wrapping round the crucifix, stem jutting out like a knife. One rule, another voice was shouting at him. Take him, but take him alive. Your only contact. Your last connection with Heiner.

Schmeltz slashed forward, desperate, tiredness pulling his body off-balance, knife still slashing at Laporte's arm. The Frenchman felt the sudden pain, reacted instinctively, moving aside, fist coming up, sharp and powerful, the stem of the crucifix burying itself in Schmeltz's stomach.

The counter, the instructor was screaming, for Christ's sake the counter. The knife was rising again, slowly and inevitably. Laporte was trying to move away, feet leaden, seeing the knife rip through his clothing, feeling the second wound, taking the forearm as it rose, twisting it back, the knife leaving the hand. Schmeltz falling back, the son on top, the bodies hitting the ground, Schmeltz's head striking hard against the concrete base of the pavement, flopping to one side.

Through the thudding in his ears Laporte heard a car. Accelerating. Coming up the hill towards them. He pulled himself up, trying to lift Schmeltz's massive frame, knew it was Jaime and Lucho, Roberto and Paco. Schmeltz was heavy in his arms. He turned. The car was still accelerating, fifty metres away, now forty. Headlights full on. Blinding him. Not Lucho, he knew, not the guerillas.

The sten was ten metres away. He began to run, leaving Schmeltz, the instructor shouting at him again. Night vision. Keep your night vision. Instinctively he shut his right eye, his left guiding him to the gun. The headlights blinding him. In one eye only. He reached the sten, picked it up, letting his almost useless left eye guide him to the target. Shutting the left, opening the right. Full night vision. Finger coming down on the trigger. One two three four. One two three four. The car out of control, sliding left. One two three four. One two three four. Mag empty. The car careering to the left, striking the pavement, turning over.

He turned, pulled himself back to Schmeltz, lifted the head. Knew it was too late. The eyes were upturned and white, a thin line of blood trickling from the corner of the mouth, a small pool already formed on the pavement where the skull had fractured in the fall. His last route to Heiner.

'Don't wait,' the instructor was shouting at him, 'no use to you, leg it.' He let the disappointment drop, the survival take over. The sirens were closer, too close. He let the head fall and broke into a pitiful run.

In the building site at the bottom of the road Corrigan shifted two metres to the left, maximising his position. Through the night sights he could see the laboured movements of the Frenchman as he struggled to make the corner. It had been a long road, he thought, a very long road. He remembered the secret. The secret which the big

298

boys in Washington had tried to keep to themselves. The secret he had taken from them.

The sirens were almost there. He could see the flashing lights. The street below was empty except for the fleeing figure. Slowly and calmly Corrigan brought the M 76 round, shifting his balance, till the graticules of the sights centred on Laporte's back. His breathing was shallow. He concentrated on the figure, no longer hearing the screaming and shouting from the neighbouring houses or the wail of the police sirens. As if nothing and nobody existed except himself and Laporte.

On the balcony in Lima, Maria knew it was the end. She turned away, felt the emptiness come upon her. Wondered if Jean knew. Remembered the house at Chaclicayo, the way she had protected him, guarded him, saved him. 'Please, God,' she prayed, 'let there be someone now.' Knew there was not. Closed her eyes and waited.

In the street below the building site the figure had almost reached the safety of the corner. Behind the building the first shaft of sunlight broke over the mountains, piercing the bowl of the city. In the sudden light, Corrigan saw the glint of the metal. He swung round, picked up the sniper on the rooftop a hundred metres away. Concentrating. Like him. Concentrating on the Frenchman. He knew who it was, why he was there. Heiner's insurance job, the back door out, the final solution if all else failed.

'Screw you, Tex,' he said, almost aloud.

The crack of the high-velocity weapon whiplashed through the streets. Laporte froze, heard the first bullet, knew it had missed him, waited for the second. Knew he was about to die. Knew that he had failed. So close, he thought, so close to the Monday. He felt the single, sickening thud as the bullet ploughed into the bone of the skull, boring its way through the brain, tearing the head apart as it exited on the other side. Then heard the clang of metal against concrete as the Ruger fell from the assassin's hands and the body of the Texan called Anderson toppled from the building.

He waited. No second bullet. Did not know who. Or why. In Lima, Maria felt the darkness lift. Laporte raised one hand in thanks and disappeared round the corner.

On the eighth floor of the building site Joe Corrigan dropped the M 76 and ran for the rear staircase. Wondered what Laporte would do next. Whether he would work it out.

3

The car was parked twenty metres around the corner, facing him. Logical, thought Laporte. Schmeltz's back door out. He remembered the Volaire parked next to the Caprice in the road behind the safe house at Chaclicayo. The same, he thought, as Schmeltz had arranged in Lima. The same, he realised, as he himself had arranged.

His arm and side hurt. He opened the driver's door and sat down, trying to fight off the mix of fatigue, pain and confusion. Reaching for the ignition key, hearing the police sirens. No key. Bastard, he cursed, the bastard. The sirens were close, very close. He cursed again, began to get out, will himself to run again, thinking he was mistaken, that the car was not even a back-up, that it had no connection with Schmeltz.

Calm down, the instructor was telling him, think it through. Nobody leaves a car like this in a place like this. Nobody leaves it unlocked. But they don't leave the key in the ignition. He looked across. On the floor in front of the passenger's seat he saw a blanket, covering something. He knew what it was, ignored it, hand reaching down, finding the key on the floor beneath his own seat. He started the engine, not knowing where to go. Hearing the sirens, at the top and bottom of the street in front of him.

He pushed the car into reverse, lurched back down the street, pulled round the corner, changed gear, and accelerated up the hill parallel to the street on which the safe house was situated. To his left he could hear the wail of more sirens. At the second intersection to his left he saw flashing lights. At the top of the hill he turned right and drove for ten minutes, not knowing where he was going, clearing the danger zone, instinctively heading north, keeping the rising sun on his right. Sensing, without knowing why, that he was heading for the city centre.

The pain in his side was getting worse. He steered with one hand, feeling down with the other. The shirt was cold and wet.

The streets were getting wider, better constructed, the buildings changing, street lights appearing. He knew he was getting closer to the centre, did not know what he would do when he got there. In front, to his left, was a small shopping area. He pulled off the road, looped behind the shops and stopped in a small parking bay at the rear, away from the road, his self-discipline beginning to impose an order of requirements upon him.

If he was driving Schmeltz's back-up car, he thought, then Schmeltz would have provided certain things with the car. He switched on the interior light and checked the blanket on the floor to his right. Beneath was a short-barrelled Heckler and Koch MP 5K, one 9mm 30-round magazine loaded, a second on the floor.

The blood was seeping through his coat. He took out the ignition key, walked to the back of the car and checked the boot. It was empty except for a spare tyre. He realised how cold he was, how much he was shivering, got back into the car, checked the rear seat and under the front driver's seat, finding nothing, then opened the spacious glove compartment of the passenger's side. Inside was a plastic box. He opened it. Inside the box were two cartons of cotton wool, three rolls of sticking plaster, and a selection of hyperdermic needles. Just like Schmelz, he thought, always thorough, always catering for every eventuality. Except for one, he thought thankfully, except for the one occasion at the house in Chaclicayo. He got out of the car, trying to stop the shivering, and took off his coat and shirt.

The wound in his side was five inches long, deep only in one place, the blood still seeping out. He wiped it with cotton wool, pulled the sides of the cut together with sticking plaster, folded a wad of cotton wool over the top, and taped the dressing in place with more sticking plaster. In the half-light he tried to read the instructions on the hyperdermic needles, failed, and discarded them. The wound on his arm was less painful. He treated it in a similar fashion then put back on his shirt and coat. Both were ripped and stained with blood.

He returned the box to the glove compartment. At the back was a street map of La Paz. He opened it, checked where he was, noting that a small cross at one intersection was probably the location of the safe house, and headed for the centre. Five minutes later, in a promenade of shops fronting onto a one-way street, he found what he was looking for. He stopped the car, leaving the engine running, and checked through the window of the men's outfitters. He went back to the car, picked up the Heckler and Koch, checked the street was still empty, then walked quickly to the door at the side of the shop window. In one clean movement he brought the butt of the gun through the glass nearest the lock, slipped his hand inside, and opened the door. The alarm sounded immediately. He ignored it, grabbed a handful of shirts, two sweaters and three coats, ran back to the car, threw them into the passenger seat, and accelerated away. The alarm was still ringing. By the time the owner reached the shattered door Laporte was ten blocks away.

The wad of cotton wool had stemmed the bleeding from his side. He stopped the car, sorted through the clothing till he found a shirt, sweater and jacket that fitted him, put them on, feeling warmer already, threw the others out of the car, and drove on. Three blocks away he emptied the pockets of his jacket and threw the bloodstained clothing away.

The city was coming to life, the first of the street traders appearing, the *ambulantes*, their bowler hats perched on their heads, bent under the load of the children strapped to their backs and the weight of their wares beneath their arms. Laporte drove into a square, noticed a café open on the opposite corner, parked the car and went in. It seemed colder inside than out. He bought a mug of tea, tasteless but hot, and a piece of bread. The tables were formica, the floor smelt of kerosene. He sat in one corner, looking out the window, keeping the car and square under observation, feeling more secure as the café filled.

Heiner, he thought, Josef bloody Heiner. He wondered where he was, how he could get to him. Josef bloody Heiner, he thought again. How the hell had Heiner known he was in La Paz, known he was in the safe house, known the exact bloody location? The first strand of a connection began to form, weaving, growing. He bought another tea, wrapping his hands round the mug, warming himself. Listing those who knew of the safe house, of his link with it.

He went through the list chronologically. Guillermo Pertierro. Guillermo Pertierro and the four guerillas in the safe house. Guillermo Pertierro, the four guerillas and Carmen. He began to eliminate them. If Guillermo Pertierro had betrayed him, he could have done it in Lima. There would have been no reason for the guerilla to send him to La Paz. Not Guillermo, he thought. Not Lucho either. Lucho had been imprisoned with Guillermo, been tortured with him. He thought of the other guerillas in the safe house. Paco had also been in the torture house with Guillermo and Lucho, had escaped with them. He eliminated Paco, concentrated on the remaining two, Jaime and Roberto. Both had left the safe house after he had arrived, to deal with the passport. Both had had the opportunity to betray him. But both had been in the safe house during the attack by Heiner's men. If either of them had betrayed him, he would not have returned to the safe house. He eliminated them from his calculations.

One other, he thought, only one other. Carmen. Not

Carmen, he knew he was thinking, please not Carmen. He remembered Guillermo Pertierro's words in the brothel at Cinco y Media. 'The *compañera* is a trusted, very dear colleague in the struggle.'

There had been something in the way the guerilla leader had spoken of Carmen, Laporte recalled, that suggested they had been more than comrades in war. Carmen, logic told him, it can only be Carmen.

Carmen, he decided.

He checked his watch. Fifteen minutes past six. Too early. He had met her at nine o'clock the morning before, assumed therefore that she would not be on duty again till nine, eight at the earliest. He sat back, trying to work out how he would approach her, how he would get through her to Heiner.

Heiner, he thought again, Josef bloody Heiner, the man in the street only two and a quarter hours before. So close, he had been so close. He sipped the tea, the strands of the web still weaving in his brain. He sat back, seeing the pattern, identifying the connections. Working out the numbers.

Four streets off the safe house, he remembered, six cars involved. The first assault car, Schmeltz and four others, including the driver. All dead. The four cars blocking off each of the roads. He went through the killings. One car containing the man who had surprised him after he had jumped from the window, and the lone gunman on the corner opposite the flat. Both dead. One car containing the two who had tried to capture him when the sten jammed. Both dead. One car containing, he assumed, two others, who had tried to take him after he had fought with Schmeltz. Both dead.

The carnage, he knew, should have horrified him. His appraisal was cold and analytic. That morning Heiner had lost ten, perhaps eleven men, including Heinrich Schmeltz. He moved on, trying to work out how many men Heiner had left in La Paz. His chauffeur and the two men in the remaining assault car. Three. Plus, he assumed, one who had been left in charge of Heiner's base during the assault. Four men left out of fifteen.

He drank some more tea, still welcoming its warmth, trying to decide what he would do in Heiner's position. There were a number of options. He analysed them till he knew there was only one thing Heiner could do. One thing, he realised, that Heiner was probably already doing. On the bar at the side of the café was a telephone. He asked to use it, checked the directory, and dialled the El Dorado. The switchboard answered immediately. He asked for reception, was relieved to hear a male voice, and asked what time Carmen was due to start work that day.

'I'm sorry, sir,' replied the receptionist, 'a gentleman phoned earlier to say she would not be in today. Are you Jean Laporte?'

The words screamed at him, the first half of the answer confusing him, the second warning him, his instinct telling him to say he was not. 'Yes,' he replied, 'I'm Jean Laporte.'

'The same gentleman left an address for you, sir. He said you needed it, and that if you phoned for Carmen, I was to give it to you.'

Laporte grabbed a pen and paper from the bar and wrote down the address, asking the receptionist to spell it twice for him.

'Did the caller leave a name?' he asked. 'No, sir, just the address. He said to tell you he hoped all was well after this morning. He said you would know what he meant.'

'What nationality was he?'

'He spoke Spanish, but I think he was American.'

Laporte put the phone down, confused. Trying to work it out. An American, he thought. He didn't know any Americans. Knew one, he corrected himself. Knew suddenly who it was. Where he had seen the man. In the breakfast bar in the Lima Sheraton. In the La Paz street when he was in the cab, with Carmen, on the way to the safe house. The man, he realised, who had saved his life that morning. The man whose name was the only one to appear regularly on the documents he had found in the house at Chaclicayo.

Corrigan. Joe Corrigan.

He sat down. Tried to work out the connections. Even more confused. The address, he knew, was Heiner's. It was the only thing he wanted. Corrigan knew it was the only thing he wanted. Corrigan had originally ordered his execution to keep the secret, to protect Heiner. Yet that morning Corrigan had saved his life. And now Corrigan had given the address to him.

Something else, he thought. Carmen. Carmen had betrayed him. And Corrigan had told him, via the hotel, that Carmen had been taken care of.

It was almost, he found himself thinking, as if Corrigan had discovered something, wanted him to survive, to win, in order to discover it himself. He wondered what was that important.

His first reaction was to go immediately to the address. Instead he bought a third tea and settled back at the table, deciding what he would do, how he would do it. The strands pulling together, the web growing stronger, reaching back, drawing in everything he had learned in the past six days. The knowledge he had gleaned from the documents he had found in the house at Chaclicayo, the additional information he had seduced out of the bookkeeper in the café by the Pacific Ocean. When he was satisfied he left the café, consulted the street map in the car, and drove to the address.

The street was quiet. He parked a block away and walked back, down the road. The house was on the right, set back. Through the iron bars of the front gate he could see three cars. In the next garden a servant was watering the lawn. Heiner plus four, he had calculated. He walked back to the corner and waited.

Laporte was warmer but stiff, his side hurting again, a pain
creeping up his arm. He wondered if he was right. And if
he was right, whether those in the house would leave
together. He had gambled they would not, relied on Heiner
seeking to avoid the mistake that had proved so costly at
Chaclicayo. Would clear the house of documents, despatch
them, but would remain behind to do one last personal
check. It was 10.35 a.m.

The front gate of the house swung open and the two
estate cars pulled out, turning left, the gate closing automatically behind them. Two men in the first car, he counted, one in the second. The cars moved slowly, heavily
laden, low on their suspensions. At the top of the road
they turned right and disappeared.

Heiner plus four, he had calculated. Now Heiner plus
one. It was his last chance. He could see it, feel it, knew
how it would happen. Heiner in his study, the last careful
scrutiny, sending the one man remaining with him to start
the Mercedes. It would be swift and silent. Then Heiner
would be his. He walked back to the car, concealed the
Heckler and Koch beneath his stolen jacket, and hurried
back to the house.

Josef Heiner checked that the wall-safe was empty, closed
it, spun the combination and pulled the oil painting back
in front. Late, he knew, it was getting late. Almost too
late. He wondered what was happening. Where the boys
were, where Schmeltz was.

He had last seen the *Hauptsturmführer* in the street
outside the safe house, diving for cover, screaming a warning as the grenade bounced off the roof of his car. The
man was OK, of course. Probably, almost certainly, still

hunting down the bastard of a son. Got him by now, he thought, knew he was not convinced, knew he was not convincing himself.

Should have phoned in by now. Schmeltz, one of the boys, even Carmen. But no news, no news from anybody. The isolation was closing in around him.

Anderson, he thought. Even if Schmeltz had not succeeded, even if the boys did not make it, there was always the Texan called Anderson, the private insurance, the back door out if all else failed. Anderson was good, he reminded himself, the best. Expensive, one of the most expensive around. But reliable. Totally methodical. Especially under pressure. Anderson had proved that at Portachuela. But no news, even from Anderson. No message left at the hotel. No check calls every hour on the half hour. Even Carmen, he thought again, disappeared without trace. No news at the hotel, no answer from her flat.

He moved to the desk, wondered again what was happening, opened the drawers and began to check for the last time that nothing had been left. Not like Chaclicayo, he thought. No mistakes like Chaclicayo. Nothing left. Nothing that would provide a clue.

He wondered again where Schmeltz was. The *Hauptsturmführer* would know, of course, realise what he had to do when he found the house empty. Would know where Heiner was heading, appreciate why Heiner could not wait for him. 'My duty was to stay,' he reminded himself of Schmeltz's description of the flight from Chaclicayo, 'yours was to leave.'

Nothing in the drawers.

He switched his mind away from Schmeltz. The boys should be out of the city by now. He should have kept them in the house, of course, held them while he made his final checks, then travelled in convoy. But there had been no time. Better to get the documents away. Santa Cruz as fast as they could make it, he had told them, an overnight in Cochabamba if anything went wrong, but Santa Cruz by the following morning.

He wondered about the significance of the next morning, knew there was a reason, could not remember what it was. He shut the drawers, imagined the road winding off the *altiplano*, dropping into the semi-tropics till it came to an end in Santa Cruz. The single road in from the west. The single railway track to Brazil in the east. The end of the world. His last refuge, an inhospitable place, but a sanctuary where he knew he would be safe. Would be able to regroup as necessary, find out how much damage had been done to the organisation, how much his former friends had discovered about him. Whether he needed another Anderson for another Portachuela.

In the driveway outside he heard the *Scharführer* start the car. He should have kept more than one, he knew, but there were few left he could summon in time. More in Lima, in Santa Cruz, but none close enough to help. He checked the desk for the last time, snapped his briefcase shut, heard the noise in the kitchen and the man enter the room behind him. Schmeltz, he hoped. Knew it was the *Scharführer*. He picked up the briefcase, rising, still facing away from the door.

The first edge of doubt mixed in the pit of his stomach, hardening to fear, rising, touching his throat. The tips of his fingers already growing cold, beginning to tremble. Not Schmeltz, he knew, not the *Scharführer*. He waited. For the *Scharführer* to tell him the car was ready. Wondered if he could reach the handgun in the briefcase, open the lock in time. Knew it was impossible.

Go for the gun, thought Laporte. Go for the gun. Give me an excuse. So long, he thought, he had waited so long. The calm of the vigil outside was giving place to anger. He tried to control it, knew he could not, knew he did not want to. Go for the bloody gun, he urged Heiner. So long, he thought, he had fought for so long. He remembered the shadow in the doorway of the schoolhouse of the *barriada*, the man reaching behind his jacket. A week ago. Almost a week ago. A week minus one day. His finger tightened round the trigger. More than a week, he thought, more than seven days the following day. Nearly thirty-nine years, thirty-nine on the Monday. He remembered the wait, the despair as the years slipped by and the act was forgotten, the anger as the injustice was left unrevenged. Remembered the cold of the earth as he waited, the loneliness of the priesthood.

Go for the gun, he thought again, go for the briefcase. The bastard was close, so close. Three paces. Less. Two paces. One pace and he could have him. Take him, as Heiner had taken so many. Knew how easy it would be. Could see it, feel it. The butt of the gun descending on the unprotected skull, splitting the bone. Knew it was what he wanted, what he had come so far for. Go for the briefcase, he thought again, go for the gun.

'Put the briefcase on the table and push it away from you.' The command was in French. Heiner did as he was instructed, confused, the fear growing in him. 'Turn around.'

The man was in the shadows, just inside the door. Heiner could hardly see him, tried to adjust his eyes to the dimness, began to make out the features. Recognised the voice. Saw the man on the train.

'*Ich fragte ihn, ob er wieder kommen würde,*' the book-keeper had told Schmeltz from his deathbed, his eyes still showing the fear of realisation, '*Ich fragte ihn und er sagte "Ich habe Ihnen gesagt, dass ich wieder komme."*'

'I asked him if he would be back and he said "I told you I would return."'

Heiner turned to the door, looking for the *Scharführer*. Laporte knew what he was thinking. 'No use,' he said, 'he's no use to you any more.' Heiner saw the gun the other man was carrying, the Heckler and Koch which Schmeltz had left in the back-up car.

'Schmeltz?' he asked, his voice barely a whisper.

'Dead,' said the man on the train.

'Anderson?'

The man on the train nodded.

'Carmen as well?' There was desperation in Heiner's voice.

'The boys,' he pleaded, 'all the boys?'

The man on the train did not reply. 'Sit down,' he said, 'away from the briefcase.'

Heiner pulled a chair forward, sat in it, his bowels beginning to turn, his hands gripping the arm rests, trying to stop the shaking.

'How did you know?' he asked, no longer recognising his own voice.

'He knew everything,' the book-keeper had told Schmeltz. 'Everything. Heidi with the big boobs. *Der Rathauskeller. "Das Horst Wessel Lied"*. Siegfried. *Die Spinne.*'

'What do you want?' Heiner twisted, changed the question.

The reply was bleak, without compromise. 'I want you,' said the man on the train.

Now, thought Laporte, do it now. Not extradition, not the justice of a court of law. Here, now. The anger was building in him again, pushing him on, taking him closer. No guarantee he could get Heiner out of Bolivia, he rationalised, no guarantee that justice would be done. Even in France. Too many secrets, too many people who would wish Heiner dead, too many political reasons why Heiner should not face trial. A heart attack, he thought, it would be a heart attack.

Now, he thought again, do it now. No excuse, something inside him reminded him. No briefcase, no gun. Every excuse, a second voice countered, every justification. Romans xiii.4. 'He beareth not the sword in vain: for he is God's minister, an avenger to execute wrath upon him that doth evil.'

He remembered the abbot's room in the monastery in Lima, the call from France, the first time he had spoken to his godfather after hearing the news. The thin, cloth-bound book lying in the circle of light, the faded lettering on the spine. Thomas Aquinas. 'The Summa Theologica.' Volume

Two, he remembered, Part Two. Question 40. War. Three conditions, he remembered, each met.

Now, the anger told him, do it now. No, the remnants of his priesthood countered, no justification, the conditions not met. His revenge was now personal, there was no longer a just cause.

Screw the just cause, his anger told him, screw the authority of the French courts. His was the suffering, not theirs. He had been the victim, not them. He remembered the events of the past week. The search for Heiner had stripped him of everything, just as Heiner had stripped everything from wherever he had passed. Forced him to lie and kill. Torn his beliefs from him as Heiner had torn his body from him thirty-nine years ago. Thirty-nine years ago at eleven o'clock the next day, he thought, thirty-nine years ago at eleven o'clock on Monday, February 7th.

'I want you,' he repeated, 'I want your extradition to France.'

Heiner was laughing nervously, his stomach churning, the fear freezing every part of his body. 'The general will never agree,' he hurried his words. 'The general, the president, is a personal friend of mine. He will never agree.'

The eyes that were looking at him did not move. An interrogation, Laporte knew, a cold, callous interrogation. Knew it was necessary, did not know why. 'The general,' he said, 'will have no option.'

'He knew everything,' the book-keeper had told Schmeltz. 'Everything.'

'The president,' said the man in the shadows, 'will not care about most things, most of your operations. Aries, Minos.' He began listing the codenames on the files, the knowledge which had both stilled and excited the old man in the café called the Atlantico a bare five yards from the mighty Pacific Ocean. 'But there are some things which he will care about.'

It was the beginning, the introduction to the one thing

312

they all feared. The first thought on Joe Corrigan's mind when he read the initial details of the exposure of Josef Heiner in the Lima newspaper. The prime concern of Dick Mayer when Corrigan had discussed the issue with his station chief. The question Bailey had put to both of them as soon as he arrived from Washington. The operation of which even the book-keeper was afraid. 'You know about that project?' he had asked incredulously in the waterfront bar at Mollendo, 'about *all* of it?'

'The first thing the general will care about,' said the man on the train, 'is Project Octavio.'

Heiner waited, no longer thinking of the handgun in the briefcase, no longer eyeing the weapon across the man's lap. Knowing what was to come. Laporte began to spin the web, drawing Heiner in, the anger still in him, feeding the information to Heiner, taunting him about how much he knew. Knowing he had to, not knowing why. Tightening the strands around Heiner.

In the chair in front of the desk, Heiner's hands were white with fear as he gripped the arm rests.

'The one thing the Americans fear most,' began the man by the door, 'is the domino theory. Once one country falls to what they call communism, the next becomes vulnerable. In South America they fear Chile, Bolivia, Peru. In Central America they're even more paranoid. Their own backyard, they call it. Now Nicaragua has gone, it's El Salvador, then Guatemala, then Mexico. And Mexico borders the United States itself.'

Heiner's shoulders were shaking uncontrollably.

'The United States knows it cannot stop opposition,' continued the man on the train, 'so it tries, in addition to propping up existing governments, to control the opposition which those governments breed. Either by influencing the leaders or, in the case of armed insurrection, by controlling the supply of arms and support to that opposition.' He paused. 'The advantage is obvious. The supply of arms is the lifeline of a group. Control it, you control the group. Wipe out the group and another will take its place. And

313

you may not be able to control its successor as well or as easily. But leave it in place, supply it, and you are safe.'

'But Project Octavio?' asked Heiner, his voice thin, almost a whimper. Afraid to know how much the man on the train knew, knowing he needed to know. Knowing already where it would take him.

'He knew everything,' the book-keeper had said. 'Everything.'

'Project Octavio was the beginning of this process. Each guerilla group has connections with groups in other countries. Control one group, you have the first step to controlling the others. The Americans had to start somewhere. They decided to start in Bolivia.' Heiner waited. 'The Americans support the Bolivian government, but at the same time they began to supply weapons to the guerillas opposing that government, the MIR. Not American weapons, weapons from the Soviet bloc, Russian and Czech weapons. Their target, of course, was not just South America, but the guerilla groups closer to home, the groups in Central America.'

'But how does that affect me?' Heiner pleaded, twisting, knowing there was no hope. 'The general is my friend.'

The man on the train continued. 'The general, the president, is indeed your friend. You work with him, for him. You have helped organise his security system, helped strengthen his intelligence-gathering operation. You penetrated the guerillas for him, caught selected members of that group for him. Even tortured them for him.'

The fear was creeping back into Heiner.

'But you were also the man who was organising them, supplying guns to them.' Heiner could see the outline of the president, in the room on the third floor of the Interior Ministry, standing just outside the ring of lights. Please God, he prayed, may the man on the train not know, not know everything, not be prepared to use it. His frame jerked convulsively, as if he knew what was about to come.

'You were the man the Americans used to penetrate the guerillas, to establish Project Octavio. It was you who arranged the purchase of the weapons, the end-users certificates, the shipments.' He pulled together the strands he had gleaned from the documents he had found at Chaclicayo, that he had drawn from the book-keeper, from the guerillas in the safe house.

'But proof,' Heiner protested feebly, 'the general will ask for proof.' Laporte pulled the strands tighter. 'The documents,' he said simply. 'They left here an hour ago. It takes ten hours to drive to Santa Cruz. The general will have plenty of time to intercept them.'

'He knew everything,' the book-keeper had said, his breath smelling of death, not knowing how much he himself had betrayed.

'Project Aries,' he had boasted confidentially, 'two birds with one stone. Bought out the politicians and set up a good deal in the white stuff.' The old man had laughed, remembering an incident, making an obscene gesture with his lily-white forearm, simulating a male erection. 'Too much of the white stuff. All right for some, helps you go all night.'

'Santa Cruz,' said the man on the train, 'is the centre of the South American cocaine business. One of your projects, Aries, was based there. Most people would assume that if you had any connections with cocaine, it would be merely to advise the traffickers on security. Your involvement, of course, is much deeper than that. Which is why you felt it safe to send the documents to Santa Cruz.'

He wondered why he was drawing out the interrogation, letting the fear sweat out of the man opposite him. Why he was stretching the web around him, tightening the connections. Why he needed to tell Heiner of Project Octavio, of Minos and Aries. Knew only that he had to tell him. Knew that in the end he would know why.

Let him not know it all, prayed Heiner, please God let him not know it all. He could no longer control his muscular movements, his bodily functions. He could hear the general's voice, giving the instructions, could smell the excrement of his own fear. 'The general is my friend,' he tried to persuade himself for the last time, 'he would not let you take me out of the country.'

'He knew everything,' the book-keeper had said. 'Everything. Heidi with the big boobs. *Der Rathauskeller.* *"Das Horst Wessel Lied."* Siegfried.' Siegfried, Heiner could not stop thinking, the Wagnerian hero, the Führer's favourite. The hero with the one fatal weakness. 'He knew everything.' He could not stop himself hearing the book-keeper's voice. 'Everything.'

'I imagine,' said the man on the train, 'that the general gets at least some of his arms and planes from the French, everybody else does, so he would not like to lose that source.' Heiner waited, the man on the train continued. 'But you are his friend, so perhaps he would not let me take you out of the country.'

Heiner knew what the next words would be, could see the general, feel the electrodes being attached to his genitals.

'He would not let me take you out of the country if he knew one thing.'

Heiner could smell the general's stale breath close to him, could see the general, nodding for the switch to be thrown. 'He would not let me take you out of the country if he knew about Portachuela.' Heiner felt the excrement, the first shock as the electricity was turned on. He knew everything, the book-keeper had said. Everything.

'The general,' said the man on the train, 'grew suspicious. Either because he was honest, which is unlikely, or because he felt he was not getting enough of the profits. It does not matter. Eighteen months ago he decided to investigate your connections. You were informed of his decision, of course, by one of his own confidantes. The details are in the documents. A month later the general was due to fly by helicopter to Portachuela.' Heiner could hardly hear the words, see the face. 'At Portachuela, you decided to kill the general.' Heiner could feel the pain of the shocks, convulsing him, sending the agony through him. 'It was an ideal opportunity, you could even make it

316

seem like an accident. You brought in an assassin, the man you call Anderson. You knew the exact timing, the precise flight plan, of the general's helicopter. You were even able to arrange a minor problem on the ground at Portachuela, just as the general was landing, so that the helicopter was forced to hover.'

It was the precision of detail which had impressed the Texan called Anderson, the efficiency which made him happy to work for the organisation.

'The man called Anderson was already in position. As the helicopter hovered, according to plan, he shot away the tail rotor. The one thing guaranteed to make the helicopter crash, the one thing guaranteed to look like an accident. The one thing nobody could prove was not an accident.' The man on the train stared at Heiner. 'It's all in the documents. Anderson's expenses, his travel movements, the purchase of the rifle he used.' He paused. 'There was only one problem. The general did not make the trip. He sent his wife instead. You killed the general's wife.'

A thin line of foam had appeared at Heiner's mouth. The muscles of his face were jerking. He could feel the pain as the general exacted his revenge. 'You wouldn't,' he pleaded, his eyes white with fear.

'Yes,' said the man on the train, speaking slowly, 'I would.'

'You know what he will do to me?'

The man in the shadows nodded. 'Yes, I know what he will do to you.'

'Is there anything?' Heiner was talking gibberishly, frantically, almost incomprehensibly. Twisting, turning, looking for a way out of the pain. 'Money,' he suggested, tasting the blood in his mouth, 'I'll pay you. Anything.' He could feel the relief, the easing of the pain as the first jolt of electricity subsided, then the horror as the flesh was torn and the rape began. 'Anything,' he let slip the last grip of control over himself, 'there must be something.'

Laporte knew why he had controlled his anger, why he

317

had spared Heiner. Why he had fed him the details he had gleaned first from the book-keeper's files, then from the book-keeper's drunken indiscretions. Why he had needed to spell out to Heiner the details of Octavio and Aries, taunted him with the secret of Portachuela. One thing, he knew, one thing he needed. Then he could do with Heiner as he thought fit.

It was both the beginning and the end. The unlocking of the secret previously known only to Washington. The secret Joe Corrigan had prised from the series of telephone calls Heiner had made from his eyrie in La Paz. The reason Corrigan had gone to La Paz. The reason he had executed Carmen. The reason he had spared the son, saved his life.

The reason Joe Corrigan had finally betrayed Josef Heiner to him.

'There must be something.' Heiner was pleading, panicking. He could see again the face of the president, feel again the pain of the electricity. The man on the train checked his watch. Remembered the date. Almost there, he thought again, it was almost there. Almost 11.00 a.m. Almost 11.00 a.m. Monday, February 7th. He checked his watch again, calculating the time in France.

'There is,' he said, 'one thing, one small thing.'

6   *6.46 p.m. France*

The land was frozen hard with winter, the snow settling from the dark of the sky. The few who braved the bleakness of the streets were hurrying home, clothes wrapped tight against the night cold, unaware of the wrath that was about to be unleashed.

Fifty-three minutes later, at precisely thirty-nine minutes to eight, the call began. Summoning those who had waited through their middle years, returning them in the cold of their age to their youth of three decades before. The first to be called was a farmer, Jean-Marc Lucien, on the

318

outskirts of Moussey, east of Paris, in the Alsace Lorraine region of the republic. He was stooped low, examining the hoof of a cow that had gone lame, in what served as the barn of his meagre smallholding, when his wife came through the door. The white of her face was not the white of winter.

'It's Marcel,' she said, her voice low with fright, 'he wants to speak to you.'

The farmer saw the fear in his wife's eyes. 'What is it?' he asked.

She could hardly speak. 'He called you Martin, he called himself Emanuel.'

The fear spread to the man. He straightened, letting down the cow's leg, and walked past his wife into the house. The names were those he thought he would never hear again, the wartime codenames of himself and his network leader in the French Resistance. His wife waited in the cold of the barn. When he returned he was dressed to leave, a thin overcoat pulled over his working clothes, the black beret on his head. In his hand was the sten gun he had last used in 1945, kept in oil-cloth in the attic of their house ever since. In the glow of the hurricane lamp his wife saw the silver of the tears on his cheeks.

'What is it?' she asked.

'It's Max.' He used the codename of the man who had died on the train to Paris thirty-nine years before. 'It's Max. He's calling us again.'

For the next two hours the roll-call continued, till all had been summoned, all answered. The survivors of the Gliéres Battalion, the remnants of the village of Vassieux on the Vercours plateau, the survivors of Oradour-sur-Glane, the men and women who had held up the elite Das Reich tanks of the 2nd SS Panzer Division in the crucial days of the Normandy landings. Through the steamy windows the grandparents watched them leave, remembering the old days, remembering the way they had watched them leave thirty-nine years before. From the bedrooms the children and grandchildren watched in wonder as the grey-faced men and women drove into the night.

By eleven, with those from the more distant regions of the country still arriving, the main body was in position. At eleven-thirty the next strand of the web was strung, the call made and the decision taken. At one in the morning, as the bell of Notre Dame de Lorette struck the hour, they moved on, swollen in numbers, waking the towns of Versaille and Coignières, Rambouillet and Maintenon as they drove south, their column taking twenty minutes to pass.

Until, in the first hours of Monday morning, they came to the mighty cathedral of Chartres.

Chapter Eight

Monday, February 7th 1983

Laporte checked the power points, pulled the roll of detonator cord into the centre of the room, measured off eight lengths, and took each to the positions he had selected. Eleven hours since he had first known. Ten hours since he had telephoned France. Five hours since the return call, since he had begun to consider how exposed he was. Since he had begun to think what he could do if they came for him. As they had done in the house at Chaclicayo, as he assumed they had done at the book-keeper's hotel in Mollendo, as they had done less than twenty-four hours before at the safe house. He checked that Josef Heiner could not move from the chair in the centre of the lounge to which he had been bound and gagged, confirmed that the torch he had taken from the Mercedes in the driveway was working and that the batteries were strong, then cut the electrical cable he had found in the garage into eight lengths, cutting seven of the eight into three equal lengths and the eighth into two.

Nothing. He had found nothing in the house. No explosives, no spare weapons or ammunition except the handgun Heiner had concealed in the briefcase and the Heckler and Koch that he had removed from the driver Heiner had kept with him. Nothing. Except the roll of detonator cord and the handful of electrical detonators which he supposed they had assumed were useless without the explosives they had presumably taken with them.

He placed each of the detonators in the positions he had chosen, cut the adhesive tape he had found in Heiner's desk into strips, then sliced the insulating coat off each

323

end of the lengths of electrical cable he had cut till he had exposed the gleaming copper wire inside.

'Dirty,' they had taught him thirty nine years before, 'think dirty.'

2 *Melleran, France*

The eyes stared at her from the two photographs in the silver frame on her dressing table. Same face, she thought, same eyes, same smile around the mouth. For three hundred and sixty-four nights of the year she knew she would be troubled in her sleep. On the three hundred and sixty-fifth she would not be haunted by the ghosts of the past. For thirty-nine years, on the night before February 7th, Madame Laporte, widow and mother, did not go to bed. In the tall bedroom of the château she sat as she always sat in the early hours of that day, refusing to let the memories torture her, waiting for the dawn, rehearsing her movements for the next morning.

She knew what she would do, how it would happen. Except that this year it would be different. This year there would be no son by her side. No news, Chalbrand had told her when he had telephoned her late the previous afternoon. No information despite his enquiries, both official and unofficial.

Charles Chalbrand woke at five-thirty, a bare four hours after the cabinet meeting had drawn to a close. It would have been earlier, he recollected, had the president not excused himself for a full half-hour the night before.

He dressed, taking care not to wake his wife, went downstairs to the warmth of the kitchen, and made himself a hot chocolate. There was another ten minutes before the official car would pick him up, time for another drink. He would travel alone, his wife would make the journey later.

The car was five minutes late. Chalbrand went to the door and peered through the spy-hole. Outside stood the personal bodyguard of the president of France. He opened the door and let the man in.

'Your car had an accident on the way,' the bodyguard explained. 'we were on call, so were sent instead. Our apologies for being late.'

Chalbrand waved the apology aside. 'I'm sorry you had to get up so early, it's good of you.'

The bodyguard returned to the car while Chalbrand picked up his coat and briefcase. On any other morning, perhaps, the foreign secretary would have taken a secret delight in being assigned the president's personal squad; a portend, he would have thought, of the future. This morning, however, was different. His mind was on the cathedral at Chartres and the events of thirty-nine years ago.

The Citroën slid through the slush, left Paris and turned south. They had been travelling for eighty minutes when the first grey began to thin the black of the sky. The car sped on, the windscreen wipers flicking backwards and forwards. The worry began to grow in his mind. No news of the son, his godson, no news at all. He wondered where he was, what he was doing.

3   *La Paz*

Seven points of entry, he had confirmed from the recce, seven places in the house he could not cover if they came for Heiner, if they came for him. Six windows, Bavarian-style with shutters, and one door. Plus the two doors and one window he could cover from the position in the lounge he had selected for himself, the position behind Heiner.

Laporte went to the first window, checked that the power point on the wall was switched off and that the two halves of the shutters were locked and would not move unless they were forced. Then he took two of the three lengths of electrical cord he had placed beneath the window, taped them end to end against each other, the insulated sections tight together, the exposed wires at the ends not touching, onto the centre of the left shutter. He let the remainder of the first length fall onto the floor, stretched the second length across the two halves of the shutters, taping it into place on the right-hand shutter so that any movement of the shutters would pull the two exposed pieces of wire together, and let the remainder of the second section fall onto the floor. He attached the other end of the first length to the detonator and the other end of the second length to the live element of the power point, then completed the circuit by connecting one exposed end of the third length of electrical cable to the earth element of the power point and the other to the detonator. When he was satisfied the connections were secure he wound most of the remainder of the detonator cord into a ball, taped it onto the shutters, connected one end to the detonator and drew the remaining length into the room in which he had placed Josef Heiner.

In France, he knew, it was almost time.

4 *France*

'Damn.' The driver swore, braking gently.

Chalbrand jerked awake. 'What is it?' The car had stopped.

'I think one of the tyres is going down, I'll have to change it.' Chalbrand looked through the condensation on the windows, recognised the woods which converged on the road where they had stopped.

'Can you drive another kilometre or so?' he asked. 'There's an *auberge* I know, we can get some breakfast.' The driver thanked him and drove on, more slowly.

The lights of the inn stood out in the bleak dawn. The Citroën stopped in front of the door and the three men got out. The driver bent to examine the tyre. Around them the snow in the fields was eighteen inches deep, the car park empty. Chalbrand followed the bodyguard inside and shut the door. The room was empty. From the back he could smell cooking.

'Wake up,' he called, 'you've got customers.' He banged on the top of the bar and called again.

The door behind the bar opened. Chalbrand began to say something, then stopped. Into the room filed five of the other six remaining members of the Melleran cell, led by Henri Bellan, the newspaper editor. The only survivor not present was Madame Laporte. Each of the five carried a gun. They fanned into a semicircle round Chalbrand and the bodyguard, never taking their eyes from him.

'What the hell's going on?' Chalbrand turned to Bellan, then to the president's bodyguard, then back to the others.

'It's no good.' Bellan spoke with a great sadness in his voice. 'We know.'

'Know what? What are you talking about? What are you doing?'

Chalbrand turned to the bodyguard. 'Do something. Do your duty.'

The bodyguard looked back at him. 'I was told to deliver you,' he said, 'I have done my duty.' He looked once at the semicircle of faces, not knowing what else to say. 'On behalf of France,' he suddenly said, 'I am ashamed.' He turned, unable to look at them, and left. One of the five moved across the room behind him and locked the door. In the still outside, Chalbrand heard the Citroën pull away.

'I think you owe me an explanation,' he began, the anger building in his voice. Bellan shook his head. 'As I said, my old friend, it's no good. We know.'

'Know what?'

'Know about you.'

Chalbrand's face had drained to chalk. 'How?' he betrayed himself.

'The priest,' said Bellan simply, 'the one everybody despised. He found The Butcher.'

'And the president's bodyguard?' There was panic in the voice.

327

'He told you himself. He was ordered to deliver you.' Bellan's mind went back. To fourteen minutes to seven the previous evening, the land locked in the grip of winter. He hesitated, not knowing what to call the son, deciding there was only one name. 'Yesterday evening, Jean Laporte phoned me from Bolivia. He said he had found The Butcher. He said The Butcher had confessed. To everything. But to one thing in particular.'

It was the beginning of the secret which had haunted Joe Corrigan. The beginning of the secret which those in power in Washington had guarded for over thirty years, irrespective of party loyalty or personal allegiance. The beginning of the secret which Washington had sought to protect by sending an assassination squad after the son.

The secret which Corrigan had prised from the web of telephone calls Josef Heiner had made from La Paz. The secret Laporte had finally confronted in Heiner's house in the same city.

The reason Corrigan had protected the son, saved his life. The reason he had executed Carmen. The reason he had given Heiner's address to Laporte.

'You were the traitor in our midst.' Bellan spoke slowly and with sadness. 'The Judas amongst us. It was you who betrayed Laporte to Heiner when he returned to France. Worse than that, you have remained in contact with Heiner ever since, profiting from the relationship, gaining from your treachery. Even when you were presiding over the committee of enquiry set up to establish the identity of the traitor.

'And when the son was in Lima, hunting Heiner, you passed to The Butcher whatever the son told you. To protect Heiner. To save yourself. As you betrayed the father, so you betrayed the son. Your own godson.'

Chalbrand began to speak but Bellan silenced him with a wave of the hand.

'As if that was not enough, you betrayed something else. Something so sacred that those of us burdened with the knowledge have sworn never to talk of it again.'

It was the reason for the secret Washington had guarded so faithfully for almost half a century. The reason president had spoken to succeeding president, Democrat to Republican to Democrat.

'You also,' said Bellan, carefully and deliberately, 'betrayed your own country.'

At his side the others were silent.

'It was ironic,' he went on, 'as you betrayed for Heiner, so Heiner betrayed you. He sold his knowledge of you, the details of your collaboration, the intimacy of your continued relationship, to the Americans.' He remembered the details of the conversation with Laporte in La Paz. 'Not the Americans in Lima, with whom Heiner was also working, but those in the highest positions of power in Washington.'

It was the final connection Joe Corrigan had made as he sat in his office in Lima on the afternoon of the previous Friday. The day Corrigan had ordered the son's execution. The day the priest had executed his own executioner. The day the son had finally gone to La Paz.

The day Corrigan had received from his sources in Washington and New York the details of the telephone calls Josef Heiner had made from his supposedly secure system in La Paz. The day Corrigan had drawn a box round the last two telephone calls Heiner had made. Call Number Five. To a private number of one of the three highest-ranking political offices in the United States of America. Call Number Six. To an equally private number of the foreign secretary of France.

'With that information,' continued Bellan, 'you were theirs. To do as they wanted. Nothing so trivial as the mere passing of secrets, of course. More subtle, more deadly. A slight change of policy here, an almost unnoticed change of emphasis there. And for them, the biggest prize still to come.' He shook his head. 'You were to be our next president.'

Bellan glanced at the others. 'I was unsure what I should do, so I spoke to the members of the cell. All except

Madame Laporte. Late last night I went to the president with the information and told him of our decision.' Chalbrand remembered the long minutes he and the other ministers had waited in the cabinet room late the previous evening, the expression on the president's face when he returned. 'The president said that France could not bring its foreign secretary to trial,' continued Bellan, 'and I said that if he could not guarantee justice, then *Le Monde* would publish Laporte's story this morning.'

'The president would not have allowed it,' Chalbrand interrupted nervously. 'He would have stopped *Le Monde*. He would have sent in the police, the army.'

Bellan nodded sadly. 'That was precisely what the president said, but by then it was too late. By then *Le Monde* was already defended.' He remembered the cars arriving, the lorries and buses, the sea of old faces, grey with cold, their eyes bright with youth. 'I told the president what would happen if he sent the police and army to stop *Le Monde*. I told him simply that the Resistance had been summoned.'

He paused. 'The president understood. I agreed with him that there would be no public trial, no publicity, he agreed with me that there should be justice.'

'And Heiner?' Chalbrand was a defeated man.

Bellan looked at his watch. 'At this moment,' he said, 'Josef Heiner is beginning his last journey.'

He drew six chairs to a table in the centre of the room, placed one chair on one side, the other five opposite, and sat down. 'This court martial,' he said, 'is now in session.'

5 *La Paz*

Laporte finished wiring the access points and returned to the lounge. Fifteen hours since Heiner had told him of Chalbrand, fourteen hours since he had telephoned Bellan in France, nine hours since the newspaper editor had phoned back, confirming that the president had agreed, detailing the plan.

In France, he knew, the court martial would be under way. He wondered what the priest was thinking, knew there was no time to dwell on the thought, pushed it away.

In the centre of the room Heiner was watching him, turning his head, unable to move his body. Laporte checked his watch. Eight hours since he had first contacted the French ambassador in La Paz, informing him of the arrangements, notifying him how and with whom the checks should be made. Eight hours, he thought, for the ambassador to act, eight hours for the general to be contacted and persuaded to agree.

Eight hours, he thought, for another betrayal.

The last two lengths of electrical cable and the one remaining length of detonator cord were on the floor. He laid the cord from Heiner's chair to the position he had selected for himself, connected one end to one of the remaining detonators and connected the detonator in turn to the two remaining lengths of electrical cable. He unscrewed the glass of the torch he had taken from Heiner's car and removed the bulb, unscrewed the other end and connected the exposed wire of one of the electrical cables to the batteries of the torch, then placed the torch, together with the other electrical cable, on the floor.

It was time for the second call to the ambassador. He pulled the telephone to his position and dialled the number with one hand, holding the Heckler and Koch with the other. The number rang twice before the telephone was picked up. He rang off, dialled again, waiting for the number to ring five times as arranged before the telephone was picked up again.

'Yes,' said the ambassador, not identifying himself, not committing either of them.

'Is it arranged?' asked Laporte. The wounds in his arm and side were beginning to hurt again.

'Yes,' said the ambassador, 'the general has agreed.'

'And you are ready?' Close, he thought, so close.

331

Already Monday, already the seventh. In France it was almost eleven o'clock. So long, he thought again, it had been so long.

'We are ready,' replied the man.

No guarantee it was the ambassador, Laporte thought. No guarantee the ambassador was loyal, was on his side. No guarantee the call was not being intercepted.

'How long?' he asked.

'That depends where you are,' replied the man who was supposed to be the ambassador. No back door, Laporte thought again, no way out. Except the precautions he had taken. No option, he reminded himself. He gave the ambassador Heiner's address.

'Twenty minutes,' said the man.

'Twenty minutes,' confirmed Laporte.

He put the phone down, looked up the street to where the cars would appear. Somewhere, he knew, Joe Corrigan was watching, waiting, seeing what he would do. He wondered what Corrigan would have done, checked his watch again. In France his mother would almost be there. In France the court martial would almost be over.

In the centre of the room Heiner strained to hear the conversation, knowing what was being arranged. A priest, Chalbrand had told him, the son had become a priest. A weakling, Chalbrand had said, not like his father. Ineffective, ineffectual. Chalbrand was good, he thought. Through fear or greed he did not know. But reliable. Had even informed him that the son was coming to Lima. Heiner himself had informed Washington immediately. Been informed equally swiftly that they had checked on the son, that there was nothing to worry about, but that they were nevertheless taking precautions. He had known of them, been informed of them, even before his flight from Lima. Had known of Father Michael even before Corrigan had heard the first news of the raid on the house at Chaclicayo.

He watched as the man on the train replaced the telephone and came towards him. Ineffectual, Chalbrand had said. No problems, Washington had told him. 'Save me,' he pleaded silently to his friends, 'for God's sake save me.' He knew what the man on the train was about to do, could feel the fear growing in him again. 'Save me,' he pleaded again. 'No. For Christ's sake, no,' he also prayed, knowing what was about to happen, 'For Christ's sake stay away. Don't try to get into the house. For God's sake leave him be.'

Slowly, taking care not to break the connections, Laporte took each of the eight ends of detonator cord and wrapped them in turn around Heiner; four round his neck, tied at the back, four round his waist. Then he went to each of the seven access points, switched on the power point at each, turned off all the lights in the house except the one light outside the front door, overlooking the drive, and the second in the hallway just inside the door, and returned to the position he had chosen for himself.

No way out now, he knew again, no back door as there had been at Chaclicayo. No escape. If they came for Heiner. If the calls to the ambassador had been intercepted. If the general had decided to pluck Heiner from him. If the ambassador himself had been instructed to betray him. No way out, he thought again. No way out for Heiner either, he consoled himself.

Det cord, he had remembered. An explosive device in itself. Not enough to kill. Unless used in the right way. Dirty, they had trained him at Arisaig, think dirty. Seven access points he could not cover. Six windows and one door. Now covered. If anybody entered them, tried to enter them, the slightest movement would pull the exposed ends of the electrical cable together. Activate the circuit. Detonate the cord. Hold up, probably injure, at least some of his attackers. Warn him. Take out Heiner. Sever his body. Either at the neck or waist.

Dirty, they had taught him thirty-nine years before. Very dirty.

He tucked the three spare magazines into his belt, placed the pistol which Heiner had carried in the briefcase in the right-hand pocket of his coat, slipped the Hockler onto automatic fire and held the torch, with its one connecting wire, in his right hand, against the metal of the sub-machine gun, his fingers holding it through the trigger. Almost time, he knew, almost time. He reached down, picked up the second electrical cable, and held the exposed end with his left hand, close to the torch, ready to make the connection with the element from which he had removed the bulb.

He checked his position for the last time. Dominate, he remembered they had taught him. The firing zone. The street. The room. The position was perfect. Back to the wall. Able to see through the window to where the cars would appear, to see the exact spot on the driveway where the ambassador would stop. Able to follow the ambassador through the open front door, into the hall, into the lounge itself. The door into the lounge opening correctly, his right to left. So that even if it closed accidentally, anybody opening it would be exposed immediately. Heiner himself in the exact position. Between him and the ambassador.

And the last trick, if they tried to take him behind the ambassador, through the open door and window. If they switched off the electricity to the house. The torch, connected to the det cord, the batteries strong enough to activate the detonator. To take Heiner with him if the end came fast upon him.

For one moment he remembered the priest. Thought of the moment Heiner had told him of Chalbrand. One thing, he had suggested to Heiner, one small thing. And Heiner had told him. Of the treachery which had betrayed his father, the treachery which had spun through the years, the treachery which had betrayed the son. He remembered the way the darkness had come upon him, enveloping him, taking away the anger, replacing it with hopelessness. Till he had become lost, till he had almost allowed Heiner to win. Then, and only then, had he remembered. Monday. Monday, February 7th. Then, and only then, had the hopelessness disappeared. Then, and only then, had the anger returned.

At the top of the road the lights of the first car appeared.

Four cars, they had agreed; the first carrying the ambassador. Alone. The others carrying the team. The lights dipped as the cars stopped. The lights of the first car flicked off and on, off and on, three times, then the car moved forward, slowly and deliberately, the other three remaining in place as arranged. So close, he thought, so close to eleven o'clock. The car moved down the road, turning right, pulling into the driveway. Stopping. Laporte moved his left hand closer to the torch. At the top of the road the other cars were still waiting.

The driver of the car got out, leaving the door open so that the interior light remained on, lighting up the inside. Slowly, carefully, he walked round the vehicle, opening each door, till Laporte could see inside, see he was alone. So close, Laporte thought again, so close to eleven. Remembered how many times he had been betrayed. In the driveway the man returned to the front of the car, stood motionless for ten seconds in the light of the headlamps, then turned to his right and walked into the house, pausing in the hallway, turning left, entering the door of the lounge.

Laporte moved the wire closer to the element, resting it on the rim of the torch. In the chair between them Heiner moved his eyes, afraid to turn his head. The man moved to the centre of the room, two yards from Heiner, holding up a passport, knowing Laporte could not see it, identifying himself as the ambassador. Half-looking at the complex of wires leading from the man in the chair to the various exits from the room.

'You are the son?' he asked.

'I am Laporte,' replied the man in the shadows.

'I am Ambassador Renier,' said the man, stiffly. Three times he had been betrayed, Laporte thought again, wondered if there was to be a fourth. Remembered what he had feared during his interrogation of Heiner, that the man knew too much to be allowed to stand trial in France.

'Is all arranged?' he asked.

'Yes,' confirmed the ambassador.

'The plane?' He waited for the first crack of the detonator cord. The first scream.

'Waiting. It has been refuelled and cleared for immediate take-off.'

'And the general has agreed?'

'So far.'

For the first time Laporte began to believe the man. 'Any complications?'

The ambassador nodded. 'The press,' he said. 'The arrival of the plane has already started a rumour. The embassy has already had enquiries. Even at this hour. The press are already on their way to the airport.'

'Do they suspect?'

'Yes,' said the ambassador, 'they suspect.'

Laporte calculated the time in France. Ten in the morning, a little after. By now, he knew, it would be over.

'That's OK,' he said.

'Can I bring in the boys?' the ambassador asked. The last flicker of suspicion crossed Laporte's mind. Too close, he knew, too close to eleven o'clock to refuse.

'Yes,' he agreed, 'bring in the boys.' The ambassador returned to the car and flicked the headlamps off and on. At the top of the road the cars moved forward.

6 *Lima*

The telephone rang in the dark. Startling her. Frightening her. Maria got off the bed, picked it up. Let it be Jean, she prayed, please God let it be Jean. Six days, she did not need to count, since she had met him. Five days since the raid on the house at Chaclicayo. Four days since he had told of the secrets he had prized from the book-keeper. Three days since she had last seen him. Two days, she thought, since Pacheco had said he thought Jean might have gone to La Paz. One day, almost twenty-four hours exactly, since she had woken in the night, screaming at him to wake.

Please God, she prayed again, let it be Jean. Knew it would not be. Recognised immediately Pacheco's voice. Phoning from his office, she knew. Knew he had been there all night, waiting as she had been waiting. Not left his office since Laporte had disappeared.

Nothing positive, he said, apologising for disturbing her at such an hour, probably nothing at all. But thirty minutes before a plane, a Hercules C-130, had landed at El Alto airport in La Paz. Nothing unusual about that, he went on, except that the plane had been refuelled instantly and cleared for immediate take-off.

Jean, she thought, tell me about Jean.

A number of people were reported to have left the plane, he said. Men, young men. Moving fast, not like ordinary passengers. As if they were soldiers, someone had said, special soldiers. Even in their civilian clothes. As if they were on a mission. Four cars had met them, inside the airport, as soon as they had stepped from the plane. Then they had left, disappeared into the darkness, before anyone could stop them, ask who they were.

But Jean, she wanted to scream at him, what about Jean?

The Hercules, he said, carried no markings, no clue to its nationality. There was a rumour, he said, that it was a military plane, that the men were commandos. Already, he said, even at five in the morning, the press and television were on their way to the airport. His men among them, sent to La Paz after the gun battle the previous day. There was a rumour, he said, that the plane was from France. There was a rumour, he said, uncorroborated he emphasised, totally uncorroborated, that the French had come for Josef Heiner.

'Jean,' she asked at last, 'any news of Jean?'

'No,' admitted Pacheco, 'no news at all.'

337

The snow was crisp, the crystals sparkling in the morning sun. Madame Laporte left the château and was driven through the country lanes, white and glistening, into Melleran, and onto the main road to the north. At ten fifteen she arrived in Chartres, climbing towards the cathedral. It was the first time she had made the journey alone. On every other occasion she had been accompanied by her son; either carrying him as a babe in arms, praying his cries would not interrupt the solemnity of the occasion; as a boy, his eyes staring at the gaunt figures of the men around him; as a youth, and then as a priest, upright but humble. She knew she would miss his presence, his arm to rest upon.

The driver stopped behind the cathedral, where he always stopped. The old woman got out, wrapped her coat round her against the sudden chill, and walked beneath the towering walls to the corner of the square in front.

The pattern was set, as she had rehearsed it in the emptiness of the château that morning. She would enter the square, see with affection the several hundred who still came, then walk slowly up the steps of the cathedral, past the two *gendarmes* who would salute her, and enter by the west door, taking her place in the front pew. At fifteen minutes to eleven, having respected her wish for solitude, Chalbrand and the rest of the Melleran cell would join her. At one minute to eleven the priest would climb the steps to the pulpit, at eleven o'clock exactly the power of the *Marseillaise* would surge through the cathedral and they would remember. It was always the same. It was marked in time.

She turned the corner.

Before her, filling the square and reaching into the streets beyond, stood a crowd of several thousands, heads bare, the high and low of the land. Waiting. They were old, as old as she was. Many of them, she saw, carried weapons. She turned to the two *gendarmes* at the top of the steps, bewildered, needing an explanation. There were no police in sight. In their place two rows of men and women, some dressed poorly, stood in a guard of honour. On their breasts were the symbols of courage that so many had forgotten. The red and yellow ribbon of the *Croix de Guerre*. The red ribbon, the white and green medal with the gold centre, of the *Chevalier de la Légion d'Honneur*. The red, white and blue of the *Médaille de déportation de Résistance*, the badge of those who had survived the concentration camps.

The old woman walked between them, through the oak doors, and into the cathedral. As she walked they fell in behind her. The men and women of Vassieux; of Bonnay, where three thousand *Maquis* had given a full military funeral to a twenty-year-old Resistance hero known simply as Nono; of Glières, rememering the rampages of the despised *Miliciens*; of Oradour-sur-Glane, where six hundred and forty-two villagers had been executed in an SS reprisal. Slowly they filled the vastness of the cathedral, till there were none outside, the last closing the huge doors. In the middle, the sten gun under his arm, was the farmer from Moussey. The old woman knelt to the Virgin, crossed herself, took her place, and waited for her friends. The cathedral was quiet. The bass of the organ rolled through the pillars of the building, the choir began a motet, their voices floating to the high vaulted ceiling. Ten-thirty passed, fifteen minutes to eleven, and they did not come. At one minute to eleven the priest mounted the pulpit, bowed his head in a moment of prayer, and opened his Bible.

It was eleven o'clock on Monday, February 7th. The massive strains of the *Marseillaise* rose to the roof, the voices of the thousands ringing with memories. The old woman looked about her, seeking her friends. Still they did not come. The anthem soared higher then died, the voices faltering, then stopping, till even the music of the organ faded. The old woman turned and looked behind her. The huge oaken doors of the cathedral swung open, creaking, allowing in the sunlight. In the sudden shaft walked the remnants of the Melleran cell. On their berets they wore the cross of Lorraine, on their left sleeves the black band of mourning. Their faces were bowed, the automatic rifles they bore were carried with dignity. Behind them, the doors were shut again. As they reached the altar each in turn bowed to the Crucifix and took their place beside the old woman.

Bellan bent over her, close to her, so that not even those in the row behind could hear, whispering quickly and urgently. The old woman nodding.

'Are you sure?' she asked, just once.

'Yes,' replied Bellan, 'it is confirmed.'

The old woman drew herself up, straightening her thin shoulders, walked forward across the sanctuary and began to mount the steps of the pulpit. Those close to her saw that her face was dry. At the top the priest stood back and let her take his place.

'I have news,' she said, her frail voice growing stronger, reaching the farthest corner of the cathedral. 'The Butcher is found.' She clutched the tiny lace handkerchief tightly in her right hand. 'He was tracked down last night in Bolivia, South America, by a *réseau* of the Resistance. We are still awaiting more news.' She looked at Bellan, needing his strength. He nodded and she continued. 'I also have to tell you that the traitor, the collaborator who betrayed us all, who worked with The Butcher, has been brought to justice. He was tried by court martial this morning and confessed.'

There was a crack of light in the huge oaken doors at the entrance of the cathedral. A solitary figure slipped through, closed the doors behind him, passed by the crowd, and gave Bellan a note. The newspaper editor read it, stood up, walked to the altar, and handed it in turn to the old woman. She looked at it, the tears blurring the writing, then put it down.

'More news,' she said. In the vastness of the cathedral the farmer from Moussey knew what she was about to say.

'Fifteen minutes ago,' she began, 'a French military aircraft left Bolivia for France. It will arrive in Paris later tonight.' She paused, almost unable to speak. 'On board,' she finally said, 'was Josef Heiner.'

She looked across the sea of faces, seeing those who were not there, remembering her youth of thirty-nine years before, remembering those who had not lived beyond it. Remembering the photographs of the two men on the dressing table in her bedroom. Suddenly, spontaneously, she tightened her hand in salute, thrusting it above her head.

'*Vive la France,*' she cried out. '*Vive la Résistance.*'

8 *Lima*

The telephone rang. Maria picked it up immediately, heard Pacheco. His voice was low and calm, she knew he was fighting to control it. 'There is news from La Paz,' he said. On the balcony the curtains were blowing in the first breeze of the morning. 'It was the French,' he said simply, 'they had come for Heiner.' Already his control was breaking. She knew he could see the scene at the airport, knew he wished he had been there. 'Twenty-five minutes ago, Heiner was taken to La Paz airport by a convoy of French commandos and put on the Hercules.' She knew he was wiping his eyes. 'I have just heard that the plane has taken off. Josef Heiner is on his way back to France.'

'Jean,' she asked, 'any news of Jean?'

'No.' She almost did not hear the word. Knew he had something to tell her, knew he was about to say that he thought Jean was dead, that he had disappeared as Herbert Weissemann had disappeared.

'But?' she asked.

'But something strange happened at the airport. After Heiner was put on the plane, it was cleared for immediate take-off. All other planes were stopped. But it waited. For

341

ten full minutes the French plane waited. When the control tower asked the pilot what was wrong, the Frenchman replied that the controller would not understand.'

'And?'

'After ten minutes, the French pilot told the control tower he was taking off.'

Maria waited.

'It was six o'clock exactly,' said Pacheco.

The realisation began to come upon her, the hope returning. 'Remember Jean's story,' said Pacheco, 'remember the times. The plane took off at six o'clock Bolivian time. Bolivia is five hours behind French time.'

She knew, knew why the pilot had waited, why they had all waited.

Eleven o'clock in the morning of Monday, February 7th.

'And Jean?' she asked again.

'Something else happened at the airport,' said Pacheco, 'perhaps important, perhaps not.'

Tell me, she pleaded silently, for God's sake tell me.

'The press and TV crews were close, very close, to the point where the French commando team brought Heiner into the airport and put him on the plane. As they led him up the steps, as he disappeared from view, the man in charge of the team turned and saluted. The press thought he was saluting them.'

'But?'

'But my people think it was something else. My people think that he knew somebody in the crowd, that he was saluting that person.' Maria waited. 'There's a story that the commando team stopped their convoy just outside the airport, that they dropped somebody off. My people think that was the person the commando leader was saluting.'

'Jean?' she could barely ask.

Pacheco knew he could not commit himself. 'One of my photographers, the one who took the pictures in the house at Chaclicayo, thought it was Jean, thought he saw him in the crowd. But before he could confirm it the man disappeared.'

Laporte turned away from the crowd of pressmen and radio
and television crews, and walked back into the airport
building. So long, he thought, it had been so long. He
looked at his watch, breathing in the thin air, smelling the
sharp tang of the burnt fuel. In the concourse the cleaners
and a handful of early passengers were staring confused at
the activity.

He walked slowly, unsure what to do, looking for somewhere to buy a coffee. The line of telephone kiosks on the
right were filled with reporters, others crowding round
impatiently. Americans trying to catch their early-morning
news programmes, Europeans their afternoon editions. In
the third kiosk from the end a reporter from *Agence France
Presse* was playing live to a news flash on French national
radio the commentary he had recorded during the past
minutes.

'The plane is moving,' Laporte listened to the voice, 'the
plane is moving. In the darkness at the end of the runway
I can see the plane moving. I can hear the engines building
up.' The reporter was lost in the memory. In France,
the man knew, in France, Laporte knew, they would be
listening, wondering: 'Fifteen minutes since the commandos came back, out of the night, into the airport,' the
voice played into the telephone, 'young men, grim-faced
men, the figure of Josef Heiner almost lost among them.
Fifteen minutes since they put him on the plane. Ten
minutes now that the plane has been waiting at the end of
the runway. Cleared for take-off. I don't know why they
are waiting.'

Laporte stood still, remembering the moment, remembering the time. Hearing again the voice of the
reporter.

'The plane is moving, I can see the plane moving, down
the runway, coming past me.' It was a moment the man
would tell his children, his grandchildren. 'The plane is
lifting off. Off the concrete. Into the sky.' The reporter

was almost in tears. 'Josef Heiner is going back. The Butcher is on his way back to France.'

Laporte moved away, ignoring the excitement, the jostling around him. The concourse was busy, suddenly full. He thought of those who had helped him. Maria. The magazine editor Ricardo Pacheco. The guerilla leader Guillermo Pertierro. Of those who had opposed him. The book-keeper, dying in his arms, the dread of realisation on his face. Father Michael, slipping peacefully into death in the restaurant in the back street in Lima. Heinrich Schmeltz, dead in the back street in La Paz. Josef Heiner.

Joe Corrigan, the enemy who had saved his life, given him the key to the one thing he needed to know.

The television crews were hurrying past. A press conference, he heard someone saying, the French ambassador is giving a press conference. He followed them up the stairs, towards the suite on the floor above the main concourse. Remembered the moments of decision. The book he had found on the abbot's desk in the monastery in Lima. The shoe-shine boy. Thought of the moments he still did not understand. The moment he had recognised the man in the street below the safe house in La Paz, the man he had last seen on the train to Paris thirty-nine years before. The moment in the street when his fingers had searched in his pocket for the comfort of the rosary, found instead the metal of the spare magazine. The voice of the instructor in the darkened room at Arisaig, shouting at him, screaming at him. Saving his life. Reminding him how to booby-trap the house in which, until less than two hours ago, he had held Heiner.

He did not understand, knew that he would probably never understand. He went into the suite, already ablaze with lights, the television crews and photographers almost fighting for position, the Americans whispering into their radios about satellite links and deadlines. At the top of the room, waiting patiently behind a table and flanked by aides, was the ambassador.

Laporte stood on the edge of the crowd of reporters,

remembering the journey from Heiner's house to the airport, remembered the moment the ambassador had asked the question they all feared. 'What if the general changes his mind,' the diplomat had asked. 'What happens if there's a problem at the airport?' Remembered the words of the commander of the snatch squad as he radioed the pilot of the waiting Hercules. 'Two minutes,' he had said, 'we're two minutes away, we're coming in.' Remembered the way the other cars had closed around them, shielding them, protecting them, the commandos flicking off the safety catches of their weapons.

He looked again at his watch. In France it was fifteen minutes past eleven o'clock. A long time, he thought again, it had been a long time. He looked around the press conference, not seeing the cameras, the lights. Seeing instead his mother, standing alone, in the mighty cathedral of Chartres. Seeing Maria, waiting alone, as his mother had waited thirty-nine years before.

No longer a priest, he knew, yet in some ways closer to the values he had held as a priest than when he had worn the cloth. The ambassador began to rise. To Laporte's right the *Agence France Press* reporter he had overheard on the telephone downstairs slipped into the room, looking for his bureau chief, began whispering to him, not letting the others hear. The man looked up, aghast. The others heard, the rumour already spreading. The ambassador hearing it, sitting down, turning to an aide for guidance. The foreign secretary of France, the hero of the Resistance, the next president of the Republic, the man who had masterminded the capture and extradition of Josef Heiner, was dead. Killed in a car crash on his way to the memorial service at Chartres.

Laporte felt the last tiredness drain from him, the final strands of the spider's web decay into the dust of age. He looked round for the last time. Saw the faces. One face.

The man next to him was smoking. He asked for a cigarette, took the packet and walked to the other side of the room.

'Do you have a light?' he asked. So many faces, he thought. One face that mattered. The man he had recognised felt in his pocket, pulled out a box of matches, and handed it to him.

'Thanks,' said Laporte.

'That's OK,' said Corrigan.

Laporte left the room, went downstairs to a travel agency, the clerk just pulling back the shutters, and asked for a ticket to Lima.

THOMAS KENEALLY

GOSSIP FROM THE FOREST

November 1918: a railway carriage in a bleak forest
in Compiègne, north-east of Paris. Six men meet
to sign the armistice that will shape the future of
Europe. Threatened by famine and anarchy at
home, the Germans struggle to mitigate the
punishing terms offered by the Allies. But both sides
are torn by battle exhaustion and a confusion that
far exceed their national differences. History,
speculation and rumour combine to riveting effect.

Post·A·Book

A Royal Mail service in association with the Book Marketing Council & The Booksellers Association.
Post·A·Book is a Post Office trademark.

THOMAS KENEALLY

CONFEDERATES

A troop of soldiers from the Army of the South led by General Stonewall Jackson were making their way north to the big battle that they thought would determine the American Civil War. By the end of their year of battles those men and women had lived through a lifetime.

'Such a magnificent book that I count it a privilege to read and keep'
Books and Bookmen

'From this book one gets the true feel of war . . . we are shown it all . . . it compels attention'
Daily Telegraph

'An excellent read . . . one need ask no more'
Auberon Waugh

CORONET BOOKS

AIREY NEAVE

THEY HAVE THEIR EXITS

Here is a story of supreme courage, of the daring
and resource of men in the bright face of danger.
Norman Birkett says in his foreword:

'None of those who have written (about World War
II) have had the unique experience that the whirlgig
of time brought to Airey Neave, and which he has
used in this book with such dramatic effect. The young
lieutenant of 1940, wounded, captured, imprisoned,
suffering intense humiliation, yet lived to be the Major
of 1945, who was appointed by the judges at the
International Military Tribunal at Nuremberg to a
position that brought him into the closest touch with
the Nazi leaders when they were, in turn, captured
and imprisoned on the collapse of the German
Reich.

'It is the vivid contrast of the escaped prisoner of
war set in authority over Keitel, Goering, Hess,
Ribbentrop and the rest, that gives to this book a
quality that no other book of the like kind possesses.'

CORONET BOOKS

AIREY NEAVE

NUREMBERG

On 18th October 1945, a day that would haunt him
forever, Airey Neave personally served the official
indictments on the twenty-one top Nazis currently
awaiting trial in Nuremberg – including Goering,
Hess, Streicher and Speer. With his visit to their
gloomy prison cells, the tragedy of an entire
generation reached its final act.

Neave, a wartime organiser of MI9 and the first
Englishman to escape from Colditz Castle, watched
and listened over the months to come as the
momentous events of the trial unfolded. Was this
victor's justice? Or was it civilisation's infinitely
painful verdict on the worst crimes ever committed?
These questions, and many others, are answered
in this definitive, eye-witness record of THE
NUREMBERG TRIAL.

CORONET BOOKS

NOEL BARBER

A FAREWELL TO FRANCE

Sonia Riccardi, impetuous and sensual, was a
woman no man could resist. And Larry Astell, heir
to a champagne fortune, knew their passion was
the most important part of his life. Until war placed
in jeopardy all they held dear – love, family,
country.

From the Left Bank of the 1930s to Nazi-occupied
Paris, A FAREWELL TO FRANCE is an epic novel of
star-crossed lovers torn apart by duty to a cause and
devotion to others.

A FAREWELL TO FRANCE – a rich, sweeping novel
destined to become one of the most cherished
stories of our time.

CORONET BOOKS

ALSO AVAILABLE FROM CORONET BOOKS

THOMAS KENEALLY

☐ 33501 7	Schindler's Ark	£2.95
☐ 33783 4	Confederates	£2.95
☐ 35474 7	Gossip From The Forest	£2.50

NOEL BARBER

☐ 28262 2	Tanamera	£2.95
☐ 34709 0	A Farewell To France	£2.95

AIREY NEAVE

☐ 10524 0	They Have Their Exits	£1.10
☐ 25450 5	Nuremberg	£2.25

All these books are available at your local bookshop or newsagent, or can be ordered direct from the publisher. Just tick the titles you want and fill in the form below.

Prices and availability subject to change without notice.

CORONET BOOKS, P.O. Box 11, Falmouth, Cornwall.

Please send cheque or postal order, and allow the following for postage and packing:

U.K. – 55p for one book, plus 22p for the second book, and 14p for each additional book ordered up to a £1.75 maximum.

B.F.P.O. and EIRE – 55p for the first book, plus 22 for the second book, and 14p per copy for the next 7 books, 8p per book thereafter.

OTHER OVERSEAS CUSTOMERS – £1.00 for the first book, plus 25p per copy for each additional copy.

Name ....

Address ....

....